I0822661

BENEATH THE RINGS

By

Joe Battaglia

ISBN: 979-8-89324-792-3

Published by Franklin Publishers
Printed in the United States of America

For permissions, inquiries, or additional copies, contact:
Franklin Publishers
www.franklinpublishers.com

For Mom

Table of Contents

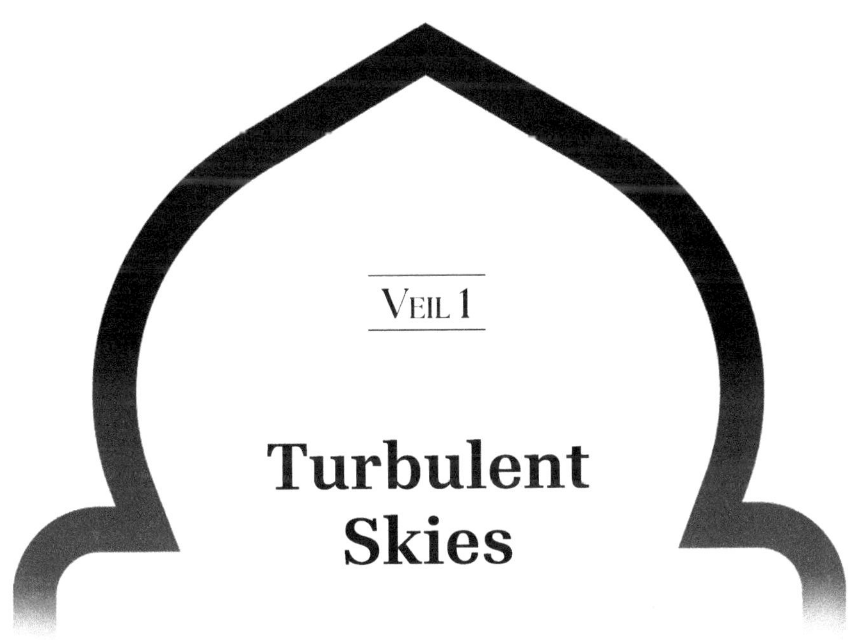

Veil 1

Turbulent Skies

The hum of the Qatar Airways A350 reverberated faintly through the cabin as Nova Mendelsohn adjusted her noise-canceling headphones. She sat in business class, a perk of her frequent flyer miles accumulated over decades of crisscrossing the globe for Olympic coverage.

She was en route from JFK to Hamad International Airport in Doha, Qatar, for the Summer Olympics—the first ever hosted in the Middle East. The flight attendants moved gracefully through the aisles, their maroon uniforms a subtle nod to Qatari elegance, but Nova barely noticed. Her focus was fixed on the glowing screen of her laptop, where she hammered out the final draft of an article for her website, OlymPulse.

After decades of chasing stories across the globe, some of the shine had worn off. The Games stirred a complicated blend of hope and skepticism.

Her piece dissected the paradox of the International Olympic Committee's sustainability rhetoric clashing with Qatar's ambitious construction spree.

Nova paused to stretch her fingers, glancing out the window at the endless expanse of clouds tinged gold by the setting sun. At 48, she still carried the sharp-edged determination of her younger self, tempered by two decades of Olympic deadlines—and a few early gray strands threading her red hair.

She leaned back in her seat, rereading the text:

OlymPulse Nova Mendelsohn

DOHA 2040: A SHINY NEW SPORTS MECCA—AT WHAT COST?

When the International Olympic Committee awarded the 2040 Summer Games to Doha, it hailed the decision as a triumph of inclusivity and a nod to the Middle East's rising global presence.

But can a city built on spectacle truly claim sustainability?

What the Qataris have created seems to fly at odds with the IOC's post-2020 pledge to prioritize that ideal.

Qatar has spared no expense to erect a constellation of state-of-the-art venues for Doha 2040, retrofitting existing ones to create a shiny new sports mecca. However, this grandeur exacts a heavy toll: sprawling construction has uprooted local communities and drained resources, while the environmental cost of such vast infrastructure casts a shadow over the IOC's green ideals. As the world prepares to marvel at this futuristic Olympic stage, the question lingers—does it represent progress, or a step backward from sustainable values?

The centerpiece is the Lusail Iconic Stadium, a 100,000-seat marvel in Lusail City, 15 kilometers north of Doha. Designed by a consortium of Qatari and international architects, its sleek, crescent-shaped roof and interwoven Islamic motifs make it a visual masterpiece. Built from scratch for the Games, it will host the opening and closing ceremonies, athletics, and football finals. Post-Olympics, it's slated to become a cultural hub—an idealistic vision, one with a $2 billion dollar price tag, should it survive inevitable budget cuts.

Nearby, the Aspire Aquatics Center in the Aspire Zone is a new aquatic jewel. With a capacity of 15,000, it boasts cutting-edge water recycling systems and a retractable roof, purpose-built for swimming, diving, and synchronized swimming.

The Doha Velodrome, another fresh addition, rises like a sculpted wave in Al Waab, its 7,000 seats primed for cycling events. Meanwhile, the Al Rayyan Gymnastics Arena, constructed adjacent to the existing Al Rayyan Sports Club, will host gymnastics and trampoline with a 12,000-strong crowd.

Qatar didn't stop there. The Education City Combat Sports Complex, a 10,000-seat venue, was erected to house judo, taekwondo, and wrestling, its modular design promising future adaptability.

The West Bay Beach Volleyball Courts, carved into Doha's waterfront, offer a 5,000-seat temporary setup for beach volleyball, with plans to dismantle it post-Games—a rare nod to impermanence. And in Al Thumama, the Thumama Tennis Center dazzles with its 8,000-seat main court and surrounding smaller arenas, built to host tennis and wheelchair tennis.

Existing venues got upgrades too. The Khalifa International Stadium, a 1976 relic reborn for the 2022 FIFA World Cup, will host archery and secondary athletics events, its 40,000 seats freshly renovated. The Aspire Dome, a multi-sport complex since 2005, will accommodate indoor events like basketball and volleyball, its 15,500 capacity unchanged but its tech modernized.

The Hamad Aquatic Centre, also in the Aspire Zone, was expanded to 2,500 seats for water polo, while the Al Sadd Sports Club—home to football and futsal—gained a polish for Olympic football preliminaries.

This construction blitz reflects Qatar's vision. But the question remains whether this vision is a beacon or a mirage: a nation once defined by pearl diving now staking its claim as a global sports titan. The government touts sustainability—solar panels power Lusail, recycled water cools the Aquatics Center—but critics point to the carbon footprint of building eight new venues in a decade.

The IOC's "New Norm" guidelines, adopted in 2018, urged host cities to leverage existing infrastructure. Doha's response? A hybrid approach—retrofitting some, building others anew, and promising legacy use. Yet, as the world descends on this desert metropolis, the gleam of these venues may outshine the sustainability debate—for now.

On July 20, Doha will unveil its creation to the world. The question is whether this sports mecca heralds a new era of Olympic ambition or a cautionary tale of excess.

Nova saved the draft and sipped her coffee, the bitterness grounding her. She knew the article would stir debate among her OlymPulse readers—some would see Qatar's boldness as a triumph, others as a betrayal of the IOC's principles. Either way, she'd be there to witness it unfold.

The captain's voice crackled through the cabin: "We'll be landing in Doha in approximately one hour." Nova closed her laptop, her mind already shifting to the opening ceremony two days away. She glanced out the window again, unsure whether what waited in Doha would inspire her, or break her heart. She'd seen a lot in her career, but something told her Doha 2040 would be unlike anything before.

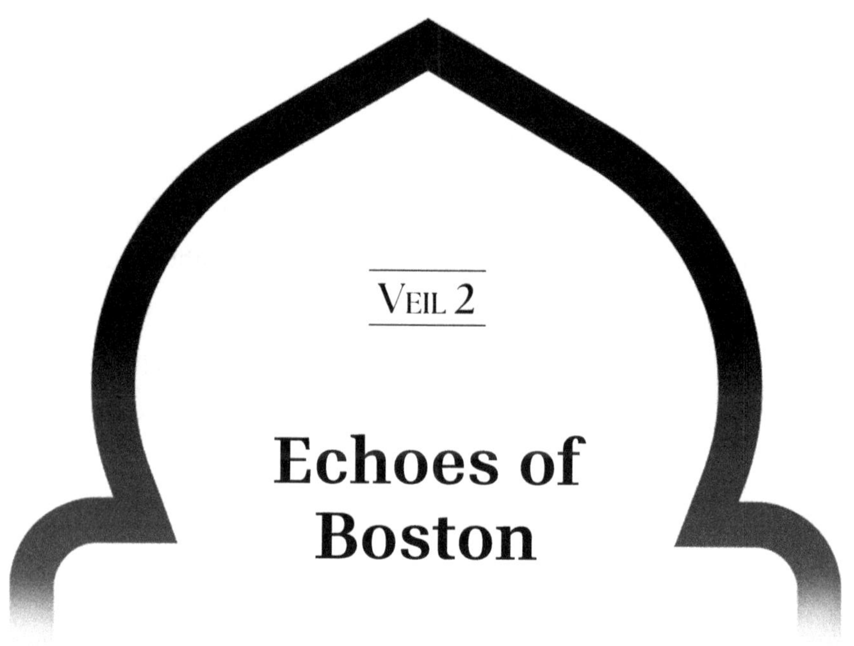

Veil 2

Echoes of Boston

Nova's pen hovered above her notepad as the stadium shimmered into life. The world held its breath as the countdown echoed through the vast expanse of Lusail Iconic Stadium. A sea of lights pulsed in perfect harmony, reflecting the shimmering brilliance of the Persian Gulf beyond the skyline. It was July 20, 2040, and Doha, Qatar, was making history as the first Middle Eastern city to host the Summer Olympics.

The stadium, a fusion of modern architecture and traditional Islamic motifs, was at full capacity, an electrified crowd of 100,000 spectators draped in the colors of their nations.

This historic event was also the first Olympic Games under the leadership of International Olympic Committee President Sheikh Tariq bin Fahd Al-Mazrouei of Kuwait. His appointment marked a new era for the Games, emphasizing inclusivity and regional representation. Now, standing beneath the Olympic cauldron, his legacy was on the line.

The significance of hosting the Olympics in the Middle East was palpable—this was a moment of pride, a testament to the region's growth, and a celebration of its rich heritage.

Inside the tunnel, athletes from every corner of the world lined up in preparation for the grand parade of nations. Dressed in sleek uniforms designed to combat Doha's notorious summer temperatures, the Olympians awaited their moment to step onto the track. Among them, the Israeli and Lebanese contingents found themselves standing side by side, their nations' flags adorning their uniforms.

Maya Ben-Ari, a sprinter from Israel, adjusted the sleeve of her white-and-blue tracksuit and exchanged a glance with her teammate, Lior Abramson, a swimmer set to compete in the 400m freestyle.

"Crazy, isn't it?" Maya murmured, shifting from foot to foot. "First Middle Eastern Olympics, and we're part of it."

Lior smirked. "Let's just hope the politics stay outside the stadium."

A few feet away, Yasmine Haddad, a Lebanese taekwondo champion, overheard the comment. She turned to her fellow countrywoman, Nadine Al-Rassi, a long-distance runner, and nudged her slightly. "You hear that?" she whispered.

Nadine sighed. "Of course. But tonight isn't about that."

Yasmine hesitated, then took a breath and stepped closer to Maya. "It's a first for all of us," she said cautiously. "Maybe we should just appreciate that we're here."

Maya blinked, surprised. In past Olympics, tension had always shadowed their nations' delegations. But this time felt different—perhaps because of the location, or maybe because the world itself was tired of division.

"Agreed," Maya finally said, offering a tentative smile. "No politics. Just competition."

Yasmine nodded, and the two exchanged a brief handshake—small, but monumental in its own way.

Suddenly, a deep voice boomed through the stadium's speakers. "And now, the Parade of Nations!"

One by one, countries were introduced alphabetically, their athletes marching into the stadium beneath a dazzling array of lights.

When Israel was announced, its athletes stepped in sync. Their flag bearer, Ronit Weissman, a decorated judoka and the first Israeli woman to win back-to-back world championships, led the team with a confident stride. She held the Star of David aloft, her expression one of sheer determination and pride.

A murmur rippled through the stadium, quickly growing into audible boos from pockets of the crowd. Some spectators remained silent, while others clapped politely, but the wave of jeers was undeniable. Maya felt her stomach tighten as she walked alongside her teammates.

Lior clenched his jaw. "Well, so much for fucking keeping politics out of the stadium," he muttered under his breath.

Maya exhaled slowly. "Just keep walking," she said. "We knew this bullshit might happen."

From a few feet away, Yasmine watched the Israeli team endure the reaction. She glanced at Nadine, who remained impassive. "Sucks to be them," Yasmine admitted.

Nadine nodded. "You don't have to like someone to respect that they trained just as hard to be here."

Moments later, the Lebanese team stepped forward, their red, white, and green uniforms gleaming under the stadium lights. At the front of the delegation, holding the Lebanese flag high, was Omar Haddad, a decorated Greco-Roman wrestler and two-time Olympic medalist. His grip on the cedar-emblazoned banner was firm, his posture dignified, embodying the pride of a nation that had endured challenges yet continued to shine on the world stage.

As they entered, a wave of cheers erupted from the stands. Lebanese expatriates, many draped in their homeland's flag, stood proudly, chanting and waving in unison. The sound of traditional Lebanese derbakke drums echoed through the stadium, adding a rhythmic pulse to the moment. Yasmine felt a surge of exhilaration, exchanging glances with her teammates as they waved to the crowd.

"Hadha ghayr waqieiun tamaman!" she exclaimed to Nadine, who walked beside her. "I didn't expect this kind of reception."

Nadine smiled, her eyes scanning the roaring audience. "Lebanon always brings passion, no matter where we are."

Omar turned back briefly, raising a fist in solidarity with his team before refocusing ahead, leading them with steady confidence. The Lebanese delegation marched forward, their steps purposeful, as the stadium announcer's voice boomed, highlighting their achievements and aspirations in the 2040 Games.

Meanwhile, in the Israeli section, the athletes watched the warm reception Lebanon received. Tamar Cohen, a sprinter, exhaled sharply. "Unbelievable," she muttered under her breath.

"It's like we're ghosts," added swimmer Noa Levi, shaking her head. "Or villains."

Weissman adjusted her grip on the Star of David banner, keeping her expression neutral. "We knew it would be like this," she said firmly. "But we're here. We earned this. That's what matters."

Tamar forced a small smile. "Guess we just let our performances do the talking."

"Exactly," Yael agreed. "We represent more than just the reaction of the crowd. We represent our country, our families, and the work we put in."

The Israeli athletes continued watching as the Lebanese delegation completed their lap, standing strong despite the lingering tension in the air.

In the media tribune, journalists from around the world scrambled to document the moment. Mendelsohn adjusted her earpiece as she exchanged glances with the reporters around her.

"Unbelievable," she muttered, shaking her head. "This celebration of unity is a total fucking farse."

A British correspondent beside her, James Cartwright, sighed. "Not exactly shocking, though, is it? Given the region's history?"

Nova exhaled sharply. "No, but you'd think, with all the emphasis on inclusivity and sportsmanship, people would at least pretend for one night."

A Qatari journalist, Layla Al-Mansoori, tapped her stylus against her tablet. "It's complicated," she said carefully. "Many people see this as political no matter what. The reception was expected."

Nova frowned. "Expected or not, it's disgusting. These athletes trained for years to be here, just like everyone else."

Layla nodded. "True, but emotions run deep. The world will interpret this moment in many ways."

Nova typed furiously, the memory of another crowd flashing through her mind. Boston, 2013. She'd crossed the marathon finish line in 3:40, flushed with triumph. Then the bombs exploded. Chaos. Blood. Her journalist instincts had kicked in—she'd recorded, helped, survived. That day had shattered her law career and launched her into reporting. Now, here in Doha, the boos felt like echoes of that blast—division masked as celebration.

The ceremony continued, but Nova's mind lingered on Boston. It had taught her: spectacle could hide horror. And Doha felt ripe for it.

Growing up in Newark's Weequahic section, in a middle-class Jewish family, she'd learned to read the world sideways—trust tone over words, spot lies behind smiles. Her parents, a teacher and an accountant, pushed education above all. At Solomon Schechter Day School, she'd been a stubborn track runner, never a star but determined. Finishing dead last in a 1500m race had sparked her epiphany: she wasn't meant for the track, but to write about it.

The parade dragged on, but Nova's thoughts raced back to Syracuse, where she'd earned her journalism degree in just three years while cutting her teeth on athletics coverage. Those days had built her reputation—sharp, fearless, with a deep love for track. But, life had detoured her into law at Seton Hall, a year of corporate drudgery in Manhattan. The billable hours suffocated her, but running kept her sane—until that Vero Beach Marathon in 2012, qualifying her for Boston, proving grit mattered.

The boos faded, but the tension lingered. Nova wondered if Doha would be her next turning point.

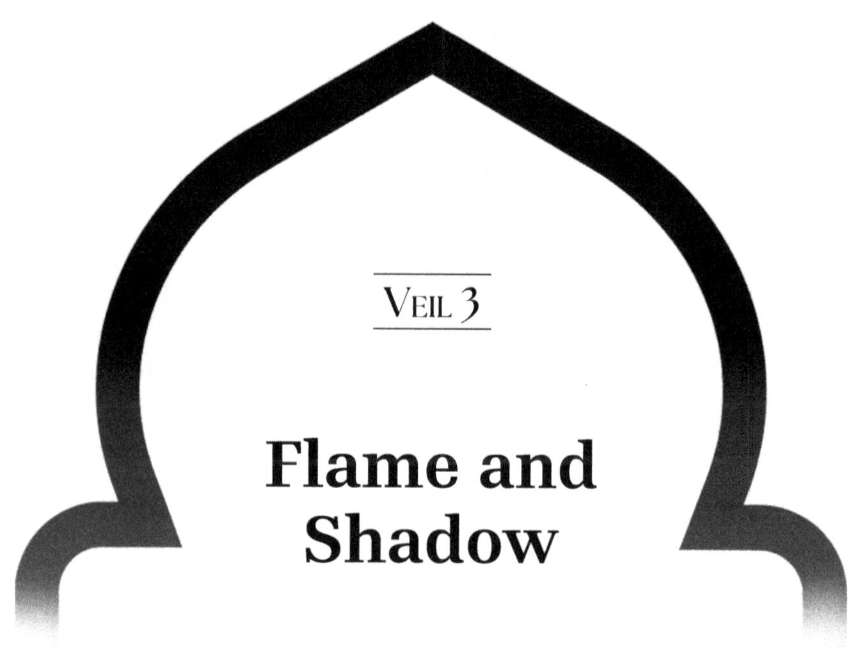

Veil 3

Flame and Shadow

A sudden hush fell over the crowd as the stadium floor transformed, revealing a massive, man-made river emerging from beneath. Gasps echoed through the stands as a grand wooden dhow, a traditional Qatari sailing vessel, glided gracefully across the water, carrying the host nation's delegation.

Their entrance was unlike anything ever seen in an Olympic Games. As the dhow reached the center of the stadium, a burst of fireworks erupted into the sky, illuminating the faces of the Qatari athletes, who waved proudly to the crowd.

In the media section, the reaction was immediate. Mendelsohn leaned forward in her seat, eyes wide. "Now that," she murmured, "is how you make an entrance."

Cartwright of the BBC whistled. "I don't think I've ever seen something this grand. Doha just rewrote the rulebook for Olympic host nations."

Emilie Laurent, a journalist at France's L'Équipe, clapped her hands together in delight. "The symbolism is beautiful—the dhow, the water, it's a tribute to Qatar's seafaring history. This is more than spectacle; it's storytelling."

Even Greg Palmer, the skeptical Australian journalist, shook his head in begrudging admiration. "Alright, I'll give it to them. That was one hell of an entrance."

Social media exploded with reactions, with hashtags like #DhowOfDreams and #Qatar2040 trending worldwide. The spectacle was already being hailed as one of the most memorable moments in Olympic history.

The stadium thrummed with anticipation as Sheikh Tariq bin Fahd Al-Mazrouei stepped forward, his robes rippling faintly in the warm Doha breeze. With a gesture both regal and serene, he presided over the ceremonial release of doves—dozens of them spiraling upward in a cascade of white wings against the indigo night.

The crowd's murmurs softened into a reverent hush as he approached the podium, the Olympic rings gleaming behind him, a symbol of global unity framed by the ultramodern arc of Lusail Stadium.

"My friends from every corner of the world," the Sheikh began, his voice steady yet resonant, carrying across the sea of faces and flickering camera lights. "Tonight, we gather not merely as nations, but as a single human family, bound by the timeless ideals of peace, excellence, and shared endeavor.

"Here, in Qatar, where the desert meets the sea, where tradition dances with progress, we welcome you to the Games of the XXXVII Olympiad. For centuries, our people have looked to the horizon—divers plunging into the depths for pearls, traders crossing dunes and waters to connect worlds. Tonight, that spirit of courage and connection lights our way forward. Let these Games be a beacon of hope, a testament to what we can achieve when we strive together."

With a final flourish, he raised his hands skyward. "I declare open the Games of the XXXVII Olympiad!" The Olympic flag snapped taut in the wind, its colors vivid under the floodlights, as the haunting strains of the Olympic hymn swelled, stirring hearts in the stands and beyond.

The oaths followed—athletes, judges, and coaches reciting their pledges with solemn pride—before the stadium erupted anew.

Mutaz Essa Barshim, Qatar's high-jumping legend and the 2020 Olympic gold medalist, bounded into view, the Olympic torch blazing in his grip. His strides were fluid, almost effortless, a testament to the grace that had carried him to global acclaim. The crowd roared, a thunderous wave of sound that seemed to lift him higher as he approached the centerpiece of the night.

The cauldron emerged from behind a curtain, a breathtaking marvel unlike any before it. Nova felt torn between admiration and the unease of what such grandeur was meant to overshadow. Crafted to evoke Doha's pearling legacy, it rose as an enormous oyster shell, its curves sculpted from shimmering steel and glass, cradling a luminous orb at its heart—a pearl reimagined as a vessel of fire. The design glittered with intricate filigree, echoing the patterns of traditional Qatari dhows, while a sculpted wave of molten metal and cascading light spiraled upward, guiding Barshim to his destiny.

As he ascended, torch held aloft, the pearl ignited—a radiant burst of flame and color that shimmered like a mirage, bathing the stadium in golden reflections. The skyline of Doha glowed in response, its towers catching the light as if the city itself were celebrating this fusion of past and future.

From the media tribune, Nova leaned forward, her voice a mix of awe and excitement as she spoke into her recorder.

"I've covered 13 Olympics, but this—this is something else entirely. That cauldron lighting? It's not just a flame; it's a story. You've got this oyster shell, massive and gleaming, holding that pearl like it's cradling history itself.

"And when Barshim lit it, the way that glow spilled out, rippling across the stadium and into the night—it's like Doha's saying, 'Look at us, look at where we've been and where we're going.' It's poetic, it's powerful, and honestly, it's one of the most stunning things I've ever seen at an opening ceremony. The legacy of those pearl divers, the resilience of this place—it's all right there in that light." She paused, her eyes tracing the shimmering skyline.

"This is going to be one for the ages."

The lights dimmed once more. A hush fell. Then, the story of a nation unfolded. From the sky, drones swirled in precise formations, their synchronized movements forming the iconic Olympic rings, then morphing into a falcon in mid-flight—Qatar's national symbol.

The crowd roared in approval. As the drones reassembled into calligraphic designs of Arabic poetry, a symphony of traditional Qatari instruments—ouds, rebabs, and daffs—filled the stadium with melodies rooted in centuries-old Bedouin traditions.

The celebration deepened, unfolding a layered portrait of Qatari heritage.

There was a pearl diving tribute where a troupe of performers dressed as pearl divers emerged from the stadium floor in a simulated underwater environment, representing Qatar's historical ties to the industry. Gasps rippled through the crowd as the arena dissolved into the depths of the Gulf.

The stage was transformed into a breathtaking underwater seascape, with projected waves rippling across the floor and holographic fish swimming between the divers.

Soft blue lighting cast an ethereal glow, mimicking the depths of the Arabian Gulf. The performers moved with fluid precision, their flowing garments creating the illusion of water currents as they 'swam' gracefully. A haunting melody played on traditional Qatari instruments, blending with the sound of distant waves.

As the performance reached its climax, the divers surfaced with glowing pearls in their hands. They presented the pearls to a central figure dressed as a merchant from the bygone era, who lifted them toward the sky, symbolizing the nation's transformation from a pearl-diving economy to a modern global powerhouse. The sequence ended with a brilliant burst of golden light, illuminating the entire stadium and leaving the audience in awe.

Then there was a stunning display of the traditional Qatari ardha sword dance, an iconic performance deeply rooted in Qatari heritage. Rows of men dressed in golden bishts, embroidered with intricate designs, moved in rhythmic unison, their swords gleaming under the stadium's dazzling lights. The steady beat of traditional drums, known as al-ras, resounded through the air, setting the tempo for the dancers' synchronized steps.

As they advanced in formation, their voices rose in a powerful poetic chant, each verse recounting stories of bravery, honor, and unity from Qatar's storied past. The poetry, known as nabati, carried deep historical significance, invoking the strength of ancestors who defended their land and upheld their traditions. Behind the performers, massive LED screens projected desert landscapes and historic battles, immersing the audience in the rich history of the Arabian Peninsula.

At the climax of the performance, the dancers raised their swords high, crossing them in a symbolic gesture of solidarity and national pride. The audience erupted into applause, moved by the electrifying display of culture. The ardha dance, a testament to Qatar's resilience and unity, in a moment became the country's most eloquent ambassador, setting the stage for the rest of the night's breathtaking performances.

Nova watched, her notepad filling with notes, but her thoughts drifted.

As the product of a middle-class Jewish family, her parents had pushed education, but she'd found her path in journalism. S.I. Newhouse School of Public Communications had honed her skills, and the brief detour into law had only confirmed her calling.

But it was Boston—the marathon, the bombs—that had forged her. She'd run it, finished it, then reported on the chaos. That day changed everything, pushing her into Olympic journalism. Now, amid Doha's spectacle, she wondered if history would repeat itself.

After five years at The New York Times, where she'd covered Sochi's human rights abuses and Russia's doping scandal, she'd launched OlymPulse for more freedom—in-depth profiles, investigations on overlooked athletes. This was her seventh Summer Games, fourteenth overall.

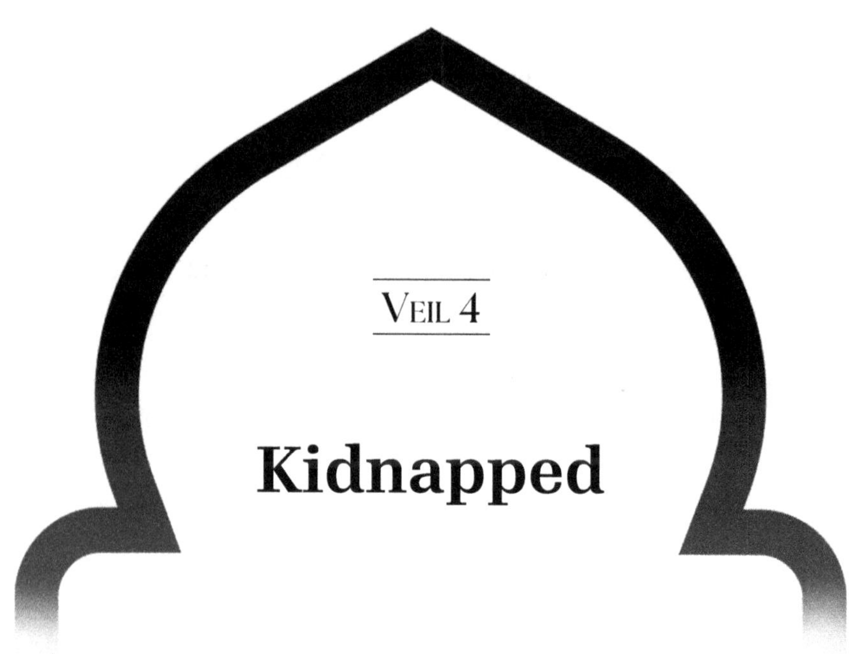

Veil 4

Kidnapped

The Olympic Village shimmered under stadium lights, its sleek glass buildings humming with the echoes of celebration. But just beneath the chorus of laughter and pounding music, an uneasy stillness clung to the air like static before a storm.

Some, exhausted from the emotional high of the ceremony, retreated straight to their rooms, eager to get a good night's rest before competition began. Others, still buzzing with adrenaline, gathered in common areas, celebrating the momentous night with drinks, laughter, and music.

In the Israeli dormitory, Tamar Cohen stretched on her bed, scrolling through social media as her roommate, Noa Levi, a swimmer, lay on the top bunk, earbuds in, listening to music.

A few rooms down, Yael Ben-Ami, a modern pentathlete, had collapsed into bed still in her ceremonial attire, too drained to change. Across the hall, teammates played a quiet game of cards, their voices hushed but lively as they reminisced about their journey to the Games.

Meanwhile, in the Lebanese dormitory, Omar Haddad sat on the edge of his bed, rubbing his sore knuckles from a celebratory fist bump gone wrong. Nadine Mansour, an equestrian competitor, joked with her roommates about their unexpected fanfare during the parade.

Yasmine Khalil, a marathon runner, leaned against the window, gazing at the glowing Doha skyline, still processing the magnitude of the event.

In another wing of the Village, other national delegations reveled in the afterglow of the ceremony. A group of Brazilian athletes played samba music on portable speakers, dancing in a circle as American and Japanese gymnasts joined in. Swedish and South Korean archers and shooters engaged in a friendly debate over who would claim the most medals, laughing between playful taunts.

A few dormitories hosted quieter gatherings, intimate moments shared between competitors from different nations—sometimes in hushed conversations about past training, sometimes in passionate encounters that would be remembered long after the Games ended.

The Olympic Village had always been notorious for its uninhibited atmosphere, and with a reported 40,000 condoms made available, many athletes took full advantage of the fleeting opportunity. Behind closed doors, bodies entwined, adrenaline and pent-up energy finding sexual release in fevered exchanges.

Some encounters were quick, fueled by mutual attraction, alcohol, and the euphoria of the night while others unfolded slowly, whispered conversations turning into shared secrets, comfort, and connection.

For some, the night blurred into passion, a brief escape from the pressures of competition. By 3 a.m., the revelry had begun to wane. Laughter and music dimmed. The last few wandering souls, reluctant to let the night end, finally retreated to their rooms. Silence slowly crept over the Village.

The music had stopped. The laughter had died. Now, only the whisper of wind against metal fencing broke the silence as twelve figures slipped through the shadows, the Village suddenly too quiet to be safe. They had arrived in unmarked black SUVs, which had been staged outside a maintenance access road near the Village's service entrance.

From there, they moved on foot, their approach synchronized with a cyber intrusion that disrupted security cameras and sensors. A perimeter fence, designed to detect the slightest breach, blinked offline for precisely 120 seconds—just long enough for the intruders to slip through.

The Olympic Village, meant to be one of the most secure locations in the world, had been compromised.

The team, clad in all-black gear with night-vision goggles and silenced firearms, operated with surgical precision. Each was equipped with a specialized loadout: subsonic weapons, tranquilizer darts, and electronic jammers to neutralize potential alarms.

They split into two groups of six, one assigned to finding the Israeli dormitory and the other to locate the Lebanese quarters. Moving in synchronized formation, they used handheld devices to override biometric locks in seconds, doors sliding open with barely a whisper.

Inside, the athletes slept, oblivious to the danger creeping upon them.

The first sign of intrusion came as muffled whispers in the dark. Then, sudden movement—shadows shifting against the dim glow of emergency exit signs. Within moments, hands were over mouths, arms wrenched behind backs.

Some athletes awoke in confusion, only to be met with fists striking their temples or knees driven into their ribs.

Lior Abramson managed to thrash against his attackers, but was swiftly subdued by brutal efficiency. Blood stained the sheets as Ronit Weissman and Yael Ben-Ami had their noses broken from the impact of rifle butts, and their muffled cries of pain were silenced by thick, gloved hands clamped over mouths.

The Lebanese dorm was breached at the same time. A similar, ruthless efficiency was displayed—athletes were dragged from their beds, their heads slammed against the walls if they resisted.

Omar Haddad, still groggy from sleep, managed to throw a punch at one of the masked intruders before a savage blow to his temple sent him crumbling to the ground.

Nadine Mansour screamed, only for a knife to press against her throat, her breath hitching as a hushed warning was whispered in her ear.

Some of the captives tried to fight back even as they were hauled from their rooms, but their struggles only earned them harsher beatings—ribs cracked beneath booted feet, arms were wrenched so violently behind backs that shoulders popped from their sockets.

Cyclist Cyrine Ghazal made it to the door before a silenced bullet buried itself in her calf, sending her crumpling to the floor as a hood was yanked over her head.

A security guard making rounds spotted movement from down the hall and hesitated for half a second before reaching for his radio. He never got the chance to call for help—a dart struck his neck, and within moments, he collapsed unconscious. Another guard, stationed near the exit, was met with a swift knife to the ribs, his breath coming out in a strangled wheeze before he, too, crumpled to the floor.

As the operation neared its conclusion, two members of the Italian women's beach volleyball team, Gabriella Russo and Martina De Luca, strolled through the dimly lit walkway leading back to their dorm. Their laughter faded as they noticed the suspicious movement near the service exit. Gabriella instinctively reached for her phone, but she had no time to react.

A masked figure emerged from the shadows and grabbed her, one gloved hand clamping over her mouth while the other wrenched her wrist back, forcing her to drop the device. Martina let out a stifled gasp before another attacker seized her, twisting her arms behind her back and forcing her to her knees.

They struggled, but their attackers were stronger, faster. Gabriella managed to break free for a second, stumbling back as she opened her mouth to scream—but the blunt end of a rifle struck her temple with sickening force, and she collapsed in a heap.

Martina's muffled pleas vanished into the dark as she was dragged behind the hedge. A shadow moved once, twice, and then there was only stillness, her phone screen blinking faintly in the gravel, her struggling form vanishing into the darkness as the blade of a cold steel sliced across her neck and plunged through her breast. Moments later, the path was empty again, save for Gabriella's shattered phone, its screen flickering weakly.

The entire operation lasted no more than five minutes. Each athlete was bound with zip ties, their unconscious or semi-conscious bodies carried out swiftly. The intruders moved with a practiced, military-like efficiency, slipping through the same path they had entered. The bodies of the fallen guards were left behind as grim warnings.

Once outside, the kidnappers loaded the captives into the waiting SUVs, which sped through a pre-planned escape route, avoiding main roads and weaving through service alleys and backstreets. Within ten minutes, they reached a concealed landing zone on the outskirts of the city, where three RAH-66 Comanche stealth helicopters were waiting, rotors barely making a sound against the desert wind.

The hostages, still unconscious or groggy, were hauled into the helicopters, secured with chains and restraints. Within moments, the aircraft lifted off, disappearing into the desert night with no radar detection, their presence masked by advanced stealth technology.

A junior technician at the security outpost blinked at his screen as the feed returned. "What the..." he muttered, scanning the blank halls. No motion. No heat signatures. Just blood, and silence. The Village remained silent, oblivious to the nightmare unfolding. As the helicopters disappeared into the darkness, the captives were gone—vanished without a trace.

Veil 5

Crisis Unfolds

A horrific discovery was made just before dawn. Coach Marco Conti, making his early rounds to check on his athletes, noticed the shattered remains of a phone near the walkway and a faint trail of blood leading toward the dormitories.

His initial confusion turned to horror as he saw the motionless bodies of Gabriella Russo and Martina De Luca crumpled in the bushes. Their lifeless eyes stared into nothingness, the ground beneath them darkened with congealed blood. His scream of terror shattered the early morning silence, sending a ripple of panic through the Village.

Security forces arrived within minutes, swarming the dormitory corridors. What they found sent shockwaves through the Olympic community.

The Israeli and Lebanese dorms had been completely ransacked—mattresses overturned, sheets torn, blood smeared on the walls. The air was heavy with the metallic scent of blood and the sharp sting of broken glass. Personal belongings lay scattered across the floor: torn uniforms, shattered water bottles, and half-packed suitcases left abandoned in haste.

One locker had been violently forced open, its contents spilling out, including a passport left behind in the chaos. A half-eaten energy bar sat on a desk beside an overturned chair, as if someone had been interrupted mid-bite before being dragged away. In the Israeli dorm, a Star of David necklace lay trampled into the carpet, its chain snapped.

In the Lebanese quarters, a team flag had been ripped from the wall and lay crumpled in a corner. Dried streaks of blood ran down one doorframe, and scratch marks were visible on a nearby wall—clear signs of a desperate struggle. A phone screen flickered weakly from beneath a bed, displaying a shattered video call frozen on the image of a horrified loved one.

Several security guards, assigned to the night patrol, were discovered slain near the exits, their throats slit with military precision. Others lay slumped in hallways, tranquilizer darts still embedded in their necks.

An emergency committee convened before sunrise. Words like 'containment' and 'optics' filled the room before 'rescue' was even uttered. The first memo to national delegations emphasized calm and cautioned silence. A headcount confirmed the worst: all six Israeli and all six Lebanese athletes had vanished without a trace.

Within the hour, Qatari law enforcement and intelligence agencies descended upon the Village. The elite Lekhwiya Internal Security Force, clad in tactical gear and armed with compact submachine guns, moved in first, securing the perimeter and establishing checkpoints at every exit. Their crimson berets, the symbol of Qatar's rapid-response counterterrorism unit, stood out against the dim morning light.

Accompanying them were officers from the Ministry of Interior's Special Operations Unit, who began combing through the dormitories with K9 units trained for detecting explosives and human scents. Police drones were deployed overhead, scanning the area for any heat signatures or unusual movement, while mobile command units set up an operational hub just outside the Village gates.

Forensic teams combed through the crime scenes, collecting shell casings, blood samples, and fragments of fabric torn in the struggle. Surveillance footage, once restored, provided a brief, grainy glimpse of masked figures moving through the dorms—ghostly shadows slipping in and out of sight. But beyond that, there was no sign of where the kidnapped athletes had been taken, nor who had orchestrated the attack.

Emergency sirens blared through the Village as panic spread among the remaining athletes. Lights flicked on in dorm rooms as groggy competitors from around the world peered out their windows, trying to make sense of the chaos. Some stumbled into the hallways, still in their pajamas, whispering nervously in their native tongues.

"What the fuck is going on?" muttered American sprinter Jason Carter, rubbing the sleep from his eyes. "I heard screams," Swedish swimmer Linnea Eriksson responded, clutching her teammate's arm. "It woke me up. Something bad happened."

In the hallway, Brazilian gymnast Rafael Nascimento stopped a passing French judoka, Antoine Lefevre. "Did you see anything?"

"Only the police. So many of them. Armed," he replied, shaking his head. "This isn't just some fight. Something bigger."

Argentinian rower Santiago Velasco pressed his face to a window overlooking the Village courtyard. "There are bodies," he whispered, voice laced with horror. "Near the bushes. Madre de

Dios! This is bad."

In one corner, a group of Kenyan runners lit small candles beneath a balcony. Nearby, a Japanese coach silently bowed at the edge of the courtyard, hands folded in grief. Religion or not, the Village had become a shrine of sorrow.

Nearby, Muslim athletes unfurled prayer mats, bowing toward Mecca, their voices rising in solemn unison as they sought divine protection for their missing comrades.

Others, without a specific religious affiliation, simply clasped hands in silent solidarity, forming circles in the courtyards and dormitory hallways.

Some wept openly, their tears glistening under the harsh fluorescent lights, while others closed their eyes, murmuring desperate pleas into the still night air. In this moment of crisis, differences of nationality, faith, and competition melted away, leaving only shared grief and hope.

The cafeteria lights buzzed faintly overhead, casting long shadows over trays of untouched food. The air smelled of reheated starch and panic.

Swimmer Natalie Brooks clutched her coffee cup, her hands trembling. "This can't be happening. Not here, not now."

Hurdler Marcus Reynolds shook his head, his jaw tight with tension. "They were taken. Just like that? Where the fuck was security?"

"I thought I heard shots," added gymnast Alyssa Park, her voice barely above a whisper. "And then the screaming started. Jesus Christ, I can't stop shaking."

Wrestler Damon Cole slammed his fist on the table, rattling the cutlery. “They’ve been warning about regional unrest for months,”

Damon muttered. “No one wanted to admit it could touch the Games.”

At a nearby table, American women’s pole vaulter Emily Dawson sat hunched over her phone, her shoulders shaking as she sobbed. “Come on, Mom, pick up…” she whispered, her thumb trembling over the call icon. “Please.”

"Please pick up, please," she begged under her breath, her voice breaking. But there was no answer—only endless ringing, taunting her with silence. She let out a strangled cry, burying her face in her hands as her teammates exchanged uneasy glances, the weight of the unfolding nightmare settling over them like a suffocating fog.

The televisions mounted around the dining area suddenly switched to a breaking news broadcast, the red scion flashing across the screen.

The anchor’s voice, usually chipper with sports updates, now rang flat and metallic, betraying the magnitude of what he had to say.

"We interrupt our coverage of the Olympic Games with breaking news out of the Olympic Village," the broadcaster announced, his voice grim. "In a shocking and tragic development, multiple athletes from the Israeli and Lebanese delegations have been kidnapped overnight in what appears to be a highly coordinated attack. Security footage remains inconclusive, but sources are reporting multiple fatalities have been discovered at the scene."

By this time, Jason Carter groggily made his way over to the table, rubbing his temples. "Now what? Do we just keep competing like nothing fucking happened? Or is this whole fucking thing about to fall apart?"

The news quickly spread to the Raffles Doha, the hotel housing all of the Olympic dignitaries, and panic surged through the ranks of the IOC. An urgent call was placed to Sheikh Tariq bin Fahd Al-

Mazrouei.

He had staked his reputation, and the region's image on these Games. Now, it all threatened to unravel before dawn. Woken from his sleep by his chief security officer, the Sheikh immediately sat up, his face draining of color as he absorbed the news. He had spent years championing the first Olympics in the Middle East, and now, in an instant, the Games had become a global crisis. The echoes of 1972 Munich filled his mind—a nightmare the Olympic movement had sworn would never happen again.

Dressing hurriedly, he barked orders to his staff, demanding every resource be thrown at the unfolding catastrophe.

Within minutes, a high-level emergency meeting was convened in a secure conference room of the Raffles Doha. Around the table sat the Sheikh, his chief security officer, members of Qatar's state security forces, the Olympic security chief, and key IOC officials, their faces pale with tension. Satellite images and grainy security footage flickered on the screen before them, showing masked figures moving with military precision through the Village.

"How the hell did this happen?" demanded Jacques Moreau, the French IOC vice president. One assistant murmured something about procedural gaps but fell silent under the weight of the room's glares. "We were assured security was airtight."

Qatari intelligence officer Colonel Faisal Al-Kuwari exhaled sharply. "We are reviewing every breach point. These men knew what they were doing—they bypassed multiple security layers as if they had inside knowledge."

Another officer, Major Hamad Al-Nasr, leaned forward, his voice low and measured. "It is too soon to confirm, but the precision of this operation suggests extensive planning. We must consider the possibility that someone within our security structure fed them details."

Captain Amal Rahman, arms crossed, added, "Or they could have been studying us for months, even years. With enough surveillance, even the tightest security can be unraveled. The question is—who would go to such lengths, and why now?" "We are reviewing every breach point. These men knew what they were doing."

“Inside knowledge?" interjected U.S. Olympic Committee President Linda Reynolds, her brow furrowed. "Are you saying this was an inside job?"

The Sheikh slammed his palm on the table. "Enough speculation! We need facts, and we need them now! Every second that passes, our athletes are in greater danger. Mobilize every available resource. Coordinate with INTERPOL and every international intelligence agency.

Lock down the borders. No one leaves this country without scrutiny.

"We cannot let this be another Munich!" he snapped, his voice cracking as he spoke the word. Munich. The kidnapping and murder of 11 Israeli athletes by Palestinian terrorists still haunted the Olympic conscience nearly seven decades later. "The world is watching. We must act swiftly."

Across the city, in hotels housing the international press, the world was already beginning to watch.

Nova Mendelsohn jolted awake in the dim glow of her hotel room, the stiff hotel sheets tangled around her legs. She had been dreaming of sand dunes and warm coffee. The ringing phone felt like an alarm from another world. Her phone, face down on the nightstand, vibrated against the artificial wood with another incoming call.

The sound barely registered—she was already staring at the screen, heart pounding as she processed the barrage of notifications. Missed calls, frantic messages, and a flood of news alerts lit up her phone:

"BREAKING: Hostage Crisis at Olympic Village" ... "Israeli, Lebanese Athletes Among Those Taken in Coordinated Attack" ... "Security Failure Raises Questions Amid Growing Panic."

"Holy shit!," she muttered, sitting up, her jet lag forgotten in an instant.

Across the hall, James Cartwright was already dressed, pacing in his room with his phone pressed to his ear. "I don't care if it's six in the goddamned morning, get me a statement from security officials now!" he barked, running a hand through his graying hair.

Meanwhile, Emilie Laurent stood at her window, staring out at the city's quiet streets, the eerie calm at odds with the chaos unfolding. She exhaled sharply, swiping through the flood of messages from her editor. Get to the Main Press Center ASAP. We need updates from the French Olympic delegation. Get confirmation on the number of hostages.

Greg Palmer, with a reputation for chasing danger, was already halfway out the door, shoving a notebook into his jacket pocket as he muttered, "If it bleeds, it leads," he muttered, checking his camera battery. "And this one's arterial."

As the sun rose over Doha, what had begun as a night of Olympic celebration had transformed into an international crisis. The world's eyes are on Qatar, demanding answers.

What they didn't yet know was how deep the shadow ran, or how long it had been waiting.

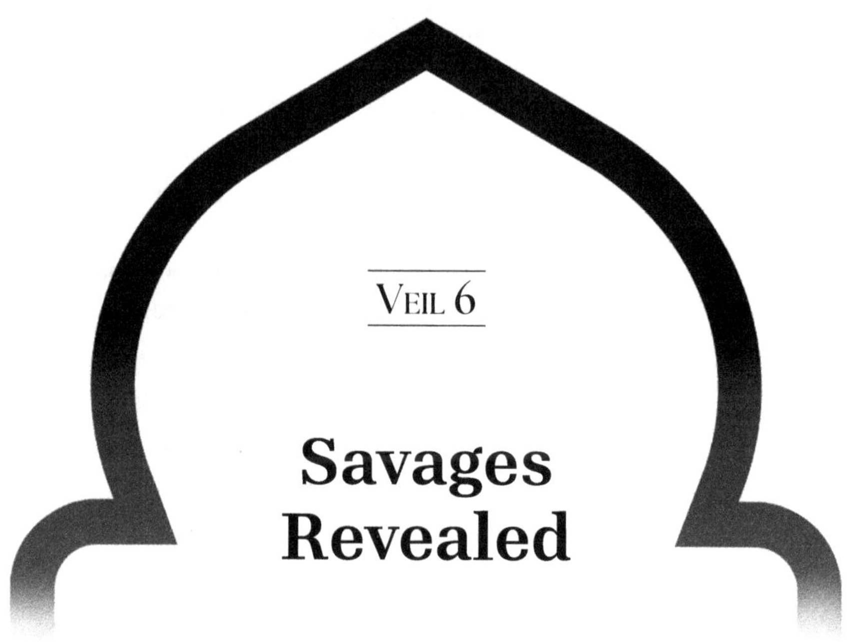

Veil 6

Savages Revealed

The captives awoke in darkness.

The air was thick with damp earth and the sour tang of sweat and blood, pressing against Maya's bruised ribs like a living thing. Her wrists burned where metal cuffs bit into raw skin, chains tethering her to the cold stone floor.

Beside her, Omar stirred, his breath ragged. Yasmine, her taekwondo champion sister, sat rigid, eyes blazing with defiance despite the blood crusting her temple. Lior slumped against the wall, unmoving, while Tamar trembled, her whispers barely audible. The silence was broken only by a distant drip of water and the faint clink of chains as someone shifted.

A single bulb flickered above, caged in rusted iron, casting jagged shadows across the cavernous chamber. The walls were rough, pockmarked stone, slick with age and neglect, the low ceiling forcing a hunch that made Maya's spine ache.

The iron door—scarred with desperate claw marks—stood as the only exit, its bolts a grim promise of entrapment. This was no ordinary prison; it felt like a tomb, carved from some forgotten war, buried deep under a barren expanse outside of Barga Al Kharaz, a remote and uncharted region on the fringes of the Rub' al Khali, or "Empty Quarter." Outside, Maya imagined endless dunes swallowing sound, stars mocking their captivity in a sky they couldn't see.

She'd heard the name before, whispered like a curse in locker rooms: The Obsidian Hand.

Now, it wasn't just a story. It was the weight in her chest, the dread pooling in her gut. As her pulse hammered, fragments of their legend surfaced in her mind, unbidden, like shards of a nightmare she couldn't shake.

The Obsidian Hand.

Born from the ashes of the Yom Kippur War in 1973, when Arab forces struck Israel and were pushed back, leaving bitterness in their wake. In refugee camps, among displaced Palestinians and betrayed soldiers, the group took root, fueled by rage against peace deals like Camp David that they saw as surrender. They drew from ancient Najdi traditions of tha'r—a blood debt, honor balanced through vengeance.

Over the years, the group had evolved, shifting from scattered cells to an organized network, funded by illicit trade, black-market arms dealings, and shadowy benefactors with vested interests in destabilizing regional politics.

What had begun as a reactionary movement fueled by the anger of a lost war transformed into a sophisticated paramilitary organization, capable of orchestrating complex operations across borders. The lessons of the Yom Kippur War had taught them one thing—never to rely on governments, only on their own unwavering commitment to their cause.

The Obsidian Hand's insignia—an intricate arrangement of cryptic Arabic calligraphy intertwined with a bleeding crescent moon—symbolized their belief that peace was an illusion, that only force and bloodshed could rectify the historical wrongs imposed upon their people. Their motto, "Through fire, we are forged," was whispered in the darkest corners of the region, a warning to those who opposed them.

The group was founded in the early 1980s by four infamous figures, each shaped by personal tragedy and radicalized by years of violence and betrayal.

Jibril al-Nasr, a former Palestinian guerrilla strategist, grew up in the shattered ruins of a refugee camp, watching his family suffer under Israeli military occupation. As a young man, he joined a militant faction, quickly rising through the ranks due to his tactical brilliance. After narrowly escaping an airstrike that obliterated his entire unit, al-Nasr vowed to dedicate his life to orchestrating a new, more ruthless resistance.

Hassan Suleiman, an exiled Lebanese militia commander, once fought in the brutal Lebanese Civil War. Originally a nationalist fighter, he saw his comrades massacred in a failed coup attempt against a pro-Western faction. Branded a traitor and forced into hiding, Hassan fled to the mountains, where he rebuilt his following from the shadows, developing a deep hatred for both Lebanese elites and foreign powers that had meddled in his country's affairs.

Fadi al-Bashir, an arms dealer with deep connections to underground terror networks, was born into a wealthy Gulf family but rejected his privileged upbringing after witnessing government corruption firsthand. While working in the illicit arms trade, he realized that war was not just an ideological struggle but a lucrative business. His radicalization was gradual, fueled by a growing contempt for Western-backed regimes and a desire to fund insurgencies that would destabilize their power.

al-Nasr met his end in a fiery ambush on the outskirts of Damascus. Suleiman's life ended in the Bekaa Valley, where his own recruits opened fire on him. al-Bashir's death came in the chaos of a double-cross. Though those three men were gone, their deaths did not mark the end of The Obsidian Hand. If anything, their violent ends only fueled the next generation of militants, who saw them as martyrs.

Maya's breath hitched as she recalled the fourth founder, Dr. Samir Haddad, the group's most twisted mind. Once a surgeon celebrated for separating conjoined twins, he'd been broken by false accusations of assault, years in a brutal prison twisting his genius into something grotesque.

She'd dismissed rumors of his "Singularity" experiments as myth—tales of nerves rewired, pain weaponized to shatter human limits. But now, in this suffocating dark, she felt the myths breathing nearby, their weight as real as the chains on her wrists.

The door groaned open, metal screeching against stone. A tall figure entered, balaclava-clad, his posture rigid like a soldier's. Two others flanked him, rifles slung casually. The leader knelt, his gaze sweeping over them with clinical detachment. Maya's stomach twisted as his eyes met hers, cold and unyielding.

"Not all of you will suffer today," he said, his accented English laced with faint amusement. "But the night is long, and pain finds the strong. Pray your overlords pay, or screams will be lost here."

No one spoke. Fear choked them. He rose, the door slamming shut behind him, locks echoing like a gavel. Maya exchanged glances with the others—Omar's jaw tight, Yasmine's fists clenched, Tamar's eyes wide with panic. The Olympics, their dreams of gold, felt like another life. Survival was their only game now.

In a shadowed room elsewhere in the compound, Khalid Al-Masri, The Commander, leaned over a monitor displaying a $500 billion ransom demand. His fingers drummed the table, his voice low and deliberate. He was a cold and calculating figure known for his ruthless intelligence and strategic brilliance.

"They think they can stall, negotiate, spy. We'll show them the cost of hesitation."

The Specter, his second-in-command, nodded, adjusting a camera in the dim light.

"The first broadcast is ready. They'll watch."

Maya didn't see the room where Ronit Weissman was dragged, but she heard the echoes—metal screeching, boots thudding, the sharp rip of fabric, a muffled cry that twisted into desperate, pleading gasps before cutting short. Her mind raced, piecing together the whispered horrors she'd heard about The Obsidian Hand's leaders and their brutal, violating appetites.

Al-Masri, a former officer turned warlord, his cold brilliance shaping the group into a paramilitary force. The Specter, a ghost who orchestrated atrocities from the shadows.

And Haddad, The Doctor, whose experiments turned human bodies into canvases of suffering. Others, too—Rashid Nazari, The Arbiter, a judge warped by loss; Adil Rahmani, The Scribe, a historian turned propagandist; Zainab Al-Fahd, The Watcher, a betrayed spy with eyes everywhere; Darius Khan, The Enforcer, a mercenary mountain; Elias Marwan, The Keeper, a shadow guarding their secrets. Each a piece of the machine that held them now.

When the door screeched open again, Maya's heart lurched. Ronit was shoved back into the cell, her face pale, eyes hollow. There was a faint tremor in her hands as she reached to pull her legs in closer, to her chest, unaware as she smeared the drip of blood on her inner thigh. She collapsed against the wall, curling in on herself, her breathing shallow.

Maya's chest tightened, her mind recoiling from what Ronit's silence implied.

The air seemed to thicken, the stench of rust and fear sharper now. She wanted to reach out, to say something, but words felt useless against the weight of what had happened.

Nadine, hunched in the next cage, met Maya's gaze, her eyes wide with dread. The Specter lingered at the door, his shadow still, the camera's red eye glinting behind him. Maya's pulse thundered, her mind flashing to Haddad's philosophy—pain as a tool to break the soul, to control.

She wouldn't let it. Not yet.

The Obsidian Hand hated more than just them. They despised Israel, born from the scars of 1982's Lebanon invasion, the bombings of Beirut, the massacres at Sabra and Shatila. They scorned Lebanon, too, for cracking down on their allies in the '90s, choosing diplomacy over resistance.

And the Olympics?

A symbol of Western hypocrisy, a stage that barred their people while preaching unity.

Maya remembered the story of a Palestinian weightlifter, banned in '96 over passport disputes—a spark that fueled their vendetta against the Games.

The door clanged shut, sealing them in darkness again. Maya's fingers traced the cold chain, her mind clinging to fragments of defiance.

The Obsidian Hand wanted to break them, to broadcast their pain to the world. She knew what was in store but refused to give them her screams.

Not yet.

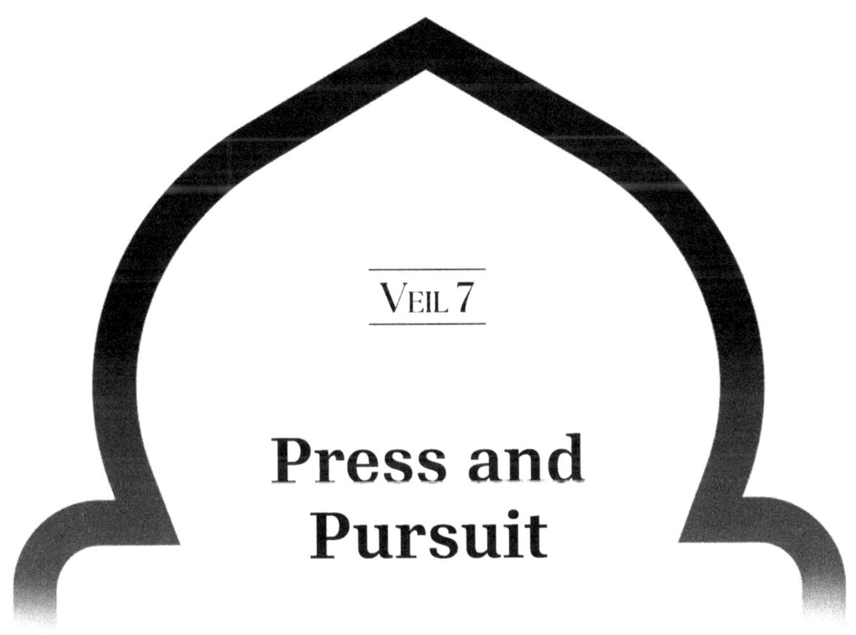

Veil 7

Press and Pursuit

The lines for the media shuttles snaked through the hotel lobby and out onto the street, dozens of reporters shifting restlessly, their faces illuminated by the blue glow of phone screens. Some barked into their devices, scrambling to confirm details with sources, while others speculated in hushed, urgent tones with colleagues, questioning what had happened—and, more pressingly, what was going to happen next.

Frustration mounted as the shuttles crawled through security checkpoints, their usual streamlined routes now blocked by roadblocks and heavily armed police. Some journalists, unwilling to wait, peeled off from the lines in search of Ubers or taxis, only to find that most rideshares had been suspended due to the lockdown. A few desperate souls started jogging toward the Main Press Center, weaving through Doha's eerily quiet streets, hoping to get close enough to walk past the heightened security cordons.

By the time Nova Mendelsohn, James Cartwright, Emilie Laurent, and Greg Palmer finally arrived at the MPC, the gravity of the situation hit them like a tidal wave. The air inside buzzed with overlapping voices and the hum of live news feeds, the scent of burnt coffee thick in the corridor. Just stepping through the front doors, they could feel it—the raw, electric charge of a world in crisis.

The story had already exploded across every news network, amplified by the relentless, instantaneous churn of modern communication. Social media was a firestorm of speculation, fear, and outrage. Hashtags trended within minutes—#OlympicHostageCrisis, #Doha2040, #MunichAllOverAgain—as users scoured the internet for scraps of new information. Some posts spun wild conspiracy theories, others stoked political tensions, while a few pleaded for calm. But the dominant emotion was terror.

Misinformation spread like an unchecked virus. Grainy, unverified footage of masked men circulated, some real, some doctored. One widely shared video falsely claimed to show the captives being loaded onto military trucks, even as officials scrambled to refute it. News broadcasts abandoned their scheduled programming for round-the-clock coverage, their anchors struggling to keep pace with the deluge of conflicting reports.

Terrorism experts were rushed onto live panels, their faces grim as they dissected the attack's eerie precision. By midday, analysts like Sahar Qadir on ION World had begun dissecting the crisis with forensic calm, her voice threaded into every living room on Earth. Former intelligence officers speculated about the possible perpetrators—was it a known extremist faction? A rogue paramilitary group? A black-ops mission gone awry? Theories piled up, but facts remained scarce.

Meanwhile, the visuals flooding the airwaves told a chilling story of their own. Live footage showed armed responders combing through the Olympic Village, weapons raised, their eyes scanning for threats. The sleek, futuristic venues, once filled with the jubilant energy of competition, now looked like a war zone.

The initial reports were disjointed and contradictory. Though officials had confirmed the number of hostages taken, almost everything else was murky. How had the attackers gotten in? How had they evaded some of the most sophisticated security protocols in the world? Some believed they had disguised themselves as event staff, slipping past checkpoints unnoticed. Others insisted this was the work of trained operatives, possibly ex-military, executing a highly coordinated strike.

One thing was clear: this wasn't a haphazard act of terror. It was precise. Chillingly efficient.

James Cartwright exhaled sharply as the four journalists made their way through the bag checks and security screenings at the MPC, his hands shoved into the pockets of his jacket. "No place is bloody safe anymore," he muttered. "Nothing is bloody sacred."

Emilie Laurent, shot him a glance – half agreement, half discomfort – but said nothing.

Adjusting the strap of her laptop bag, she frowned. "Are we all so obsessed with athletic competition that we've blinded ourselves to the dangers beneath the surface?"

Greg Palmer let out a dry laugh, devoid of humor. "I don't know," he said, shaking his head. "But one thing is for sure. Forget unity. These Olympics aren't a celebration anymore. They're a battleground."

Nova Mendelsohn barely heard them. Her mind was already miles ahead, dissecting the facts, or lack thereof. As they entered the grand press conference hall and found their seats, she stared at the empty stage where officials would soon deliver their first statements.

Her heart pounded.

Twelve hostages.

Two countries.

The math didn't add up unless someone wanted chaos on camera.

Her heart pounded harder.

Who was behind this? And what did they want?

A hush fell over the room as the doors at the back of the stage opened, and the press conference speakers filed in. IOC President Sheikh Tariq bin Fahd Al-Mazrouei led the way, his normally poised demeanor carrying an air of unease. At his side, Jacques Moreau, the IOC Vice President, adjusted his tie with sharp, nervous movements. Flanking them was Colonel Faisal Al-Kuwari, a senior Qatari intelligence officer, his expression unreadable beneath the sharp lines of his uniform.

They took their seats behind the dais, cameras flashing wildly as reporters jostled for position. The air was thick with tension.

Sheikh Tariq gripped the edges of the table, his voice steady but heavy with the weight of the crisis.

"Ladies and gentlemen of the press, and to the millions watching around the world—I address you this morning under the most difficult of circumstances. In the early morning hours, a coordinated attack took place within the Olympic Village. Twelve athletes—six from Israel and six from Lebanon— have been taken. We are deploying every available resource to bring them back safely."

He paused, exhaling through his nose before continuing.

"We are working closely with international intelligence agencies, security forces, and the highest levels of government to determine the perpetrators and their motives. This is an attack not just on these athletes and their nations, but on the very spirit of the Olympic Games. We will not allow this tragedy to define Doha 2040."

Across the room, pens stalled mid-sentence. A few reporters exchanged uneasy looks.

His words were measured, deliberate. But they did little to soothe the storm brewing in the room.

Jacques Moreau leaned into his microphone next.

"We will provide updates as the investigation unfolds. However, at this time, speculation will not serve the interests of those taken, nor will it aid in the pursuit of those responsible. We ask for patience, diligence, and cooperation from the media as this investigation progresses."

A murmur rippled through the crowd—restless, unconvinced. Then came Colonel Faisal Al- Kuwari, his presence commanding even in silence. He surveyed the sea of journalists before speaking.

"Security protocols are being reviewed and reinforced at every Olympic venue and facility. We are treating this with the highest level of urgency and priority. No effort will be spared in ensuring the safety of all remaining athletes and personnel."

He did not elaborate further. The vagueness of his words was not lost on the journalists in the room. Nova didn't even bother writing it down. Just another polished phrase for a botched crisis.

The floor opened for questions.

James Cartwright of the BBC was first, his voice sharp with accusation. "Colonel Al-Kuwari, you say security protocols are being reviewed—how do you explain the failure that allowed this to happen in the first place? Are you acknowledging that there was an internal breach?"

Al-Kuwari's jaw tightened. "This investigation is ongoing. We are considering all possibilities, but I will not engage in speculation at this time."

Greg Palmer, the blunt Australian, didn't wait for permission. "Given the history between Israel and Lebanon, do you believe this was politically motivated?"

Jacques Moreau interjected. "At this moment, we are not assigning motives. Our priority is securing the safe return of the athletes."

"Are the kidnappers in contact?" asked Emilie Laurent of L'Équipe, pushing forward. "Has there been any ransom demand?"

Al-Kuwari's response was immediate, firm. "I cannot comment on ongoing intelligence matters."

A new voice rang out—Layla Al-Mansoori, a Qatari journalist, her tone urgent. "With all due respect, Colonel, if this was so meticulously planned, how do you respond to accusations that this was an intelligence failure?"

A muscle twitched in Al-Kuwari's cheek. "The perpetrators exploited vulnerabilities. Those vulnerabilities are being addressed as we speak."

Nova's turn. She leaned forward, her voice laced with controlled frustration.

"You ask for patience, but the world remembers Munich. You have an audience of millions waiting for answers. Can you at least confirm whether this group has been identified?"

Sheikh Tariq exhaled through his nose, his expression unreadable. "At this time, we are following multiple leads. That is all I can say."

Nova sat back, her mind racing. This wasn't enough. She needed more.

As questions flew, Nova's thoughts turned inward. After Boston, she quit law, joined The Times, covering Sochi's anti-LGBTQ policies and Circassian activism, drawing parallels to her own grit.

Then the doping scandal—Rodchenkov's revelations, medals stripped, Russia banned. It battle-tested her, teaching hard questions and meaningful stories.

Now, this crisis felt like those days—pressure building, truth hidden.

VEIL 8

Shadows of Justice

As the last echoes of tormented cries reverberated through the underground labyrinth, fading into the oppressive silence of the desert's hidden veins, the true architects of chaos gathered in seclusion. Far from the bloodstained holding cells where vengeance was meted out in raw, visceral strokes, the Obsidian Hand assembled in their sanctum, ready to weave the next thread in their grand tapestry of retribution.

Eight figures sat around a weathered wooden table, their faces obscured by smooth, featureless masks—black as obsidian, each etched with a single crimson rune that glowed faintly in the flickering light.

The clandestine group, born from the ashes of forgotten wars and unheeded cries, was united by a shared disgust for a world they saw as rotten to its core. The Obsidian Hand had gathered in full: The Commander, The Arbiter, The Scribe, The Watcher, The Enforcer, The Keeper, The Specter, and The Doctor.

The tallest among them, The Commander, sat at the head, exuding authority as gloved hands rested on the table's edge. "The time is now," came a voice, deep and resonant through the mask's modulator.

"The demand must be delivered soon—five hundred billion dollars. The IOC will falter, and we need a voice they can't silence."

Beside them, The Arbiter leaned forward, hands steepled beneath shadowed vents. "It's not negotiable. The Olympics are a festering wound—corruption, exploitation, complicity in atrocities. We need someone to bear our message, someone they'll heed."

Across the table, The Scribe—a wiry figure with fingers stained from years of ink and blood—tapped a pen against a stack of papers. "It's more than the money. It's the reckoning. The IOC's propped up tyrants, ignored genocide, and profited off broken bodies. Our conduit must know that rot—someone who's tasted it."

The Watcher tilted their head, a faint hiss escaping the mask. "We've narrowed it to three: diplomat, politician, journalist. Diplomats drown in red tape, politicians in compromise. A journalist, though—independent, credible, but not untouchable—could work."

The Arbiter nodded slowly. "Who, then?"

The Scribe slid a dossier across the table, edges worn from handling. "Nova Mendelsohn. Forty-seven. American. Independent Olympic beat reporter since 2008. Not a star, but respected. She's curious, persistent, and naive enough to mold."

The Enforcer grunted, arms crossed. "Why her? Bigger names—NBC, ESPN, BBC, The New York Times—carry more weight."

"Because she's perfect," The Watcher countered, voice sharp. "Big names have teams—editors, security, noise. Nova's lean—freelances, travels solo, no baggage. Vulnerable yet connected.

She's already grazed our target."

The Commander tilted their mask, considering. "What do we know?"

The Scribe flipped open the dossier, revealing a meticulous collage of Nova's life. "Eight years of bylines—hundreds archived. Doping scandals, athlete exploitation, IOC ties to dictators. Tokyo 2020: displaced workers buried under stadium budgets. Paris 2024: sanctioned nations waved through. She's close to the truth."

The Watcher interjected, "Her email—hacked last year via a phishing link in Frankfurt. Inbox, contacts, drafts: she's pitching an IOC finance exposé—offshore accounts, shells. No bites yet, but she's got whispers."

"And personally?" The Arbiter pressed.

The Specter, silent until now, spoke in a whisper that chilled the air. "Social media's sparse—travel shots: Doha, Rio, Tokyo. Sister in Trenton, parents dead—car crash, 2017, from an obituary. Brooklyn one-bedroom. X posts: press freedom, airline gripes. Her DMs, spoofed via burner, tie her to a Lebanese coach—harassment in Beirut camps. It fits."

The Enforcer shifted, unconvinced. "A nobody. How's she leveraging half a trillion?"

"She doesn't," The Doctor said, voice clinical, cutting through. "She's the spark, not the vault. Credible enough to rattle the IOC, small enough to control. She's in Doha now—Gulf Cup. Hotel booking tracked via app. Isolated. Ripe."

The Keeper, gravelly and low, broke their silence. "How do we reach her?"

The Scribe tapped the table. "Her phone—number from a 2022 Beijing credential leak. Encrypted burner text: vague, then specific.

She's a journalist—curiosity's her flaw."

The Commander drummed a slow rhythm. "Delivery?"

"Dual approach," The Watcher said. "Physical drop—Al-Ruwais, remote, symbolic. SD card: hostages Weissman and Mansour—proof of life, stakes. She'll watch, and it'll hook her."

The Enforcer snorted. "If she bolts to the cops?"

"She won't," The Scribe said firmly. "Rio 2016 favela piece—sat on it for weeks, cautious. She'll dig first. The video ensures compliance."

The Doctor leaned in, analytical. "Psychologically, she's primed—idealistic but worn. She'll carry it."

The Specter's mask gleamed. "She's a shadow we'll wield."

The Commander raised a hand, silencing them. "Nova Mendelsohn it is. The IOC's filth, Israel's impunity, Lebanon's strings—she's brushed it all. She's our voice. We ignite the blaze."

The eight masks nodded, a pact sealed in the dim glow. The Obsidian Hand had their pawn. Now, they would strike.

A desert away, Nova sat unsuspectingly on the edge of the hotel bed, her laptop balanced on her knees, the glow of the screen illuminating her face in the dimly lit room. The television was on, volume low, the CNN banner rolling across the bottom of the screen in a bold, urgent red: **BREAKING NEWS: Diplomatic Crisis Unfolds as Kidnapping Shakes International Relations.**

On the screen, two pundits were locked in a heated debate, their voices rising over one another.

"This is a direct consequence of the Vance administration's reckless and short-sighted foreign policy," said Mark Ellison, a man in a navy suit, gesturing emphatically. "They abandoned diplomatic norms, cut funding to key stability initiatives, and left a power vacuum that has now made U.S. citizens vulnerable to these kinds of incidents."

His opponent, a blonde woman in a stiff blazer, shook her head. "This is the result of longstanding instability in the region, not just one administration's actions. You can't pin every international crisis on J.D. Vance—"

"But you can point to the dismantling of alliances that would have prevented this exact scenario," Ellison interrupted. "The rollback of strategic aid, the failure to reinforce diplomatic ties—this kidnapping isn't happening in a vacuum. It's the ripple effect of years of neglect."

The woman, Rachel Martinez, pursed her lips. "Let's not forget that the administration has also had ample opportunity to address these concerns, and yet, here we are."

Nova sighed and shifted her focus back to her laptop. News tabs were open in a cluttered mess, each headline more frenzied than the last.

The Guardian: Western Governments Silent as Crisis Deepens—

What Are They Hiding?

Al Jazeera: Revenge or Ransom? Theories Swirl Over Mysterious Abduction

Le Monde: Un Scandale Diplomatique: Le silence troublant des États-Unis

She clicked on an article from The Guardian, skimming rapidly. It was riddled with speculation, hinting at secret negotiations happening behind closed doors, anonymous sources claiming there had been "hesitation at the highest levels" regarding a response. Another piece from Al Jazeera suggested the kidnapping might be tied to a retaliation effort, possibly linked to a covert operation that had gone unreported.

Nova's stomach twisted. Every article painted a different story. Every take was laced with an undercurrent of uncertainty, of something larger looming just beneath the surface.

Her phone buzzed beside her. A message from an unknown number.

You're looking in the wrong places.

Nova's breath caught.

She stared at the screen, the noise of the television fading into a distant hum.

Outside her window, the city stretched dark and endless, the world unraveling in real time, and somewhere out there—someone was watching.

A chill ran through her spine. She looked around the room, suddenly hyperaware of the silence pressing in. She reached for the curtain, hesitated, then pulled it aside just enough to peek out. The street below was empty—too empty for a city this size. No late-night wanderers, no taxis cruising by. Just shadows stretching unnaturally beneath the streetlights.

Her fingers hovered over the screen. Should she respond? Block the number? Call someone?

Before she could decide, her phone buzzed once more. A final message.

Do you want to see them again?

This wasn't just fear anymore. This was war.

Her heart pounded. Her fingers moved before she could second-guess herself.

Who are you? she typed, pressing send.

Seconds passed. Then her phone lit up again.

We are the ones who decide what happens next.

Nova swallowed hard then typed, **What do you want?**

The response was almost immediate. You want the truth. We want what is owed.

Her breath hitched. **Where?**

Find your way to the place where the water touches stone, where echoes speak louder than words. Come alone.

She read the message twice, her pulse quickening. A riddle. A destination she had to figure out on her own.

Her mind raced through possibilities. A fountain? A pier? A cave? She had no idea.

Another message arrived.

No police. No hesitation. Or, the truth disappears. You disappear.

Nova glanced at the door, then back at her phone. Every instinct told her this was a bad idea. But the alternative? Losing everything.

She took a deep breath, stood up, and got dressed.

The hotel lobby was nearly empty, save for the lone receptionist scrolling through her phone behind the front desk. Nova settled into a chair near the large bay windows, her laptop open once again as she feverishly searched for clues.

"Where the water touches stone," she murmured under her breath, typing variations into a search engine. She pulled up maps of the city, scanning for locations that might fit.

The waterfront?

The Pearl-Qatar?

The Corniche?

She scrolled through historical landmarks, her mind snagging on a name that stirred like a half-remembered tale—Al-Ruwais, a quiet coastal whisper at Qatar's northern edge, where the sea kisses jagged stone and the wind carries secrets older than the desert itself.

In the style of the old storytellers, the elders would say, "Al-Ruwais is where the sea speaks to the soul, and the stones guard the truths of those who came before." Its rocky shores, kissed by the waves, were said to hold the memory of a thousand voyages, each wave a verse in an endless poem of salt and survival.

Once, Al-Ruwais thrived as a beating heart of trade, a fishing and pearling village where dhows swayed like dancers under the moon, their sails catching the breath of the Gulf. Merchants, sailors, and Bedouins wove their lives into its tapestry, their footsteps etched into the stones like verses of a qasida.

The elders spoke of it as mawqif al-asrar, the place of secrets, where the wind carried not just salt but the murmurs of the past—promises made, oaths broken, and the cries of those who sailed and never returned. At night, the silence was heavy, broken only by the sea's restless song against the rocks, a rhythm that locals swore held the voices of djinn al-bahr, the spirits of the sea, whispering warnings to those who dared listen.

Nova's pulse quickened. Where echoes speak louder than words. It was an Arabic saying, sada al-makan, the echo of the place, where truths linger in the air like a falcon circling its prey. Al-Ruwais was no mere location—it was a riddle wrapped in the desert's lore, a place where the past and present met like lovers at dawn.

It had to be Al-Ruwais.

She pulled up satellite images, the rocky coastline stark against the Gulf's dark expanse. Far from Doha's glittering towers, it crouched like a Bedouin tent under the stars, hidden yet exposed. A perfect stage for a clandestine meeting, where the sea's whispers could drown out footsteps and the rocks could hide a thousand eyes.

Her fingers trembled as she closed the laptop. There was no turning back now.

Nova rose, her decision made, and stepped out into the night.

The moment she exited the hotel, the air felt different—cooler, heavier, as if the city held its breath, waiting for her to unravel its secrets. The streets were quiet, the hum of traffic reduced to a faint murmur, like the sigh of a camel settling into the sand.

She considered a taxi but dismissed it. A tracked ride was a thread for her pursuers to tug. Instead, she pulled her jacket's hood over her head and walked briskly toward the Doha Metro station, her steps quick as a desert fox.

The train to Al-Ruwais would carry her only so far; the northern reaches were a land apart, where roads dwindled like a fading mirage. She boarded, choosing a seat at the back, her eyes scanning the carriage like a hawk. The train's hum did little to calm the nervous energy coiling in her chest, sharp as a Bedouin's dagger.

At every stop, she watched the platform, searching for shadows that lingered too long. A man in a dark suit boarded two stops later, his gaze brushing hers before he turned away. A commuter? Or a hunter in disguise? Her fingers tightened around her bag's strap, her heart drumming a rhythm older than fear.

As Doha's lights faded and the train sped into the vast emptiness, Nova's resolve hardened like desert stone under the sun. But at a near-deserted station just before her stop, the man in the suit rose. His movements were too smooth, too deliberate, like a snake gliding over sand. He stepped off without a glance, yet the air grew colder, as if the djinn had stirred.

Was he truly gone? Or was he waiting, hidden in the folds of the night?

She forced calm into her veins. At the final station, she disembarked, her steps slow and deliberate, eyes sweeping the empty platform. No sign of him. Only the wind, whispering like a storyteller beginning a tale.

The road to Al-Ruwais stretched ahead, long and lonely. Taxis were as scarce as rain at this hour. She had mapped a secondary route—a Lime bike rental station just beyond the platform. If she was followed, the bike would be her wings.

She unlocked one with swift motions, the electric motor humming like a soft zajal, a poet's chant. As she pedaled into the dim road, Doha's glow shrank behind her, swallowed by the desert's embrace. The sea shimmered to her right, its surface catching starlight like pearls scattered across a merchant's cloth.

The further she rode, the louder the silence grew, broken only by the wind's mournful howl, as if it carried the grief of Al-Ruwais's forgotten sailors. Her mind played tricks—a shadow darting across the sand, a glint in the distance. Was it the moon's reflection, or the gleam of eyes watching from the dunes? She gripped the handlebars, her senses sharp as a falcon's cry.

The road roughened, sand creeping onto pavement like an encroaching tide. She swerved, glancing back—nothing but the desert's black expanse, vast as the tales of Sindbad. Yet the stillness felt alive, as if the land itself whispered, "Inti thariya, ya bint al-hikaya"—you are hunted, daughter of the story.

Al-Ruwais loomed closer. The air thickened with salt and the scent of ancient tides, a reminder of the Gulf's eternal dance with the shore. The town lay quiet, its streets bathed in the faint glow of scattered lamps, like lanterns left by travelers long gone. Waves lapped the rocks, their rhythm a heartbeat in the night.

Nova slowed her bike near the old fishing port, where a rusted gate creaked like an elder reciting a forgotten verse. Beyond it, wooden docks jutted into the dark waters, their splintered forms like the bones of a shipwrecked dream. She dismounted, her heart pounding like a daf drum at a zar ritual.

She pulled out her phone—no new messages, only the riddle that had drawn her here, sharp as a scimitar's edge. Her breath misted in the cool air, a fleeting cloud in the desert night.

A sound—a scrape against stone. Nova froze, her pulse spiking like a storm over the Gulf. She turned, eyes piercing the darkness. Nothing. Only the wind, only the sea. Yet the feeling of being watched clung to her like damp sand.

She stepped forward, her boots crunching softly, each step a challenge to the unseen. If this was a trap, she was its prey. If it was a test, she would meet it, as the Bedouins met the desert—with courage born of necessity.

The truth—or its shadow—awaited. And so did the one who had

summoned her to this place of whispers and stone.

The wait stretched, time slow as a caravan crossing the dunes. Nova's breath steadied, though her fingers twitched, itching to check her phone. She resisted. They were watching, testing her resolve, as if she were a pearl diver facing the deep.

The wind howled, rattling the docks like a storyteller's pause before the tale's heart. A creak echoed, then another scrape—closer now, deliberate as footsteps on a moonless night.

Nova's muscles tensed. "I'm here," she called, her voice steady despite the tightness in her chest, ringing clear as a call to prayer across the sands.

Silence. Then, footsteps, slow and measured, emerging from the shadows beyond the pier. A tall figure appeared, face hidden beneath a dark mask, its smooth surface gleaming like the black stone of a mihrab. The voice that spoke was distorted, mechanical, like a djinn trapped in iron.

"You came alone." The words cut through the night, sharp as a Bedouin's blade.

Nova exhaled, steadying herself. "Wasn't that the deal?"

The figure stepped closer. A gloved hand reached into a pocket, withdrawing an envelope, small as a folded misbah bead. It landed in the sand between them, a challenge thrown.

"Inside is your next step. No questions. No delays."

Nova hesitated. "And if I refuse?"

A pause, heavy as the desert's heat. The voice crackled, low and cold. **"Then you'll never see them again."**

Her stomach twisted, but she kept her face a mask of stone. Slowly, she bent, retrieved the envelope, and stood. The figure was already fading into the shadows, as if swallowed by the sea's own tale.

"You'll hear from us soon," the voice drifted back, a whisper on the wind.

Nova gripped the envelope, its weight heavier than a thousand pearls. She had found her messenger. And now, the story had no path back.

Nova dropped onto the damp sand, her hands trembling slightly as she stared at the envelope. The wind tugged at the corners, threatening to snatch it away, but she held firm. The air smelled of salt and something else—something old and forgotten. Her pulse pounded in her ears.

She ran a finger along the edge of the envelope, hesitating for a moment longer before finally tearing it open. A small object tumbled onto her lap—a micro SD card. Her brow furrowed as she reached inside and pulled out a folded piece of paper, its edges creased and slightly damp from the night air.

Her breath hitched as she unfolded the paper, only to be met with a script she didn't recognize. The ink was dark and bold, looping into intricate, ancient Arabic calligraphy.

سَلِّموا ٥٠٠ مليار دِينَار. لا شُرطة. لا تأخير. وإلّا ماتوا.

هذا هو العدل. لقد استفادت اللجنة الأولمبية الدولية طويلاً من الفساد والاستغلال، متجاهلةً معاناة الرياضيين من بلاد مزقتها الحروب. إسرائيل تواصل انتهاك القوانين الدولية بلا حساب، ولبنان لا يزال أداة في يد القوى الإقليمية، يقمع الأصوات المعارضة ويخدم أسياده الأجانب. العالم يغض الطرف، لكنّنا لن نفعل.

أمامكم ٧٢ ساعة. التفاصيل لاحقًا.

Her heart pounded harder. She couldn't read it.

She turned the note over, as if the answer might be hiding on the other side, but it was blank. The realization sent a fresh wave of panic through her.

What did it say?

Was it instructions?

A warning?

Or something worse?

Her mind raced. Who could she trust to translate this? Anyone she asked would inevitably have questions—questions she wasn't prepared to answer. If she made the wrong move, she could tip off the wrong people. But if she did nothing, she would be running out the clock on something she couldn't yet understand.

She clenched the SD card in her palm. Maybe it held the answers. Maybe it was another dead end. The uncertainty clawed at her, making her stomach turn.

The waves crashed against the rocks as she sat there, frozen in the dim moonlight. The weight of the envelope had been insignificant. But the weight of her next decision felt impossible.

The ride back to Doha was a blur, her mind replaying every second of the encounter at Al-Ruwais. The masked figure. The cryptic ransom note. The SD card now burning a hole in her pocket. Every flickering streetlamp she passed on the highway felt like a spotlight trained on her, each shadow a lurking threat just out of reach.

When she finally reached her hotel, the familiarity of the brightly lit lobby should have been a comfort, but instead, it felt artificial—too safe, too detached from the storm raging inside her mind. She walked past the receptionist, still glued to her cellphone, without a word, heading straight to her room, locking the door behind her with a shaky breath.

She pulled the note from her pocket, staring at the indecipherable script once more. Could she trust someone to translate it? What if it revealed something even more dangerous than she already feared?

Her fingers traced the SD card. Should she check its contents first?

Why had they chosen her? The thought gnawed at her, refusing to be ignored. She wasn't a diplomat, wasn't a government official or a corporate executive. She was a journalist, yes, but she hadn't published anything controversial—at least, nothing that should have put her in the crosshairs of kidnappers demanding half a trillion dollars.

They knew her name. They knew how to contact her. But how? Had she been watched for longer than she realized? Had she unknowingly stepped into something much larger than herself?

A chill ran down her spine as she considered the possibility that her reporting, something she had written months ago, had drawn the wrong kind of attention. Or was this personal? Had someone from her past fed her name to the captors?

A sudden vibration against the nightstand made her jump. Her phone screen lit up. A message from an unknown number.

The clock is ticking.

A cold dread settled in her stomach. They were still watching. And they knew she was hesitating.

Her breath caught in her throat as she stared at the message, the words The clock is ticking searing into her mind like a brand. It wasn't just a threat—it was a countdown, a relentless pressure tightening around her chest. She set the phone down slowly, as if moving too quickly might trigger whatever invisible trap she'd stumbled into.

The SD card sat on the desk beside the crumpled ransom note, its unassuming plastic shell mocking her indecision. She had to know what was on it. Whatever game this was, the answers—or at least the next piece of the puzzle—were likely hidden in its files. Ignoring it wouldn't make the masked figure or the cryptic demands disappear. It wouldn't stop the ticking.

Nova's hands shook as she snatched her laptop from her bag, a surge of urgency overriding her earlier hesitation. She couldn't wait any longer—she needed to see what they'd given her. The familiar hum of the machine booting up felt absurdly mundane against the chaos swirling in her head. She jammed the SD card into the port, her fingers fumbling for a moment before it clicked into place.

A single folder appeared on the screen: "For Your Eyes Only." Her stomach twisted. The title was a taunt, a deliberate echo of espionage clichés that somehow made the situation feel even more surreal.

She double-clicked, bracing herself. Inside was a lone video file: "WatchMe.mp4." No text, no additional clues—just the video, sitting there like a coiled snake. Her pulse thudded in her ears. What if it was a trap? Malware? Something that would brick her laptop—or worse, signal her location to whoever was behind this? But they already knew where she was. The hotel. The message. They were steps ahead of her.

With a shaky breath, she opened QuickTime Player and dragged the file in. The screen flickered to life, and what she saw made her blood run cold.

Grainy footage filled the frame—a dimly lit room, concrete walls, no windows. Two women were there, their wrists bound, their faces contorted in terror.

Nova's breath hitched as she recognized them—bruised, bound, eyes wide with terror. Then came the sounds—muffled cries, inhuman grunts. She couldn't watch. She didn't need to. The horror was already lodged in her chest.

The video spared no detail. Masked figures took turns moving into frame, their movements deliberate, brutal. Nova's stomach churned as she watched the violent rapes unfold—Ronit's muffled screams, Nadine's desperate thrashing against her restraints. The camera lingered, unblinking, capturing every agonizing second. There was no sound beyond their cries and the guttural grunts of their attackers, no narration, no explanation—just raw, unrelenting horror.

Nova slammed the laptop shut, her hands flying to her mouth as bile rose in her throat. She stumbled to the bathroom, barely making it to the sink before retching. The images seared into her mind, inescapable even with her eyes squeezed shut. Ronit. Nadine. Athletes she felt she knew. And now this—evidence of their suffering, dropped into her lap like a poisoned gift.

She gripped the edge of the sink, her reflection in the mirror pale and hollow. Why them? Why her? The SD card wasn't just a clue—it was a weapon, wielded to break her. And it was working. Her legs trembled as she forced herself back to the desk, the laptop still closed, the ransom note staring up at her with its unreadable script.

The phone buzzed again. She flinched, glancing at the screen. Another message from the unknown number: **You've seen it. Now move. 48 hours.**

A cold dread settled in her stomach, heavier than before. They knew she'd watched it. They were still watching. And they were waiting for her next move.

Her mind churned, grasping for options in the suffocating fog of fear. She could go to the police—the note had warned against it, and the video made the stakes brutally clear, but at some point she would have to.

Ronit and Nadine's lives hung in the balance, and any misstep could end them. She could try to decipher the ransom note's script, find someone discreet to translate it, but that would take time. But it was her only lead, a tangible thread in this nightmare.

But could she realistically do this alone? She wasn't a hero, and wasn't trained for this. Yet doing nothing wasn't an option—not with their screams still echoing in her head.

She thought of her work, her stories. Had her reporting on corruption in the Olympic movement crossed some unseen line? Or was this revenge, a personal vendetta from someone she'd forgotten? The pieces didn't fit, but she couldn't dwell on it—not now. The clock was ticking, and every second of indecision was a second closer to failure.

Nova straightened, wiping her clammy hands on her jeans. She couldn't save Ronit and Nadine by falling apart. She'd start with finding a translator. She wasn't sure she could trust anyone, but she had no choice but to roll the dice. She had to. For them. For herself.

With a deep, steadying breath, she opened her laptop again, the SD card's folder still glaring at her. She wouldn't watch the video again—she couldn't—but she'd use it. She'd move forward. The resolve hardened in her chest, fragile but real.

She wasn't broken – yet.

Veil 9

Lost in Translation

Nova's fingers trembled as she jammed the SD card into a concealed slit in her bag, her laptop snapping shut with a sound that echoed like a gunshot in the stifling silence of her hotel room.

The air pressed against her lungs, heavy with an unseen menace. Someone was watching her—too close. Not yet at her door, perhaps, but near enough that the walls seemed to pulse inward, conspiring to trap her.

She had to flee. *Now.*

Doha wore a fractured mask: its glittering towers and sterile glass corridors gleamed like a predator's grin, while the old districts festered below—tangled, ancient arteries where the scent of rot clung to crumbling stucco, and heat pressed like breath from an open grave.The note's jagged script, etched in a language older than the city itself, wasn't something she'd unravel in a pristine office or a sterile university hall.

No, she needed someone festering in Doha's underbelly—a dealer in dead tongues, a keeper of secrets too vile for the light of day.

But finding them meant plunging into the abyss.

Her mind snagged on Omar.

She'd first stumbled into Omar's orbit in 2010, a naïve reporter chasing the IAAF World Indoor Championships. The Aspire Dome had shimmered with cold perfection, but the real story gnashed at the fringes—doping rings, crooked federations, athletes erased by scandals woven in silence.

She'd hunted whispers of a pay-for-play scheme, shadows muttering of "injuries" that weren't chance.

It was a story that could kill, and she'd been too reckless to care.

That's when she'd blundered into Omar's spice shop, where the trail didn't just twist, it split open and swallowed her whole.

The memory clawed at her—a sweltering night, the souq choking on the stench of grilled meat and spice-heavy air. His shop and café crouched in an alley like a trap waiting to spring. She'd strode in, bold and foolish, hunting a source. Instead, she'd found Omar, leaning against the counter, his eyes glinting with a predator's amusement.

"You're not lost," he'd rasped, voice a blade dipped in honey. "So you're either law, or you're begging for a grave."

"I'm a journalist," she shot back, meeting his stare.

He sneered. "Same difference."

Omar had waved her off at first, warning her to let the story bleed out. But she'd pressed—too hard—and it had nearly ended her. Two nights later, after meeting a skittish source in West Bay, she'd felt the weight of eyes. She hadn't seen them until it was too late—

cut off from the lights, trapped in the dark. The men who closed in didn't speak. Their intent was etched into their knuckles.

She'd been a breath from ruin when Omar emerged, his voice slashing the night in guttural Arabic. No blows fell, but whatever he'd snarled made them slink away like whipped curds. She never learned what leash he'd yanked—only that he'd spared her hide.

Later, in the dim fog of his café, he shoved a chipped cup of tea into her hands and growled, "Learn when to quit."

She'd stared into his shadowed gaze. "You knew they wouldn't let me."

That was when she'd glimpsed it—Omar wasn't just a survivor. He was a serpent, coils of power slithering into corners she couldn't fathom.

Now, a decade later, she was back, pleading for his fangs to shield her again. As she slipped away from his café into the treacherous sprawl of old Doha, dread tightened its grip. This time, even Omar's venom might not fend off the jaws snapping at her heels.

She yanked a tattered Golda Och hoodie over her head, a scarf strangling her hair as she melted into the humid night. Doha pulsed with a deceptive rhythm—life cloaking the decay beneath. She clung to the margins, head bowed, skin prickling under an unseen stare.

Was she followed?

The urge to glance back seared her nerves, but she fought it. Seeing nothing would only hone her paranoia. Seeing something—she didn't know if she'd bolt or collapse.

The café loomed ahead, its faded sign a taunt in the gloom. She stepped inside, qahwa's bitter sting and the acrid bite of clove smoke clawing at her lungs. Omar's eyes pinned her instantly—

dark, unreadable voids in a face hewn from suspicion. Sixty-something, broad as a barricade, his silver beard glinted like a sharpened edge. He wiped his hands on a rag, slow and deliberate, leaning on the counter as if daring her to breathe.

"This isn't your haunt, journalist," he murmured, voice a low, venomous drip.

She slid onto a stool, ignoring the hostile glares drilling into her spine. "I need a translator," she whispered, words barely escaping her lips. "Something ancient. Something dangerous."

His face didn't shift, but his fingers twitched—a serpent coiling. "That's not a favor you beg for," he said, each word laced with menace. "Not without blood."

"I don't have a choice," Nova said.

He studied her, exhaling a slow hiss, then jerked his head toward a curtain of rattling beads. She followed him into a backroom that reeked of ruin—old maps peeling like flayed flesh, scrolls yellowed and brittle, a radio spitting a warped Egyptian dirge from a buried age.

"You're after Alim," he said at last, voice a gravelly undertone. "They say he's older than the sands, speaks the tongues death devoured. But he doesn't deal with strays. You need a key."

Her gut twisted into a knot. "Can you get me in?"

Omar's eyes narrowed, his silence a blade pressed to her throat. "Not without knowing why. You don't drag me into your messes blind."

Nova's pulse hammered, her mouth dry as ash. She couldn't tell him—not yet—but the weight of eyes beyond the walls pressed harder. She leaned closer, voice a desperate hiss.

"It's about the Olympics. The kidnapping. I met the captors – face-to-face – so to speak. They gave me this." She patted the bag, the SD card, a live wire against her hip. "It's bigger than me, Omar. And they're here."

His gaze sharpened, but he didn't budge. "Words don't buy trust. Show me."

She hesitated, dread pooling in her chest. But the air crackled with danger—she had no time. With a trembling hand, she fished out a battered portable drive, plugged it into a cracked tablet from her bag, and slid it across the table. "Watch it. But don't say I didn't warn you."

Omar's jaw tightened as he tapped the screen. The video flickered to life—grainy, shadowed footage from a concrete cell. Screams tore through the static, raw and guttural. Figures moved in the gloom, silhouettes of captors circling their prey—athletes, bound and broken, faces twisted in terror.

The camera lingered as hands ripped at flesh, as pleas dissolved into sobs. The rapes unfolded in merciless detail, each frame a fresh wound. Blood streaked the floor. One captor turned, his eyes glinting through a mask—cold, deliberate, *knowing.*

Omar's breath hitched, but he didn't flinch. When it ended, he shoved the tablet back, his face a mask of stone. "You've brought hell to my door."

"And it's already at mine," she snapped, voice cracking. "They're tailing me. I feel them. I need Alim now, or we're both dead and they're all dead."

His eyes flicked to the door—not at her, but *past her.*

Something was there. Silent. Stalking.

Her heart slammed against her ribs, a frantic tattoo. The presence slithered closer, a noose tightening with every breath. Whoever hunted her didn't need her alive—just the card, the note, the secrets she hadn't yet pried open.

Omar saw it in her face—the naked terror—and his resolve cracked. "Alim's in the Old Port," he muttered, voice barely audible. "A shack by the fish docks, marked with a red anchor. Knock three times, then once. Tell him I sent you. But if they catch you first, I never saw you."

She nodded, throat tight, and slipped the tablet back into her bag. "One hour?"

"Less," he growled. "Lose them, or don't come back."

She stumbled back through the beads, the night's jaws yawning wide. The streets pulsed with malice, every shadow a threat. She felt the tail now—closer, hungrier. One wrong step, and they'd have her.

All she had to do was reach Alim before the darkness swallowed her whole.

Nova lurched out of Omar's café, the bead curtain's clatter a skeletal rattle chasing her into the night. Doha's humid grip tightened around her throat as she yanked the hoodie over her head, the scarf strangling her hair into a damp knot.

Her pulse roared, a relentless tide hammering her ribs, drowning the city's distant pulse. They were out there—watching, waiting, their unseen claws grazing her spine. She couldn't see them, but their presence festered in the air, a venomous weight that promised no mercy. One hour—less, Omar had warned. She had to reach the Old Port before they decided her blood was cheaper than her compliance.

The Old Port—Mina'a Al Doha Al Qadeema—hunkered along Doha's northern rim, where the Corniche's polished arc surrendered to the jagged remnants of a forgotten era. In its prime, through the

1920s and 30s, it had throbbed as the lifeblood of Qatar's pearling trade, wooden dhows slicing the Gulf's turquoise skin, their holds swollen with lustrous treasures that bartered survival for a coastal people.

Fishermen mended nets on sun-bleached quays, their chants weaving with the cries of gulls and the groan of rigging, while merchants haggled over pearl weights in the shade of palm-thatched sheds.

By the 1950s, oil's black tide had swept in, choking the pearling fleets and leaving the port to rot—a decaying husk of crumbling stone, rusted iron, and memories drowned in salt. Now, it was a spectral fringe, a warren of sagging docks and abandoned wares where the past gnawed at itself, a haven for those who fed on the shadows.

Nova darted north from the souq's edge, her boots scraping uneven cobblestones slick with spilled tea and fish oil. The city's neon halo dimmed as alleys constricted around her, walls leaning in like conspirators. The air thickened—cardamom fading to the briny reek of the Gulf, laced with the sour rot of seaweed and gutted catch.

Her skin crawled; she was a prey animal, exposed, every nerve screaming flight. A hunched man bartering over a crate of mackerel, a woman in a billowing abaya melting into a side street, a boy kicking a deflated ball with hollow thuds—she couldn't trust any of them.

Were they *them?*

She kept her head bowed, fighting the itch to look back. Seeing nothing would sharpen her dread. Seeing something would snap her taut thread of control.

Her phone jolted in her pocket—a buzz that punched her chest like a fist. She ducked into the lee of a shuttered stall, its splintered slats peeling like flayed skin, and clawed the device free with shaking hands. The screen flared: a new message from an unknown number. Her breath snagged as she opened it:

"You think distance hides you. It doesn't."

The words sank talons into her, dread pooling cold and viscous in her gut. They knew her path. They knew her fear. Were they pinging her signal? Shadowing her breath? She mashed the power button, killing the phone, and shoved it back into her bag. No time to ditch it—not yet. The Gulf's restless growl reached her now, a low dirge beneath the creak of dhows straining at their ropes. The Old Port was near—she just had to survive the crossing.

The alleys spat her onto a fractured promenade, the Old Port sprawling before her like a beast baring its decayed maw. To her left, the Gulf shimmered under a sickle moon, its surface a shattered mirror pierced by the dark spines of moored boats—traditional dhows with curved prows, their timbers weathered to a ghostly gray.

To her right, a jagged line of low buildings crouched—once storehouses for pearlers' hauls, now hollowed-out husks, their stone facades pocked with salt scars and streaked with rust. Nets sagged over warped railings, snarled with dried kelp and crab shells.

Eastward, the fish docks sprawled in chaotic disarray—crates stacked like tombstones, gutting tables slick with scales and blood, the air a choking stew of brine and offal. Lanterns dangled from crooked poles, their jaundiced glow twitching against the encroaching black, leaving pools of shadow deep enough to swallow a scream.

She scanned the docks, chest constricting. Omar's words echoed: a shack by the fish docks, red anchor on the door. Her gaze snagged—there, where the pier thrust out like a gnarled talon into the Gulf. A squat, listing structure clung to the edge, its corrugated roof buckled, walls smeared with mildew and salt crust. A faded red anchor bled into the wood, its paint chipped like old wounds.

That was it. But the stretch between her and the shack yawned—a barren gauntlet of open ground, no cover, no mercy.

A scrape of gravel rasped behind her. She froze, breath a jagged shard in her throat.

The wind?

A stray dog?

Her instincts shrieked no. She flicked her eyes back—a figure loomed at the promenade's rim, half-veiled by a teetering stack of crates. Tall, motionless, a statue carved from night. The lantern's reach fell short, leaving their face a void, but their stare sliced through her, cold and unyielding. Her stomach plummeted. They'd tracked her.

She bolted, legs churning as she zigzagged through the dock's refuse—past barrels oozing fish oil, around a heap of shattered planks, boots skidding on slime-slick stone. The shack loomed closer—fifty yards, thirty, ten. Her lungs seared, each gasp a ragged plea.

The figure didn't shout, didn't sprint—just advanced, a relentless specter, boots crunching gravel in a steady, deliberate rhythm that echoed like a death knell.

She slammed into the shack's door, fist hammering—three sharp raps, then one, as Omar had drilled into her. The wood shuddered, frail and hollow, splinters biting her knuckles. "Alim!" she rasped, voice a shredded whisper. "Omar sent me!" Silence answered. She pounded again, the red anchor blurring as panic clawed her vision.

The footsteps halted—too near. She whirled, back flattening against the door, eyes raking the dark. The figure had vanished—or melted into the shadows. The stillness was a trap, a predator's pause before the lunge.

Her phone buzzed again, a dead thing twitching in her bag. She didn't touch it—couldn't. The door groaned open behind her, a sliver of blackness yawning wide. A voice, dry and ancient as wind-scoured dunes, hissed from within: "Inside. Now."

She stumbled backward, the shack swallowing her as the door banged shut, iron bolts scraping into place. The air inside was stale, thick with the musk of old paper, incense, and something metallic—blood or rust, she couldn't tell.

Dim light seeped from a single oil lamp perched on a warped table, its flame guttering against walls lined with shelves. Scrolls and leather-bound tomes teetered in stacks, their spines cracked and yellowed, some gnawed by time into illegible husks.

A rug, threadbare and stained, sprawled across the floor, its patterns faded into a labyrinth of muted reds and browns. In the corner, a narrow cot sagged under a heap of coarse blankets, and a rusted brazier smoldered, spitting faint tendrils of clove-scented smoke.

The figure before her was a wraith—Alim, she presumed. He was gaunt, his frame swallowed by a tattered robe the color of storm clouds, its hem frayed to threads. His face was a map of crevasses, skin like parchment stretched over sharp bones, eyes sunken but glinting with a feral sharpness beneath a tangle of white hair. His hands, gnarled and spotted, clutched a cane carved with spiraling runes, its tip grinding into the floor as he shifted.

He didn't speak, just stared, his gaze peeling her apart layer by layer.

"You're late," he croaked finally, voice a rasp that scraped her nerves raw. “And you’ve brought death to my door.”

She swallowed, throat sandpaper-dry. “I didn’t have a choice. They’re after me—after this.” She patted her bag, the SD card and ransom note burning like coal against her hip.

The shack’s darkness pressed against Nova like a living thing, the brazier’s ember glow casting jagged shadows that danced across Alim’s hollowed face.

Her phone trembled in her hand, the captors’ last message—**“We see you. The old man won’t save them.”**—burning into her retinas.

Outside, the night growled with menace: a faint scrape of boots on gravel, a muffled thud against the pier’s edge, circling, tightening. They were out there, coiling closer, their patience fraying. She had seconds, maybe less.

Alim’s sunken eyes bore into her, sharp and unyielding despite the tremor in his cane-gripping hand. “What do you carry that’s worth their hunt?” he rasped, his voice a dry wind rattling through bones. The air between them crackled, thick with the musk of old parchment and the metallic tang of rust—or blood.

Nova’s throat seized, but she forced the words out, her voice a shredded whisper. “A note. And a video. They gave me both—proof of what they’ve done and I presume of what they want. I need you to read it. It’s old—older than anything I’ve seen.”

She fumbled in her bag, the SD card a scalding weight against her fingers, but it was the note she pulled free—a crumpled scrap of paper, its edges frayed, stained with sweat and time. The script scrawled across it was jagged, ink bled into the fibers, a haunting dance of curves and slashes that felt alive, sinister.

She thrust it toward him, her hand shaking. “Please. They’re coming. Translate it—now.”

Alim's gnarled fingers snatched the note, his cane clattering against the table as he hunched over it in the emberlight. His breath hitched, a sharp, involuntary sound, as his eyes traced the text.

The shack seemed to shrink, walls groaning under an unseen pressure, as if the words themselves carried a curse. Outside, a low creak—wood bending, or a blade testing the door's frame—sent a jolt through her spine.

Her gaze darted to the bolted entrance, then back to Alim. "Hurry," she hissed.

He muttered under his breath, a guttural string of syllables she couldn't catch—prayer, curse, or something older—before his voice steadied, low and grave.

It's Arabic," he said, voice strained. "But ancient. Pre-Islamic… Sabaean roots, maybe." His hand trembled as he continued, the ink on the note seeming to shimmer beneath the oil lamp's glow. "This… this isn't just language. It's a curse disguised as ransom."

"'Deliver five hundred billion dollars. No police. No delays. Or they die.

"This is justice. The International Olympic Committee has long fattened itself on corruption and exploitation, feasting while athletes from war-torn nations choke on their suffering.

"Israel spits on international law with impunity, and Lebanon dances as a puppet to regional lords, crushing dissent, bowing to foreign thrones. The world blinds itself, but we will not.

You have seventy-two hours.

Details to follow.'"

The silence that followed was a void, swallowing the shack's stale air. Nova's stomach twisted, bile clawing up her throat.

Five hundred billion.

A deadline ticking down—less than three days now, if they'd started the clock when they'd cornered her in that shadowed meeting. And the video—those screams, the blood, the masked eyes glinting with cold intent—flashed behind her lids. This wasn't just a ransom. It was a manifesto, a blade aimed at the world's throat, and she was tangled in its edge.

Alim's face hardened, the lines deepening as he folded the note and slid it back to her.

"You've brought a war to my door," he growled, his voice laced with something feral—anger, or fear. "This isn't just money they want. It's vengeance. And you're their messenger."

"I didn't ask for this," she snapped, snatching the paper, her pulse a frantic tattoo. "They found me. Gave me this, the card—said I'd know what to do. But I don't. That's why I'm here."

His eyes flicked to the door, where a shadow briefly blotted the sliver of light seeping through the cracks. A soft thud—flesh or steel against wood—rattled the frame.

"They're done waiting," he muttered, hobbling to a shelf, his cane tapping a staccato rhythm. He yanked a rusted tin box free, spilling its contents across the table—yellowed maps, a dagger with a chipped blade, a small clay vial stoppered with wax.

"You've got the video. Show me. If it's as bad as this—" he tapped the note "—we're both dead unless I know what they're holding over you."

Nova hesitated, the memory of the footage clawing at her—those athletes, bound, broken, the captors' hands tearing at them, the relentless cruelty captured in grainy frames. But the boots outside shuffled closer, a low murmur of voices seeping through the walls, clipped and foreign. No time. She fished the SD card from her bag, her fingers slick with sweat, and jammed it into the cracked tablet she'd used with Omar. The screen flickered, casting a sickly glow across Alim's craggy features as she tapped play.

The screams erupted again, tinny but visceral, slicing through the shack's gloom. Alim's jaw tightened, his knuckles whitening around his cane as the video unspooled—concrete walls, flickering light, the athletes' faces contorted in agony, the rapes unfolding in merciless detail. Blood smeared the floor, pooling under a woman's limp hand. A captor turned, mask askew, his eyes locking with the lens—knowing, taunting. The footage cut to black, leaving only the echo of a final, choked sob.

Alim exhaled, a slow hiss, his gaze snapping to Nova. "You've seen hell," he said, voice barely above a whisper. "And they've made you carry it."

Before she could respond, the door shuddered—a hard, deliberate blow, splintering the frame. A voice barked outside, low and guttural, in a tongue she didn't know. Alim lunged, surprisingly swift, shoving the tablet into her bag and snatching the dagger from the table.

"Back wall," he hissed, pointing to a sagging plank near the cot. "Loose board—leads to the pier. Go. I'll hold them."

Nova's heart slammed against her ribs. "You can't—"

"They want you, not me," he cut her off, eyes blazing. "Move, or we're both meat."

The door buckled again, a crack splitting the wood as a blade's tip punched through. Nova stumbled to the cot, clawing at the plank—it gave with a groan, revealing a narrow gap, the Gulf's briny reek flooding in.

She squeezed through, splinters tearing at her sleeves, and dropped onto the pier's slime-slick boards. Behind her, Alim's voice roared—a guttural challenge in that ancient tongue—as steel clashed against steel.

She ran, the note's weight searing her pocket, the captors' 72-hour clock ticking louder than her ragged breaths. The night stretched ahead, a black abyss swallowing her flight, but she knew one truth: they wouldn't stop.

Not until they had their vengeance.

Veil 10

The Architect's Abattoir

As Nova fled the Old Port's briny decay, the Gulf's restless churn and the fish docks' rancid stench clung to her like a second skin, the night's humid chaos swallowing her desperate footfalls. The fractured promenade, alive with the creak of dhows and the flicker of dying lanterns, receded into a suffocating memory as she vanished into Doha's shadowed veins.

Hundreds of miles away, in the desolate heart of Barga Al Kharaz, the Obsidian Hand's subterranean lair festered, a chilling counterpoint to the port's raw, rotting pulse. This carved out sepulcher was set to morph into a surgical theater where human potential was twisted into a grotesque experiment. The air was heavy with the sharp tang of antiseptic and the faint hum of flickering fluorescent lights, a clinical contrast to the horror unfolding within.

Twelve steel tables formed a stark half-circle, each holding an athlete—once proud Israeli and Lebanese Olympians—now strapped down with leather restraints, their bodies limp under the weight of heavy sedation. The chamber was quiet, save for the soft beeping of medical monitors and the occasional groan from a drugged captive.

Dr. Samir Haddad, the orchestrator of this nightmare, moved with cold precision, his lab coat pristine despite the hours spent in the lair. His tools were arrayed on a gleaming tray: scalpels, sutures, syringes filled with sedatives, and a monitor displaying vital signs. The athletes—Maya Ben-Ari, Lior Abramson, Tamar Cohen, Noa Levi, Yael Ben-Ami, Ronit Weissman, Yasmine Haddad, Nadine Al-Rassi, Omar Haddad, Nadine Mansour, Yasmine Khalil, and Cyrine Ghazal—lay unconscious, their breathing shallow, their minds clouded by drugs.

Haddad had sedated them all upon capture, using a cocktail of Rohypnol, midazolam, and propofol to ensure compliance. Their restraints were more for protocol than necessity; the drugs kept them docile, their Olympian strength dulled into a haze. He saw them not as victims but as components in his grand design—a perverse unification of Israeli and Lebanese athletes, symbols of a conflict he despised.

"You thought you were untouchable," he muttered, his voice a low, venomous hiss. "Medals, glory, nations cheering. Now you're mine to reshape."

He glanced at a diagram on the wall, a clinical schematic of his plan: a chain of bodies, surgically linked in a grotesque parody of unity. The design was precise, almost academic, inspired by a blend of historical cruelty and modern surgical technique.

As a young surgeon in Damascus, Haddad had studied banned texts—medieval surgical manuals, accounts of Roman punishments, and a Dutch film, The Human Centipede, that fueled his obsession with merging bodies to erase division. His hatred for the Israeli-Lebanese conflict had crystallized this vision: a single organism, forged from suffering, to mock their endless strife.

"Conflict ends in me," he had written in his journals, pages filled with sterile sketches of connected forms. "I will bind them into one—a monument to my will."

He turned to his captives, eyes glinting with cold fervor. "Time to begin."

The surgery began at midnight, a meticulous procedure under harsh lights. Haddad worked alone, his hands steady, guided by years of surgical training and a twisted imagination. Each athlete was kept under deep anesthesia, their bodies unmoving as he performed the delicate, horrific task of linking them. The process was clinical, blood minimized by precise incisions and cauterization, the gore restrained to avoid unnecessary mess. He sutured tissue with fine stitches, ensuring the chain was functional yet stable, a perverse testament to his skill.

Lior Abramson, the first in the chain, lay still as Haddad whispered, "You're the head, Lior. The start of my creation." His incisions were clean, the connections made with surgical efficiency, monitors confirming stable vitals. Omar Haddad followed, then Yael Ben-Ami, Tamar Cohen, Noa Levi, and the others, each linked in sequence, their bodies arranged in a grim procession. The drugs kept them unaware, their pain dulled, though their faces twitched in unconscious distress.

The athletes' resistance had been crushed before the surgery. Omar had lunged at Haddad during capture, only to be subdued with a sedative dart. Yasmine Haddad had screamed defiance until a needle silenced her. Cyrine had tried to flee, collapsing under a dose of midazolam as The Spectre dragged her back. Now, they were all pliant, their spirits buried under layers of chemical fog.

Haddad stepped back, surveying the completed chain—a writhing, sedated mass of twelve bodies, stitched into a single, grotesque form. The lair's sterile air carried no stench, only the faint hum of machinery and the soft drip of IV fluids.

But the horror wasn't over.

As dawn broke over Qatar's Empty Quarter, Haddad prepared for the next phase. He whispered to his creation, "Let's see what you can do."

The Spectre, his enforcer, approached with a tray of nutritional paste, a clinical mix designed to sustain the chain without taxing their systems. He inserted a feeding tube into Lior's mouth, the paste flowing slowly, ensuring the chain's survival without the chaos of forced consumption.

Ronit Weissman, at the chain's end, stirred faintly, her eyes fluttering under the sedation. "Stop…" she mumbled, her voice a weak rasp, lost in the haze. The others remained still, their bodies processing the paste, the chain's connections holding under the strain.

Haddad watched, his expression one of cold satisfaction. "Perfect," he murmured, adjusting an IV drip to deepen their sedation. "You'll live to serve my purpose."

This was no celebration of human achievement—it was a calculated mockery of the Olympic ideal, a political statement carved in flesh and ambition.

The lair's sterile air grew tense as The Commander gathered The Obsidian Hand's eight: The Arbiter, analytical and detached; The Watcher, scanning for flaws; The Enforcer, restless for action; The Keeper, her ledger a map of secrets; The Spectre, a towering shadow; and The Doctor, hands clean but mind stained with his creation.

The Commander's voice was a low growl. "Truck 17 from Aspire Katara Hospitality is our ticket—concessions rig for the Aspire Arena, pre-dawn drop before the gymnastics all-around. We hijack it, load the crate, and roll into their bay. Five hundred billion, forty-eight hours, or they see it live via OBS."

Haddad nodded, his mind already on logistics. "Katara's refrigerated units will keep them stable, mask any signs until the reveal. How's the grab?"

"The Spectre leads," The Commander said, pointing to the hulking figure. "The Enforcer's muscle, The Keeper's eyes. Depot's five miles out—Truck 17 stages there, loaded with soda, flatbread, frozen goods. We hit it en route, no trace."

The Spectre's voice was gravel. "Layout."

The Keeper opened her ledger, voice crisp. "Katara's depot is low-security—chain-link fence, two guards, lax. Truck 17 departs 3 a.m., cleared for a 4 a.m. arena drop. Driver's Hassan, 40s, contractor, no radio check until on-site. Route's Al Waab Road—quiet, dark, half a mile from the depot. Logs show 20 pallets, refrigerated, transponder AKH-17."

The Arbiter leaned forward. "Staging a breakdown—how?"

The Spectre's eyes narrowed. "Spike strip—retractable, dropped from a bike I ride ahead. Hits the front tire, slow leak, he pulls over. I signal The Enforcer in a blacked-out van. We box him in."

The Enforcer cracked his knuckles. "I'll drag him out."

"No," The Spectre snapped. "I lead, I neutralize. Panic button's under the dash, links to dispatch. I choke him—silent, ten seconds. You ditch him in the scrub."

The Keeper cut in. "I've cloned Hassan's ID—photo swapped for The Spectre. Transponder's spoofed, pings clean. I ride in the van, jamming cell signals within 50 yards."

The Watcher frowned. "Depot's gate cam logs departures. If the truck's late, they'll check."

The Spectre smirked. "Bike's plate fakes AKH-17. I ride out 2:55 a.m., cam logs 'Truck 17' leaving. Spike hits 3:05, driver's down by 3:07, we're in by 3:10. Five minutes to load the crate—false wall's pre-cut, bolts ready. We roll by 3:15."

The Commander nodded. "Crate's in the van—steel, vented, sedatives keep it quiet. Transfer?"

The Enforcer flexed. "I move it—800 pounds, straps, dolly. Slide it from the van, secure it in the truck's false wall. Pallets cover it—guards see catering, not our cargo."

Haddad spoke, voice clinical. "They're sedated—breathing steady, vitals monitored. Reefer masks any trace until the arena. Floodlights, locks, mic on Lior—ready to wake when I signal."

The Spectre grunted. "I spike, I choke, I drive. The Enforcer hauls, The Keeper jams. Van tails, crate swaps, peels off. Truck hits the bay 4 a.m., crate drops center-floor."

The arena, a symbol of triumph, would become their stage of infamy.

The Commander's scar twitched. "The Doctor films a teaser—sedated faces, stitches clear. Send it tonight—'Wire the cash, or they awaken live.' The Watcher hacks OBS, loops static until the reveal—NBC, BBC, Al Jazeera, all see it. Crate sits until morning, gymnasts warm up, then we trigger."

The Arbiter glanced at The Spectre. "Contingency?"

"Driver fights, I end him faster," The Spectre said. "Van's got a spare tire—worst case, we swap, roll late. Semtex's in the crate—troops rush, we detonate remotely. No traces."

The Keeper smirked. "Exit's the van—'Katara maintenance,' parked in the vendor lot. We ditch Truck 17, slip out as the arena reels. Money hits, we burn this place. No pay, they get the show, we vanish."

Haddad adjusted his glasses, calm. "Antibiotics, sedatives, monitors—they'll last. My creation will shock the world."

The lair's sterile hum swallowed their words, the chain's faint breaths a grim countdown.

The Spectre's hijack was locked: a silent strike on Truck 17, a clean swap, and a nightmare set to unravel the Aspire Arena.

For the world, it would be a crisis that wrote its own headlines. For the athletes, they had fallen directly into a political trap—a final stretch of hell they might not escape.

Veil 11

Don't Shoot The Messenger

Nova's boots slammed against the pier's splintered planks, each frantic stride a gamble as the Gulf's inky maw churned below, its waves gnashing like teeth eager to claim her. The humid night plastered her hoodie to her skin, the fabric a sodden shackle dragging at her shoulders, but she couldn't pause—not with Alim's final roar still ringing in her ears, a guttural cry severed by a wet, choking gurgle and the brutal clang of steel on steel.

That sound was a gunshot in her skull, a death knell for the old man who'd bought her seconds with his blood. Her lungs burned, each breath a ragged scrape, the SD card a searing ember against her hip, the ransom note a crumpled fuse in her pocket. The kidnappers' warning clawed at her mind, venomous and absolute: "No authorities, or they all die—slowly, screaming your name." Every step toward the truth threatened to become a step toward someone's grave.

She burst off the pier onto the Old Port's crumbling fringe, the spectral sprawl of Mina'a Al Doha Al Qadeema fading into shadow as she veered south toward the Corniche. The Raffles Doha flickered in her fevered gaze—a crystalline fortress piercing the skyline, its glass and steel facade a cruel mirage of sanctuary. Inside its opulent walls, the International Olympic Committee's titans—President Sheikh Tariq bin Fahd Al-Mazrouei, Vice Presidents Jacques Moreau and Viktor Mikhailovich Borodin—huddled, cocooned in luxury while twelve Israeli and Lebanese athletes bled in a concrete abyss.

She had to reach them—now, before the captors' 72-hour clock, already hemorrhaging down to 60 or less, ran dry. The SD card felt radioactive in her pocket—too dangerous to hold, too damning to lose. On it, was proof—grainy, soul-shredding footage of two captives raped, their guttural shrieks tearing through static—a Molotov cocktail she couldn't clutch alone.

The note, scrawled in a pre-Islamic snarl Alim had deciphered, demanded five hundred billion dollars and promised slaughter if the world didn't bend. Every second she wasted was a blade inching closer to their throats.

But the kidnappers' eyes were everywhere, a suffocating presence stalking her through Doha's fractured veins. Her phone jolted in her pocket—a venomous buzz that punched her ribs like a fist. She skidded into an alley's shadow, the fetid reek of fish guts, salt, and rotting seaweed choking her as she clawed the device free with trembling hands.

The screen flared, a dagger of light in the gloom: **"We see you running."** Her breath snagged, panic spiking her veins like shards of glass. They knew—tracked her every gasp, every faltering step.

Were they the silhouette lurking by that weathered dhow, its curved prow a dark sickle against the Gulf? The pair of eyes glinting in the rearview of a passing sedan?

She smashed the power button with a shaking thumb, killing the phone's glow, but nearly fumbled it to the slime-slick stones below. No time to ditch it—not here, not yet. The Raffles was her only lifeline, and the captors were tightening the noose with every heartbeat.

The Old Port's decay surrendered to the Corniche's polished arc, its crescent sweep glittering under sodium lamps that cast long, claw-like shadows from swaying palms. The Raffles Doha loomed ahead, a glass dagger thrust into the night sky, its facade a mosaic of wealth and power that mocked her desperation. But a fortress of security stood between her and its doors—a gauntlet of checkpoints bristling with Qatari police in starched uniforms, private guards in sleek suits, and metal detectors humming with menace.

The kidnapping had shredded the Olympic illusion, and now the Raffles was a citadel under siege, its defenses coiled tight as a cobra. Nova had no credentials, no badge, no name to trade—just a battered bag, a hoodie streaked with sweat and grime, and a truth that sounded like a madwoman's fever dream. Her pulse roared, a relentless war drum battering her ribs, as she yanked the scarf tighter over her damp hair, ducking her head to melt into the thinning crowd—chauffeurs idling by Bentleys, a tea seller's clattering cart fading into the humid haze, a handful of late-night strollers oblivious to the storm bearing down.

Her boots scraped the pavement as she neared the first checkpoint—a snarl of black SUVs and cops with radios spitting Arabic like machine-gun fire. Beyond, journalists swarmed the velvet rope at the hotel's grand entrance, their camera flashes glinting like vultures' eyes, ravenous for any scrap of the crisis.

Nova's gut twisted—she was a ghost in this world, a prey animal darting through a predator's den, and every wasted moment sharpened the captors' blade. She veered left, eyes locking on a service entrance—a loading bay tucked in shadow, its steel door ajar as a janitor in a gray jumpsuit wrestled a trash bin through the gap. Her chest tightened, breath shallow and sharp; this was her only breach in the wall.

She bolted, timing her move—his grunt of effort, the bin's scrape against the frame—and slipped past, her shoulder slamming the door frame with a jolt of pain as she plunged into a fluorescent-lit corridor. The air snapped cold, sterile with lemon polish, a stark shift from the Gulf's briny reek, but her flicker of relief died fast.

A guard loomed ahead—hulking, broad-shouldered, his hand resting on a holstered pistol, eyes narrowing to slits as they pinned her. "Credentials!" he barked, his accented English a whip-crack, advancing with a stride that swallowed the distance between them.

Nova froze, her throat locking tight, her voice a shredded plea tumbling out too fast. "I don't have them—I need Sheikh Tariq! The athletes—they'll die if I don't get through!" Her hands shook, adrenaline flooding her veins, words tripping over themselves in a frantic rush.

"No badge, no pass!" he snapped. His hand drifted to his weapon. Her pulse slammed against her throat. A single twitch would tip this from threat to disaster.

"It's the kidnapping—proof!" she yelled, her voice shrill with terror, cracking under the strain. "Video—a note—they've got hours, not days! Please!" Her chest heaved, each breath a jagged shard, her desperation a live wire sparking in the air.

His jaw clenched, a flicker of doubt shadowing his glare, but he tapped his earpiece, growling rapid Arabic—"Intruder, no ID, screaming about hostages, mushkila kabeera…"— and jabbed a thick finger at her. "Don't move! One step, and you're on the floor!"

Time bled away, each second a scream clawing at her skull, the captors' deadline tightening like a garrote. Footsteps echoed down the corridor—sharp, relentless—two more guards rounding the corner, their hands on weapons, followed by a woman in a crisp blazer, her badge glinting like a blade: Captain Amal Rahman, Qatar Police.

Nova's stomach plummeted, dread pooling cold and viscous in her gut. The kidnappers' warning screeched in her head—no authorities, no police—but she was cornered, a rat in a trap with no way out. Rahman's dark eyes dissected her, sharp as a scalpel, her voice ice cutting through the chaos. "You claim evidence. Show me—now."

Nova's hand jerked to her bag, hesitating, dread a lead weight crushing her chest. Showing it here, under police eyes, was a death sentence—the captors would know, they always knew, their messages a constant lash—but refusal meant cuffs, a cell, or a bullet in this sterile hallway.

"It's for the IOC, not you!" she rasped, her voice a frayed thread. "They said no cops, or they're dead—I'm begging you!"

"Show it, or you're mine," Rahman snapped. For a fraction of a second, something flickered in her eyes—doubt, maybe, or fear. Then it vanished beneath cold steel. The guards shifted, weapons glinting, their stares boring into her spine, closing the net tight. The air crackled, her nerves fraying to raw threads, the weight of twelve lives crushing her resolve.

"If they die, it's your fault!" she spat, tears of fury burning her eyes as she ripped the tablet from her bag, the SD card already slotted. Her fingers, slick with sweat, stabbed play, and the screams erupted—raw, visceral, a jagged slash through the corridor's silence. The video unspooled in merciless clarity: the concrete cell's flickering gloom, the athletes' faces twisted in agony, their bodies violated as captors' hands tore at flesh. Blood smeared the floor, pooling under a trembling hand, the rapes unfolding frame by brutal frame.

Rahman's eyes darkened, her face a mask of granite, but she didn't flinch as the footage cut to black, leaving a void filled with the echo of a final, broken sob.

"Upstairs," she hissed, shoving past Nova with a force that nearly knocked her off balance. "Now!"

The guards flanked her, guns drawn, their boots a staccato beat as they marched her to a service elevator. The doors clamped shut, sealing her in with Rahman's cold silence and the suffocating hum of machinery. The captain's radio crackled to life—"Al-Kuwari, live intel, hostages confirmed, escalate to Al-Nasr…"—and Nova's dread spiked, a white-hot lance through her chest.

Qatari intelligence was sinking its claws in, Colonel Faisal Al-Kuwari and Major Hamad Al- Nasr looping into the web she'd tried to evade. The captors would smell the betrayal—her defiance was a death warrant unfurling in real time.

The elevator jolted to a halt on the 15th floor. For all she knew, this floor wasn't salvation—it was the final misstep they'd warned her against. The door opened and spit her into a plush hallway—cream carpets plush underfoot, gold sconces casting pools of warm light, IOC security posted at every door, their insignias glinting like fangs. Rahman strode to a suite marked Presidential, her fist pounding the wood with a force that rattled the frame.

The door flew open, revealing Sheikh Tariq bin Fahd Al-Mazrouei—tall and imposing in a tailored thobe, his silver-streaked beard framing a face carved with strain and fury. Behind him, Jacques Moreau—wiry, pale, his suit rumpled—lurched up from a leather sofa, while Viktor Mikhailovich Borodin—a bearish figure with a vodka-roughened glare—loomed beside a glass table strewn with papers, maps, and half-empty coffee cups. The room reeked of tension, a pressure cooker ready to blow.

"Who the hell is this?" Tariq roared, his voice a low thunder rolling through the suite, his dark eyes boring into Nova like drills.

Rahman gestured sharply. "She's got video, a note—claims it's from the kidnappers."

Nova stumbled forward, her legs trembling but her jaw set, her voice a desperate torrent spilling out in a rush. She was no negotiator, no hero. Just a journalist who'd followed the story straight into a nightmare.

"They've got twelve athletes—Israeli, Lebanese! This—" she thrust the tablet toward them, her arm shaking so hard it nearly slipped "—shows two raped, tortured—proof they're alive, but not for long! And this—" she yanked the crumpled note from her pocket, Alim's translation searing her memory "—demands five hundred billion dollars in under sixty hours, or they're all dead! They blame you—the IOC—for corruption, exploitation—it's a manifesto! They warned me no police, but I had to come—they'll know I'm here—"

Tariq snatched the note from her grasp, his fingers tightening as Moreau and Borodin crowded in, their faces ashen as they scanned the jagged script and its translated venom: "Deliver five hundred billion dollars. No police. No delays. Or they die. This is justice…"

Nova stabbed the tablet alive, the video flaring to life—screams tearing through the suite's opulence, the cell's filth a stark wound against the room's silk and gold. The IOC leaders watched, transfixed, as blood streaked the screen, as masked eyes glinted with cold intent.

Moreau gagged, pressing a hand to his mouth, Borodin cursed in guttural Russian, and Tariq's fist slammed the table, cutting the footage mid-scream with a crack that echoed like a gunshot.

"Why you?" Tariq snarled, his voice a blade slashing the air, his gaze pinning her where she stood. "Why not us directly?"

"They didn't need me," she rasped. "They needed a symbol. Someone expendable, but loud.

"They found me—masked—gave me this!" Nova's shout cracked, raw with exhaustion and terror. "I'm a journalist—they knew I'd run to you! But they're watching—texted me minutes ago—they'll know I'm here, with her—" she stabbed a trembling finger at Rahman "—and they'll kill them all!"

Borodin bellowed, "We don't bow to terrorist scum!" his voice a growl that rattled the glassware, but Moreau's trembled, high and tight, "We can't let this spread—the Games, our legacy—it's crumbling before our eyes!"

Tariq slashed a hand through the air, silencing them both, his glare shifting to Rahman. "Your people—what's your move?"

"Al-Kuwari's briefed—tracing signals, mobilizing—" she began, her tone clipped and professional.

"No!" Nova lunged forward, her voice a raw scream, tears of fury and fear burning her cheeks. "No cops—they'll butcher them! You've got to move the money—now—before they—"

The suite's phone shrieked, a banshee wail that sliced through her plea. Tariq grabbed it, his face twisting into a mask of rage as he listened, the receiver trembling in his grip. He slammed it down with a force that cracked the base, his eyes blazing into Nova's soul.

"They called. Forty-eight hours now—because you ran here. Sent a finger with it—ring still on, blood still wet." Nova's knees buckled, a sob ripping free from her chest—whose finger? The athletes' faces flashed behind her lids—pleading, broken, their blood pooling under her failure. She'd gambled everything, and they'd paid the price. The kidnappers' jaws were snapping shut, her defiance a death sentence she'd dragged the IOC into with her.

Tariq whirled on Moreau, his voice a whip. "Get Mazar and el-Khoury on the line—now! Israel and Lebanon need to see this."

Moreau fumbled with a secure phone, his pale fingers shaking as he punched in codes. "Eitan Mazar's in Jerusalem—Ziad el-Khoury's in Beirut. They're not going to like being dragged here at this hour."

"They don't have a choice," Tariq snapped, his tone brooking no argument. "Their people are dying."

Minutes later, the suite's video screen flickered to life, split between two grim faces—Eitan Mazar, Israel's prime minister, his hawkish features taut with exhaustion, and Ziad el- Khoury, Lebanon's leader, his silver hair disheveled, eyes bloodshot from a sleepless night. Both men glared into the feed, their voices crackling with impatience.

"What's this about, Tariq?" Mazar demanded, his Hebrew accent clipped. "You pull me from a security briefing for what?"

"Same here," el-Khoury growled, his Arabic sharp. "Beirut's a powder keg already—give me a reason not to hang up."

Tariq didn't flinch. "Your athletes—six from each of your nations—are hostages. We've got proof." He nodded at Nova, who, trembling, replayed the video. The screams filled the room again, the footage unspooling its horrors—blood, terror, violation. Mazar's jaw tightened, el- Khoury's hand clenched into a fist, both men's faces paling as the screen went black.

"And this," Tariq thrust the note forward, reading aloud, "'Five hundred billion dollars, forty- eight hours, no police—or they die. Justice for corruption, exploitation, your regional games.' A finger's already here—bloody, with a ring."

Mazar's voice exploded through the speakers. "Who are these bastards? Hezbollah? Hamas? Someone's getting a missile up their ass for this!"

"We don't know," Borodin cut in, his growl heavy with vodka and rage. "No name, no claim—just masks and threats." El-Khoury's eyes narrowed, his tone icy. "Forty-eight hours? Where's the money coming from? Lebanon's broke—our economy's a corpse. You expect me to magic up half a trillion?"

"Israel's not a bank either," Mazar snapped. "Our budget's stretched fighting wars, not paying off thugs. IOC—you're the target here. You cough it up."

Tariq's face darkened. "The IOC doesn't have five hundred billion liquid. Our funds are tied in sponsorships, infrastructure—not ransom slush piles."

"Then borrow it!" el-Khoury barked. "Your corruption's what they're raging about—your golden parachutes, your private jets. Sell something!"

"Borrow?" Moreau's voice pitched high, incredulous. "From who? Banks don't move that fast, and sponsors will flee the second this leaks. The Games are already teetering—"

"We don't pay," Borodin interrupted, slamming a fist on the table. "We hunt them. Russia's got Spetsnaz ready—give me coordinates, I'll end this."

"And risk twelve corpses?" Mazar shot back. "You don't even know where they are!"

Nova's voice broke through, hoarse and shaking. "They're watching us—right now. They cut the deadline because I came here. Paying might be the only way—"

"Paying?" El-Khoury scoffed. "You think they'll stop at five hundred? They'll bleed us dry, then slit their throats anyway."

"Or they're serious," Mazar countered, his tone grim. "This 'justice' rant—could be ideologues, not just greed. We need intel—who are they? Where's the cash going?"

Tariq rubbed his temples, his voice strained. "Qatar's tracing signals, but it's slow. We've got no ID, no location—just a clock and a finger."

"Then we stall," el-Khoury said, leaning closer to the screen. "Demand proof of life—all twelve—buy time to track them."

"And if they send more fingers?" Moreau whispered, his face ashen. "Or, God forbid, worse?"

"Then we're damned either way," Mazar growled. "Pay, and we fund terror. Don't, and we bury our own. Tariq—what's your call?" Tariq's gaze swept the room, landing on Nova's tear-streaked face, then back to the screen.

"We need to know who we're dealing with. That note—ancient Arabic, pre-Islamic. Who uses that?"

"Scholars? Fanatics?" Borodin mused, his brow furrowing. "Could be a splinter group—ISIS remnants, maybe, cloaking themselves in history."

"Or a state actor playing dirty," Mazar said, his voice low. "Iran's got the motive—hit Israel, destabilize Lebanon, smear the IOC. That dialect could be a feint."

El-Khoury shook his head. "Not Iran's style—they'd claim it, gloat. This feels personal— 'justice' for the Olympics? Maybe ex-athletes, coaches, someone burned by the system."

"Or mercenaries," Moreau offered, his voice trembling. "Hired by someone with a grudge— Qatar's got enemies in the Gulf. UAE? Saudi?"

"The video," Nova rasped, clutching the tablet. "Those masks—plain, no symbols. And the cell—concrete, no markings. They're hiding everything."

Tariq's eyes narrowed. "That accent in the call—guttural, clipped. Rahman, your people hear it?"

Rahman nodded, terse. "Al-Kuwari's analyzing—could be Levantine, maybe Syrian. But it's masked, distorted."

"Syrian?" Mazar seized on it. "Assad's dogs? Or rebels looking to fund a comeback?"

"Or neither," el-Khoury countered. "Could be a diaspora cell—Europe, America— radicalized, with cash and tech. That signal trace—where's it pinging?"

"Still working it," Rahman said. "Bouncing through proxies—could be anywhere."

Borodin snorted. "Forty-eight hours, and we're guessing? We need their throats, not their shadows."

"We need both," Tariq said, his voice steel. "Scrape the money—quietly. Stall them with proof of life. And dig—every frame, every word. They slip, we strike."

Nova's knees trembled beneath her, the weight of the severed finger—a grotesque token of her failure—crushing her resolve as the suite's opulent silence pressed in. The IOC leaders, Sheikh Tariq bin Fahd Al-Mazrouei, Jacques Moreau, and Viktor Mikhailovich Borodin, stood in a tense knot, their faces etched with fury and dread, while the video screens flickered with the stern visages of Israel's Prime Minister Eitan Mazar and Lebanon's Ziad el-Khoury.

The air crackled with desperation, the kidnappers' 72-hour deadline—a relentless guillotine—slicing through every breath. She clutched the tablet, its cold edges biting into her palms, the

SD card and note searing her mind with their brutal truths. She'd brought this hell to their door, and now she had to claw her way out—for the athletes, for herself.

She lurched forward, her voice raw and splintered, cutting through the simmering debate. "You can't just sit here guessing! I need time—access—to figure out who they are. Let me investigate!"

Tariq's dark eyes snapped to her, his silver-streaked beard glinting like a blade in the sconce light. "You? A journalist? You've already cost us a finger and twelve hours—what makes you think you can do more than stumble into another trap?"

"Because I've seen them!" Nova shot back, her shout cracking with exhaustion and terror. "Masked, yes, but I was there—face-to-face! I heard their voices, felt their intent. I can dig where your suits and soldiers can't—I've got contacts, instincts. Give me a chance to track them before they carve up the rest!"

Mazar's voice boomed through the screen, his Hebrew accent sharp with skepticism. "You're a liability, not an asset. You ran here against their orders—now my people are bleeding. Why should we trust you?"

"Because I'm the only one they've talked to!" Nova's fists clenched, tears of fury streaking her face. "They picked me for a reason—I don't know why, but I'm in this whether you like it or not. I can use that—reach out, bait them, anything to get a lead. You're blind without me!"

El-Khoury's bloodshot eyes narrowed, his tone icy. "Bait them? And what—get another finger mailed to us? You're a loose cannon, not a detective."

"I'm not asking to play hero," Nova rasped, her voice breaking. "I'm asking for resources— phone logs, signal traces, whatever Qatar's got. I've chased shadows before—doping rings, corruption—I know how to find cracks. Please, let me try before the clock runs out!"

Borodin's bearish growl rumbled through the room. "We've got Spetsnaz, Mossad, Qatari intelligence—professionals. You're a scribbler with a death wish. Sit down."

"No!" Nova's scream tore free, raw and desperate, silencing the room. "Professionals follow rules—these bastards don't! I can move faster, quieter—off the books. You need someone they won't see coming. Give me access—two hours, even one—I'll find something!"

Tariq rubbed his temples, his voice a strained thunder. "And if you fail? If they catch you sniffing around? We're down to forty-eight hours because of you already."

"Then you lose nothing," Nova pleaded, stepping closer, her eyes locking with his. "I'm already a target—they're watching me, not you. Let me use that—turn their surveillance into a weapon. I'll report back, every step. But I need your trust, your data—now!"

Moreau's wiry frame shifted, his voice trembling. "She's right about one thing—they're fixated on her. Those texts—'We see you running'—they're personal. Maybe she can draw them out."

"Or get us all killed," el-Khoury snapped, his fist slamming his desk off-screen. "We don't even know who they are—Hezbollah? ISIS? Some Gulf rival? She's grasping at ghosts!"

"Then let's narrow it down," Nova pressed, her voice steadying despite the quake in her chest. "That note—pre-Islamic Arabic—Alim said it's rare, tribal. I can hit the streets, talk to linguists, historians—someone's got to recognize it. The video's masks—no logos, but the cell's concrete, the lighting—there's clues. I'll analyze it, frame by frame, with your tech.

Give me a shot!"

Mazar's hawkish glare softened, just a fraction. "You're reckless, but you've got guts. If we give you this—what's your first move?"

"Back to Doha's underbelly," Nova said, her mind racing.

Tariq exhaled sharply, his gaze flicking to Rahman. "Captain, your team's on the trace. Can you feed her intel—discreetly?"

Rahman's jaw tightened, her voice clipped. "Al-Kuwari's running it—proxies everywhere. I can route it through a burner, keep her off our grid. But if she's caught—"

"She won't be," Nova cut in, fierce. "I've dodged worse. Just get me the data—now."

Tariq nodded, reluctant but resolute. "Two hours—max. You report every thirty minutes, or we cut you off. Understood?"

Nova wasn't just racing a clock. She was threading a needle between diplomacy and death.

"Yes," she breathed, relief warring with dread. "Thank you."

Borodin slammed his hand on the table, the echo sharp. "This is madness! While she plays detective, we've got a press conference in two hours. The world's watching—what the hell do we say?"

Moreau paled, his hands wringing, the grandeur he'd spent a lifetime protecting now teetered on a screen of screams. "We can't show this—the video, the finger—it'll tank the Games, spark panic—"

"No," Tariq snapped, his tone steel. "We control the narrative. Say we're 'still 'working with authorities'—vague, calm. No ransom, no details."

"Bullshit," Mazar growled. "My people will demand blood—vague won't cut it. Say we've got leads, that we're hunting them—give them hope."

"And lie?" el-Khoury scoffed. "Beirut's streets will riot if they think we're hiding bodies. We need something concrete—say we're negotiating, buying time."

"Negotiating?" Borodin's voice rose, incredulous. "That's admitting weakness! Say we're mobilizing—force, not words."

Nova's voice sliced through, urgent. She didn't hesitate. Clarity was her only weapon in a room full of power. "Say both—'actively pursuing all avenues, cooperating with international partners.' It's true enough—covers me, your traces, everything. Stall the press, keep the kidnappers guessing."

Tariq's eyes met hers, a flicker of grudging respect. In that moment, she wasn't just a reporter—she was a pivot point in the crisis. "Fine. 'Pursuing avenues' it is. Moreau, draft it—ten minutes. Captain, get her that burner and the trace feed. Nova—you move now."

She nodded, adrenaline surging, the tablet a lifeline in her grip. This wasn't courage—it was compulsion, the kind that left scars. "I'll find them—or die trying." "Don't," el-Khoury said, his tone grim. "We've got enough corpses."

The screen blinked out, Mazar and el-Khoury vanishing, leaving the suite a cauldron of tension. Rahman handed Nova a sleek burner phone, her stare cold. Their eyes locked for half a second—trustless, necessary. "First ping's in—it's messy, but it's yours. Don't screw this up."

Nova pocketed it, her heart pounding as she bolted for the door, the clock's relentless tick echoing in her skull.

Two hours to unearth the kidnappers' identity—two hours before the world's eyes turned to the press conference, and the athletes' fate hung in the balance.

Outside, Doha's lights glittered. It looked like a jewel from above.

But Nova knew better—jewels cut deep.

VEIL 12

The Silent Strike

The night over Doha was a thick, like a lid pressed tight over a city about to suffocate. Perfect for a strike meant to go unnoticed. The sky a bruised indigo bleeding into the desert's edge, where sodium-lit sprawl gave way to sand and silence.

It was 2:45 a.m., and the Katara Hospitality depot—a squat, utilitarian scar on the city's fringe, five miles southwest of the Aspire Arena—hummed with the faint clatter of pre-dawn prep.

Chain-link fencing sagged under years of neglect, barbed wire curling like rusted thorns, enclosing a yard of cracked concrete stained with oil and tire marks. Bay 3 cradled Truck 17: a white refrigerated rig, 20 feet of dented steel, its side emblazoned with "Aspire Katara Hospitality" in faded green cursive over a peeling palm logo. It looked like any other logistics rig. By dawn, it would carry a nightmare into the heart of the Games.

The cargo bay brimmed with 20 pallets—Pepsi cans stacked in shimmering silver towers, their aluminum glinting under the reefer's cold light; foil trays of flatbread, edges crimped, exhaling a faint yeast tang through microtears; and plastic crates of frozen kebabs, frost crusting their shrink-wrap, dripping condensation onto the rubber-matted floor.

The cab was a cramped cave of worn brown vinyl and despair—a crumpled Marlboro pack wedged in the cupholder next to a chipped mug emblazoned with "Best Dad" in chipped red letters, a cheap air freshener (pine, long faded) dangling from the rearview, swaying as the engine idled.

Hassan bin Faisal slumped in the driver's seat, a wiry figure in his mid-40s, his polo shirt— once beige, now a map of sweat and grease—clinging to his bony frame. His stubbled jaw worked a piece of gum, the mint long gone.

The brew was bitter, gritty with grounds, sloshing as he scrolled a cracked Samsung phone, squinting at Al Rayyan's latest match highlights through smudged glass. "Fucking referee," he muttered, voice a dry rasp, thumb swiping past a blurry goal replay. The radio crackled faintly—oud music weaving through static—its dial stuck at 92.3 FM, a loose wire buzzing in the dash. He yawned, rubbing bloodshot eyes, oblivious to the shadows tightening their noose.

Sixty six miles away, The Obsidian Hand's lair festered in a concrete hollow beneath Doha's skin—a bunker of damp rot and despair, its walls slick with black mold, streaked with rust where pipes wept. The air was a noxious stew: blood's copper bite, shit's rancid bloom, and the sharp sting of antiseptic from a spilled bottle on the floor.

The centipede sprawled in its corner—Lior's face, now a purpled mask, oozed against the floor. Once, he'd blazed down Tel Aviv's pools, his strokes fluid, jaw sharp under stadium lights. Crowds had roared his name. Now, only his moans echoed, a dirge in the lair's pulse.

Ronit's necrotic hindquarters seeped into a glistening puddle. Above, the bulb flickered, casting jagged shadows on rusted surgical tools scattered across a table. A clipboard hung on the wall, its pages yellowed, scrawled with numbers—vitals, perhaps, or a tally of suffering.

The Doctor hovered over his creation, a gaunt figure in a stained lab coat, blood crusting his knuckles, fingernails jagged from biting. This wasn't madness to him. It was art. Evidence that humanity was as fragile and perverse as he'd always suspected.

He adjusted an IV line—clear tubing snaking from a rusted stand into Lior's arm—dripping midazolam, 10 mg, a sedative to keep them limp but alive.

"Stay with me, my beauties," he crooned, voice a jagged hum, stroking Ronit's matted hair with a gloved hand. "You're gonna sing for the world."

The steel crate loomed beside them—8 feet long, 4 feet wide, 800 pounds of cold metal, its base sealed with rubber gaskets, top vented with slats for air. Floodlights were bolted to the frame, wires dangling, their glare unlit but poised. Semtex bricks—four, each a dull gray slab—nestled in a hidden panel, red and black wires snaking to a remote detonator, its button capped in The Doctor's pocket. He grinned, flaking gore from his nails, imagining the reveal.

The Commander paced the lair's filth-caked floor, his boots—black, scuffed leather— squelching in a puddle of congealed slime, leaving prints that glistened briefly before sinking. He didn't need to revel in gore. His violence lived in numbers and timing. His tall frame, draped in a black tactical jacket, cast a jagged shadow, his scarred face—left cheek a lattice of white tissue from an old blade—taut with cold fury.

"Five hundred billion, wired in forty-eight hours," he growled, voice a blade slicing the stench, "or they choke on this live. Every bastard from Washington to Beirut will pay or puke." He stopped, fists clenching, scar twitching as he glared at the crate.

The Arbiter stood by the rusted table—its surface pocked with dents, streaked with dried blood—syncing comms on a handheld rig, a matte-black box with eight green LEDs blinking. She was lean, her dark hair pulled into a tight bun, eyes sharp behind wire-rimmed glasses, fingers deft as she paired earpieces—small, curved, encrypted for short-range chatter.

"Comms are live," she said, tone clipped, testing hers with a tap. "Spectre, you copy?" A faint crackle, then two clicks—his signal. She nodded, sliding the rig into a pocket of her cargo pants.

The Watcher hunched over a battered Dell laptop, its screen glowing a sickly blue in the dimness, keys worn smooth from use. Her hoodie—gray, frayed—hung loose on her wiry frame, hood shadowing a face pocked with acne scars.

He'd phished an OBS tech's credentials weeks ago—username: qatarvision23, password: !Doha2025!—and his hack was primed: static loop ready, hijack set to flood NBC, BBC, Al Jazeera, CBC come 8 a.m.

One glitch, and the eyes of the world would stay blind. That wasn't acceptable.

"Feed's mine," he muttered, voice a low hum, fingers hovering over the trackpad. "They'll see every stitch when I say go."

The Commander spun, boots grinding filth. "Spectre's on the truck. No fuck-ups—clean grab, clean drop. Doctor, that thing better crawl when we unveil it."

The Doctor smirked, wiping a bloody glove on his coat. "Sedatives are dialed—midazolam's keeping 'em quiet, adrenaline's on deck for the show. Lior's gagging'll be crystal clear through that mic, Ra'īs. Ronit's rot's fresh—smell'll hit a mile off when the trap pops."

"Good," The Commander snapped. "Watcher, you miss that OBS splice, I'll carve your eyes out."

The Watcher didn't flinch, tapping a key. "Won't miss. Static's queued—ten-second loop, seamless. Trigger's mine at 8."

The Arbiter adjusted her glasses. "Timing's tight. Truck's gotta hit the bay by 4, crate down, us out. Spectre's got 60 minutes to jack it and roll."

The Commander's scar twitched again. "He'll make it. Spectre doesn't bleed time. Not after what he pulled in Istanbul. Not after the embassy van."

Across the city, at 2:50 a.m., The Spectre straddled a matte-black Kawasaki Ninja 400, its frame stripped of decals, exhaust muffled to a guttural purr with a custom silencer. He counted seconds in heartbeats. Every sound was a variable, every turn a knife edge.

The plate—AKH-17—matched Truck 17's, screwed on with rusted bolts, edges chipped from hasty swaps. He tugged a black balaclava over his face, leaving only his eyes—yellow, glinting like a predator's—visible beneath a tinted visor.

His tactical gloves—leather, worn thin at the knuckles—gripped a retractable spike strip: six inches collapsed, steel teeth honed to puncture rubber, coiled in a leather pouch clipped to his belt. His right hand twisted the throttle, the bike snarling awake, tires spitting gravel as he rolled from the lair's jagged mouth into the night's maw. The depot's chain-link gate loomed at 2:54, its posts leaning from years of wind, barbed wire sagging in loops. A single guard—mid-20s, paunch spilling over a too-tight uniform—slouched in a booth, breath fogging a cracked window as he swiped through a dating app, profile pics blurring past.

The Spectre slowed, engine idling to a soft rumble, and leaned into the cam's grainy eye—a cheap dome lens bolted to the booth, its feed fuzzy with dust. The guard glanced up, squinted at the plate—AKH-17—and tapped a log on his tablet: "Truck 17, out at 2:55."

He waved a lazy hand, muttering, "Move it," and returned to his screen. The Spectre gunned the bike, its hum fading into Al Waab Road—a half-mile ribbon of cracked asphalt flanked by sand dunes and thorny acacia, unlit save for the depot's faint bleed behind.

In the chase van—a blacked-out Toyota HiAce, no plates, windows tinted to ink—The Enforcer gripped the wheel, his meaty hands—scarred from bar fights, knuckles swollen— dwarfing it. He didn't like waiting. And when The Enforcer got bored, mistakes happened.

His buzzed scalp glistened with sweat under the dome light, a vein pulsing at his temple as he chewed a toothpick to splinters, splinters catching in his beard stubble.

"This better go quick," he growled, voice a bass rumble, shifting in the seat, his bulk—6'2", 250 pounds—straining the springs.

Beside him, The Keeper perched on the passenger seat, a wiry figure in a hooded jacket, her laptop—stickers peeling, keys smudged—balanced on her knees.

The screen flickered with green code: jamming software live, a 50-yard cell blackout radius primed, transponder spoofing AKH-17's signal to Katara's servers.

"Depot's blind," she said, voice a clipped hiss, fingers dancing across keys. She tapped the Enter key like a detonator—cool on the surface, but her pulse ticked faster. "Hassan's badge is cloned—Spectre's face, his name. GPS fuse is next—three seconds when we hit."

The Enforcer spat the toothpick out the window, a wet plink on asphalt. "Spectre better not fuck around with that spike. I'm not hauling that crate all night."

"He won't," The Keeper snapped, eyes on her screen. "Spike's clean—six teeth, slow bleed. You just keep this heap steady—truck's ours in ten."

In the van's rear, the crate squatted under a tarp—steel edges dented from rough handling, 800 pounds strapped to a dolly with fraying nylon, hydraulic lift cables coiled beside it like sleeping snakes. The reefer's hum from Truck 17 would mask its stench—Lior's rasps, Ronit's rot—until the arena drop.

At 3:00, Truck 17's engine coughed awake, a diesel sputter rattling the cab. Hassan tossed his mug onto the dash—coffee sloshing over the rim, staining a crumpled Doha map pinned under a half-eaten shawarma wrapper. He shifted into gear, the rig lurching forward, tires crunching gravel as it cleared the gate, hazard lights off, headlights dim from a weak battery.

The guard didn't look up, swiping left on a profile—"Too much makeup," he mumbled. Hassan turned onto Al Waab, beams slicing the dark, radio crackling oud music through a loose wire buzzing in the dash. He yawned again, scratching a stubbled jaw, muttering, "Gonna be late," as the speedometer crept to 35 mph.

The Spectre rode low, a quarter-mile ahead, wind whipping his jacket—black, Kevlar- lined—against his frame, eyes locked on the rearview. At 3:03, he eased off the throttle, coasting to a stop on the road's shoulder—50 yards past a gnarled acacia, its branches clawing the sky, roots buckling the asphalt's edge.

He thumbed the pouch open, the spike strip unspooling with a soft clink—six teeth gleamed, each an inch long, angled to shred, their edges glinting faintly in the Kawasaki's taillight. He dropped it across the lane, a thin line blending with the road's grit, then kicked the bike forward, circling back 100 yards to wait, engine idling to a purr.

His earpiece buzzed—two clicks from The Keeper: "He's rolling."

"Spike's down," The Spectre rasped, voice low, barely audible over the wind. "Van, close in—ten seconds."

The Enforcer grunted, flooring the Toyota, tires whispering on sand. "'Bout time. This crate's rattling my damn spine."

"Shut it and drive," The Keeper shot back, tapping her screen. "Signal's jammed—50 yards out. He's got no bars, no SOS."

Truck 17 hit the strip at 3:04, a faint pop-hiss as the front left tire took the puncture—a slow bleed, rubber peeling back like skin. He hesitated. Could be nothing. Could be trouble. The wheel tugged again—too much to ignore.

Hassan cursed—"Ya haram!"—feeling the wheel drag, the rig veering slightly right. He flicked on the hazards, orange pulses staining the dark, and pulled to the shoulder—10 feet off the lane, dust billowing around the cab in a gritty haze.

The tire sagged, a black flap slapping the rim, air hissing out in a slow whine. Hassan grabbed a flashlight from the glovebox—batteries rattling loose, beam flickering—and stepped out, boots scuffing sand, muttering, "Fucking nails again," as he crouched by the wheel, poking the gash with a calloused finger. The Spectre tapped his earpiece—two clicks back—and swung the bike around, tires whispering on sand as he parked 20 yards behind, dismounting in one fluid motion, boots silent on the roadside grit. His breath fogged the inside of his visor. He didn't blink.

The van crept closer, The Enforcer cutting the lights, easing to a stop 10 yards from the truck's rear—boxing it against the scrub, engine ticking as it cooled.

The Spectre stalked forward, breath steady, a shadow stretching long under the rig's pulsing hazards—left, right, left, right. Hassan's flashlight bobbed, its weak beam jittering across the tire, his back turned, muttering about a spare as he stood to grab a jack from the cab's passenger side.

"Got him," The Spectre whispered into the comms, closing the gap—eight strides, each a muffled crunch on gravel, his 6'4" frame a silent wall of intent. "Enforcer, ready the dolly. Keeper, kill his signal now."

"Jamming's live," The Keeper replied, voice sharp, fingers slamming Enter—50 yards of dead air locked in. "He's cut off."

The Enforcer cracked his knuckles, a loud pop-pop. "Dolly's set—let's rip this bastard out." "No noise," The Spectre hissed, three strides from Hassan. "I kill, you haul. Clean."

At 3:05, he struck. His left arm snaked around Hassan's throat from behind, elbow locking under the chin like a vice, forearm crushing the trachea with a dull crunch. Hassan crumpled without a sound. Just as Spectre liked it—no noise, no memory.

A gurgle choked out, coffee breath sour and hot in the air, legs kicking dust in frantic arcs— left boot scraping a shallow trench. The Spectre's right hand braced Hassan's skull, fingers digging into greasy hair, twisting just enough—six, seven, eight.

Hassan's eyes bulged, glassy and red, tongue lolling purple as his chest heaved once, twice, then stilled. At ten seconds, the body slumped, 150 pounds of dead weight sagging in The Spectre's grip—no scream, no blood, just silence. The panic button under the dash—red, thumb-sized, glowing faintly—stayed unpressed, five feet away in the cab.

"Down," The Spectre rasped into the comms, dragging Hassan's frame to the van's rear, boots scuffing sand. "Enforcer, take him."

The van's door slid open with a soft thud, The Enforcer lumbering out, boots thudding on asphalt, a grin splitting his bearded face—teeth yellowed, one chipped. "Fucker's light," he growled, hefting the corpse over his shoulder, a grunt escaping as he adjusted the weight— arms like tree trunks flexing under the tank top. He trudged 30 yards into the scrub, sand puffing underfoot, sweat beading on his brow, and dumped Hassan behind a thorn bush—body crumpling, polo riding up to expose a pale, hairy gut speckled with sandflies.

The flashlight's beam stabbed skyward, flickering; The Enforcer kicked dirt over it—three quick scoops with his boot—snuffing the glow, then snapped a brittle acacia branch, draping it over the face. One missed flicker, and the whole plan could ignite.

"Sleep tight, asshole," he muttered, spitting into the dust.

The Keeper leapt from the van at 3:06, laptop slung in a battered case over her shoulder, Hassan's cloned badge in hand—photo swapped for The Spectre's scarred mug, name intact, laminated edge curling. Her pulse thudded in her ears, but her fingers never trembled. She slapped it onto his chest, clipped it tight to his jacket, plastic glinting faintly under the hazards.

"Signal's dead—50 yards, no calls," she said, darting to the cab, her sneakers—black, soles worn—slapping concrete. She popped the hood—hinges squealing, rust flaking off—and peered into the engine bay, flashlight beam from her pocket cutting through shadows: wires tangled, oil-slicked, a faint hiss of coolant.

She fished needle-nose pliers from her jeans—handles chipped blue—and yanked the GPS fuse, a tiny black rectangle: three seconds, a faint click, tracker dead. She slammed the hood—bang—wiped greasy hands on her thigh, and nodded. "Transponder's spoofed— AKH-17's live on their system. Move it."

"Fuse out—good," The Spectre said, voice low, stepping back to the truck's rear. "Enforcer, crate—now."

At 3:07, The Enforcer circled to the van's rear, yanking the doors wide—hinges groaning, tarp rustling. The crate squatted there—steel edges dented from rough drops, 800 pounds strapped to a dolly with fraying nylon, rubber wheels scuffed black. Inside: twelve groaning links in a nightmare chain, doped but not dead.

He untied it, muscles bulging under the tank top—veins popping like cords—grunting as he wheeled it out, tires squeaking on the van's ribbed floor, a low rumble as it hit asphalt.

"Heavy as shit," he snarled, shoving it 15 feet to Truck 17's back end, sweat dripping onto the dolly's handle, staining it dark. The Spectre unlatched the rig's rear door—clank—a cold gust spilling out, Pepsi cans glinting six feet high, foil trays stacked unevenly, bread sacks sagging with humidity, yeast mingling with the desert's dry bite.

"False wall—open it," The Keeper said, stepping up, laptop case banging her hip. "Crate's gotta lock tight."

The Spectre gripped a hidden lever—metal cold, slick with condensation—sliding the false wall aside: a 4-foot panel, plywood painted white, groaning as it shifted on unoiled tracks, exposing the hydraulic bed's steel frame, its surface scratched from test runs. "In," he rasped, nodding to The Enforcer.

The Enforcer tilted the dolly, crate teetering—steel scraping steel—and muscled it in, arms straining, a bead of sweat splashing the floor, his breath a ragged growl. "Fuckin' stitches better hold," he panted, shoving it flush against the bed, dolly wheels locking with a click.

The Spectre knelt, bolting it down—four 3-inch bolts, a cordless drill whining in his gloved hand: thunk, thunk, thunk, thunk—each turn a sharp twist, metal biting metal, two minutes ticking by, clock hitting 3:09. He double-checked every bolt. There was no next time if one came loose.

“Secured,” he said, standing, drill buzzing to a stop.

“Pallets—move ’em,” The Keeper ordered, peering in, flashlight beam bouncing off aluminum. Cheap carbs and cold cans—enough to cover a horror no eye should meet. “Cover’s gotta look legit.”

The Enforcer grabbed two Pepsi pallets—50 pounds each, cans rattling—stacking them back with a grunt, aluminum clinking like loose change, then slung a bread sack over the gap—20 pounds, plastic crinkling, yeast puffing out.

“Good enough?” he asked, wiping his brow with a forearm, smearing grease.

“Perfect,” The Spectre said, voice flat, slamming the door—thud—latch clicking shut. “Cab—let’s roll.”

He climbed into the cab at 3:10, key dangling from the ignition—brass, scratched— Hassan’s coffee pooling on the seat, acrid and brown, soaking the cracked vinyl. He swiped it with a rag from the floor—gray, oil-stained—tossed it out the window into the dust, a wet plop as it landed.

“Tire’s shot,” he said into the comms, twisting the key—engine sputtering, then roaring, reefer kicking on with a low, steady hum.

The Keeper tapped her laptop, screen glowing green in the van’s dimness. The tire fought her like everything else tonight. She growled back. “Spare’s in the back—swap it. We’re five minutes off.”

“On it,” The Enforcer growled, hauling the spare from the van—40 pounds, tread worn thin, rubber cracking—jack in one hand, wrench in the other. He jacked the front left wheel— metal creaking, rig tilting—bolts clattering as he loosened them: five turns each, a clank- clank-clank rhythm, hands black with grease. The flat tire slumped off, rubber shredded, and he slammed the spare on—bolts tightened, wrench slipping once, slicing his knuckle, a thin red line welling.

"Done," he spat, kicking the flat into the scrub, clock hitting 3:15. "Let's move, Spectre."

The Spectre tested the pedal—rig steady, no wobble—and nodded. "Rolling," he said, voice gravel over steel, shifting into gear, headlights carving Al Waab's gloom at 40 mph. The crate's weight shifted faintly—Lior's mic'd throat rasping under sedatives, a faint guk-guk through the comms, Ronit's rot seeping pus into a sealed tray, stench trap primed with a chemical latch—sulfur and decay locked tight. The reefer's hum masked it, a mechanical drone syncing with the rig's rumble.

"Van, peel off at 3:50," The Spectre said, eyes on the road, hazards off. "Vendor lot—stay low."

"Got it," The Enforcer replied, flooring the Toyota, dust swirling in its wake. "This better fuckin' work, Keeper."

"It will," she shot back, hood up, laptop stashed. "Transponder's holding—arena's blind 'til we drop."

Back in the lair, The Doctor chuckled, tweaking the mic's gain—Lior's rasps sharpening. "Hear that, Raʾīs? My baby's ready to sing."

The Commander smirked, scar stretching. "Send the teaser—let 'em squirm."

The Arbiter nodded, pulling a burner phone—black, scratched—from her pocket, uploading the GoPro clip: Lior's sobs, Ronit's rot, shit oozing in close-up. "Wired to the dropbox—'Wire the cash, or they crawl live.' They'll see it by dawn."

The Watcher grinned, static looping on her screen. “OBS is mine—8 a.m., world’s gonna gag.”

At 3:50, the van diverted, sliding into the Aspire Arena’s vendor lot—a sprawl of parked rigs, floodlights buzzing, workers shuffling with coffee cups. The Enforcer killed the engine, slapped a “Katara Maintenance” magnet on the side—crooked, peeling—and slumped low, toothpick back between his teeth.

“We’re ghosts,” he muttered, cracking his neck.

The Keeper stashed her laptop in a duffel, hood shadowing her face, blending into the crowd—exit locked in. “Bay’s next,” she said into the comms. “Spectre, you’re on.”

Truck 17 hit the arena’s loading bay at 3:58, transponder pinging AKH-17 on the guard’s handheld—green light flashing, a soft beep. The guard—a lanky kid, patchy beard, eyes half-shut—yawned, clipboard smudged with thumbprints: “Concessions, 4 a.m. slot.”

One wrong look, one nosy clipboard, and the whole game went up in smoke.

The Spectre leaned out, gravel voice low—“Hassan, bulk refreshments”—badge glinting under the bay’s flickering fluorescents, balaclava stashed, face shadowed by the cab’s angle. The kid waved him through, scratching his neck, mumbling, “Hurry up,” as he turned back to a folding chair.

“Cleared,” The Spectre said into the comms, backing the rig into Bay 6—tires squealing on polished concrete, echoes bouncing off steel girders overhead, a faint drip-drip of condensation from pipes above. He killed the engine at 4:00 sharp—key yanked, dashboard lights fading—flipped a switch under the dash, hydraulic bed whirring to life, a slow hiss as it tilted, cables groaning under the weight.

The crate slid—800 pounds grinding metal on metal—hitting the floor with a dull clang, dust puffing around its edges, a faint tremor rippling through the concrete. Center-stage, under the arena's dim prep lights—yellow, buzzing—it sat: steel gleaming, locks armed, floodlights dark, Semtex silent 'til The Doctor's trigger.

"Down," The Spectre rasped, locking the cab—key pocketed, door thudding shut—slipping out a side exit past a stack of folding chairs, their plastic seats cracked, a faint whiff of bleach lingering from a janitor's mop. He melted into the vendor crowd by 4:03—balaclava off, badge stashed in a pocket, jacket zipped to his chin—steps silent on the asphalt, a shadow among shadows.

"Out," he said, final click into the comms, voice fading as he vanished.

Back in the lair, The Commander's scar twitched as he replayed the teaser—Lior's purpled face sobbing, Ronit's black flesh splitting stitches, shit oozing from every seam in grainy close-up. He'd won nothing yet. Not until the world choked on what they'd built.

"They'll pay or burn," he growled, tossing the burner to The Arbiter.

The Arbiter caught it, smirking faintly. "Message sent—governments'll scramble. 8 a.m. is ours."

The Watcher leaned back, static looping on her screen—ten seconds of gray fuzz, seamless. "OBS'll beam it—NBC, BBC, Al Jazeera, CBC—every screen, every gag. My hack's tight."

The Doctor rubbed his hands, blood flaking off onto the floor. "My centipede's ready— crawling, moaning, shitting when we hit the button. World won't forget."

The Commander paced again, boots squelching. "Spectre's done his part. Morning's the kill shot."

The Aspire Arena slept, quiet, cavernous, unaware. Beneath it, horror waited. Its breath shallow. Its scream inevitable.

Veil 13

The Spotlight and theShadow

The Main Press Center buzzed like a live wire, one breath from a spark, its glass walls refracting the dawn's pale gold over Doha's skyline.

It was 6:00 a.m., July 22, 2025, and the room—a stark, modern expanse of white panels, tiered seats, and blinking LED screens—bristled with over 200 journalists, their laptops casting a blue glow across tense faces, cameras perched like vultures on tripods, cables tangling the floor in a chaotic web.

The air was a stale cocktail of burnt coffee from a sputtering machine in the corner, sweat clinging to pressed shirts, and the faint ozone buzz of overheating equipment. Microphones crackled—"Testing, one-two-three"—as techs darted through the back, adjusting feeds, while a low murmur of speculation rippled through the crowd, punctuated by the sharp clack of a dropped pen or the rustle of hastily flipped notebooks.

At the front, a navy-draped table faced the throng, three microphones clustered like sentinels atop it, wires snaking to a soundboard manned by a harried tech. Sheikh Tariq bin Fahd Al-Mazrouei sat center, his tailored thobe pristine despite the sleepless night, silver- streaked beard glinting under halogen spots, his dark eyes hard as polished stone.

To his left, Jacques Moreau slumped in his chair, wiry frame drowning in a rumpled gray suit—tie askew, collar stained with sweat—his pale hands fidgeting with a water glass, condensation pooling on the cloth.

To his right, Viktor Mikhailovich Borodin loomed, a bearish hulk in a navy blazer stretched tight over broad shoulders, unshaven jaw set in a vodka-roughened scowl, meaty fists resting like hammers on the table. Behind them, a blue backdrop bore the IOC logo—five rings interlocking—a hollow symbol against the crisis's weight.

A digital clock on the wall ticked to 6:01, each second a silent whip-crack in the charged silence.

James Cartwright, BBC's seasoned Middle East correspondent, rose first—tall and lean, his tweed jacket patched at the elbows, gray hair swept back, voice a crisp British drawl slicing through the din.

"Sheikh Tariq, it's been nearly twenty-four hours since twelve athletes—Israeli and Lebanese—vanished from Doha. The world's on edge—parents weeping on air, governments demanding action. What's the IOC's progress? Have you pinned down who's behind this?"

Tariq leaned into his mic, voice steady but taut, a low rumble rolling out. "We're actively pursuing all avenues, working closely with international partners to resolve this swiftly and ensure the athletes' safety. That's our stance at this time."

Cartwright's brow creased, pen tapping his notepad with a staccato tap-tap-tap. "All avenues? That's a politician's dodge, Sheikh. Rumors are flying—ransom demands, body parts in boxes. Can you confirm or deny anything? Give us a shred of substance—people are losing their minds out there."

Behind the microphone, Moreau's heart skittered. They were too close.

He shifted, his chair creaking, voice high and reedy as he cut in. "We're working tirelessly—day and night. Our priority is the athletes' well-being. Speculation only muddies the waters; it doesn't help. We ask for patience while we—"

"Patience?" Emilie Laurent, L'Équipe's sharp-eyed Parisienne, surged to her feet—petite, her black bob framing a face tight with indignation, her French accent a blade through the noise. "Monsieur Moreau, your 'priority' is a hollow word when sources whisper a finger arrived—bloody, ringed, delivered to your doorstep. Is this true? Are they butchering them while you serve us platitudes?"

The room erupted—gasps, muttered curses, a wave of restless shifting. Borodin's fist slammed the table—crack—rattling the mics, his growl thick with Russian gravel. "No comment on rumors! We're mobilizing—best resources, best people. You want blood? Ask the scum who took them, not us!"

Laurent's eyes blazed, unyielding, her pen jabbing like a dart. "Mobilizing how? Military? Interpol? You sidestep ransom talk, but what's the ask—money, a manifesto? The public deserves clarity—athletes are dying, and you're choking on vagueness!"

Moreau shifted again. The tablecloth twitched beneath his hand.

Tariq raised a hand, palm out, his tone steel over silk. "We're coordinating with Qatari authorities and global agencies. Details jeopardize the effort—endanger lives. We won't fuel panic with unverified claims."

Greg Palmer, the Australian reporter—broad-shouldered, sunburned, khaki shirt rolled to the elbows—leaned forward from the third row, voice a dry Outback drawl laced with irritation. "Unverified? You're stonewalling, mates. Word's out —Nova Mendelsohn— stormed your suite last night with proof. Video, a note—where's she at now? Why isn't she up there spilling the goods?"

Borodin's jaw ticked, eyes flicking to Tariq, a beat too long. Moreau's glass trembled, water sloshing onto his cuff, his reply a stammer. "We—uh—we don't discuss individuals. Our focus is the situation, not… not speculation about—"

"She's a reporter, yeah?" Palmer cut in, voice rising, his pen stabbing the air. "Heard she had footage—nasty stuff, real evidence. If she's got the scoop, why's she dodging this circus? What're you lot hiding?"

Tariq's jaw clenched, a flicker of strain cracking his calm. "We're not hiding. We're managing a crisis—one question at a time. Next."

Rashida al-Hakim, Al Jazeera's Doha bureau chief, stood—mid-30s, her burgundy hijab framing a face carved with resolve, her Arabic crisp and commanding.

"Sheikh, with respect, 'managing' isn't cutting it. My sources say the kidnappers slashed their deadline—72 hours to 48—after a breach last night. Was that Nova's doing? Are you negotiating or gearing for a fight?"

Borodin snorted, a harsh bark that drew glares. "We don't kneel to terrorist filth! We're hunting—hard, fast, global. That's what you need to know."

Rashida's gaze held steady, unflinching. She had walked these streets at dawn. She knew when silence turned sour.

"Hunting where? Qatar? The Levant? The Gulf? You've got twelve lives dangling—families begging on live feeds. Toss us a bone, or we'll dig deeper—Al Jazeera's already got crews sniffing."

Tariq's voice hardened, fatigue threading its edge. "We're pursuing leads with international cooperation—Qatar's leading, others follow. Dig if you must, but operational specifics stay off the table. Lives hang in the balance."

Carlos Mendes, Brazil's Globo Esporte reporter—stocky, salt-and-pepper beard bristling, his Portuguese accent thick with urgency—rose next, his chair scraping loud.

"Señor Borodin, you talk hunting, but what about the Games? Women's gymnastics kicks off today—Aspire Arena, 10 a.m. Parents back home are screaming—cancel it, or let it roll while their kids bleed? What's the call?"

Moreau fielded it, voice quavering as he gripped the mic. "The IOC's assessing—safety is paramount. No final decision yet, but we're committed to the Olympic spirit, to—"

"Spirit?" Mendes roared, incredulous, his fist slamming his thigh.

"You've got a finger in a box—maybe more—and you're bleating about spirit? Postpone it— grow a spine! Brazil's got two athletes in that hell—families are torching effigies of you lot!"

The room surged—shouts overlapping, "Postpone!" "Ransom!" "Where's Nova?"—cameras flashing like gunfire, a wave of frustration cresting. A new voice cut through—Priya Patel, The Times of India, slim and poised, her sari a flash of teal, her English lilting but fierce.

"Sheikh Tariq, India's got no skin in this—yet—but the subcontinent's watching. If this is political—Hezbollah, Hamas, Gulf rivals—say it! Are we next? Is this a regional vendetta spilling over?"

No one on stage moved. For a moment, the microphones hummed alone.

Tariq's eyes narrowed, his reply measured but sharp. "We've no evidence of specific groups—only threats. Our focus is rescue, not geopolitics. Assumptions help no one."

Priya pressed, undeterred, her pen poised. "Threats with a deadline—72 hours now, per Rashida's scoop. That's not random; it's calculated. What's the trigger? Nova's breach, or something you're not telling us?"

Borodin growled, leaning forward, his bulk shadowing the mic. "Enough guessing games! We're tracking—airtight ops. You'll get facts when we've got 'em."

The crowd bristled again—groans, hissed expletives. Cartwright stood once more, voice rising over the chaos. "Facts? You're feeding us fog, Sheikh! That finger—whose was it? Israeli? Lebanese? And Nova—where's she gone? She's the only one who's seen these bastards—why's she not here?"

Moreau flinched, glass clinking as he set it down too hard. "We—we can't confirm identities or… or individuals' whereabouts. It's sensitive—"

"Sensitive?" Laurent snapped, her tone venomous. "You're shielding her—or she's dead. Which is it? She had video—rape, torture, per leaks. If she's missing this, she's either running or silenced."

Someone in the back cursed under their breath. A camera light blinked red.

Palmer nodded, his drawl cutting in. "Yeah, mate—Nova's a bloodhound. Chased that doping ring 'til it cracked wide open. She'd be here, front row, unless you've gagged her—or worse."

Tariq slammed a palm on the table—thwack—the sound a gunshot, silencing the uproar. “Enough! We’re doing everything possible—trust that. No one’s gagged, no one’s dead. Updates when we have them—dismissed.”

The press screamed after them, but the silence Nova left was louder.

The trio rose, chairs scraping in unison—Moreau’s squeaking, Borodin’s thudding, Tariq’s a sharp drag—exiting through a side door flanked by Qatari security in black suits, earpieces glinting. The press exploded—cameras clicking, voices shouting—“Sheikh, one more!”

“Give us a name!” “Aspire’s still on?”—but the door slammed shut with a hollow boom, leaving a wake of grumbling discontent.

Cartwright snapped his notebook shut, muttering to Laurent beside him, “Bloody wall of nothing. Nova’s the hinge—they’re dodging her hard.

“And if she breaks,” he added, “the whole story cracks open.”

Laurent’s pen paused, her eyes narrowing. “Oui, she’s a terrier—sniffed out that EPO scandal in ‘23. If she’s not here, she’s either got a lead or they’ve buried her. Either way, they’re scared.”

Palmer slung his bag over a shoulder, smirking grimly. “Reckon she’s out there chasing ghosts. Hope she’s quick—these vague pricks’ll smother her story if she blinks.”

Rashida adjusted her hijab, voice low to Mendes beside her. “Forty-eight hours, and they’re still blind—or lying. Aspire’s a red flag—gymnastics today, and they won’t budge.

Something’s off.”

Mendes nodded, his beard bristling. “They’re sweating—Moreau’s a wreck. Nova’s the wildcard—wherever she is, she’s stirring the pot."

The press center churned on, a beast ravenous and unappeased, its questions ricocheting off the glass walls as the clock hit 6:30 a.m., the world beyond still groping in the dark. Outside those glass walls, the truth ran faster than the headlines

Five miles away, Nova slipped through the Old Port's fractured veins—Mina'a Al Doha Al Qadeema—a decaying sprawl of weathered dhows, rusting cranes, and crumbling warehouses hugging the Gulf's edge. No cameras here. Just grit, blood, and ghosts.

It was 6:15 a.m., the sky a bruised gray bleeding into gold, the air thick with salt, fish guts, and diesel. Her boots splashed through oil-slicked puddles, scarf tight over matted hair, hoodie clinging damp.

The burner buzzed—Rahman: **"Katara Hospitality truck, fake plates—depot raided, nothing yet"**—a splinter of dread she couldn't shake, Aspire Arena looming in her mind.

She'd bolted from Omar's shop in Souq Waqif, his warning—"Old Port, Jaber, scarred nose"—a lifeline, Alim's death throbbing in her memory—his blood a ghost under her soles. The tablet in her bag—SD card slotted—burned against her hip, its footage (rape, blood, screams) a relentless echo, the note's pre-Islamic snarl (Hijazi, Najdi, per Omar) her only thread. The Old Port pulsed—fishermen hauling nets, a tea seller clattering a samovar, a stray dog gnawing a fish head. Shadows moved—silhouettes in doorways, eyes glinting from skiffs, a sedan's tinted window rolling slow. Nova's breath quickened with each pulse of the harbor—every shadow felt like it knew her name.

"We see you running," their 4 a.m. text had hissed—The Watcher's work. Were they here? That hooded figure by the dhow? The man flicking a cigarette into the water?

She ducked behind crab traps—wood splintered, reeking of brine—breath shallow, pulse hammering. The burner buzzed—6:17 a.m., Rahman: **"Aspire footage—truck backed in, dropped cargo, driver gone. Blurry face, checking IDs."** Her gut twisted—Katara Hospitality, Aspire, 4 a.m.—a truck staging something,

Omar's "chaos" theory clawing at her.

She needed Jaber. If she didn't find him now, the truth—and everyone it could save—would vanish with the tide.

The pier stretched south, warehouses gray and sagging. She darted through an alley— narrow, slimed with algae—boots slipping, a shout—"Ya bint!"—sending her sprinting onto a quay littered with ropes and oil drums. "Jaber," she muttered, scanning—scar over nose, skinny, Omar's lead. A tea stall ahead, three men hunched over cups; a warehouse door ajar, oud music crackling; a skiff bobbing 20 yards out.

The burner tugged her pocket—6:19 a.m., 11 minutes to her IOC check-in, 47 hours left. A figure emerged from the warehouse—thin, wiry, keffiyeh loose, a jagged scar slicing his nose bridge, eyes darting. Jaber? She froze, breath snagging—too exposed. He lit a cigarette—match flaring, sulfur sharp—glancing her way, then past, hand patting a pistol's grip at his hip.

"Jaber?" she hissed, five yards out, hand on the tablet. He turned—sharp, sudden—scar glinting, cigarette dropping, embers scattering.

"Who's asking?" he snapped, Arabic rough, hand twitching to the gun.

"Nova—Omar sent me," she said, low and fast, palms up. "Script—Najdi, Hijazi maybe—twelve athletes, they'll die unless…"

His jaw tightened, scar stretching, a flicker in his eyes—fear, recognition? "Omar's a fool," he growled, glancing past her—quay, dhow, sedan rolling slow. "That script's dead—Hijazi, Najdi, tribal shit. Smugglers don't touch it—too rare."

"Then who?" she pressed, desperation cracking her voice. "Fanatics? Exiles? Someone's got a grudge—Olympics, five hundred billion. Tell me!"

He stepped back, hand on the gun, eyes darting. “Not here,” he muttered, nodding to the warehouse—door creaking, shadows pooling. “Too many ears—move.”

She hesitated—trap? Lead?—but the sedan’s engine growled closer, headlights dim but piercing. Her gut screamed—run or follow?—but Jaber was her thread. She nodded, darting after him, the warehouse swallowing her—air cold, dank, smelling of rust and rot—door slamming shut with a clang.

Inside, crates loomed—stacked high, marked with faded Arabic, relics or contraband?—a single bulb swinging, casting jagged shadows across a concrete floor streaked with oil and slime. Jaber turned, gun half-drawn—a scratched Makarov—voice a hiss. “Show me— script, now. I don’t talk blind.”

Her hand shook, ripping the note from her bag—crumpled, sweat-stained—thrusting it at him. “Here—‘justice,’ they said. Who writes this?”

He snatched it, eyes scanning, scar twitching. “Najdi—old blood, vengeance vibe. Not smugglers—too clean.” He paused, then darted to a crate—six feet tall, marked “Fragile” in peeling paint—prying it open with a grunt, wood splintering. Inside, a leather satchel, cracked and ancient, spilled out—scrolls, yellowed, edges crumbling, tied with frayed cord. He yanked one free, unrolling it—script jagged, ink faded but sharp, matching the note’s snarl.

“Found these last month—Najdi ruins, deep desert,” he rasped, voice low, eyes flicking to the roof—a creak, metal shifting. “Old grudges—vengeance in the sand, disdain for Western pride on ‘our’ soil. Oaths broken, forgotten kings—centuries of wait, Najdi blood boiling.” He tapped the scroll, finger trembling. “They curse invaders—‘gold rings on stolen dunes,’ they call it. Olympics—five hundred billion—it’s their trigger.”

Nova swallowed hard—every gold medal now felt like a bullseye.

Her breath caught, mind racing—Aspire, the crate, a vendetta centuries old. "Who's 'they'?" she whispered, heart slamming, eyes darting—roof, door, a sliver of dawn through a cracked window.

"Exiles—Syrian, Iraqi—Najdi kin," he snarled, rolling the scroll tight, shoving it back. "Burned by wars, by deals—'Obsidian Hand,' they whisper. That script's their oath—justice, not cash."

Nova's pulse surged. This wasn't about ransom. It was revenge—scripted in blood.

A thud above—boots on tin—froze him, gun snapping up, cocked with a click. "Someone's here—you brought 'em!"

Nova's hand twitched toward the tablet. If they were coming, she'd take them down with the truth.

"No!" she hissed, ducking behind a crate—wood splintered, salt-reeking—tablet clutched tight. "I'm clean—Omar vouched! Who's up there?"

"Them—your kidnappers," he rasped, backing toward a crate, sweat beading on his scarred brow. "Old Port's their haunt—exiles, crazies. That script's their flag—Najdi hate, pure."

The burner buzzed—6:42 a.m., Rahman: **"Aspire crate—steel, locked, guards spooked. Al-Nasr's moving in"**—her thumb smudging the screen, glowing in the dimness.

Time was thinning—forty-seven hours now felt like minutes.

"Crate," she muttered, eyes on Jaber. "Aspire—steel box, dropped 4 a.m. That's them— staging chaos. What's in it?"

His face paled, scar stark. "Chaos? Could be anything—bomb, gas, worse. Scrolls say 'scourge the pride'—Western games, Najdi vengeance. Five hundred billion's their insult." A scrape above—metal grinding—jerked his gun higher. "They're coming—move!"

She scrambled left, crate's edge tearing her knee—denim ripping, blood stinging— crouching behind burlap sacks, fish oil seeping through. "Where?" she hissed, bulb's swing casting her shadow jagged.

"Back exit—there," Jaber snapped, nodding to a rusted door—padlocked, chain dangling, gray light leaking through. He edged toward it, gun sweeping—creak, thud, creak— footsteps pacing. "They've got the roof—perch. You're dead if they drop."

Her pulse roared—window too high, front door a trap, sedan a wildcard. "Names—give me names!" she demanded, inching after him, sacks shielding her, stench choking her.

"No names—ghosts," he rasped, yanking the chain—links clanking, rust flaking. "Najdi exiles—war dogs, Olympic burnouts. 'Obsidian Hand'—black vengeance." A bang above— metal buckling—froze him, eyes wide. "They're through!"

She lunged, slamming into the door—shoulder jarring—as the chain snapped, door groaning open—Gulf air rushing in, briny and cold—an alley beyond: crates haphazard, a dumpster spilling nets. "Go!" she yelled, shoving him.

A crash—tin ripping, boots hitting concrete—spun her back. Two figures dropped—hooded, black-clad, one wiry (The Watcher?), one hulking (The Enforcer?)—15 feet off. The wiry one raised a silenced pistol—thwip—a dart burying in Jaber's shoulder. He gasped, gun clattering, knees buckling—sedative—crumpling into the alley, keffiyeh tangling in dirt.

"Jaber!" Nova screamed, diving after him—a second thwip grazing her arm, fabric tearing, pain flaring—sprawling beside him, tablet skittering.

The Enforcer charged—hand snatching her hood, yanking her back—scalp burning, hair tearing—pinning her, knee grinding her spine, wrists twisting in his grip.

"Got her," he growled—voice deep, muffled—breath sour through his mask. The Watcher loomed—pistol steady, her yellow eyes were impossible to forget—predator's eyes, watching everything—voice a rasp: "She's the runner—Raffles bitch. Crate's set—tie her, move."

"No!" she roared, kicking—boot glancing his shin—clawing the tablet, fingers brushing its edge. The Watcher knelt, zip ties snapping tight—blood welling as she twisted—her legs flailing, his hand clamping her ankle, twisting until pain shot up her calf.

"Stop squirming," The Watcher hissed, tightening the ties—yellow eyes flicking to Jaber, then back, a smirk tugging his mask. "Feisty—won't help. Crate's live—your mess."

"Then let the world see it," Nova hissed, the pain sharpening her voice.

The burner buzzed—6:25 a.m., Rahman: **"Aspire breached—crate's live, guards down, chaos"**—screen glowing, unreachable. The Watcher snatched it—crushing it under her boot—crack—shards scattering. "No more pings," she rasped. "Lair—now. She's leverage."

"Names!" Nova gasped, lungs screaming, ribs creaking under The Enforcer's knee. "Obsidian… who?"

The Watcher paused, pistol tilting—her rasp deliberate. "You'll meet 'em—Commander'll like your fight. 'Obsidian Hand'—Najdi justice, sand's revenge. Crate's the proof—scrolls promised it."

Nova had thought this was about money. It wasn't. It was about memory—and rage. She tapped the tablet—scooping it up, SD card intact—tucking it into a pouch.

The Enforcer hauled her—arm wrenching, legs kicking air—slinging her over his shoulder, warehouse spinning: crates tilting, bulb flickering, Jaber's sprawl blurring. She hung like dead weight in his grip, the same way the truth hung in that steel box.

"Let me… go!" she choked, clawing his Kevlar—useless—blood trickling down her forearms.

"Shut it," he grunted, stride heavy—thump-thump—toward the front door, sedan's purr louder. The Watcher followed—rope in hand—voice cutting: "Alley's clear—Jaber's out, won't talk. Truck's waiting."

She bucked—knee slamming his chest—his grip faltering, cursing as he tightened his hold. "Fucking stop!" he roared, slamming her against a crate—wood splintering, ribs flaring— dumping her, head cracking concrete, stars bursting.

The Watcher loomed—rope snapping taut—lassoing her ankles, cutting circulation. "Enough games," she rasped, yellow eyes glinting—checking the ties, cinching tighter. "You'll see the centipede—live, screaming. Forty-seven hours—your clock."

A thud outside—sedan door opening—drew her up. The Enforcer heaved her—shoulder digging her gut—her body limp, warehouse blurring. But then—a crackle on The Watcher's comms, static slicing, a voice barking: "Abort—truck's compromised, heat's inbound. Leave her."

The Watcher froze—eyes narrowing—then nodded. "Drop her," she snapped, turning toward the door. The Enforcer grunted, flinging Nova down—body slamming concrete, ribs flaring, head cracking—blood pooling under her cheek, vision swimming.

"Forty-seven hours," The Watcher rasped, dart gun dangling, boots fading. The Enforcer lumbered past, sedan peeling away—tires screeching, gravel spraying—silence settling. Nova lay—bound, battered—lungs clawing air, each gasp a knife.

Minutes bled—pulse thudding, blood sticky—until Jaber stirred, groaning, dragging himself up—eyes bleary, spotting her. "Nova..." he croaked, crawling—knees scraping—reaching her, fumbling the ropes free, ankles tingling as blood rushed back. He hauled her up—her body screaming, a groan tearing loose.

"Gotta... move," he muttered, slinging her arm over his neck—steps unsteady, her weight dragging. The docks loomed—Old Port's mist curling, waves slapping—each stumble jarring her ribs, vision fading. He found a shed—door ajar, reeking of salt—easing her against the wall, her back scraping planks.

"Stay awake," he said, voice sharper, shaking off the daze—kneeling, checking her pulse. "You're a mess... but here." He glanced out—docks quiet—then back, eyes hard.

"Scrolls—they're real. They've been waiting a hundred years," he said, voice low. "Now, the world will watch them strike."

Nova nodded—weak, pain searing—but alive, the crate's shadow five miles off, its pulse a distant threat in the dark.

Veil 14

The Unveiling

The Aspire Arena's gymnastics hall gleamed under its vaulted dome at 7:45 a.m. on July 23, 2025, its polished hardwood floor reflecting crisp LED beams. Chalk dust swirled faintly, mingling with a subtle, unsettling odor—sharp, chemical, barely noticeable but enough to prickle the senses.

Somewhere beyond the sealed doors, a crackle of static whispered on an unsecured comms line, a sign of Nova's surveillance net tightening, her attention drawn to the anomaly at the arena's heart.

The space thrummed with pre-competition energy: sneakers squeaked, practice vaults thudded, and athletes stretched—muscles flexing, wrists popping—amid the faint scent of sweat and resin. Navy blue mats lined the walls, edges curling slightly, while the uneven bars stood in shadow, steel frames cold. The all-around competition, an Olympic qualifier, was 90 minutes away, the air taut with focus.

At the center, beneath the dormant scoreboard, sat a steel crate—8 feet long, 4 feet wide, 800 pounds of dented metal. Its bulk jarred against the arena's polish. Floodlights on its frame were dark, wires tucked neatly, a hidden panel concealing a remote detonator linked to The Doctor's control, 66 miles away in The Obsidian Hand's lair.

The crate arrived at 4:03 a.m., its hydraulic bed groaning as The Spectre positioned it center-stage, logged as "equipment surplus" on a forged manifest, unnoticed amid pre-dawn setup. In a shadowed loading dock corner, a discarded tablet flickered, showing a grainy feed of the crate's arrival—Nova's hack into the arena's CCTV, a clue she'd soon unravel.

The U.S. team warmed up 20 feet away, six gymnasts in star-spangled leotards, chalk dusting their palms. Alyssa Park—23, compact, eyes sharp—led, her vault skills renowned, though Maya Ben-Ari's absence nagged her. Mia Torres—19, wiry, freckled—adjusted her wrist wraps, muttering, "This floor's too slick," voice tinged with nerves. Katie Nguyen—25, lean, bangs framing her face—stretched silently, their coach, Dan Novak, barking, "Eyes up!" over a chalk block's clatter. The crate's shadow felt heavy, unspoken.

Across the floor, the Italian team stretched in blue uniforms. Giulia Rossi—24, lithe—led drills, movements precise but tense. Sofia Conti—25, poised—adjusted her grips, fingers restless. Elena Ricci—26, lean—stretched her calves, breaths uneven. Their coach snapped, "Concentratevi!" but the crate gnawed at their focus.

Judges milled near their table, clipboards rustling, badges glinting. In the luxury box, Sheikh Tariq bin Fahd Al-Mazrouei, IOC President—mid-50s, robes pristine, silver cufflink catching light—sipped tea. His phone buzzed—an anonymous tip about "irregular cargo," dismissed by his aide but flagged by Nova. Jacques Moreau—lean, silver-haired, suit sharp—fiddled with a pen, muttering about delays. Viktor Borodin—barrel-chested, ruddy-faced—swiped through athlete stats, pinky ring clinking.

At 7:50, Alyssa drifted to the crate, chalk smudging her thighs, water bottle in hand. "What's this?" she muttered, kicking its base—sneaker scuffing steel, a dull thunk. A low rasp answered—guk-guk—muffled, like a distant machine. Her pulse quickened, bottle slipping, cracking on the floor, water pooling. "You hear that?" she called to Mia, stretching nearby, freckles stark against unease.

Mia frowned, stepping closer, chalk puffing off her leotard. "Sounds like… air escaping?" she said, crouching near a vent. The rasp grew—guk-guk—strained, living. A faint smell hit—sharp, medicinal, sour. Mia recoiled, coughing, hands on knees. "That's not right," she gasped, eyes watering.

Alyssa shouted—"What is this?"—drawing the Italians. Elena Ricci grabbed her arm, whispering, "Cosa c'è?" as the smell spread, tightening throats. Sheikh Tariq's cup hit the table, tea splashing his robe. "Who authorized this?" he barked. Jacques Moreau muttered, "Mon Dieu, qu'est-ce que c'est?" Viktor Borodin growled, "Open it—now!"

Alyssa found the latch—a rusted lever, cold—and pulled. Gears whined, the lid slid back, floodlights snapping on, bathing the floor in harsh white. Inside lay the centipede—a 20-foot chain of twelve sedated athletes, stitched together, faces pale under the glare.

Lior's chest rose faintly. Omar's head lolled. Yael's eyes fluttered. Tamar lay twisted. Noa breathed shallowly. Yasmine Haddad stirred. Nadine Al-Rassi groaned. Nadine Mansour twitched. Yasmine Khalil was limp. Cyrine's fingers trembled. Maya's breaths were ragged. Ronit's face was slack, a faint moan escaping.

The gymnasts' screams shattered the air—a raw, collective cry echoing off the dome. Alyssa stumbled back, hands shaking, chalk smearing her face, gasping, "No… no way…" Her knees buckled, catching herself on a mat, eyes wide, locked on Lior's pale form. Mia gagged, doubling over, breaths sharp, choking out, "What the hell is this?" as she backed into a beam, wood thudding her shoulder.

Sophie Laurent, French gymnast—petite, blonde braid—screamed, "Mon Dieu!" hands covering her mouth, stumbling into a mat, tearing its edge with a rip. Her eyes darted to Omar's still face, voice trembling, "They're… alive?" Sophie's teammate, Amélie Dubois, froze, whispering, "C'est pas possible…" as she clutched Sophie's arm, nails digging in.

Sakura Tanaka, Japanese gymnast—small, dark ponytail—gasped, "Kuso…" backing away, tripping over a water bottle, plastic crunching. She sank to her knees, hands shaking, staring at Yael's fluttering eyes, muttering, "This can't be real…" Her teammate, Hana Mori, clutched her shoulder, voice breaking, "Sakura, don't look!"

Elena Vasquez, Mexican gymnast—muscular, dark ponytail—shouted, "Dios mío!" lurching back, crashing into a vault, wood creaking. Her hands trembled, covering her face, voice hoarse, "They did this to them?" Her teammate, Sofia Ramírez, grabbed her, whispering, "Elena, breathe," as tears streaked Sofia's chalk-dusted cheeks.

Lia O'Connor, Irish gymnast—freckled, red hair—bellowed, "No way!" charging the crate, fists pounding steel—bang-bang—skin reddening, voice raw, "Who did this?" She sank to her knees, sobbing, staring at Tamar's twisted form, her teammate, Erin Kelly, pulling her back, murmuring, "Lia, stop, you can't…"

Anya Petrova, Russian gymnast—tall, blonde bun—cried out, a high wail, spinning into a teammate, gripping their shoulders, gasping, "Nyet… this is wrong…" Her eyes locked on Noa's shallow breaths, hands shaking as she whispered, "They're suffering…" Her teammate, Irina Volkov, steadied her, voice low, "Anya, we can't help them here."

Jade Williams, Australian gymnast—tanned, short curls—screamed, "No!" collapsing to her knees, palms skidding in chalk, sobbing, "This is sick!" She stared at Yasmine Haddad's stirring form, her teammate, Chloe Harris, kneeling beside her, whispering, "Jade, look away," as Chloe's hands trembled.

Isabela Nascimento, Brazilian gymnast—lean, dark eyes—shouted, "Caralho!" kicking a bench, wood creaking, her voice breaking, "Monsters!" Her gaze fixed on Nadine Al-Rassi's groan, her teammate, Larissa Silva, grabbing her arm, voice soft, "Isa, we'll get them help…"

Zara Khan, Indian gymnast—braid loose, hennaed hands—gasped, "Bhagwan…" sinking to her knees, hands clutching her face, tears falling, whispering, "How could they?" She stared at Nadine Mansour's twitch, her teammate, Priya Sharma, touching her shoulder, voice steady, "Zara, stay strong."

Lena Müller, German gymnast—stocky, blonde ponytail—screamed, "Nein!" lurching forward, stopped by a teammate's grip, her voice cracking, "They're Olympians!" Her eyes fixed on Yasmine Khalil's limp form, her teammate, Anna Schmidt, murmuring, "Lena, they're coming for them."

Aisha Diallo, Senegalese gymnast—wiry, braids—wailed, "Allahou akbar!" staggering back, ankle twisting on a mat, hitting the floor, palms slapping wood. She sobbed, staring at Cyrine's trembling fingers, her teammate, Fatou Ndiaye, helping her up, whispering, "Aisha, they'll save them."

Klara Svensson, Swedish gymnast—pale, freckled—shrieked, "Herregud!" doubling over, hands in her hair, gasping, "This is evil…" Her eyes locked on Maya's ragged breaths, her teammate,

Emma Lind, steadying her, voice soft, "Klara, they're getting help."

Katie Nguyen, American gymnast—lean, bangs—wailed, "Holy shit!" punching a water cooler, water splashing her legs, stumbling into a beam. She choked, "They're our friends!" staring at Ronit's moan, Alyssa pulling her back, voice firm, "Katie, we'll fight for them."

The arena erupted—shouts, gasps, equipment clattering as mats toppled, water bottles rolled. The smell intensified—antiseptic, sour—clinging to the air. Sheikh Tariq stood rigid, robes stained, voice hoarse: "This is an outrage!" Jacques Moreau sank into a chair, muttering, "Inhumain…" Viktor Borodin slammed the table, roaring, "Sabotage!"

Athletes scattered, coaches shouting into radios—static hissing as The Keeper's jam faded. Medical teams rushed in at 8:02—Qatar Civil Defence medics in yellow hazmat suits, boots thudding, carrying trauma kits. Dr. Fatima al-Sayed, trauma lead—40s, hijab under her suit—led, voice sharp: "Get them out—carefully!"

She knelt by Maya, cutting an IV tube—milky fluid dripping, pooling on the crate's base. Maya's face was pale, pulse weak, monitor beeping—48 bpm. Dr. Fatima applied gauze, securing it, checking her airway, gloves slick with sweat.

Hassan al-Abdulla worked on Ronit, cutting stitches—snip-snip—thread snapping, revealing swollen skin. "Stable but critical," he called, hooking an IV with saline, bag swaying. Ronit's leg twitched, pulse monitor at 50 bpm.

Medics moved fast, suits rustling, masks fogging. Sara al-Najjar freed Tamar, slicing stitches, applying pressure to minor bleeding. "She's holding," Sara said, securing a tourniquet. Khalid bin Hamad worked on Noa, cutting her free, stabilizing her neck with a collar—plastic snapping—breaths shallow but steady.

By 8:07, six stretchers lined the floor, wheels squeaking, athletes secured—IVs reinserted, saline dripping. Maya's stretcher rolled, monitor beeping—52 bpm. Ronit's gurney followed, IV secure, antibiotics flowing—ceftriaxone, 2 grams—pulse at 55 bpm.

"Al Wakra Hospital—now!" Dr. Fatima ordered, directing three ambulances. Sirens blared, speeding from the loading dock, weaving through traffic. Inside Ambulance 1, Dr. Fatima monitored Maya, adjusting IV, saline flowing, pulse at 50 bpm. In Ambulance 3, Ronit lay still, tech checking vitals—58 bpm—antibiotics working.

Ambulance 2 carried Tamar and Noa. Tamar's tourniquets held, pulse at 60 bpm. Noa's collar aligned her spine, breathing even, monitor—62 bpm. The 12-mile drive was tense, medics focused, equipment humming.

At Al Wakra Hospital, trauma bays sprang to life at 8:20 a.m.—gurneys rolling, medics shouting, "Critical but stable!" Air smelled of antiseptic, floor clean but tense. Dr. Omar Khalifa, chief of surgery, directed Maya to Bay 1. Pulse at 50 bpm, IVs pumping, ventilator hissing—12 breaths per minute—stable.

Ronit, in Bay 3, prepped for surgery. Dr. Khalifa checked her leg—swollen but viable—ordering antibiotics, fluids. Pulse at 60 bpm, monitors steady. Lior, in Bay 2, breathed through a chest tube, pulse 55 bpm, sutures clean. Tamar, in Bay 4, stabilized at 62 bpm, wounds dressed. Noa, in Bay 5, spine braced, pulse 60 bpm, vitals holding.

ORs buzzed—surgeons stitching, monitors beeping, air sharp with antiseptic. Athletes prioritized, survival ensured, infection managed.

At 8:30, 66 miles away, The Watcher hit Enter, OBS feed flickering live to NBC, BBC, Al Jazeera. Maya's faint rasps, Ronit's moans, the centipede's sedated form filled screens. In the media room, reporters froze. James Cartwright—tweed rumpled—dropped his mug, coffee pooling. "Unthinkable," he croaked, typing: HORROR IN DOHA.

Emilie Laurent, L'Équipe, whispered, "Impossible," streaming Tamar's still form. Greg Palmer, Seven Network, shouted, "Turn it off!" as Lior's pale face flashed. Rashida al-Hakim, Al Jazeera, faltered—"Ya Rab…"—mic live, voice shaking. Carlos Mendes, Globo, muttered, "Caralho," as Ronit's stitches gleamed. Priya Patel, The Times of India, gasped, "Bhagwan," typing: OLYMPIC CRISIS UNFOLDS.

Sheikh Tariq grabbed a radio, shouting, "Shut down OBS!" Robes clung, sweat-soaked. Jacques Moreau slumped, muttering, "Ruined…" Viktor Borodin smashed his tablet, growling, "Find them!"

IOC scrambled—Sheikh Tariq's statement at 9:05, voice unsteady: "We condemn this atrocity." Jacques Moreau, on Paris call, choked, "The Games are sacred…" Viktor Borodin, to Moscow, snarled, "They'll pay."

PA blared at 8:40: "Evacuate—hazard on the floor!" NBC cut to black at 8:42, BBC at 8:43, Al Jazeera at 8:44, but the image lingered—X erupting with #DohaHorror, clips spreading.

In the lair, The Commander grinned. "Five hundred billion, thirty-nine hours," he said, burner buzzing—Beirut: Negotiating.

The arena emptied—chalk dust settling, crate sealed by hazmat, its echo a political firestorm no broadcast could contain.

Veil 15

Threads in the Dust

The Old Port's dawn mist had burned off into a clammy haze by the time Jaber dragged Nova from the fisherman's shed, his wiry arm hooked under her shoulders, her boots scuffing wet planks as she stumbled through the splintered doorway.

Twelve hours had passed since she'd bolted from the Main Press Center's electric chaos— Sheikh Tariq's stonewalling, Moreau's trembling platitudes, Borodin's vodka-roughened roar still echoing in her skull—her sprint through Doha's shadowed veins a desperate bid to chase the kidnappers' trail before it went cold. The air outside the shed hung heavy with salt, fish guts, and the sour tang of diesel from idling skiffs, the Gulf's gray churn slapping against rotting pilings a low, restless growl.

Inside Omar's shack—a ramshackle lean-to of corrugated tin and scavenged wood at Souq Waqif's edge—the atmosphere was thicker still: a stale brew of kerosene from a sputtering lamp, the acrid bite of Jaber's cigarette smoke, and the lingering anise sting of arak, its bottle uncorked and gleaming dully on a shelf.

The crescent-scarred door slammed shut, the tin shack sealing them into a stale tomb of fear and rot—Omar's meaty hand sliding the bolt with a dull clank—sealing them into a cramped cocoon of survival. Shelves sagged under a clutter of yellowed books—Arabic poetry curling at the edges, nautical charts stained with coffee rings, a dog-eared Quran wedged beside a tin of loose tea leaves.

A cot, its frame rusted and sagging, groaned under a pile of threadbare blankets—reds and browns faded to rust—as Nova collapsed onto it, springs squeaking in protest, her body a battered map of pain. A crate doubled as a table, its surface scarred and littered with cigarette butts, a chipped teacup ringed with old stains, and a rusted tin of arnica salve, its lid dented from years of rough handling. The kerosene lamp flickered amber across peeling tin walls, casting jagged shadows that danced with each breath of the humid air seeping through cracks.

Nova's ribs throbbed—each stab of pain tried to drown her resolve– but the centipede's shadow loomed larger in her mind than her broken body. Her left shoulder pulsed hot and swollen, sprained beneath a makeshift sling of torn blanket, the joint stiff and screaming from his fist's brutal crunch—a blow that had rattled her teeth and left a bruise blooming purple under her hoodie.

Her wrists bore raw, red welts—zip ties' jagged bite crusted with blood, the skin chafed and oozing where plastic had cut deep—while her head pounded, a concussion's fog blurring her vision's edges, a sticky smear of crimson matting her hairline from repeated slams against the floor. Her hoodie clung damp—sweat-soaked, streaked with dock slime, and tinged with the faint copper tang of her own blood—her boots scuffed and caked with Old Port mud, one ankle twinging sharp from The Watcher's twist, a dull fire licking up her calf with each step.

She was a wreck—functional but teetering on collapse—pain a constant hum beneath her skin, her breath a shallow rasp as she slumped, the cot's coarse blanket scraping her neck.

Jaber dropped her tarp—a stiff, fish-gut-stained shroud that reeked of brine and decay—into a corner with a wet slap, the sound echoing off the tin walls as he sank onto the crate, his wiry frame slumping with exhaustion. His keffiyeh hung loose around his neck, mud- streaked and damp, the scar slicing his nose bridge a stark white against sallow skin still flushed from the sedative dart's lingering haze. He'd taken it in the shoulder—Watcher's silenced thwip burying the dart deep, dropping him like a sack of wet sand—and though the fog had mostly burned off, his hands still trembled faintly as he struck a match, the flare of sulfur biting the air.

He lit a cigarette—cheap, local, the paper yellowed and crinkled—exhaling a plume that curled lazily toward the tin roof, his dark eyes darting to Nova, then Omar, voice a rough rasp scraping over the shack's stillness: "She's busted—dock fight, their goons. Watcher, sneaky bitch—darted me, nearly took her. Tablet's gone—video too. Said 'centipede'— Aspire's live, chaos brewing."

Omar loomed over Nova—mid-40s, stocky, his grizzled beard framing a face carved with fatigue and resolve, kaftan stained with tea, sweat, and the faint yellow of spilled turmeric from a souq deal gone messy days back. He knelt beside her, thick fingers probing her wrists—the cuts swollen, oozing a thin pinkish fluid—then her shoulder, her sharp wince drawing a grunt from his throat, a sound half-disapproval, half-concern.

"Ribs cracked, shoulder's a mess, head's concussed—foolish, Nova, running blind into their web."

His voice was gruff, weathered by years of haggling in the souq and dodging knives in darker corners, but his eyes softened briefly—a flicker of something paternal—before hardening again as he rummaged a shelf. Glass jars clinked—a faint rattle of loose pills echoing—as he pulled out gauze, the arnica tin, a cloudy bottle of arak, and a dented tin box of medical odds: iodine in a chipped vial, a frayed bandage roll shedding threads, a needle and spool of black thread for stitching if her cuts turned worse.

"Drink—small, slow," he said, uncorking the arak—its anise stink sharp, stinging her nose as it wafted up—pouring a splash into the chipped teacup, its rim catching the lamp's weak glow, the liquid shimmering faintly golden. She took it—hands trembling, a grimace twisting her face as the arak burned down her throat—three sips, each one a fiery jolt that made her cough, the sting cutting through her concussion's haze like a blade, grounding her scattered senses.

Omar worked with brusque efficiency, his thick fingers surprisingly deft despite their calluses. He soaked a wad of gauze in arak—liquid dripping, pooling on the crate with a faint plink—swabbing her temple where blood had crusted in dark, flaky clumps, the cut shallow but jagged, stinging sharp as alcohol bit into raw flesh, her hiss swallowed by the shack's hum.

She bit the inside of her cheek, swallowing every hiss of pain—there was no room left for weakness. Arnica salve came next—cool, greasy, scooped from the tin with a blunt fingernail— smeared thick over her wrists, its herbal tang mixing with the arak's bite, easing the heat of torn skin as he rubbed it in, the welts glistening under the lamp. Iodine followed—brown liquid splashed from the vial onto her ankle, pooling in the creases of scraped skin, a sharp twinge flaring as it seeped in—then wrapped tight with bandage strips torn from the roll, the fabric rough and slightly mildewed but snug as he knotted it, his breath puffing out in short bursts from the effort.

Her shoulder sling he adjusted—tearing a fresh strip from a

blanket, gray and moth-eaten, knotting it tighter with a faint creak of cloth—easing the joint's weight, though pain still flared with each shift, a dull roar radiating down her arm.

Jaber fetched water—tin cup, tepid, tasting faintly of rust and metal—tilting it to her lips with a gentleness that clashed with his scarred, hard-edged look, her sips slow and deliberate, washing the arak's burn from her throat, a faint relief unclenching her jaw. She exhaled— shaky, ragged—her good hand clutching the mug's edge, the warmth seeping into her palm as she fought the urge to collapse fully, her body begging for rest but her mind clawing for answers.

"Better?" Omar asked, voice gruff but threaded with a softening edge, sitting back on his heels, wiping iodine-stained hands on his kaftan, the brown smears blending with older stains.

She nodded—slight, pain pinching her features, a twitch at the corner of her mouth—but her gaze sharpened, adrenaline fading to a cold, focused steel, the fog lifting enough to let her think.

"Enough to think," she rasped, voice steadier despite the crack, leaning forward—ribs protesting with a grinding ache, a groan stifled in her throat—as the cot's springs squeaked beneath her shifting weight. "Aspire—what's 'live'? They said crate, centipede—Jaber heard it. Tell me—everything."

Omar's jaw clenched, a shadow darkening his face, his thick hands clasping tight—knuckles whitening, veins bulging under weathered skin—as he traded a glance with Jaber, who dragged deep on his cigarette, ash flaking onto the crate like gray snow, smoke spiraling upward in lazy coils. Even Omar—battered by a life of back alleys and betrayals—seemed to flinch at the memory clawing from his throat.

"Twelve hours since you ran," Omar began, voice low and deliberate, each word measured as if prying it loose from a locked chest, “from that press circus—Sheikh Tariq dodging Cartwright’s barbs, Moreau sweating through his suit, Borodin roaring threats. IOC wouldn’t bend—games rolled on despite the press clawing, parents weeping on live feeds, no postponement called.

Then it hit—Aspire Arena, women’s gymnastics slated for morning, but it blew apart hours ago, right after you bolted. Crate dropped—steel, padlocked, unmarked truck—middle of the night, guards clocked it, spooked, called it in, but too late. Broadcast hijacked—Olympic feed, global—NBC, BBC, Al Jazeera, CBC, Globo, all of ’em, live to millions. Floodlights snapped on—crate split open like a gutted beast. Twelve athletes, Nova—your Israelis: Lior Abramson, Yael Ben-Ami, Tamar Cohen, Noa Levi, Maya Ben-Ari, Ronit Weissman—and Lebanon’s full squad: Omar Haddad, Yasmine Haddad, Nadine Al-Rassi, Nadine Mansour, Yasmine Khalil, Cyrine Ghazal. Stitched—mouth to ass, a writhing chain—alive but rotting, midazolam dripping through IVs, keeping ’em limp, breathing, barely.”

His voice dropped to a gravelly whisper, each detail a hammer strike against the shack’s tin walls, his eyes distant as memory clawed up from the depths. “Lior’s head—mic taped to his throat, rasping guk-guk-guk, wet and choking—eyes rolled back, blue gone yellow, shit streaking his tongue from Omar stitched behind, his broad chest sagging gray and slick.

Yael’s neck oozed—blood and filth dripping down her throat, thread tearing her lips—legs twitching like a pinned bug under the floodlights’ glare.

Tamar’s knees cracked—twisted back, popping loud as bone strained—skin chafed raw where Noa’s spine bulged, green with sepsis, her moans a gurgle through the muck, vertebrae knobbed beneath thinning flesh. Yasmine Haddad’s chest shuddered—sweat and pus gleaming under the lights—stitches fraying as Nadine Al-Rassi’s head jerked, her flesh blackening, necrosis chewing her thighs into a glistening ruin. Nadine Mansour's legs swelled—purple, grotesque—screaming muffled by Yasmine Khalil's rear, thread snapping, blood welling in dark streaks down her chin.

Cyrine's tail—black ruin, pus oozing in thick yellow streams—flies swarming bone peeking through peeling flaps, their buzz a high-pitched drone. Maya's face—purple, bloated—lips cracked and oozing, tongue lolling shit-streaked from Cyrine, drool pooling brown beneath her. Ronit's end—rotting meat, sinew glistening pink and gray—moans threading Lior's rasps, a duet of despair blasted live, the mic's cruel clarity amplifying every wet, guttural note."

Nova's breath snagged—her body recoiling hard. The truth slammed into her like a hammer to bone, her body jerking as if she'd been stitched into the grotesque chain herself. Slamming back against the crate with a heavy thud, a raw groan ripping free as her ribs flared, a white-hot lance of pain shooting through her chest. Her hands clawed the rug—nails tearing into the wool, threads snapping loose, a faint puff of dust rising as her fingers dug deep, desperate to anchor herself against the flood of horror.

"No…" she whispered, voice fracturing into shards, head shaking slow—denial twisting into a visceral, gut-wrenching dread, then surging into rage, a scream building in her throat but choking into a sob, her good fist pounding the floor—thud-thud-thud—pain ignored, knuckles whitening as the wood bruised her skin. "Stitched—alive? Broadcast—global?

Those sick fucks…"

Her eyes burned—tears streaking hot down her cheeks, carving tracks through the blood crust caked on her face—her chest heaving, each breath a jagged, ragged fight against the images searing her mind: Lior's wet guk-guk drilling through the mic, Maya's purpled, oozing lips peeling back, Ronit's fly-swarmed rot shimmering in the floodlights' glare.

She retched—dry, convulsive, her stomach clenching hard—The taste of bile flooded her mouth, bitter and metallic, dragging the centipede's screams back up from her gut. As she doubled over, good hand gripping her hair, pulling hard until strands snapped loose, fluttering down to stick in the rug's weave.

Her mind spun—fragments of the press conference clashing with Omar's words— Cartwright's crisp drawl demanding answers, Laurent's venomous "butchering them," Palmer's gruff "where's Nova?"—all drowned now by the centipede's grotesque tableau, a nightmare stitched from flesh and vengeance. She'd chased leads—Rahman's texts, Jaber's scar-faced whispers—only to crash into this, her tablet's SD card, its screams of rape and blood, now a taunting prize in The Watcher's hands.

Her sobs choked off—rage hardening her spine, eyes narrowing to slits, a glint of steel piercing through the haze as she forced herself upright, ribs screaming, breath steadying into a low, furious growl.

Jaber exhaled smoke—slow, deliberate, the cigarette's ember glowing red in the dimness— his voice cutting through her spiraling descent, calm but edged with ice, a blade unsheathed. His smoke drifted like a funeral shroud between them as he muttered, "You wanted the truth. Here it rots."

"Centipede—their art, their brag. 'Obsidian Hand'—Watcher said 'justice,' not cash. Five hundred billion's the lure, but it's vengeance fueling 'em—old hate, deep cuts, festering scars. Broadcast was the knife—world gagging, IOC frozen, X exploding—clips looping, millions retching, hashtags bleeding out: #ObsidianHand, #DohaHorror."

Omar nodded, leaning closer—his kaftan rustling, the lamp casting his shadow long and jagged across the tin wall—voice a growl rumbling deep in his chest.

"Aspire Arena, once a shrine to human excellence, was now smothered under quarantine tents and the stench of death—Qatar Civil Defence in yellow hazmat suits, boots thudding, medics hauling stretchers through chalk dust and vomit, IOC scrambling like rats in a flood. Press is feral—Cartwright's BBC feed spitting fury, Laurent tearing into Moreau on L'Équipe, al- Hakim's Al Jazeera crews sniffing every corner—but no one's got faces, no names. They're ghosts—exiles, Syrian, Iraqi maybe—war-scarred, Olympic burnouts with grudges carved in bone. That Najdi script—pre-Islamic, tribal venom—marks 'em, pure spite, a flag waved in blood."

Nova's sobs stilled—rage hardening into a cold, unyielding resolve, her eyes narrowing further, a predator's glint piercing her pain-fogged haze. Memories of Alim's gurgled last breath and Ronit's broken sobs flickered through her mind, forging her grief into a weapon sharper than any blade.

"Ghosts with a crate—planned, surgical, a goddamn theater of cruelty. They've got lairs, muscle—Watcher's yellow eyes glinting behind that mask, Enforcer's tobacco reek choking the air, Commander's shadow barking 'abort' through static. Military moves—trained, ruthless, not some ragtag fanatics.

"We unmask 'em—flush 'em out, no IOC, no Interpol—us, quiet, under their skin, cutting deep." She shifted—wincing as her ribs ground together, a vise tightening, but sat straighter, voice firm despite the tremor threading through it. "They've got my tablet—video, proof—rape, screams, maybe their faces caught in a blur. We get it back, we break 'em wide open. Centipede's their taunt; we turn it—their fucking grave."

Jaber flicked his switchblade open—steel glinting under the lamp's amber glow. He spun it once, then leaned forward, a grim smirk tugging his lips.

"No authorities—smart, clean, the only way this works. IOC's a sieve—leaking to press, tripping over their own vague bullshit—Interpol's worse, red tape strangling anything fast, loud boots scaring off ghosts. We're shadows—me, Omar, you—slipping where they can't see.

"Old Port's their turf—I've got ears there, starting with Faisal, a dock rat, mid-30s, pockmarked face like a cratered moon, runs crab traps off Pier 7. Owes me—caught him fencing looted Iraqi gold last year, sweaty hands trembling as I held a blade to his gut, let him slide for silence. I'll hit him tonight—9 p.m., dark's cover, fog rolling thick off the Gulf— fifty riyals, grubby and folded, cash first to loosen his tongue.

"He'll know sedan sightings—black, late model, tinted windows cutting through the mist— crew movements, skiffs slipping out past curfew with no lights. If he balks, blade tip at his throat—quiet in the fog, just a nudge, his Adam's apple bobbing as he spills."

He paused, blade stilling in his grip, eyes narrowing as he mapped it out in his mind, voice dropping to a low, guttural growl, memory sharpening his words.

"Next—Hassan al-Kindi, cx-Syrian militia, 40s, bald as a stone, gold tooth glinting when he snarls, deals scrap metal in a Pier 3 warehouse—rusted hulks piled high, oil drums leaking into the dirt. Smelled him near that sedan two weeks back—cigarette stink, harsh and unfiltered, same as Enforcer's mask when he pinned you. He's twitchy—war deserter, paranoid, eyes darting like a cornered dog—sells to smugglers, knows exiles who skulk in the shadows.

"I'll corner him—midnight, his yard's edge, behind oil drums stacked like a barricade— hundred riyals, some stolen Iraqi dinars mixed in, nostalgia bait to crack him open, remind him of Damascus nights before the bombs. If he's dry, I'll break a rib—fist, not blade—keep it silent, his wheeze my leverage, breath rattling as he gives me lair hints—exile traffic, crate movers—or points me where they're hiding."

Jaber's smirk deepened—a predator's grin—as he flicked the blade shut with a sharp snap, tucking it into his boot, the leather creaking faintly. He pulled a rusted tin from his pocket— fishhooks and tangled line clinking as he dumped it onto the crate, the sound a faint, metallic jangle.

"Lair's my third play—Pier 5, abandoned warehouse, big and rusted, roof sagging but solid, corrugated tin dented by years of storms. Trucks fit through its wide bay doors, skiffs dock quiet at its crumbling pier—Watcher's 'roof perch' vibe from the docks, where she dropped through that panel to nab you. I'll scout it post-midnight—binoculars stolen from a fisherman's haul last month, scratched lenses but sharp enough, lamp for signals—two flashes if it's hot, you roll in fast.

"Tools are simple—blade's mine, always sharp, Makarov's backup, five rounds in the clip, scratched but live—Faisal gets twitchy, it's his gut, a quick pop muffled by the fog.

Crowbar's stashed at Hassan's yard—buried under scrap, blunt force if he swings, metal cold in my grip. Rope—fifty feet, crab trap haul, salt-stiff but strong—ties 'em if we catch 'em, Gulf's deep for corpses, no trace left behind."

He leaned back, exhaling another plume of smoke, eyes glinting with a cold, calculated edge.

"Contingencies—Faisal balks, I tail him—quay's maze, fog's my cloak—he'll stumble to someone, panic leading me straight. Hassan fights, I knock him cold—fist to the temple, drag him to a skiff, tie him with that rope, wake him wet—Gulf's chill cracks stubborn faster than fists, his teeth chattering as he spills. Lair scout—binocs sweep the shadows, lamp signals if it's live—two flashes, you flank, no hesitation. If guards are thick—hoods, guns—I hide, fog's my shield, wait 'til they thin, then creep closer."

Omar leaned in—his kaftan brushing the crate's edge, the lamp's glow catching the gray streaks in his beard—voice a low rumble as he cracked his knuckles, the sharp pop-pop echoing in the shack like distant gunfire. Doubt gnawed at Omar—trust was a luxury none of them could afford—but desperation carved its own risks.

"Souq's my web—I'll tap its veins, chase Aspire's echo through the chatter. First—Khalid ibn Saqr, spice trader, late 50s, hunchbacked from years bent over sacks, stall near the falcon souq, canvas tarp flapping in the breeze. Hears everything—traders gossip over saffron, smugglers barter under his awning when the moon's low.

"Saw a Katara Hospitality truck—white, logo peeling, rust creeping along its fenders—idling near his stall a day back, 3 a.m., driver hooded, unloading sacks that didn't smell like food, more like oil or metal. I'll hit him—dusk, 6 p.m., when the souq hums with early buyers— twenty dirhams, a sack of cardamom as cover, chat over tea, his samovar steaming with bitter mint. He's greedy—slips for coin, palms itching—might know truck routes, drop points, where that crate staged before Aspire. If he lies, I'll squeeze his supplier—old Yemeni, turmeric man, 60s, leathery skin, knows truckers who haul off-books—ten dirhams, a nudge over his grindstone, he'll sing."

He cracked his neck—another sharp pop, the sound reverberating off the tin walls—eyes glinting with a predator's focus as he layered his plan, hands gesturing slow and deliberate, thick fingers tracing invisible threads in the air.

"Second—Bilal al-Najjar, fixer, 30s, skinny as a reed, missing two fingers from a Homs blast years back—left hand a stump, pink scars puckering the skin—runs a tea stall at the souq's north end, chipped cups clattering on a warped plank counter. Exiles trust him—Syrian, quiet, keeps his head down—heard 'Obsidian' whispers, bragged it drunk a week back over cheap arak, his stump twitching as he slurred. I'll go—8 p.m., crowd's thick with hagglers— fifty dirhams, arak bottle tossed in to loosen his tongue, the anise stink wafting as I pour.

"Soft first—lean close, laugh at his bad jokes, pour him a shot—his stump twitches when he's nervous, a telltale tic. If he clams, I'll grip his wrist—twist 'til he squeaks—drag him to the alley behind his stall, no eyes, just shadows and the stink of spilled tea. He'll name names—exiles, contacts—or point me to who does. If he bolts, I've got boys—souq kids, fast, ten years old, barefoot and sharp—track him for five riyals each, report back where he scurries."

Omar slid a drawer open—wood scraping against rusted runners—revealing a dented Nokia 3310, pre-paid, its screen scratched and fogged, and a slim dagger—curved, hilt worn smooth by years of grip, steel glinting faintly in the lamp's light. He tossed the phone to Nova—its weight light but solid in her trembling hand—keeping the dagger close, resting it on his thigh as he continued, voice steady and low.

"Third—Rahman, your lifeline. He's near Aspire—saw the crate live, guards down—texted 'til they smashed your burner hours ago, his last ping a frantic 'Aspire breached—crate's live.' I'll ping him—new burner, dusk, 6:30 p.m.—my code: 'O, spice safe, crate pulse?'— he'll know it's us, sharp as he is, ex-Al Jazeera lensman with a nose for blood. Meet him— 10 p.m., Al Bidda Park—dark, trees thick, no cams—blindfolded, bring him here, his boots scuffing the dirt as I guide him.

"He's got shots—truck, lair fringe, blurry or not—I'll pull him in safe, trust's thin but he's ours. Burner's fifty dirhams, souq stall—tea lures him, dagger's last if he runs—quiet cut, alley's dark, blade slipping between ribs if he turns."

Nova caught the Nokia—fingers fumbling, pain spiking up her arm as her shoulder flared— keying Rahman's code—+974-555-9821—text draft trembling on the tiny screen: "N alive, Old Port hit, truck end, lair edge? 47h, no grid, you?" She slid it to Omar, voice a rasp as she sipped tea—scalding, arak-laced—from a chipped mug he'd handed her, warmth seeping into her palm, the bitter mint and anise cutting through her fog.

"Watcher's my mark—yellow eyes glinting like a cat's behind that mask, rasps like sandpaper—tablet's her prize, pouch left side, SD card slotted tight. Lair's close—Old Port's likely, Aspire's too hot now, locked tight with hazmat and sirens. I'll rest 'til 9 p.m.—two hours, cot, tea, painkiller if you've got it stashed—then map it." She nodded to Omar's shelves—charts peeking from books, edges curling, stained with salt and time—good hand tracing air, plotting invisible lines as her mind churned.

"Gulf coast, Old Port grid—warehouses, piers, skiff lanes—I'll mark possibles: Warehouse 12, Pier 8, Skiff Dock C—big enough for a crate, truck access with ruts in the mud, roof perch like Jaber saw, tin buckling under boots. Cross-check Faisal, Hassan—lair signs: sedan tracks crunching gravel, exile chatter over cheap cigarettes, Semtex stink lingering like kerosene."

She shifted—ribs groaning, a hiss escaping through clenched teeth—tea mug steadying her tremble, pain dulling to a hum as she leaned forward, voice sharpening like a blade unsheathed. Every movement carved new wounds into her resolve, a brutal reminder that survival here demanded more than just endurance—it demanded fury, precision, and sacrifice.

"Rahman's my second—he might've tailed the truck's retreat, snapped plates, faces, blur or not, his camera always clicking. Omar, send that text—6:50 p.m., dusk—he's quick, photojournalist instincts honed sharp. Code him short—'N alive, 47h'—he'll bite, trust me. Pull him in—shots to sketch, memory's sharp even concussed—I'll draw Watcher's blur, sedan link, yellow eyes etched in my skull. If lair's hot—guards, guns—I'll signal—three knocks, shack door—bait 'em, wounded, loud—limp in, draw 'em out, you flank fast.

Tools—charts, pen—sketch pad if you've got it buried in that mess—brain's my blade, cuts deeper than steel. If it's a bust, pivot—Aspire's crate, guards talk—bribe 'em, twenty riyals slipped quiet—Semtex source, truck path, they'll crack for cash."

Jaber stood—stretching, joints popping like dry twigs—grabbing a burlap sack from a corner—damp, salt-crusted, reeking faintly of fish—stuffing binocs, lamp, rope inside, the faint clatter of metal and glass muffled by the fabric as he slung it over his shoulder. Each tool he packed was more than gear—it was a debt, a silent vow to those already lost to the sand and silence.

"Timeline—9 p.m., I'm quay-bound—Faisal first, then Hassan—back by 2 a.m., lair ping or bust. Sleep 'til then—cot's yours, Nova—ribs need it, limp's no good if we're moving fast. Contingencies—Faisal balks, I tail—fog's my cloak, quay's twists hiding my steps—he'll lead somewhere, panic's a map. Hassan fights, I knock him cold—fist to the jaw, drag him to a skiff, tie him with that rope, wake him wet—Gulf's chill'll loosen his tongue, teeth chattering truths. Lair scout—binocs sweep the shadows, lamp signals if it's live—two flashes, you roll in, no delay."

Omar rose—kettle clanking as he refilled it from a dented jug—tea leaves scattering across the crate, arak bottle glugging as he laced the brew, eyes flicking to the door where the souq's hum filtered through tin, a distant pulse of voices and clattering carts.

"6 p.m., I hit Khalid—8 p.m., Bilal—10 p.m., Rahman if he bites—back by midnight, kids on watch, their bare feet silent in the alleys. Khalid lies—Yemeni supplier, ten dirhams slipped over his turmeric sacks—Bilal runs—kids track, five riyals each, eyes like hawks. Rahman's silent—ping again, 8 p.m.—park scout, no meet—kids sniff his trail through Doha's dust.

Tea's yours—rest, Nova—two hours, then charts—brain's no use fogged, pain'll dull with this brew."

Nova eased back—cot creaking, blanket rough against her neck—tea mug cradled in her good hand, warmth seeping into her palm, arak's bite dulling her ache as she sipped, the scalding liquid grounding her resolve.

"9 p.m.—charts, Rahman's ping—plot 'til you're back—lair list, Watcher's shadow narrowing to a point. Forty-seven hours—they boasted it, we're faster—Obsidian Hand bleeds, not us."

Her eyes drifted shut—pain a low hum beneath her skin, the centipede's rasp (Lior's wet guk-guk, Ronit's festering rot) a dark fuel igniting her core—resolve steeling into an unbreakable vow as the shack settled around her: lamp flickering, Jaber's smoke curling thick, Omar's tea hissing on the hotplate, three shadows weaving a net in Doha's underbelly, threads tightening against a faceless horror.

Veil 16

The Broken Reverberation

The trauma bays of Al Wakra Hospital pulsed with urgency at 8:25 a.m., sunlight streaming through windows onto tiles streaked with antiseptic and faint traces of blood. The air carried a sharp mix of iodine and sterile solution, a clinical shield against the crisis unfolding. Steel gurneys rattled as medics wheeled in the twelve athletes, freed from the grotesque human centipede unveiled at the Aspire Arena hours earlier.

Each athlete was a fragile case, their skin pale and slick with sweat, breaths shallow under ventilators' hiss and monitors' erratic beeps. Once symbols of Olympic glory, they now lay as evidence of a twisted design, their survival a desperate fight.

Surgeons in green scrubs moved swiftly, their gloved hands working with precision—cutting, stitching, stabilizing—amid shouted orders and the hum of medical equipment.

Lior Abramson lay in Bay 2, chest heaving under halogen lights, a collapsed lung supported by a chest tube. The suction machine whirred, pulling up clear fluid with faint pink traces, collecting in the canister with a steady glug-glug. His skin, once bronzed, was now ashen, sweat beading where adhesive tape had been removed, leaving raw patches. His throat rasped faintly—guk… guk—vocal cords strained from the ordeal.

Dr. Omar Khalifa, chief of surgery, leaned over, goggles fogging slightly, voice sharp: "More suction!" A nurse adjusted the tube, its hum intensifying as it cleared fluid, a small amount spilling onto the table. Khalifa's scalpel moved carefully, parting muscle with a soft sound, exposing a lung darkened but stabilizing. He clamped an artery—steel jaws clicking—stopping a minor bleed, a thin trickle of blood staining his sleeve.

"Epi—1 mg!" Khalifa ordered. A nurse injected epinephrine into Lior's jugular, the needle piercing with a soft pop, his chest jerking slightly as the drug took effect. His pulse monitor beeped—44 bpm, erratic—then climbed to 52 bpm by 8:40. Sepsis loomed, but Lior held on, his prognosis fragile but hopeful.

Omar Haddad's stretcher steadied in Bay 3, shoulders slumped, skin clammy. His lips, freed from stitches, were swollen, a thin line of blood-tinged saliva tracing his chin. His breaths wheezed softly. Dr. Amina al-Jamer, a Lebanese surgeon, worked over him, her hijab tucked under her scrub cap, scalpel cutting into his abdomen with a faint sound, parting tissue carefully.

She clamped a vein—click-click—halting a small bleed, the metallic scent faint. The suction tube hummed, clearing minimal fluid, the canister steady. Omar's liver appeared swollen, a nurse mopping excess fluid with gauze, the fabric absorbing quickly. Amina hooked a ventilator, tubes hissing, ensuring steady breaths. By 8:45, Omar's pulse held at 48 bpm, kidneys weak, urine slightly cloudy in the catheter bag, but he clung to life.

Yael Ben-Ami lay in Bay 5, limbs still, chest rising faintly, a punctured lung stabilized by a chest tube hissing softly. Her lips, once stitched, were swollen, a thin drool pooling at her neck. Dr. Sara al-Najjar cut into her chest, scalpel moving precisely, clearing an abscess with minimal fluid release, quickly suctioned. She inserted a chest tube—steel piercing with a soft sound—fluid draining steadily, the canister clear.

"Intubate!" Sara called, threading a laryngoscope down Yael's throat, metal guiding carefully past teeth. The suction cleared light mucus, maintaining her airway. Yael's pulse dipped to 40 bpm, then rose to 48 bpm with epinephrine, her body stabilizing by 8:50, though infection lingered, a persistent threat.

Tamar Cohen lay in Bay 4, legs angled awkwardly, tourniquets tight around swollen limbs, fluid minimal but present. Dr. Khalifa cut into her abdomen, scalpel parting tissue smoothly, controlling a small bleed with a clamp—click. The suction tube cleared light fluid, gauze absorbing excess. Her pulse flatlined at 8:52—beep-beep-flat—a tech applying defibrillator pads—zap-zap—her body jerking, but no rhythm returned. "Time of death, 8:52," Khalifa rasped, stepping back, gloves clean but heavy with loss. Tamar's body lay still, eyes half-open, a silent marker of the horror.

Noa Levi's spine arched slightly in Bay 5, a cervical collar creaking, vertebrae stable but strained. Dr. Khalid bin Hamad cut into her back, scalpel precise, exposing vertebrae for pinning—steel rods sinking with a faint crunch, blood minimal, gauze absorbing quickly. Her catheter drained cloudy urine, the bag steady, while a chest tube cleared light fluid from her lungs, the canister humming. Her pulse wavered—45 bpm—stabilizing at 46 bpm with epinephrine by 9:00, infection a looming threat.

Yasmine Haddad's torso glistened in Bay 3, breaths rattling, lips swollen with faint blood traces. Dr. Amina cut into her abdomen, scalpel steady, clamping a small bleed—click-click. The suction cleared minimal fluid, the canister stable. Her pulse held at 50 bpm, kidneys weak, catheter bag slightly cloudy, but she endured, organs fragile by 9:45.

Nadine Al-Rassi lay in Bay 3, skin pale, stitches removed, minimal fluid weeping. Dr. Hassan al-Abdulla used a bone saw to remove necrotic tissue from her thigh, its hum low, cutting cleanly, minimal blood controlled with gauze. Her pulse dipped to 42 bpm, flatlining at 9:10—beep-beep-flat—defibrillation failing, sepsis claiming her. The bay grew quiet, her loss heavy.

Nadine Mansour's knees were swollen in Bay 4, lips freed from stitches, saliva faintly bloody. Dr. Sara cut into her chest, scalpel precise, clearing a small abscess, suction managing light fluid. Her pulse faded—40 bpm, then 30, flat at 9:15—sepsis overwhelming, her body still, the air heavy with defeat.

Yasmine Khalil's chest rose faintly in Bay 3, lips swollen, minimal blood. Dr. Amina stabilized her lungs with a chest tube, suction clearing light fluid. Her pulse stopped at 9:20—beep-beep-flat—defibrillation failing, sepsis taking her quietly, her form motionless under the lights.

Cyrine Ghazal's legs twitched in Bay 2, minimal fluid from stitches. Dr. Hassan amputated necrotic tissue, saw humming, cutting cleanly, gauze controlling blood. Her pulse flatlined at 9:25—beep-beep-flat—organ failure ending her fight, the bay silent but for ventilators.

Maya Ben-Ari's face was pale in Bay 1, lungs supported by a chest tube, suction clearing light fluid. Dr. Khalifa stitched her diaphragm—needle piercing softly, thread taut—her pulse crashing to 38 bpm, then flat at 9:30, infection too deep, her eyes sunken, monitor silent.

Ronit Weissman's stump oozed slightly in Bay 3, gauze absorbing fluid. Dr. Hassan packed the wound, but her pulse stopped at 9:35, sepsis too advanced, her moans silenced, body still.

By 9:40, six survivors—Lior, Omar, Yael, Noa, Yasmine Haddad, Nadine Al-Rassi—teetered on ventilators, tubes and scars marking their fight, pulses weak but steady. The dead—six in total—were wheeled to the morgue, sheets clean, air heavy. Nurses swabbed fluids, the floor sterile, chaos ebbing into a fragile stalemate.

Above the blood-soaked bays, politics moved faster than grief.

Outside, the world was erupting, the Aspire Arena's conference room a crucible of tension by 10:45 a.m.

Fluorescent lights flickered overhead, casting harsh shadows across the oak table where coffee cups trembled, their contents cold and forgotten, the air thick with cigarette smoke, and the faint tang of vomit that lingered from the morning's horror. Sweat-stained cuffs, bloodshot eyes, trembling hands—power didn't make them immune.

Sheikh Tariq bin Fahd Al-Mazrouei stood at the head, his pristine white robes now stained with tea and sweat, the brown streaks stark against the fabric as he slammed a fist onto the table, pens rattling against the wood like scattered bones.

"This is an attack on the Olympics—on humanity itself!" he roared, his hawkish nose casting a sharp shadow across his face, eyes blazing with fury. "We demand Interpol—now! The world cannot stand idle while this abomination festers! Suspend the qualifiers—secure the athletes—we're a target!"

Jacques Moreau, silver hair disheveled, nodded grimly from his seat, his Montblanc pen tapping a frantic rhythm against the table, the sound a nervous tic that grated against the room's silence. "The Games are sacred," he said, his French accent thick with strain, "this requires global action—I agree, suspend everything until we've got control. I've alerted Paris—the IOC's reputation hangs by a thread, and we can't risk another strike."

Beside him, Viktor Borodin's ruddy face flushed darker, his barrel chest heaving as he growled, "Whoever did this pays in blood—I've got the Kremlin on the line, and they're ready to crush skulls. Suspend the Games, fine—but we need military here, boots on the ground, not just cops." His gold pinky ring glinted as he clenched a fist, the metal catching the light in a brief, menacing flash.

At 9:50, a speaker crackled to life, Interpol's Lyon HQ patching in with a crisp, authoritative voice—Director Sabine Leclerc, 48, wiry and sharp, her tone cutting through the static like a blade.

"We're deploying a task force," she said, her words clipped and precise. "Agent Lukas Keller, 39, ex-Swiss Guard, is leading—en route to Doha, ETA 14:00. This is a war crime— biological, psychological, unprecedented. We need jurisdiction from Israel, Lebanon, the U.S., and any nation with a stake. The Semtex in that crate didn't blow, but the intent was clear—terror on a global stage. Suspension's your call, Sheikh, but I'd back it—secure the site first."

Sheikh Tariq's jaw tightened, his voice a low rasp as he replied, "Six alive, six dead—half the centipede's Israeli, half Lebanese. The broadcast reached billions. We'll grant access,

but you move fast—qualifiers are halted, effective now. Military's an option—Qatar's army is mobilizing, but we need international teeth."

In Jerusalem, by 10:00 a.m., Prime Minister Eitan Mazar paced his office, the windows overlooking the Knesset framing a city humming with unease. At 62, he was lean and wiry, his gray hair cropped tight, a photo of his late wife on the desk a quiet anchor amid the storm.

His phone buzzed incessantly—Sheikh Tariq's voice crackling through: "Eitan, six of your athletes—three dead, three critical. Qualifiers are suspended; we're locking down. We need your intel, your cooperation—military if you've got it." Mazar's jaw clenched, his eyes flinty as he gripped the receiver, the plastic creaking under his fingers.

"This is a Zionist nightmare—stitched to Lebanese? It's a message, a grotesque provocation. Mossad's on it—I want Keller briefed the second he lands. Military's on the table—IDF can deploy to Doha if NATO green-lights. Suspension's right—protect what's left."

He hung up and dialed Mossad chief Avi Cohen, 55, whose gravelly voice cut through the line like a saw. "Eitan, we've got chatter—Obsidian Hand, Barga Al Kharaz cell. The ransom's at five hundred billion—insane, but they're serious. This isn't just terror; it's a power play."

Mazar growled, pacing faster, his polished shoes clicking against the hardwood. "Find the bastards, Avi—Barga's the key. Military's itching—get me options for a strike if it's there. Five hundred billion? They're daring us to blink—we won't." Cohen's voice hardened, "We're tapping Barga—SIGINT's picking up whispers from the desert. Ransom's a distraction—next strike's the real blow."

In Beirut, at 10:05 a.m., Prime Minister Ziad el-Khoury stood on his balcony, the Mediterranean glinting beyond the hazy skyline, a faint breeze doing little to ease the heat pressing against his broad shoulders. At 58, his barrel chest strained his suit jacket, his beard streaked gray, his fists tightening until his knuckles whitened as an aide burst in, phone thrust forward.

"Sheikh Tariq, sir—five Lebanese athletes, three dead. Qualifiers suspended, military's in play." Ziad snatched the phone, his voice a low rumble: "Tariq, what the hell is this? A centipede with Israelis? This is Hezbollah's stench—or worse. Get me Interpol—I want answers, not platitudes. Lebanon's army can reinforce—say the word."

He hung up and called General Hassan Nasrallah, 60, commander of the Lebanese Armed Forces, whose voice boomed through the line like artillery.

"Ziad, this reeks of external hands—Syria, maybe Barga Al Kharaz, stirring the pot. We're locking down borders, ports, everything. Suspension's smart—keeps our kids alive. Military's ready—50th

Brigade can roll to Doha if NATO backs it. I want those survivors breathing—they're our witnesses."

Ziad nodded, his eyes narrowing as he stared at the sea, the horizon blurring with his thoughts. "Coordinate with Keller when he lands—no leaks, Hassan. That ransom—five hundred billion? Who's got that cash, and what's the endgame? Dig into Barga—Hezbollah's denying, but I don't trust it." Nasrallah grunted, "If it's Barga, they're deep— desert's a black hole. I'll shake the trees."

In Washington, D.C., the White House Situation Room buzzed at 10:15 a.m., its screens flickering with the OBS footage that had hijacked the world's airwaves—Maya's rasps looping in a haunting refrain, a sound that clawed at President Logan Calder's ears. At 54, he was broad-shouldered, his hair thinning under the weight of office, his fingers tapping a pen against the table in a steady, restless beat.

Victoria Langford, Secretary of State, 49, sat across from him, her sharp suit pristine despite the hour, her blonde bob framing a face set with determination.

"Mr. President," she said, her voice steady, cutting through the room's hum, "Alyssa Park's team was yards away—U.S. honor's tangled in this. Six Israeli athletes, five Lebanese—half dead, half clinging. Nova Mendelsohn's missing, presumed dead by the IOC. She's a name you should know—independent Olympic reporter, born and raised in New Jersey, lives in Brooklyn now. Covers the Games for her own website—sharp, connected, last seen digging into doping scandals. Her disappearance raises questions—victim or something else?"

Calder's eyes narrowed, the pen stilling in his hand as he leaned forward, his voice a low growl. "This is a global shitstorm—terrorism on steroids. Five hundred billion in 39 hours? That's not a demand, it's a declaration of war. Qualifiers suspended—good.

Military's next— get me Mazar and el-Khoury. Special Forces boots in Doha, now—what's NATO saying?"

Langford nodded, dialing DNI chief Mark Reyes, 52, whose gruff voice crackled through: "Logan, SIGINT's got Obsidian Hand claiming it—Barga Al Kharaz chatter. Five hundred billion's the ask, leverage or lunacy. Military's hot—Pentagon's pushing for a task force, NATO's on the fence but leaning in."

Calder slammed the pen down, the sound a sharp crack. "Then we push harder—Delta Force to Doha if NATO green-lights. No payment—not a dime—until we've got them by the throat."

Back in Doha, by 10:30 a.m., Agent Lukas Keller's boots hit the tarmac at Hamad International Airport, the heat shimmering off the asphalt in waves that distorted the horizon. Keller wasn't just backup—he was the blade they would point into the heart of the storm. At 39, he was 6'2" of lean muscle, blond hair cropped close, his ice-blue eyes scanning the scene through a scar that traced his jaw from a Kabul blast—a memento of a life spent in shadows.

His team followed—Analyst Priya Sharma, 34, Indian, her dark braid swinging as she clutched a tablet, tech-savvy and sharp; Medic Jonas Weber, 41, German, broad- shouldered, his trauma kit clanking against his hip, his face grim from years in war zones.

Sheikh Tariq met them at the arena's loading dock, his voice hoarse as he gestured to the hazmat-sealed crate, throbbing in the sun, a sealed confession too monstrous to bury for long.

"Qualifiers are done—suspended indefinitely. Crate's locked down—Semtex inside, unignited. Six alive, six dead—half Israeli, half Lebanese. Military's mobilizing—Qatar's got armor rolling in. World's watching, Keller—millions saw it live."

Keller's jaw tightened, his gaze flicking to the crate, its dented steel glinting under the sun, the faint sour whiff seeping through the vents a grim reminder of its contents.

“This is surgical—planned to the second,” he said, his voice low, clipped with a faint Swiss accent. “Suspension buys time—smart. I need hospital access, survivor statements, and that broadcast source—now. Military’s a hammer—use it if it’s Barga Al Kharaz.”

Priya tapped her tablet, fingers flying across the screen, her voice tight. “OBS hack traced— Barga IP, encrypted to hell. I’m cracking it—hours, not minutes. X’s screaming— #DohaHorror, #PayOrDie—ransom’s everywhere.”

Jonas grimaced, adjusting his kit, his German accent thick as he muttered, “Sepsis, necrosis, midazolam—miracles they’re alive. Half won’t make it.”

By 11:00 a.m., Keller stood at the ICU’s glass wall in Al Wakra Hospital, the survivors laid out like broken dolls under the hiss of ventilators. Lior’s chest rose and fell—tubes snaking into his lungs, saline dripping, pulse 50 bpm. Omar groaned faintly, restraints creaking, urine bag dark and bloody, pulse 48 bpm.

Yael’s chest tube gurgled, eyes fluttering, pulse 48 bpm. Noa’s spine pins gleamed, breaths shallow, pulse 46 bpm. Yasmine’s lungs rattled, catheter trickling, pulse 52 bpm. Nadine’s stump oozed, gauze soaked, pulse 44 bpm. Nurses moved like ghosts, swapping fluids with trembling hands, the air sharp with iodine and decay.

“They’re evidence—living or dead,” Keller said, hands clasped behind his back. “Guard them—every breath’s a clue.” Priya leaned in, tablet glowing. “X’s exploding—Obsidian Hand’s gloating, clips spreading. Ransom’s the pulse—five hundred billion, 38 hours.”

Inside the arena’s media bay, evidence trickled slower than panic spread—every second, the storm outside grew teeth. The investigation roared to life as Keller's team fanned out. Priya set up in the arena's media room, her tablet linked to Interpol's servers, fingers dancing as she dug into the OBS hack.

"Barga's the hub," she muttered, voice tight with focus, "signal's bouncing—proxies in Damascus, Tehran, Moscow. Military-grade encryption—not a lone wolf." She pulled up a still—Maya's purpled face, mid-rasp—and cross-referenced X posts: #ObsidianHand, #DohaNightmare.

"They're pushing the ransom—half want payment, half want war." Jonas pored over the crate with hazmat, gloved hands trembling as he cataloged the Semtex—four gray slabs, wires snaking to a dormant detonator. "No blast yet—a threat," he said, voice muffled, the sour whiff seeping through. "Range is 70 miles—Barga fits. IVs had midazolam—surgical precision."

Keller's fingers hovered a fraction too long over the map – Barga was a noose, but it was slipping fast: "Lock down the arena—every manifest, every crew from 4:00 a.m. Forged as 'equipment surplus'—trace the truck." Captain Ahmed al-Thani, 35, wiry, nodded. "CCTV's got it—hydraulic bed, blacked-out plates, 4:03 a.m. Driver's a ghost—hooded, no prints. Crew's under scrutiny—someone's dirty." Keller's eyes glinted. "Bribes or threats—dig into bank records, phones. They're close."

By 11:30 a.m., the political threads tightened, a secure line buzzing with voices. Mazar's growl crackled to Calder: "Logan, three of my kids dead, three critical—IDF's ready to roll if NATO says go. Suspension's right—military's next. Five hundred billion? They're taunting us—we don't pay."

Calder rumbled back, "Eitan, Delta Force is prepped—NATO's wobbling, but I'll push. No cash—war first." El-Khoury cut in, voice thunderous: "Three daughters gone, two fighting—Lebanon's army can hit Doha or Barga. Ransom's a fantasy—UN won't touch it. Military's the play."

Langford, on a line to Leclerc, pressed: "Sabine, Barga's the nexus—tie it there. Military's heating up—NATO's debating strikes. Ransom's a test—what's the move?" Leclerc snapped back: "Keller's on it—evidence tight, survivors guarded. No payment—trace first, strike second."

In the White House, Calder leaned back, chair creaking, eyes on a map—Doha red, Barga a shadow. "Five hundred billion," he muttered, "they're betting we blink—UN, NATO, G20.

Treasury's screaming no—Dow's down 800. Military's our fist—NATO's got to move." Langford's lips thinned. "UK's in, France too—China's quiet. Suspension's holding—Games might be done for good."

In Jerusalem, Mazar stared at the Knesset, voice low to Cohen: "Five hundred billion's a taunt—they know we can't pay. Barga's the nest—IDF's primed. Tell Keller—strike ready." Cohen rumbled, "SIGINT's hot—Barga's buzzing. Ransom's bait—next hit's the fire."

In Beirut, el-Khoury paced, sea breeze rattling blinds, to Nasrallah: "Barga, not Hezbollah— 50th Brigade's on standby. Ransom's a ghost—track the money." Nasrallah grunted, "Desert's dark—survivors might talk. Military's go."

At noon, in the Obsidian Hand's lair beneath Barga Al Kharaz's dunes, The Commander stood over a console, his scar stretching across his face, boots squelching in blood and rot that stained the concrete floor. At 45, he was a hulking figure, his presence a coiled threat, His boots carved trails through the rot-slick floor, as if even the blood recoiled from him. His grin a jagged slash as he watched the monitors flicker with chaos—X posts, news feeds, the world unraveling.

“Five hundred billion—let them watch the sun rot the clock down to the bone,” The Commander muttered, eyes gleaming, his voice a low rumble, the burner buzzing on the table—negotiations humming from unseen contacts. “World’s choking—38 hours left. They’ll suspend, they’ll scramble—then we burn it down.”

The Scribe stopped pacing, his voice a nervous hiss. “What if they trace us? Keller’s no fool—Barga’s hot.” The Commander laughed, a guttural sound that echoed off the damp walls. “Let them come—crate’s clean, signal’s buried. Ransom’s the spark—next strike’s the blaze.”

The world teetered—six survivors clung to life, six lost, the Games halted, military gears grinding, and a ransom demand echoing like a war drum, its shadow stretching from Barga’s sands to the capitals of power, the clock ticking toward an abyss no one could yet fathom.

Their breaths rattled against the heavy silence, a heartbeat away from slipping into the sand along with the ones already swallowed.

Veil 17

The Hunt Begins

The air in the Main Press Center auditorium was a suffocating stew of tension, stale coffee, and the acrid tang of sweat-soaked fabric, all underscored by the faint, maddening buzz of a fly battering itself against a flickering fluorescent light.

It was 12:30 p.m.—four hours since the Obsidian Hand had unleashed its grotesque terror, stitching twelve athletes—six Israeli, six Lebanese—into a human centipede and beaming the nightmare live to millions.

Now, Sheikh Tariq bin Fahd Al-Mazrouei stood at the podium, his white thobe, once a symbol of unassailable authority, now hung from him like a battlefield banner torn by unseen arrows.

For a moment, even the fly stilled, the room holding its breath for what it feared to hear.

"Ladies and gentlemen of the press," he began, his words slicing through the room's restless hum like a blade through flesh, "at

11:45 a.m. today, the International Olympic Committee, in coordination with the governments of Qatar, Israel, Lebanon, and the international community, has made the unprecedented decision to suspend the Olympic Games indefinitely. This follows the barbaric act of terror that unfolded here at Aspire Arena in the early hours—an atrocity that claimed lives, shattered bodies, and seared itself into the world's conscience."

The room detonated—pens scratching furiously across notepads, cameras whirring like cicadas, a tidal wave of shouted questions crashing against the podium.

James Cartwright, the BBC's silver-haired veteran, rose first. Even his clipped civility, frayed at the edges, his pen poised like a weapon rather than a tool. "Sheikh Tariq, what's the status of the survivors? And is this suspension a prelude to cancellation?"

Tariq's jaw clenched, a shadow darkening his coal-black eyes as he raised a hand, palm out, silencing the clamor with the authority of a man who'd stared down worse storms.

"Of the twelve, six remain alive at Al Wakra Hospital, under heavy guard and intensive care. The Israeli athletes—Lior Abramson, Yael Ben-Ami, and Noa Levi—survive, though critically injured: collapsed lungs, sepsis, spinal damage. The Lebanese—Omar Haddad, Yasmine Haddad, and Nadine Al-Rassi—also cling to life, battling organ failure and necrosis. The deceased—Tamar Cohen, Maya Ben-Ari, Ronit Weissman of Israel, and Nadine Mansour, Yasmine Khalil, Cyrine Ghazal of Lebanon—were lost to septic shock and multi-organ failure between 8:52 and 9:35 a.m. Their bodies lie in the morgue, evidence in this ongoing nightmare."

He paused, his breath escaping in a sharp hiss through clenched teeth, the silence that followed heavy as lead, broken only by the fly's futile, buzzing dance against the windowpane. "This is not a cancellation—not yet. It is a suspension to secure the Games, the athletes, and this city. The IOC will not bow to terror, but we will not gamble with more lives."

Emilie Laurent of France's L'Équipe stood next, her sharp cheekbones catching the light, her voice dripping with venomous precision. "Sheikh, the ransom demand—five hundred billion in 38 hours—has the IOC considered payment? And what of Nova Mendelsohn, the missing reporter?"

Tariq's fist slammed the podium—thud—the impact reverberating through the room, a coffee cup tipping over, cold sludge oozing across the oak in a slow, dark crawl that mirrored the dread seeping into the reporters' faces.

A ripple of skepticism stirred among the press—promises sounded brittle when stitched bodies still haunted the screens.

"Payment is not under discussion—the IOC stands with Interpol and global leaders to crush this 'Obsidian Hand.' Nova Mendelsohn's whereabouts are unknown—last seen fleeing this arena 12 hours ago. She's presumed a victim, possibly dead, though no body has surfaced. We urge anyone with information to come forward."

Greg Palmer, the grizzled Australian reporter, leaned forward, his gravelly voice thick with skepticism, his sunburned hands braced on his knees. "Military's mobilizing—Qatar, Israel, Lebanon, the U.S. What's the IOC's stance on turning Doha into a war zone?"

"The IOC supports all measures to ensure safety," Tariq snapped, his eyes glinting like polished steel, cold and unyielding. "Qatar's Armed Forces are deployed, and international forces are in talks. This is no longer just sport—it's survival."

Rashida al-Hakim of Al Jazeera rose, her hijab framing a face etched with resolve, her tone measured but piercing as a needle. "The broadcast—hijacked globally—came with Najdi script and a Semtex threat. Is this a regional vendetta, and who's behind it?"

Tariq's lips thinned to a razor's edge, a vein pulsing at his temple like a metronome of rage. "The Najdi script points to pre-Islamic tribal roots—Obsidian Hand claims it. It's vengeance, not just terror—a message carved in blood. We're tracing the hack with international aid."

Carlos Mendes of Brazil's Globo Esporte jumped in, his Portuguese accent clipped with urgency, his notebook trembling slightly in his hands. "Six dead, six dying—parents are screaming on social media. What's the IOC doing for the families?"

"We've opened channels—counselors, travel aid," Tariq said, his voice softening for a fleeting moment, a flicker of humanity piercing the armor of his resolve. "The families will see their children, living or dead. This is our vow."

Priya Patel of The Times of India closed it out, her dark eyes sharp behind wire-rimmed glasses, her posture rigid with purpose. "Five hundred billion—38 hours. Is this a bluff, or are we facing a second strike?"

Tariq exhaled, a ragged sound that hung in the air like the toll of a cracked bell. "It's no bluff Semtex sat dormant in that crate, a warning. Interpol's on it, and we're bracing for more. The clock ticks for us all."

The briefing dissolved into a storm of flashes and shouts, Tariq stepping back as aides swarmed like ants around a kicked nest, the room buzzing with frenetic energy.

Outside, the world churned—social media ablaze with #DohaHorror, #ObsidianHand, clips of Lior's guttural choking looping in a grotesque requiem that clawed at the edges of sanity.

While the world gawked at hollow podiums and stammered promises, the true architects of terror carved new horrors into the sand.

Half an hour later, 70 miles away in the shadow-haunted dunes of Barga Al Kharaz, the Obsidian Hand's lair festered beneath the desert's skin—a cavern carved from ancient rock, its walls glistening with damp and streaked with rust-colored stains that might have been blood or mineral weep.

The Commander paced before a bank of monitors, their screens flickering with X posts, news feeds, and the IOC briefing looping in grainy detail—a symphony of chaos he'd orchestrated with surgical precision. At 45, his scar a jagged slash across his face from brow to jaw, a souvenir of a knife fight in a Riyadh back alley decades ago, now puckered and white against his sun-scorched skin.

His boots squelched in the mire of blood and rot that stained the concrete floor, each step a wet, deliberate thud that echoed off the cavern's walls. The floor wasn't just slick—it breathed rot, a living organism of decay that seemed to feed on the lair's violence. His grin was a predator's bared teeth, sharp and merciless, as he watched Sheikh Tariq's controlled fury play out on the screens, the suspension a sweet note in his discordant tune.

"Twenty eight hours," he snarled, his voice a low rumble that seemed to shake the stale air, the burner phone buzzing on the console like a trapped insect—contacts humming from unseen corners in Damascus, Tehran, and beyond, their voices a chorus of coded whispers. "They've suspended—scrambling like rats in a trap. Five hundred billion's the bait—next strike's the fire, and it'll burn them to ash."

The Scribe, wiry and twitchy, stopped pacing near a crate of Semtex bricks, his fingers drumming a nervous tattoo against the wood, splinters catching under his nails, his voice a hiss that barely masked his unease. “Keller’s landed—Interpol’s digging, sniffing too close. Barga’s hot—traces?”

The Commander laughed—a guttural bark that bounced off the damp walls like a gunshot, his scarred hand slamming the console, the burner skittering an inch across the metal. “Crate’s clean, signal’s buried—proxies in Damascus, Tehran, layered deep. Let ’em sniff— military’s their hammer, too slow for our blade, too clumsy for our shadows.”

The Watcher leaned against a crate, yellow eyes glinting behind her mask like twin lanterns in the gloom, Nova’s tablet spinning lazily in his gloved hand, the SD card slotted tight in its pouch—a prize he’d plucked from her satchel during the arena chaos, her blood still flecked on its edge from their scuffle.

“She’s alive—limped off with Jaber,” he rasped, his voice sandpaper on stone, rough and grating, each word scraping the air. “Old Port’s their hole—dock rats’ll squeal, scurrying for crumbs.”

The Commander’s grin widened, a glint of steel flashing in his gaze as he crushed a cigarette butt under his heel, the ember hissing out in the blood-slick floor, leaving a black smear.

“Flush her out—dock’s ours, their little net’s a toy. Tablet’s bait—she’ll bite, clawing for it. Enforcer—Pier 5, warehouse perch—eyes sharp, tobacco ready. We move when they do, and we bury them.”

Back in Doha, the air in Omar’s shack hung thick and heavy, a stew of kerosene fumes, salt-soaked wood, and the faint tang of arak clinging to the chipped enamel mug Nova cradled in her good hand.

Pain spiderwebbed through her ribs with every breath, but Nova clung to consciousness with the stubborn ferocity of someone who knew too much to die.

The Old Port's dusk chorus filtered through the tin walls—a distant hum of bartering voices from the souq, the creak of fishing skiffs bobbing against their moorings, the rhythmic slap of waves against the Gulf's gray expanse, each sound dulled by the encroaching fog.

Inside, the kerosene lamp flickered atop a crate, its amber glow casting jagged shadows that danced across the peeling paint and rusted shelves stacked with nautical odds and ends—coils of rope stiff with salt, a cracked sextant dulled by time, a jar of cloudy pickles glowing faintly green in the half-light.

It was 5:00 p.m., nine hours since the attack, and the clock was bleeding down—less than 27 hours remained until the Obsidian Hand's ransom deadline, a guillotine's blade hovering over the world.

Nova shifted on the cot, the springs groaning beneath her like a chorus of rusty ghosts, each movement a fresh stab through her bruised ribs and the throbbing ache of her dislocated shoulder, now slung tight against her chest in a makeshift bandage of torn cloth stained with sweat and blood. Her chestnut hair clung to her sweat-damp forehead, strands matted from hours of flight and a concussion's lingering haze, her scalp tender where a chunk had been ripped out by a splintered beam in the arena's collapse.

She'd escaped at dawn—a frantic sprint through the service tunnels—her ribs cracked by a falling support beam, her shoulder wrenched as she'd vaulted a barricade into the fog- choked night, her boots slipping in the mud as she ran. Now, her hazel eyes burned with a cold, unyielding fire, sharpened by two hours of fitful rest—snatches of sleep haunted by the stitched-together screams of the athletes—and the scalding, anise-laced tea Omar had pressed into her trembling fingers.

The bitter sting of it coated her throat, cutting through the fog in her skull, grounding her as she clutched the scratched Nokia 3310, its faint green glow a lifeline in the dim shack, the plastic warm against her palm, its edges worn smooth from constant use.

The phone buzzed—5:55 p.m.—and Rahman's text flickered across the screen: "N, alive— truck blurred, Aspire edge, sedan south, 27h ticking. Al Bidda, 10 p.m., lens sharp." Her good hand tightened around the device, knuckles whitening until the skin stretched taut, her mind racing as she mapped his intel against the Old Port's labyrinthine grid—pier numbers, warehouse outlines, the snaking paths of smugglers' tunnels etched into her memory from months of chasing stories in Doha's underbelly.

Rahman, her photojournalist ally, had eyes like a hawk and a nose for the unseen—his cryptic shorthand told her the Obsidian Hand's trail was still warm, threading south from the arena's outskirts, a breadcrumb trail she could taste on the back of her tongue, metallic and urgent. His messages came like heartbeat bursts—quick, coded, survival compressed into keystrokes.

Every step Jaber took was a wager against the odds he knew were tilting toward death, his wiry frame coiled with restless energy, a switchblade spinning between his calloused fingers like a dancer's pirouette, the blade's rhythm a hypnotic counterpoint to the shack's stillness. The steel glinted in the lamp's glow, catching the light in fleeting, razor-sharp flashes, a faint clink punctuating the air each time it snapped shut, the sound as familiar to him as his own heartbeat.

His keffiyeh hung loose around his neck, streaked with mud from their dawn scramble through the arena's outskirts, the scar across his nose bridge a stark slash against his sallow skin, puckered and pale from an old knife fight in a souq brawl years back, the memory of it a dull ache he carried like a badge.

He slung a burlap sack over his shoulder—binoculars, a battered lamp with a cracked lens, and a coil of rope clattering inside with a dull, metallic thunk—and exhaled a plume of cigarette smoke that curled upward like a wraith, the acrid scent mingling with the kerosene's bite, stinging the eyes.

"Faisal's first—Pier 7, soon as the fog rolls thick," he rasped, voice rough from exhaustion and a lifetime of cheap tobacco that left his teeth stained a dull yellow, his breath a faint wheeze. "Fifty riyals, grubby, up front. He'll spill on sedans, skiffs—or I'll nudge him, blade tip quiet in the mist, right where it hurts."

Once, Omar had sailed for hope. Now he scavenged among ruins, clinging to lost tides. A bear of a man with a grizzled beard that caught the flickering light in silver threads, his kaftan rustling like dry leaves as he stuffed a canvas pouch—twenty dirhams and a small sack of cardamom—into its voluminous folds, the fabric bulging slightly under the weight.

His thick fingers, scarred and calloused from years at sea hauling nets and wrestling storms, slid a curved dagger into his belt, the hilt worn smooth from decades of use, its steel a dull gleam against the stained fabric, etched with faint arabesques from a Yemeni smith long dead, a relic of a life before the port became his cage.

“Khalid’s at the souq now—dusk’s cover,” he growled, his voice a low rumble that seemed to vibrate the shack’s walls, deep and resonant as a ship’s horn cutting through fog. “Truck whispers—oil, metal, not spice. If he’s dry, Yemeni’s next—ten dirhams over turmeric, he’ll talk, or I’ll make him.”

He cracked his knuckles—pop-pop—the sound sharp and deliberate against the hiss of the kettle as he refilled it, tea leaves scattering across the crate like dark confetti, their earthy scent cutting through the room’s fug, a fleeting reprieve from the kerosene’s sting.

Nova rose from the cot, a hiss escaping through gritted teeth as her ribs flared, the pain a white-hot jolt that radiated up her spine and lodged behind her eyes like a splinter, her vision blurring for a heartbeat before she blinked it clear. Each step wasn’t just agony—it was a ticking clock, each nerve screaming a countdown she couldn’t afford to lose. She swallowed it down, tasting copper on her tongue where she’d bitten her lip, and grabbed a nautical chart from the shelf—its edges curled and brittle, stained with coffee rings and salt, the paper yellowed from years of damp air, its creases worn thin from constant folding.

She spread it across the crate, the parchment crackling under her fingers like dry bones, and her chipped pen, scavenged from the clutter of Omar’s hoard—a jumble of rusted nails, faded logbooks, and a broken compass. Every line she drew felt like a guess carved into crumbling stone—a hope that might shatter with the next wrong move. She scratched across the weathered surface as she traced the Old Port’s veins—Warehouse 12, Pier 8, Skiff Dock C—muttering under her breath in a voice hoarse from shouting over the arena's collapse, her throat raw and scratched.

"Big enough for a crate, truck ruts in the mud, roof perch for Watcher's drop. Rahman's truck south—sedan link—trail's here, Old Port's pulse." Her voice steadied despite the tremor in her hand, the pen's ink bleeding faintly into the paper, leaving a smudged halo around each mark, her fingers cramped from gripping it too tight.

"Jaber, Faisal's sedan sightings—Hassan's exile stink—cross it with this. Omar, Khalid's truck—Rahman's shots—we triangulate."

Jaber nodded, ash flaking from his cigarette onto the chart like gray snow, dusting the creases with a fine, gritty veil that he brushed away with a flick of his wrist.

"Pier 7 first—Faisal's a rat, but he sees everything, skulks in the shadows like a cockroach with eyes in the back of his skull. Then Hassan by midnight—exile's bitter, might know the Hand's shadow, nursing grudges with cheap arak and a chipped glass. Lair scout after— binocs sweep, two flashes if it's hot. Back by 2 a.m., intel or blood, depending on how they play."

Omar leaned over the chart, his shadow swallowing half the map, tea steam curling around his weathered face in ghostly tendrils, his beard damp with condensation, the scent of cardamom clinging to his skin.

"Khalid now—souq's humming, kids on watch—five riyals each, barefoot, sharp as hawks, darting through the stalls. Bilal after, then Rahman at Al Bidda by 10 p.m. Threads pulled tight by midnight, no slack."

Nova tapped the chart, the pen scratching Warehouse 12's outline in a jagged loop, her nails bitten to the quick and crusted with dirt from clawing through the arena's rubble.

"Watcher's yellow eyes—tablet's hers. Trail's close—Semtex

stink, crate echo. I'll plot 'til night—rest, then move with Rahman's shots. Three knocks if it's live—bait 'em, you flank." She slid the Nokia to Omar, her text draft glowing on the scratched screen: "O, spice safe, N alive, 27h—Al Bidda, 10 p.m., lens?" "Send it—dusk. He'll bite, he always does."

The shack settled into a tense rhythm—lamp flickering, smoke curling, tea hissing—as the three wove their net, threads tightening in Doha's underbelly against the Obsidian Hand's faceless horror. Beyond the tin walls, the city festered and flexed, a tightening noose they couldn't see but could feel pressing against their skin. Outside, the fog thickened, rolling in from the Gulf like a shroud, muffling the world beyond the tin walls, the air growing heavy with the promise of secrets waiting to be pried loose from the damp and the dark.

While three hunted in the dark with hope and desperation, armies of the world sharpened their knives for a war that might already be too late. At 7:00 p.m., Agent Lukas Keller stood at Al Wakra Hospital's ICU, his ice-blue eyes scanning the survivors through the glass wall—six broken dolls under the ventilators' relentless hiss, tubes snaking into gray flesh like parasitic vines, the room a sterile tomb of beeping monitors and antiseptic glare.

Lior Abramson's chest tube gurgled, a sluggish bubble of bloody froth rising with each labored breath, his pulse a weak 50 bpm, his skin clammy and translucent. Omar Haddad's restraints creaked against the gurney's frame, his pulse 48 bpm, his fingers twitching faintly as if clawing at nightmares that wouldn't let go.

Yael Ben-Ami's lungs wheezed, a wet rattle audible through the glass, pulse 48 bpm, her chest rising and falling in shallow, uneven gasps. Noa Levi's spine pins gleamed under the harsh lights, pulse 46 bpm, her face a mask of waxen stillness, lips parted as if frozen mid- breath. Yasmine Haddad's catheter trickled with dark urine, pulse 52 bpm, her lips cracked and peeling, a faint moan escaping as a nurse adjusted her IV.

Nadine Al-Rassi's stump oozed a sickly yellow pus, pulse 44 bpm, the bandage sodden and curling at the edges, the air around her thick with the sour reek of infection. Nurses moved like phantoms, swapping fluids with trembling hands, their faces drawn and pale behind surgical masks, the air sharp with iodine and the cloying stench of decay that clung to the tiles like a second skin, a miasma that no amount of bleach could erase.

Priya Sharma tapped her tablet beside him, her braid swinging with each furious swipe, her voice tight with urgency, barely above a whisper as if afraid to wake the ghosts.

"OBS hack's Damascus proxy—Barga's core, buried deep in the noise. X's screaming— #PayOrDie trending, ransom's splitting them—half beg payment, half demand strikes, posts piling up like a digital landslide, thousands every minute."

Jonas Weber knelt by a gurney, gloved hands tracing Lior's chest tube with clinical precision, his trauma kit clanking softly as he shifted—a stethoscope, scissors, a vial of morphine rattling in their slots, the leather worn from years in the field.

"Midazolam kept 'em alive—surgical dosing, not amateur, precise to the milligram. Semtex's range—Barga fits, chemical markers match. They're close—70 miles, dunes swallowing the signal, a black hole in the sand."

Keller's jaw tightened, a muscle twitching under his stubbled cheek, his radio crackling as he barked to Captain al-Thani, his voice a whipcrack of command: "Truck manifest—4:03 a.m., blacked-out plates. Crew's dirty—bank records, phones, now, every transaction, every ping."

Al-Thani's voice buzzed back, clipped and urgent through the static: "Two guards flagged— cash deposits, burner pings, fat stacks from nowhere. Raiding homes—11 p.m., rifles ready, doors coming down."

Keller turned to Priya, his gaze piercing, eyes like shards of ice. "Survivors' statements— when they wake, every word, every gasp. Barga's the nest—crack that hack, every byte, every relay."

To Jonas: "Crate's Semtex—trace the batch, chemical signature, origin, down to the factory floor. Military's coming—NATO's debating, but boots hit soon, and we'll be ready."

Half a world away, at 8:00 p.m. Doha time, the White House Situation Room thrummed with a different kind of tension, the air thick with the scent of burnt coffee and the faint hum of encrypted comms, maps and screens casting a bluish glow over the faces of the weary.

President Logan Calder looked less like a leader now and more like a man drowning on dry land, clinging to maps like they might rewrite the reality bleeding across them —Doha marked in red, Barga a shadowy smudge amid the dunes—his pen tapping a relentless beat against the table, the rhythm a metronome of his fraying patience, the wood dented from hours of it.

"Suspension's locked—Games might be dead," he growled, his voice rough with fatigue, his tie loosened and stained with a smear of mustard from a forgotten sandwich hours old, the collar of his shirt damp with sweat. "NATO's wobbling—Delta Force prepped, itching to move, locked and loaded. Five hundred billion's a taunt—no payment, not a goddamn cent."

Victoria Langford nodded, her blonde bob steady, voice crisp as she adjusted her glasses, the lenses catching the room's stark light in a brief flare.

"UK's in—France, Germany leaning, diplomats squabbling over timelines like it's a goddamn tea party. Israel's IDF, Lebanon's 50th

Brigade—ready if NATO green-lights, tanks fueled and restless, barrels hot. Treasury's firm—no cash, not even a negotiation. Dow's bleeding—900 down, markets jittery as hell, traders panicking."

DNI Mark Reyes cut in via secure line, his voice gruff and edged with static, a faint crackle underscoring his urgency like a storm on the horizon. "SIGINT's hot—Barga chatter spiking, coded bursts on dark channels, whispers of 'next' and 'fire.' Ransom's bait—second strike's the play, timed to break us, to shatter resolve. Military's the fist—push NATO, Logan, or we're blind, groping in the dark."

Calder's fist clenched, the pen snapping—crack—ink bleeding across his hand like a dark omen, dripping onto the map in a splatter that pooled over Doha's outline, a black stain spreading like a prophecy. "Then we swing—Delta to Doha, IDF, 50th Brigade if NATO blinks. Barga's the head—cut it off, root and stem, before it bites again."

Back in Doha, Qatar's Armed Forces rolled through the streets, vehicles rumbling past the Old Port's edge, their engines a low growl that vibrated the shack's tin walls, headlights slicing through the fog like searchlights, tires chewing the asphalt. Israeli and Lebanese forces were mobilizing too, their borders bristling with tension—IDF tanks grinding across desert tracks, treads kicking up clouds of sand, the 50th Brigade's artillery units rolling into position under a darkening sky, barrels glinting in the last light.

U.S. Delta Force prepped in staging areas, their black gear gleaming under floodlights, the clatter of weapons checks a distant percussion, rifles locked, night-vision goggles humming to life. The world was coiling tight, a spring ready to snap. And when the spring snapped, it wouldn't just break—it would rip flesh and bone from the earth.

but Nova, Jaber, and Omar cared only for the thread they held—the Obsidian Hand's trail, a faint pulse they chased through Doha's veins, a lifeline leading beyond the city's grasp into the desert's maw.

Jaber slipped into the mist at 6:30 p.m., every step felt like slipping into a loaded gun's barrel, breath held for the trigger's inevitable twitch. His boots strode silent on the wet planks of Pier 7, the Gulf's gray churn a low growl against the pilings, the water oily and restless under the fog's weight, ripples spreading like secrets whispered in the dark. The mist was a living thing, clammy and dense, swallowing the silhouettes of moored skiffs and the faint glow of lanterns swinging from their masts, their light diffused into sickly halos that bled into the gray.

His keffiyeh was pulled tight over his mouth, filtering the damp air that tasted of salt and diesel, the burlap sack slung low against his hip, its contents shifting with each step—a muted clatter of metal on metal, the rope's hemp fibers brushing his thigh. The switchblade rested in his palm, its weight a familiar comfort, the handle worn smooth from years of restless twirling, its blade nicked but lethal, a silent partner in every shadow he'd walked. He scanned the pier for Faisal—a wiry dockhand with a limp and a reputation for selling secrets as easily as he sold fish, a man who thrived in the cracks of the Old Port's underbelly, his ears tuned to every whisper the Gulf carried.

A shadow shifted near a stack of crates, the wood splintered and slick with algae, the air around them heavy with the reek of rotting seaweed, and Jaber tensed, his fingers tightening on the blade until the grip bit into his skin, a faint sting he ignored.

"Faisal," he hissed, voice barely above the waves, a whisper swallowed by the fog, his breath misting in the chill. "Show your face, or I'll carve it out, piece by piece."

A low chuckle answered, raspy and wet, and Faisal limped forward, his oil-stained galabiyya clinging to his thin frame like a second skin, a cigarette dangling from his cracked lips, the ember a dull orange glow that pulsed with each drag. "Jaber, ya dog—always with the knife," he muttered, his good eye glinting in the dim light, the other clouded white from some old injury—a bottle fight, a fishhook, no one knew—his breath a sour mix of tobacco and rot that curled in the air. "Fifty riyals, you said?"

Jaber tossed a crumpled wad of bills at Faisal's feet, the paper fluttering in the damp breeze, sticking briefly to the wet planks before Faisal's grimy hand snatched it up, his fingers trembling slightly from the cold or the arak he'd downed earlier.

"Sedans—black, fast, southbound from Aspire this morning. Skiffs too—anything heavy, moving odd. Talk, now."

Faisal counted the money with grubby fingers, nails black with filth, before pocketing it with a grunt of satisfaction, his lips curling into a smirk.

“Saw one—black sedan, tinted, no plates, peeled out of Warehouse 12 ‘round 4 a.m. Mud on the tires, deep ruts—headed south past Skiff Dock C, engine roaring like it was pissed, tearing through the fog. Heard an engine later—skiff, big, throaty, cutting through the Gulf, hull low in the water like it was hauling lead. Crate on board, maybe—canvas tarp flapping, caught a glimpse in the lantern light. Dock rats said it stank—oil, metal, sharp like fire, not fish or fuel, something that burns the nose.”

Jaber’s pulse quickened, a drumbeat in his chest that drowned out the Gulf’s murmur, the pieces snapping into place—Warehouse 12, Rahman’s truck south, Nova’s hunch threading tighter, a noose pulling taut.

“Who loaded it? Faces, names—give me something, Faisal, or I start cutting, and you’ll be limping worse.”

Faisal shrugged, exhaling a plume of smoke that hung in the fog like a Spectre, his shoulders hunching against the damp, his galabiyya sagging where it clung to his bony frame.

“Shadows—three, maybe four, moving fast, quiet as ghosts. One had yellow eyes—creepy bastard, mask up, moved like a snake, all fluid and quiet, no wasted steps. Heard ‘em mutter ‘Barga’—old tribal shit, pre-Islam echoes, Najdi tongue. That’s all I got, Jaber. Take it and piss off before I regret it.”

Jaber’s blade flicked open, a whisper of steel that gleamed wetly in the lantern light, and Faisal flinched, his good eye widening as the tip hovered an inch from his throat, close enough to nick the stubble, a bead of sweat rolling down his temple despite the chill. In the Old Port, secrets didn’t just cost money. They cost flesh, blood, and names whispered to the tide.

“Sure about that?” Jaber growled, his scar twitching in the flickering glow, his breath hot against the fog, his voice a low snarl that promised violence.

"Swear it!" Faisal yelped, hands up, palms stained with fish guts and grease, his voice cracking like dry wood. "Yellow Eyes—Watcher, they call her. Dock's her haunt, slinks around like she owns it, owns the shadows. Check Warehouse 12—roof's got a perch, fresh cigarette butts, menthol stink hanging thick. Najdi script—scribbled on a crate corner, saw it flash before they covered it. Now let me breathe, ya lunatic!"

Jaber lowered the blade, snapping it shut with a clink that echoed faintly off the crates. In the stillness that followed the echo, a chill slithered up his spine—the sense that solving one puzzle had only drawn him into the jaws of another. His eyes narrowed as he filed the details away—Watcher, Warehouse 12, Barga, Najdi script— a knot of clues tightening in his mind. "Hassan next—where's he hiding?"

"Pier 8, shack by the fuel drums—exile's sour, drinks alone, arak and regrets in a tin cup. Watch your back—he's twitchy, got a shiv of his own, rusty but sharp." Faisal limped off into the fog, muttering curses under his breath, his silhouette dissolving into the gray like a wisp of smoke, leaving Jaber alone with the Gulf's restless churn, the Najdi whisper a splinter in his thoughts.

Omar trudged through the souq's dusk bustle at the same time, his kaftan blending with the sea of robes as vendors hawked spices and fish under swaying lanterns, their voices a rhythmic cacophony—shouts of "Saffron, fresh!" and "Tuna, two riyals!" cutting through the haze, blending with the clatter of coins and the sizzle of frying dough.

The air was thick with cardamom and sweat, the ground slick with spilled tea and fish scales that gleamed like scattered coins underfoot, the crowd a shifting maze of bodies that parted around his hulking frame as if he were a ship cleaving waves, his shadow a dark tide.

Khalid waited by a turmeric stall, a lean man with a pockmarked face and a nervous tic that jerked his left eye every few seconds, his fingers drumming on a sack of saffron, the yellow dust staining his cuticles, his robe patched and fraying at the hem.

"Omar," Khalid greeted, voice low, eyes darting to the shadows beyond the stall as if expecting ghosts to lunge from the alleys, his tic twitching faster under the lantern's sway. "Souq's buzzing—trucks don't belong here, not with that weight, not rumbling like that. What you chasing?"

"Black truck, Aspire dawn—oil, metal, not spice," Omar rumbled, sliding ten dirhams across the stall, the coins clinking softly against the wood, their edges worn smooth from years of trade, his hand steady despite the weight of the dagger at his belt. "Tracks, whispers— where'd it roll?" Khalid pocketed the coins, leaning closer, his breath sour with coffee and a hint of clove, his voice dropping to a conspiratorial hush.

"Saw it—4 a.m., heavy, blacked-out plates, rumbled south from Warehouse 12, tires sinking deep in the mud, leaving ruts like scars. Mud caked, engine growling—loaded, not empty, chassis groaning under it like it'd snap. Dock kids said it parked near Skiff Dock C—smelled like fire, sharp, chemical, not diesel or salt, a sting that lingers. Sedan followed, black, fast, headlights off—ghosting it south, a shadow on its tail."

Omar's fist clenched, the dagger's hilt pressing into his palm until the worn arabesques bit into his skin, a faint ache he welcomed as a focus, his knuckles popping faintly under the strain. "Crew?"

"Didn't see—fog was thick, swallowed 'em whole, like the Gulf eating a ship. Heard a voice—gravelly, barking 'Watcher' and 'Barga,' sharp like a command, Najdi accent, old and hard. Old Port's got ghosts, Omar—check the warehouse. Roof's a nest—cigarette stubs, fresh, menthol tang still in the air, a scrap of paper with Najdi scrawl, half-burnt."

Khalid stepped back, melting into the crowd as a vendor's shout drowned his retreat— "Spice, best price!"—leaving Omar with the weight of the words sinking into his bones— Warehouse 12 again, Watcher's name a recurring scar, Barga a whisper from the desert's edge, Najdi script a thread to pull.

Nova hunched over the chart in the shack, the lamp casting her silhouette against the tin wall in a jagged, wavering dance, her shadow stretching to touch the shelves as if reaching for answers, her breath shallow from the pain she refused to acknowledge. Every throb in her ribs was a reminder: twelve lives depended on her getting it right—pain wasn't permission to stop. Despite the exhaustion creeping into her bones like damp rot, her fingers trembled faintly as she gripped the pen.

The Nokia buzzed—Omar's reply from Rahman: "Lens sharp, N—truck south, sedan tail, Warehouse 12 mud. Al Bidda, 10 p.m."

She traced the lines again—Warehouse 12, Pier 8, Skiff Dock C—a triangle tightening around the Old Port's heart, her chipped pen scratching the paper with a sound like a match striking flint, each stroke a spark in her mind.

The Watcher's yellow eyes haunted her thoughts, her stolen tablet a taunt in her hands, its SD card packed with footage—grainy clips of masked figures moving in the arena's undercroft, Semtex crates stacked in shadows, a glimpse of a scar slashing across a face—she'd captured before the world exploded around her. If she could reclaim it, it'd be a dagger in the Obsidian Hand's throat, a blade to carve out their secrets.

Jaber burst in at 8:00 p.m., fog clinging to his keffiyeh like a second skin, his breath sharp with tobacco and the salt of the Gulf, his boots leaving wet prints on the shack's warped floorboards, the wood creaking under his weight.

"Faisal sang—sedan from Warehouse 12, 4 a.m., southbound, skiff loaded after, crate aboard, stinking of fire. Yellow Eyes—Watcher—roof perch, cigarette butts, menthol. Barga slipped out—tribal ghosts, Najdi script on a crate. Hassan's next."

Omar followed minutes later, tea leaves clinging to his beard like burrs, his voice a low growl that rattled the kettle on the crate, his kaftan damp with souq mist.

"Khalid too—truck, Warehouse 12, south to Skiff Dock C. Chemical stink, Watcher's name dropped, Barga again, Najdi accent and scrawl. Roof's key—menthol trails."

Nova's pen froze mid-scratch, her pulse hammering in her ears like a war drum, drowning out the lamp's faint sputter, her breath catching as the threads wove into a tapestry of dread and revelation. And every wasted second was another stitch tightening around the captives' throats.

"Three hits—Warehouse 12's the hub. Roof's their perch—Watcher's nest. Skiff's their relay, sedan's their scout. Barga's the thread—70 miles southwest, dunes and rock, not here. Old Port's a staging ground—trail's pointing out, not down. Najdi script—pre-Islamic, vengeance roots, it's their mark."

Her voice cracked with realization, the pieces slotting together with a brutal clarity—Doha was a feint, a launchpad, the lair buried beyond the city's reach, and the script was the key to its heart.

Jaber grinned, blade spinning in his hand with a hypnotic rhythm, the steel a blur of reflected light, his eyes glinting with the thrill of the hunt.

"Fog's our cloak—roof sweep, binocs, two flashes if it's hot. Hassan after—exile might know Barga's holes, old grudges spilling over arak."

Omar nodded, dagger gleaming as he adjusted his belt, the blade catching the lamp's glow in a dull, menacing sheen, his fingers brushing the hilt like a prayer.

"Kids on watch—five riyals, eyes sharp, darting like minnows through the docks. I'll flank— skiff's trail might whisper more, oil and fire leading south." Nova stood, wincing as her ribs screamed, a hiss escaping her lips as she slung a battered satchel over her good shoulder—pen, chart, Nokia rattling inside like loose teeth, the strap digging into her collarbone.

"I'll climb—ribs be damned. Watcher's tablet's up there—I feel it, itching in my bones. Three knocks if it's live—bait 'em, we pounce. Barga's the endgame—Najdi's the map—we trace it tonight."

The trio slipped into the fog at 8:30 p.m., the Old Port a ghostly maze of shadows and muted sounds, the distant rumble of Qatar's Armed Forces a faint tremor underfoot, a reminder of the world tightening its noose beyond their focus. Warehouse 12 loomed ahead, a hulking relic of corrugated steel and cracked concrete, its roof a jagged silhouette against the mist, rust streaking its sides like dried blood, the air around it heavy with the tang of salt and decay.

Jaber led, scaling a rusted ladder with catlike grace, his sack clinking faintly as he hauled himself onto the perch, the metal groaning under his weight, flakes of rust drifting down like red snow. Nova followed, her good hand gripping the rungs, each step a grind of pain she bit back with a snarl, her breath shallow and ragged, her sling snagging briefly on a jutting bolt, the fabric tearing with a faint rip. Omar took the flank, melting into the dockside shadows, his dagger a silent promise as he scanned the skiffs, their hulls slick with condensation, bobbing like restless spirits in the fog.

Jaber crouched on the roof, binoculars pressed to his eyes, sweeping the perimeter with slow, deliberate arcs, the lenses fogging slightly in the damp air, his breath misting as he adjusted the focus.

“Cigarette butts—fresh, menthol, scattered like breadcrumbs, still damp with spit. Boot scuffs—two sets, deep, heels worn, one pair dragging like a limp. Crate marks—dragged, not lifted, gouged into the tar, splinters caught in the grooves.”

He froze, glass glinting below in a sudden flare, his voice dropping to a hiss. “Yellow Eyes— Watcher—Pier 5, tobacco flare, mask catching the light, head tilted like she smells us. She’s watching.”

Nova knelt beside a dented vent, her fingers tracing a faint scratch—her tablet’s edge, she’d swear it on her life, the groove still holding a fleck of her blood from the arena scuffle, the metal cold and slick under her touch.

“He’s got it—close, taunting. Air’s wrong—Semtex faint, but no rot, no lair stink here. This is a drop, not the nest—relay point.” She tapped the roof—three sharp knocks—her signal echoing in the fog, a challenge thrown into the night, her hand trembling faintly from the effort.

Omar’s shadow shifted below, a low whistle answering through the mist, his voice a growl carried on the wind, rough and urgent. “Skiff’s gone—oil slick, fresh, swirling in the current, black as ink. Tunnel mouth—Dock C, grate loose, but shallow—smuggler’s cache, not a base, barely a crawlspace. Tracks south—desert mud, not port, red and gritty, caked in tire treads, heading southwest.”

Jaber’s blade flicked open, his grin feral, teeth bared like a wolf’s as he pried at the vent’s edge, the steel scraping with a faint screech. “Watcher’s bait—playing us, dangling the tablet. Barga’s the lair—70 miles, dunes swallowing it. Skiff’s a ferry, sedan’s a runner— Warehouse 12's their pivot, not their heart."

He froze, his blade catching on something—a crumpled cigarette pack wedged in the vent, menthol-stained, its paper damp but intact. He fished it out, unfolding it under the lamp's glow, revealing a scrawl in Najdi script: Barga Al Kharaz, 70km, dusk drop. "Najdi—old as the sands, tribal mark. This is it."

Nova's breath caught, her good hand snatching the pack, her eyes tracing the angular, slashing glyphs—letters like knife cuts, stark and ancient, a dialect of Arabic rooted in the Najd plateau, pre-Islamic, pre-conquest, a relic of Bedouin clans who'd carved their oaths in stone and blood.

This was why she'd spent years chasing buried truths no one else wanted to see—because sometimes the past bled into the present, and only those who knew the old wounds could stop the new ones.

She'd seen it before—on smuggler manifests, in museum archives, a script tied to vengeance pacts, tribal wars that spanned centuries, feuds that never died but smoldered under the desert's skin.

"Najdi script—Najd's heart, central Arabia, pre-600 AD," she muttered, her voice a fevered thread, her mind racing through fragments of history she'd chased as a reporter—tales of the Banu Hanifa, the Kindah, clans who'd defied empires and nursed grudges into legend.

"This isn't random—it's a claim, a banner. Obsidian Hand's not just terror—it's revenge, old as the dunes, tied to Barga Al Kharaz. Interpol said tribal roots—Najdi's the vein, Barga's the pulse."

Omar loomed closer, his dagger glinting as he peered at the scrawl, his growl a rumble of recognition.

"Najdi—heard it in the souq, old men cursing in it, spitting on the ground. Barga's 70 miles southwest—rock caverns, smugglers' dens, old tribal ground. Truck tracks—desert red, not port muck—

southwest, not looping back. They're staging here, shipping there."

Jaber spun his blade, the steel a blur as he pieced it together, his grin sharpening.

"Watcher's perch—relay, not lair. Najdi script's their signature—Barga Al Kharaz, vengeance nest, 70 miles out. Skiff hauls, sedan runs—desert's the endgame, not the dock. We've got their scent."

Nova's eyes narrowed, the chart burned into her mind, her voice a low, fierce thread as she clutched the pack, the paper crinkling under her grip. "Watcher's here—tablet's proof, bait to keep us spinning. Barga Al Kharaz—cavern rock, Najdi roots, Semtex home. Truck south, sedan tail—desert trail, 70 miles southwest, not dock. Roof's a relay—Watcher's eyes, not their heart. Najdi's the map—pre-Islamic clans, blood oaths, a grudge against the world, carved in script and flesh. We've got the thread—Rahman's shots at 10 p.m., we chase it now."

She typed furiously on the Nokia, her thumb smudging the screen: "Barga confirmed— dunes, 70 miles SW, Najdi script ties it. Lens sharp, 10 p.m."

The fog thickened, behind them the Gulf roared like an ancient god hungry for the sacrifices to come—Jaber's blade glinting, Omar's dagger drawn, Nova's fire unyielding despite the ache gnawing her ribs. The grate at Skiff Dock C yawned open, a shallow smuggler's hole exhaling oil and damp earth, but the real clue lay in the mud—desert red, not port gray, caked in tire treads heading southwest, flecked with sand that glittered faintly under the lamp.

The Najdi script on the cigarette pack was their beacon—Barga Al Kharaz, 70 miles away, a lair rooted in pre-Islamic vengeance, its origins a ghost of the Najd plateau's tribal wars, now resurrected in blood and Semtex.

They'd cracked it—the Obsidian Hand's heart wasn't beneath

Doha but buried in the desert's ancient grudge, 27 hours ticking down as the world's militaries coiled tighter, oblivious to the trio's breakthrough.

The fog swallowed their retreat, the Gulf's churn a requiem for the hunt now turning toward the dunes.

VEIL 18

Dash To The Consulate

The fog draped the Old Port like a shroud spun from the Gulf's dank exhalation, a clammy, suffocating veil that smothered sound and sight, reducing the world to a labyrinth of half- glimpsed silhouettes and muted echoes.

23 hours left – the world tethered on a blade's edge, a second strike poised to shatter it.

The crumpled cigarette pack in Nova Mendelsohn's satchel—its Najdi script jaggedly scrawled with Barga Al Kharaz, 70km, dusk drop—clung to her side like guilt made tangible, pressed against her hip like a shard of smoldering coal, its damp paper a tether to the desert lair festering 70 miles southwest, a cavern of ancient rock where pre-Islamic vengeance melded with Semtex into a modern nightmare pulsing with intent.

The trio slipped from Warehouse 12's rust-streaked shadow, the Gulf's oily churn a relentless growl at their backs, its waves hammering the pilings with a rhythm that synced with the frantic thudding in Nova's chest. Her ribs throbbed, a searing ache that ignited with each shallow breath, her dislocated shoulder slung tight in a blood-crusted rag, the pain a ravenous beast she forced down with clenched teeth and a snarl she kept caged in her throat.

Jaber moved ahead, his keffiyeh streaked with dock mud and glistening with mist, his switchblade spinning in his hand like a steel whirlwind, its glint swallowed by the fog's greedy embrace. Omar flanked them, his grizzled beard dripping with condensation, his kaftan rustling as his dagger gleamed dull against the stained fabric, his hulking frame a dark tide carving through the haze.

They dropped behind a stack of fish crates near Pier 6, the wood slick with algae and reeking of rotting entrails, the air a noxious stew of salt and the acrid bite of diesel from a skiff coughing to life somewhere in the mist, its engine a guttural sputter that vibrated the damp planks beneath their boots.

Nova's hazel eyes, still piercing despite the concussion's lingering haze – her vision still blurred at the edges, each footfall a battle to stay upright – flicked between her companions, her voice a hoarse rasp torn from a throat raw with arena dust and hours of whispered plotting.

"Barga Al Kharaz—70 miles southwest, Najdi script tying it to a grudge older than empires. The centipede wasn't just terror—it was a war cry, stitched in flesh for the world to choke on. We've got the lair, the script, the trail. U.S. Consulate's our play—get this to them, they'll hit it with Delta, not our knives."

Jaber's blade snapped shut with a sharp clink, his scar twitching as he sneered, his breath a sour plume of tobacco and arak that curled in the fog like a wraith.

"Consulate? You've lost your damn mind, Nova—Watcher's yellow eyes are on us, slinking through this mist like a jackal with our scent. We'll be gutted before we hit Corniche— Obsidian

Hand's got claws in every shadow from here to West Bay. We take a skiff, strike Barga ourselves—blades in the dark, burn their Semtex stash before they even blink."

Omar's knuckles cracked—pop-pop—a stark report slicing through the Gulf's low murmur, his shadow swallowing the crates as he loomed over them, his growl a rumble of skepticism that seemed to shake the damp air.

"Jaber's right—Consulate's a fortress, sure, but it's locked tight with Qatar's military crawling the streets like ants on a corpse. Fog's our cloak—skiff southwest, slit throats, grab your tablet, torch their explosives before it's ash over Doha. We don't need diplomats tripping over their polished loafers."

Nova's good hand balled into a fist, her chipped nails digging into her palm until blood welled under the dirt-crusted edges, a sharp sting she welcomed as a tether to focus, her voice rising despite the dagger it drove into her cracked ribs.

"You're both thinking dockside brawls—this is bigger than us, bigger than blades. Six dead, six dying, a crate of Semtex they haven't even cracked open yet. The centipede was a declaration of war—Israelis, Lebanese, beamed live to millions, a giant middle finger to the world. Interpol's sniffing, NATO's gearing up, Delta's staging. We've got coordinates, Najdi script—pre-Islamic vengeance, tribal clans reborn in blood and bombs. Consulate's the nerve center—get this to them, they'll flatten Barga with Hellfire. We're the spark, not the blaze."

Jaber's blade flicked open again, spinning slower now, a metronome ticking out his simmering fury, his eyes narrowing to slits in the faint glow of a lantern swaying on a distant mooring.

"Spark? You'll torch us alive—Watcher's taunting you, Nova, dangling your tablet like a bone for a stray dog. Consulate's a beacon—they'll see us coming, carve us up in the streets before we knock. Barga's 70 miles—skiff now, we hit 'em while they're smug, laughing in their cave."

Omar's fingers brushed his dagger's hilt, the worn arabesques biting into his calloused palm, his voice a low thunder that rolled through the fog.

"Military's loud but slow—Delta's not here yet, NATO's still jawing. 23 hours—fog's our edge, skiff's silent. We gut the snake ourselves, not wait for suits to fumble the kill."

Nova's jaw tightened, a muscle twitching under her sweat-slick skin, her chestnut hair plastered to her forehead as she glared back, her Nokia glowing faintly in her grip as she clutched it like a lifeline.

"Row into a Semtex nest with a blade and a prayer? That's a death wish. This is war— global, not some portside grudge. I've got Lila Hayes, attaché, owes me from a Syria scoop three years back. She'll get us in, get this to Keller at Interpol, to Delta. Barga's theirs to crush—we just point the cannon."

The argument hung there, a live wire sparking in the fog, their breaths steaming in the damp chill like ghosts of their resolve. Jaber spat into the mud, the glob vanishing into the slick planks with a faint plop, his growl reluctant but bending.

"Fine—Consulate, but if Watcher's shadows snag us, it's your blood, Nova. I'm not dying for a desk jockey's handshake."

Omar nodded once, slow and heavy, his beard dripping as he rumbled, "Lila better be quick—23 hours, and Barga's brewing something worse than ash. Fog's our skin—move, or we're done."

Nova slung her satchel tighter, the cigarette pack's Najdi script a pulse against her side, her voice a fierce thread cutting through the pain. Fail here, and the world would choke on the cost of her silence.

“Corniche to West Bay—Consulate’s 5 miles, locked down since the attack. Military’s thick, fog’s our veil—Al Bidda for Rahman’s shots, then straight to Lila. Three knocks—she’ll know it’s me.”

The escape was a gauntlet of shadow and steel, the fog their only shield against a city bristling with paranoia and the Obsidian Hand’s unseen eyes. They darted from the crates, the Gulf’s gray churn a war drum at their heels, its waves crashing against the pilings like a countdown etched in water. Qatar’s Armed Forces rumbled along the port’s edge— Humvees snarling through the mist, their headlights slashing futile arcs that danced across the wet wood, tires chewing asphalt with a wet screech that vibrated through their bones. Each checkpoint reeked of wet sand, diesel, and the slow stink of dying hope.

A patrol truck roared past Pier 5, its engine a guttural bellow that drowned the Gulf’s growl, its spotlight sweeping the fog as Jaber dove behind a rusted oil drum, his sack clanking against the dented metal, his blade poised as the beam grazed the frayed edge of his keffiyeh, painting it briefly in stark white before the mist swallowed it again.

Nova flattened against a piling, her ribs screaming as the damp wood pressed her sling, a jagged splinter jabbing her good hand until blood trickled warm down her wrist, pooling in the creases of her palm, her breath a ragged hiss swallowed by the fog’s embrace.

The truck’s radio crackled—“Dock’s hot, eyes open”—and a soldier’s silhouette loomed, his rifle swinging lazily, his boots crunching gravel ten feet away, close enough that she could smell the tobacco on his breath, a sour tang cutting through the salt. Omar melted into a skiff’s shadow, his kaftan pooling in the mud like spilled ink, his dagger low as the soldier’s flashlight danced across the water, its beam glinting off the blade’s arabesques for a heartbeat—a frozen moment where Nova’s pulse stopped—before the fog snuffed it out, the soldier cursing the mist as he trudged on, his silhouette dissolving into the gray.

The soldier's retreat was a fleeting reprieve, and they slipped north, the Old Port's maze unraveling into Al Bidda Park at 9:50 p.m. The fog thickened here, rolling off the Gulf in suffocating waves that drowned the city's pulse—car horns bleating, muezzin wails rising, the static of military comms buzzing—all reduced to a ghostly hum that seemed to emanate from the earth itself. Rahman waited by a gnarled tree, its branches clawing at the mist like skeletal fingers, his hooded jacket slick with dew, his camera's lens a wet gleam under the hood, his hawkish eyes locking with Nova's in a silent pact forged over months of chasing shadows.

She hadn't earned his faith—but she'd damn well carry it.

"Shots—truck south, sedan tailing, desert red mud, not port gray," he muttered, pressing a USB drive into her palm, its plastic scratched and warm from his pocket, his voice a clipped urgency that cut through the haze. "Warehouse 12—roof scuffs, crate drag, Najdi scrawl on a tarp corner, caught it in a flash before the fog ate it. Barga's southwest—70 miles, signal's dead there, dunes swallowing it like a grave."

Nova zipped the drive into her satchel beside the cigarette pack, her good hand trembling as she rasped, "Consulate—now. Dock's burning, Watcher's prowling—vanish, Rahman, fog's your shield." He melted into the mist without a word, his silhouette dissolving like smoke into the gray, leaving the trio alone with the park's twisted trees and the weight of his intel sinking into their bones.

The U.S. Embassy, three miles away, floated like a mirage in a city choked with soldiers, sirens and sweat, its floodlights faint pinpricks piercing the fog, its perimeter a fortress of sandbags, razor wire, and jittery guards coiled tight with adrenaline.

They cut west off Al Bidda, skirting the Corniche where the military presence thickened like a noose tightening around Doha's throat—

Humvees idling with engines growling low, soldiers barking into radios with voices edged with panic, their rifles sweeping the mist with nervous twitches that betrayed their fear of the unseen. A checkpoint flared ahead, its floodlight slicing the fog like a blade, and Jaber dove behind a dumpster, its metal dented and stinking of rotting fish, his breath held as a Qatari soldier's boots crunched past, a cigarette's ember glowing inches from his hiding spot, the acrid smoke curling into the fog as the soldier muttered a curse in Arabic—"This damn mist hides devils."

Pain clawed at the edge of Nova's vision, but she forced it back – another breath, another step. She pressed against a shuttered storefront, its glass fogged and cracked from some forgotten riot, her ribs a furnace of pain as she flattened herself against the cold surface, the sling snagging on a jutting nail that tore a fresh rip in the cloth, a bead of blood welling as the soldier's radio buzzed—"Perimeter breach, south sector"—and his flashlight swung her way, its beam grazing the matted strands of her chestnut hair plastered to her forehead.

She ducked, the light lingering for an agonizing heartbeat, her pulse a thunder in her ears as it painted the wall above her in stark yellow before sliding away, the soldier grumbling as he moved on, his silhouette swallowed by the haze. Omar crouched behind a parked van, its tires flat and windows shattered, glass crunching faintly under his boots as he shifted, his dagger poised as a Marine's silhouette loomed through the fog, the rifle barrel glinting wetly, the fog warping his shout—"Clear it!"—into a hollow echo that seemed to bounce off the unseen towers beyond.

A second patrol rolled closer, its Humvee's engine a low snarl that vibrated the asphalt, its headlights twin spears cutting through the mist, and the trio froze, pressed low against their cover. Jaber's blade stilled, his scar a pale slash as the beam swept the dumpster's edge, rust flaking off in the light like dried blood. Nova's breath caught, her good hand clutching the Nokia as the Humvee slowed, its tires squealing faintly on the wet road, a soldier leaning out with a thermal scope that hummed to life, its red lens glinting like a predator's eye.

Omar's kaftan blended with the van's shadow, his dagger flat against his thigh as the scope's beam danced across the street, grazing the mud-caked hem of his robe for a split second before the soldier barked—"Nothing, just fog"—and the Humvee rumbled on, its taillights fading into the gray.

The fog thinned near West Bay, the neon towers shimmered like a false promise against a backdrop of blood and smoke. The Embassy's outer checkpoint emerged at 10:45 p.m.—sandbags stacked chest-high, razor wire glinting with condensation, two U.S. Marines in flak jackets sweeping M4s across the street with mechanical precision, their night-vision goggles humming faintly, green lenses glinting like insect eyes in the gloom.

A Qatari soldier flanked them, his AK-47 slung low across his chest, his comms crackling as he paced, his breath misting in the chill air, the scent of gun oil and sweat mingling with the fog's damp bite. Beyond the checkpoint, the Consulate's floodlights cast a harsh glare, illuminating a concrete wall topped with more wire, a generator's low growl pulsing through the ground like a heartbeat.

Jaber hissed, his blade flicking open as he crouched behind a burned-out sedan. The cold steel of the sedan pressed against Nova's ribs, the scrape of unseen boots hissing louder through the thick fog. "Watcher's out there—yellow eyes in the fog, smelling our blood. Marines'll shoot first, ask later—your Lila's a ghost, Nova, and we're sitting ducks."

Nova's Nokia glowed faintly as she thumbed a text—Lila, N, 3 knocks, now. Every keypress felt like a gun cocked to her head, but she tapped the message anyway, her breath hitching as she sent it, her good hand slick with sweat and blood. "Three knocks—she'll know, Damascus signal from '22. Fog's our skin—move quiet, stay low."

They crept forward, the floodlights casting long, jagged shadows that writhed in the mist like living things, the air a stew of diesel fumes and the faint tang of damp earth churned by military boots. Jaber slunk along the sedan's blackened edge, his sack muffled against his hip, the rope inside shifting with a faint clunk as he moved, his blade poised as a Marine's rifle swung lazily, its barrel a black void cutting through the haze.

Nova followed, her boots slipping on the wet asphalt, a hiss escaping through gritted teeth as her ribs jolted, pain lancing up her spine like a white-hot wire, her vision blurring as she stumbled, catching herself on a sandbag with a muted thud, her sling smearing a streak of blood across the rough canvas. Omar hugged the curb, his kaftan pooling in the mud like a dark tide, his dagger low and steady as a Qatari soldier's flashlight swept the street, its beam glinting off the blade's arabesques for a fleeting second before he ducked, the light passing inches overhead, painting the asphalt in a sickly yellow glow.

A Marine barked—"Who's there?"—his rifle snapping up with a metallic click, the safety disengaging like a gunshot in the fog, and Nova froze, her heart slamming against her cracked ribs, her sling snagging on a coil of razor wire as she dropped to a knee, mud soaking through her jeans and chilling her skin. Jaber's blade stilled mid-spin, his scar a pale slash as he pressed flat against the sedan's husk, his breath held as the Marine's goggles glinted, scanning the shadows.

Omar's growl rumbled low in his chest, barely audible, his bulk a shadow melding with the sandbags as the Marine advanced, boots crunching gravel with deliberate menace, his comms crackling—"Possible contact, west side"—the static a harsh buzz that seemed to claw at the air.

The Qatari soldier swung his AK around, his finger hovering near the trigger, his eyes darting nervously as he muttered into his comms—"Movement, west gate"—and the second Marine flanked him, his M4's barrel trained on the fog, the green glow of his goggles cutting through the mist like twin lasers. Nova's pulse roared in her ears, a deafening drumbeat drowning out the generator's hum, her good hand shaking as she tapped the gate—three sharp knocks—her chipped nails scraping the steel with a faint scritch, the sound a desperate plea swallowed by the fog's deadening grip.

The Marines froze, rifles steady, their breaths misting in tight, controlled bursts, the Qatari soldier's AK twitching as he barked—"Identify, now, or we fire!"

Nova rose, her good hand raised, her voice a raw thread torn from a throat scratched bloody by the arena's collapse, her body trembling but her eyes blazing with unyielding fire. "Nova Mendelsohn—Aspire survivor. My crew knows the Obsidian Hand's lair. Get the ambassador–move now or answer to the world!"

The lead Marine's rifle held steady, its barrel a black tunnel aimed at her chest, his jaw tight under the helmet's shadow, his voice a cold bark cutting through the fog. "Mendelsohn's presumed dead—arena collapse, 12 hours ago. Prove it, or you're a ghost—or worse, one of them. Hands up, all of you—slow!"

Jaber's blade vanished up his sleeve, his hands rising with a scowl, his voice a growl as he spat into the mud. "Jaber ibn Faisal—dock rat, Old Port. She's alive, you blind bastard— check her story, or Watcher's yellow eyes'll be the last you see."

Omar loomed, his dagger sheathed with a faint clink, his hands up but his stance coiled, his rumble a warning that vibrated the air. "Omar al-Khatib—fisherman, smuggler, her shadow. Barga's real—Najdi script, Semtex stench. Test us, and you're wasting time."

Nova's satchel hit the ground with a wet thud, the cigarette pack and USB spilling onto the asphalt, her good hand pointing as blood dripped from her wrist, staining the Najdi scrawl with a dark smear.

"Najdi script—Barga coordinates, Obsidian Hand's mark! USB's got shots—truck south, sedan tail, Warehouse 12 relay, roof perch. I ran Aspire's tunnels—ribs cracked, shoulder popped, scalp torn, but breathing. Lila Hayes knows me—Damascus, three years back, three knocks, check it! Call her, or the next centipede's on you!"

The Qatari soldier's AK wavered, his comms buzzing as the lead Marine hesitated, his goggles scanning her battered frame—mud-caked jeans torn at the knees, bloodied sling hanging loose, the fire in her hazel eyes burning through the exhaustion.

The second Marine keyed his radio—"Hayes, west gate, unknown claiming Mendelsohn, three knocks"—his voice clipped and skeptical, the static crackling like a storm on the horizon. A beat passed, the fog thickening as the generator's growl pulsed louder, the rifles steady, the air taut with the promise of violence—then Lila's voice cut through, sharp and urgent—"It's her—let her in, now!"

The lead Marine's rifle dipped, his jaw twitching as he waved them through, grudging and slow, the gate grinding open with a harsh buzz of steel on steel, the sound scraping Nova's nerves like a blade on bone.

Jaber's blade stayed hidden, his scowl deepening as he stepped past, while Omar's bulk filled the gap, his kaftan dripping mud onto the concrete threshold. The gate slammed shut behind them with a clang that echoed in the fog, sealing them inside the Consulate's fortress as the Marines resumed their sweep, their goggles glinting like sentinels in the mist.

Inside, the lobby was a sterile hum of fluorescent lights flickering overhead, their buzz a maddening counterpoint to the crackle of encrypted comms echoing from unseen rooms. The air was sharp with antiseptic and the bitter tang of burnt coffee from a pot congealing on a counter since dawn, its surface a scummy black mirror reflecting the tension.

Lila Hayes emerged from a side corridor, her petite frame dwarfed by the concrete walls, her blonde hair disheveled from hours on duty, her blue eyes widening behind glasses as she took in Nova's condition—mud-caked jeans shredded at the knees, a sling soaked with blood and sweat, her chestnut hair matted with grime and streaked with crimson where a chunk had been torn from her scalp, her face pale and drawn, lips cracked and trembling with each shallow breath.

"Jesus, Nova—you're a wreck," Lila gasped, her voice a mix of shock and urgency as she waved them forward, her heels clicking on the tiled floor. "You're bleeding—ribs, shoulder, head—how are you even standing? We've got a medic—move, now!"

Nova waved her off with her good hand, a sharp gesture that sent a jolt of pain through her ribs, her voice a hoarse thread.

"No time—Ambassador first, intel's burning. Patch me after."

But Lila's eyes flicked to the blood dripping from Nova's wrist, pooling on the floor in dark, glossy drops, and she grabbed a passing staffer—a wiry young man in a wrinkled shirt, his badge reading Consular Aide—her tone brooking no argument. "Get Dr. Patel, trauma kit, this room—five minutes ago!"

The aide bolted, and Lila ushered them into a secure room, its walls lined with monitors flickering with chaos—#DohaHorror trending on X, Tariq's briefing looping in grainy loops, posts piling up like a digital landslide. Ambassador Richard Voss waited behind a steel table, a wiry man in a rumpled suit, his gray hair thinning to wisps, his eyes piercing behind bifocals perched on a hawkish nose. His pen tapped a relentless beat against the table, denting the metal, his voice a whipcrack slicing through the hum.

“Who the hell are you three? Consulate’s on lockdown—Aspire’s a war zone, and you waltz in like ghosts. Give me something concrete, or you’re out—or worse, detained.”

Before Nova could answer, the door swung open, and Dr. Dalia Al-Hassan—a compact woman in a white coat, her black hair pulled into a tight bun, her hands gloved and steady— strode in, a trauma kit slung over her shoulder, its contents clanking faintly—gauze, scissors, vials rattling in their slots. Her dark eyes scanned Nova with clinical precision, her voice calm but firm.

“You—sit, now. You’re bleeding out, and I’m not arguing. Talk while I work.”

Nova slumped into a chair with a hiss, her ribs flaring, the edges of her vision fuzzed, her head lolling sideways, consciousness a frayed wire as she dropped her satchel onto the table, its contents spilling out—the cigarette pack, its Najdi script stark; the USB drive, scratched and muddy; the nautical chart, stained and curled.

“Nova Mendelsohn—reporter, Aspire survivor, missing since dawn,” she rasped, wincing as Al-Hassan cut away the sling with a swift snip, exposing her shoulder, swollen and purple, the joint grotesquely misaligned. “Jaber ibn Faisal and Omar al-Khatib, dock runners, my eyes in the Old Port. Barga Al Kharaz—70 miles southwest, Obsidian Hand’s lair, Najdi script tying it to pre-Islamic vengeance, a grudge reborn in Semtex and blood. Truck south, sedan tail, Warehouse 12 relay—shots on the drive, roof perch, Watcher’s nest. The centipede was war—22 hours ‘til ransom or fire. Get the Secretary of State, President, Defense—now!”

Al-Hassan’s gloved hands moved fast, probing Nova’s shoulder with a firm touch that drew a sharp gasp, her voice steady as she worked.

“Dislocated—anterior, bad. Ribs—cracked, maybe broken, bruising’s deep. Scalp laceration—four inches, clotted but oozing. You’re concussed—pupils sluggish. Hold still— shoulder’s going back, then I brace it.”

She gripped Nova’s arm, her other hand on her collarbone, and with a quick, practiced jerk—pop—the joint snapped into place, a sickening crunch echoing in the room as Nova’s vision whited out, a choked scream escaping before she bit it back, her good hand clawing the table’s edge, leaving bloody smears.

Jaber flinched, his blade spinning in his hand, his growl cutting through. “Watcher’s yellow eyes—dock’s her web, taunting us with her tablet. Barga’s the head—Najdi’s their oath, Semtex their fist. Cut it off, or it bites deeper.”

Omar’s rumble followed, his dagger gleaming as he loomed, his shadow swallowing half the room. “Fog’s thinning—military’s loud, Barga’s quiet, brewing hell. Second strike’s coming— Najdi script’s their banner, vengeance older than the sands.”

Al-Hassan swabbed Nova’s scalp with antiseptic, the sting sharp as she stitched the gash with a needle and thread—five quick sutures, the thread pulling tight through torn skin, blood welling and wiped away with gauze that piled crimson on the table.

“Scalp’s closed—concussion’s mild, but you’re pushing it. Ribs need wrapping—breathe shallow, or you’ll puncture something.” She taped a compression bandage around Nova’s torso, the fabric tight and cold against her bruised skin, each wrap a fresh jolt she endured with gritted teeth, her breath hitching as Al-Hassan secured it with a final tug.

Voss’s pen stilled, his eyes narrowing as he scanned the pack’s scrawl, the USB, the chart, his breath a sharp hiss. “Najdi—tribal roots, pre-Islamic… Barga's off-grid—Interpol's sniffing, but this…"

He grabbed the secure line, his fingers cracking the plastic as he barked—"Patch me to State—Logan, Langford, Reyes, Renshaw, Strickland, live, now! Mendelsohn's alive, intel's burning—Barga Al Kharaz, 70 miles southwest, Obsidian Hand's core, 22 hours ticking!"

Al-Hassan finished, sliding a sling over Nova's shoulder—clean, white, stiff with starch—her voice low as she packed her kit.

"You're patched—shoulder's braced, ribs wrapped, scalp stitched. Painkillers—take two, no more, or you'll fog out. You're a mess, but you'll hold—for now." She stepped back, her gloves snapping off, stained red, as the line crackled to life.

The White House Situation Room bled through, static and urgency thick in the air, the scent of burnt coffee and the hum of screens casting a bluish glow over weary faces. President Logan Calder's voice growled, rough with fatigue, his tie stained with mustard, his pen snapping—crack—ink bleeding as he leaned over a map, Doha in red, Barga a smudge.

"Voss, what's this—Barga Al Kharaz? Mendelsohn's a ghost. Give me something solid, or we're chasing shadows while the Dow bleeds—900 down."

Secretary of State Victoria Langford cut in, her voice crisp, glasses glinting. "Najdi script— pre-Islamic vengeance? A leap, Richard. Interpol's got chatter—Damascus, Tehran—but Barga's thin. Delta's staging, IDF and 50th Brigade on edge—UK's in, France and Germany waffling. Blind move, we risk blowback."

DNI Chief Mark Reyes crackled through, gruff and static-edged. "SIGINT's spiking—Barga's alive, 'next' and 'fire' on dark channels. Ransom's bait—second strike's the play.

Coordinates alone? We need eyes—military's a hammer, this is a scalpel."

Secretary of Defense General Alex Renshaw's voice was steady, medals glinting. "Delta's 50 miles out—boots in six hours if green-lit. IDF's tanks, 50th Brigade's artillery hot, but Barga's a black hole—70 miles, no recon. Storm blind, we lose men, trigger Semtex. Intel's thin—Najdi's a relic."

Chairman of the Joint Chiefs Admiral Jordan Strickland's tone was sharp, his cap tilted. "Semtex matches Barga's range—Soviet stock, but no satellite lock, dunes eating our eyes. Rush in, it's a trap—pull back, they strike. We need more, Calder—time's bleeding."

Calder's fist slammed—thud—coffee sloshing onto the map. "Five hundred billion's a taunt—no payment, but Barga… Najdi, Semtex—it's something. Delta moves, we risk a bloodbath—hold, we risk fire. Langford, diplomacy's dead—Reyes, SIGINT's vague— Renshaw, Strickland, you're split. Call it!"

Langford tightened. "Hold—buy time, stall ransom, let Interpol crack the hack. Military's loud, we're blind—Barga could be a feint."

Reyes countered. "Move—surgical, Delta scout. SIGINT's hot—Barga's the nest. Waiting's weakness—they'll hit harder."

Renshaw hardened. "Scout—Delta recon, drones if fog lifts. Barga's real, but we need eyes—Najdi's a clue, not a map."

Strickland nodded. "Recon—small team, confirm the lair. Rush, we detonate it—hold too long, they do. Middle ground—probe."

The debate spiraled, voices clashing, the clock ticking—22 hours shrinking.

Nova's patience snapped, her good hand slamming the table—

bang—pain flaring as she rasped, "Enough—Nova Mendelsohn, alive, bleeding, with the truth! You're circling while Barga brews hell—Najdi's their soul, vengeance in flesh and Semtex! Announce ransom's paid—bait 'em, buy time. Jaber, Omar, and I infiltrate—Old Port's our skin, we've tracked Watcher, cracked their relay. Track us—Delta, drones, silent. We flush 'em out, drag 'em open—then you hit, no blind storm, no ash. 22 hours—use us, or lose it!"

Silence fell, Calder's breath rasping, ink dripping. Langford exhaled. "Mendelsohn—bold… Fake payment—diplomacy's mask. Infiltration's risky, but she's got the scent."

Reyes calculated. "SIGINT backs her—track her, drones, Delta shadow—flush 'em, then strike. Ballsy—scalpel first."

Renshaw nodded. "Delta tracks—10-man, silent. She's bait, they're the net—confirm Semtex, then cut."

Strickland agreed. "Announce ransom—8 hours to stage, drones up, Delta on her. She's the spear—pierce, expose, end it."

Calder growled, "Do it—Voss, she's your asset. Announce payment talks, 8-hour window— Langford, sell it. Reyes, SIGINT—Renshaw, Strickland, Delta tracks. Mendelsohn, flush 'em—22 hours, go!"

Voss cut the line, bifocals glinting as he turned. "You're in—tracked, bait and blade. Delta's prepping—drones, comms, 8 hours. How do you get into Barga? Lay it out."

The clock was already bleeding minutes—eight hours slipping to seven before anyone even moved.

Nova traced the chart, voice steady despite the ache. "Barga—70 miles southwest, rock caverns, tribal ground. Truck tracks, skiff hauls—southern wadi, dry, deep cover. Skiff from Old Port, 20 miles south to Umm Al Houl—paddle the last mile, dusk cloaks us. Jack a truck—smuggler rigs, rusted, hotwire easy. 50 miles overland, Jaber's dune cuts.

"Wadi at midnight, park half-mile out, crawl in—sand muffles. Two entrances—main cavern, guarded; vent shaft, narrow, high, butts below. Climb—rope, grit—drop inside. Tablet's footage—Semtex east, monitors west, Commander central. Smoke 'em out—fumes, spark—Delta catches the scramble."

Jaber's blade spun, his growl doubtful. "Vent shaft? Barga's a death trap—you're busted, Nova. Watcher'll spot us—dunes bare at dusk, wadi's a choke. Skiff's loud, truck's a crapshoot. One guard, we're done—Delta lags, we're ash."

Omar rumbled, tracing the wadi. "Wadi's ingress, vent's sneak—but 70 miles of sand's a gauntlet. Skiff's a risk—truck's noisy, vent's tight. Smoke's clever, but Semtex blows, we're gone—Delta's the hinge."

Nova slammed the chart—thwack—"Skiff's quiet paddled—truck's there, I've jacked worse. Dunes—Jaber's trails. Vent's their slip—Watcher's cocky. Spark the fumes, they bolt— Delta's live, comms in our ears. We're bait—22 hours, we crack it."

Jaber grinned, convinced. "Lunatic—you've pulled crazier. Smugglers' rigs, dune ruts— vent's their mistake. Delta's fast—scar-face is mine."

Omar nodded, "Skiff's a ghost—wadi's quiet, vent fits. Delta's Yemen hunts—steel holds. Barga burns, or we do."

Lila stepped forward, her voice sharp with disbelief as she grabbed Nova's good arm, her fingers trembling slightly.

"Nova, this is insane—you're walking into a terrorist lair with cracked ribs and a prayer? This isn't sniffing out Syrian athletic corruption in '22—this is a suicide run against a death cult with bombs!"

Nova met her gaze, her hazel eyes unyielding despite the pain. “Syria was a warm-up, Lila—this is the real fight. I’ve got Jaber and Omar, Delta’s shadow, and 22 hours to stop a war. Insane’s my edge. We take Barga down – or it buries us all.”

Voss scribbled, “Skiff, truck, wadi, vent—smoke and flush. Delta’s on—10-man, drones, comms, 8 hours. Rest, gear up—Barga’s yours.”

VEIL 19

The World's Gambit

The Situation Room thrummed with tension, the air heavy with burnt coffee, overheating electronics, and sweat. Encrypted screens pulsed a cold blue across exhausted faces.

It was 11:30 p.m. EST—6:30 a.m. in Doha, where the dawn fog still draped the Gulf's edge like a shroud—and the secure video feed flickered to life, bathing the room in a cold, bluish glow that etched deep shadows across the faces of President Logan Calder, Secretary of State Victoria Langford, DNI Chief Mark Reyes, Secretary of Defense General Alex Renshaw, and Chairman of the Joint Chiefs Admiral Jordan Strickland.

Calder's tie hung loose, a mustard stain smeared across its silk from a ham and swiss sandwich he'd abandoned hours ago, his ink-smeared fingers gripping a fresh pen as he leaned into the microphone, his voice a gravelly rumble that sliced through the low buzz of machinery.

"No time for ceremony. Mazar, el-Khoury, Al-Mazrouei, Moreau,

Borodin—listen close. We have a plan. It's already live. Barga Al Kharaz, 70 miles southwest of Doha, is the Obsidian Hand's lair—confirmed by Nova Mendelsohn, alive, battered but sharp, with intel cutting like a blade through the fog. We're announcing ransom talks, faking payment to buy an eight-hour window. Mendelsohn's team—her and two dock runners—will infiltrate, tracked by Delta Force, micro-drones, silent as shadows. They flush the bastards out, we strike hard and fast. Questions—hit me now."

Israeli Prime Minister Eitan Mazar's image snapped onto the split screen from Jerusalem, ex-military steel in his eyes, voice as taut as a drawn bow, his gray eyes narrowing behind rimless glasses, his voice clipped with the precision of a former IDF general, the faint clatter of a distant telex machine threading through his feed.

"Calder, you're staking this on a half-dead reporter and a pair of dock rats to crack a terrorist stronghold? How do you know Barga's not a feint—smoke to mask something bigger? My 50th Brigade's artillery is hot, IDF tanks are rolling toward the border, but we're flying blind without satellite confirmation. What's your fail-safe if Mendelsohn's crew collapses—or worse, gets turned?"

Calder's jaw tightened, his pen tapping the table once—tap—before he leaned closer, his growl steady but edged with impatience. "You think satellites win wars? Mendelsohn's fought on their turf with blood. That's our edge. Barga's no feint—SIGINT's got 'next' and 'fire' lighting up those coords like a damn flare. Satellite's blind 'cause of the dunes and fog, but her intel's got Najdi script tying it to the Obsidian Hand's core. Fail-safe? Delta's 50 miles out—if she collapses, they roll in hot, Semtex's the target. Turned? She's got no love for these bastards—her ribs are cracked from their last dance."

Lebanese Prime Minister Ziad el-Khoury appeared from Beirut, its streets already rumbling with unrest, loomed like a powder keg behind him. His dark beard streaked with silver, his tone a weary blend of exhaustion and skepticism, the distant hum of morning traffic and a muezzin's call seeping through his window.

"And what about escalation, Calder? Hezbollah's antennae are up—Tehran's whispering in their ears. You flush this Obsidian Hand north into my territory, and Beirut's a tinderbox waiting for a match. How tight's your Delta leash—eight hours enough to choke this before it spills over my border?"

Calder's eyes flicked to el-Khoury's screen, his voice dropping to a controlled rumble. "Ziad, we're not flushing 'em north—Delta's got orders to pin 'em in Barga, cut their legs off before they crawl your way. Hezbollah's twitchy, sure, but we're looping your army in post-call with exact grids—your boys can plug the gaps if they bolt. Eight hours is tight, but Delta's leash is iron—they've run ops in worse hellholes than this. Tehran whispers all it wants; we're not giving 'em a spark."

IOC President Sheikh Tariq bin Fahd Al-Mazrouei's image flickered from a fortified office in Doha's Aspire Zone, his keffiyeh pristine despite the sleepless night, his deep voice resonating with a barely contained fury, his hands folded over a tablet streaming X posts— #DohaHorror trending, clips of the centipede looping in grotesque silence.

Beside him stood Vice President Jacques Moreau, his wireframe glasses slipping down his nose, his suit rumpled from pacing the crisis room, and Vice President Viktor Mikhailovich Borodin, his broad frame rigid, his gray eyes cold as he clutched a coffee mug, the steam curling in the dim light. The three IOC leaders, united in Doha's crucible, faced the world's scrutiny together.

Tariq spoke first, his voice a thunderclap over the faint hum of air conditioning battling the Gulf's heat. The Games had been Qatar's promise to the world. Now they teetered over an abyss.

"This is my soil, my Games—six athletes butchered, six more

dying, a nightmare broadcast to billions. Mendelsohn's intel—Najdi script, pre-Islamic vengeance—it's solid, I'll grant you, but infiltration? How do you guarantee they don't detonate their Semtex stockpile the second she breaches their lair? The IOC's neck is on the guillotine—Qatar bleeds, and the G20's eyes are boring into us."

Calder's pen stilled, his gaze locking on Tariq, his tone gruff but deliberate. "Tariq, I get it—your Games, your blood. Mendelsohn's not storming in guns blazing—she's flushing 'em with smoke, not sparking Semtex. Guarantee? There's none in war, but her plan's got drones mapping every crate before we hit. They detonate early, we've got EMP bursts to fry their triggers mid-breath. Qatar's bleeding, yeah, but this stops the hemorrhage—eight hours, and Barga's ash, not your neck."

Moreau adjusted his glasses, his French accent sharp with unease, his hands trembling slightly as he gripped the edge of Tariq's desk, the faint clink of his watch against the wood audible.

"Oui, Calder, execution is the devil here. Micro-drones, Delta shadows—how do you keep this covert in Doha's chaos? One leak, one jittery finger on a trigger, and the Obsidian Hand either bolts or strikes early—I've seen the streets out there, military everywhere, fog barely lifting. What's your contingency if Mendelsohn gets burned before the trap springs?"

Calder's lips twitched, a grim half-smirk fading fast as he leaned back, his voice a low growl. "Moreau, covert's the whole damn point—drones are the size of flies, Delta's ghosts in the sand. Doha's chaos is our cover—military noise drowns the hum, fog hides the tracks. Leak? We've got Mendelsohn's comms locked tighter than Fort Knox—encrypted implants, no chatter. She burns, Delta's contingency kicks in—10-man team shifts from shadow to strike, hits Barga before they blink. Eight hours isn't a luxury, it's a blade—we wield it."

Borodin's voice followed, a low growl thick with Slavic weight, his mug slamming down on the desk with a dull thud, his gray eyes glinting as he leaned closer to the camera, the distant wail of a siren threading through Doha's morning.

"And this ransom bluff—G20 footing a phantom bill? Russia's in, but my FSB's picking up chatter here—Najdi clans, ancient blood feuds, Semtex trails snaking from Chechnya's black markets to this damned desert. Eight hours is a razor's edge—Delta's elite, but dunes swallow signals like graves swallow bones. How do you track if comms go dark with all this sand and fog?"

Calder's pen tapped twice—tap-tap—his eyes narrowing as he met Borodin's stare, his growl sharpening. "Viktor, the ransom's a ghost—no G20 wallet opens, just words to buy time. Your FSB chatter's gold—we've got it too, Najdi clans and Chechen Semtex lining up with Mendelsohn's script. Eight hours is razor-thin, but Delta's got ATVs to chew the dunes, drones with redundant relays—comms go dark, they've got thermal scopes and boots on sand. Fog's a bitch, but it cuts both ways—hides us as much as them. We track 'til the end, signal or no."

Langford leaned forward, her blonde bob steady despite the fatigue carving lines around her eyes, her glasses glinting as she adjusted them, her voice crisp and measured, cutting through the cacophony of doubt.

"Mazar, el-Khoury—Barga's no feint; SIGINT's screaming—coded bursts, 'next' and 'fire,' pulsing from those coordinates. Mendelsohn's team isn't just survivors—they're Old Port-hardened, dock rats who breathe shadows better than our satellites pierce sand. IDF, Hezbollah—we're briefing your intel post-call, keeping this surgical, no spill. Fail-safe's Delta—10-man team, night-vision, silenced weapons, staged 50 miles out, ready to pivot. Tariq, Moreau, Borodin—Semtex's the wild card, but she's flushing, not fighting; drones map the lair, we hit when they break, not before. Comms implants have redundant channels, drones relay if signals drop. G20's briefed after the announcement—payment's a mask, no cash changes hands."

Mazar's jaw tightened, his finger tapping a map off-screen with a rhythm like a war drum, his voice a growl. "Surgical's a pretty word, Calder, but my Knesset's howling—six Israelis stitched into that abomination. Delta pivots how—extraction if she's nabbed, or full assault if she's dead? Eight hours is tight—dunes eat time like they eat men."

Calder's grip on the pen tightened, ink smearing further as he leaned in, his voice a gravelly bark. "Eitan, your six don't die for nothing—Delta pivots to assault if she's nabbed or dead, no hesitation. Extraction's Plan B if she's breathing and Semtex's still cold—otherwise, it's full throttle, Hellfire and boots. Dunes eat time, sure, but Delta's eaten worse—eight hours is enough to bury Barga, not us."

El-Khoury's brow furrowed, his voice rising over the distant wail of a siren piercing Beirut's dawn. "And my border's not a suggestion—you flush them north, I've got militias itching for blood. Delta's leash—give me Barga's exact grid, I'll loop my army in, keep this contained before it's a regional blaze."

Calder nodded sharply, his growl softening just enough to carry reassurance. "Ziad, you'll get the grid—exact coords, meter by meter, post-call. Your army's the wall, not the spear— Delta's leash is tight, they're not flushing north unless we've misread the wind. Eight hours keeps it in Qatar—your militias won't need to fire a shot if we play this right."

Tariq's hands unclenched, his eyes blazing like coals, his voice a controlled thunder as he gestured to the window, where Doha's fog-choked skyline loomed. "Containment's my nightmare—my military's roaring through these streets, but Barga's a silent void

70 miles out. Mendelsohn's vent shaft—smoke plan—how do you know they don't blow their stash the second they smell her? IOC's credibility's ash if this craters—Qatar's bleeding now."

Calder's pen dropped to the table with a faint clatter, his hands flattening as he leaned forward. In his head he knew containment was a dream, but in war dreams burned fast. "Tariq, containment's the goal—Barga's a void 'til we light it up. Smoke's a calculated risk, not a matchstick—drones spot the Semtex first, EMP's ready if they twitch. They blow it early, we're still ahead—Delta's close enough to choke the blast zone. Your credibility holds if we pull this off—eight hours, Qatar's whole again."

Moreau nodded, his tone urgent, his glasses slipping further as he leaned into the frame, the faint clatter of a dropped pen echoing from his jittery hands. "Exactement—smoke's clever, but Semtex's a beast. Drones catch the scramble—then what? Ground strike, air barrage? Timing's a guillotine's drop—one misstep in this desert, and it's carnage."

Calder's eyes flicked to Moreau, his growl softening but firm. "Jacques, drones catch it, we choose—ground strike if they dig in, Hellfire if they run. Timing's locked—Delta syncs to the second with drone feeds. Misstep? We've got layers—EMP, thermal, boots on sand. Eight hours isn't a gamble, it's a clock—we don't miss."

Borodin grunted, his thick fingers drumming a slow tattoo on the desk, his growl heavy with pragmatism as he glanced at Tariq. "Timing, yes—eight hours to stage, infiltrate, flush. Delta's fast, but dunes are slow—trucks bog down, sandstorms brew unbidden. Contingency if Mendelsohn's caught—alive or dead? She's your spear—what if the shaft snaps out there?"

Calder's gaze hardened, meeting Borodin's, his voice a low, unyielding rumble. "Viktor, dunes slow 'em, not us—ATVs cut through, drones ride the wind. Mendelsohn's caught, alive or dead, she's bait—comms stay live, Delta tracks her signal 'til the end. Shaft snaps, we've got the head—10-man team shifts to kill mode, Semtex's ours. Eight hours, sand or storm, we finish this."

Renshaw's medals glinted as he leaned into the mic, his gravelly voice steady as granite, cutting through the storm of questions. "Mazar—Delta pivots to assault if she's compromised; extraction's secondary, Semtex's the prize—six Israelis don't die for nothing. El-Khoury—coordinates drop post-call, your army's a backstop, not the spearhead; we'll grid Barga to the meter. Tariq—smoke's a spark, not a blast; drones confirm crate positions, we hit with precision—Hellfire if they bolt, ground teams if they dig in. Moreau—air strike's queued, synced to drone feeds, timing's locked to the second. Borodin—sand's hell, but Delta's got ATVs, drones adjust for storms; if she's caught, she's bait 'til the end—comms stay live, we adapt, alive or dead."

Strickland's naval cap tilted slightly, his scarred finger tracing an invisible line on his own map, his voice sharp and decisive. "Fail-safes layered—Delta's got thermal scopes, drones carry EMP bursts to fry their triggers if Semtex twitches. Eight hours—dusk hits, Mendelsohn's in, we're poised. Contingency's fluid—sand shifts, we shift faster."

Calder's pen tapped once, hard—thwack—the sound a gavel's fall, his growl final, brooking no further dissent. "It's set—announcement's at 6 p.m. Doha time, IOC fronts it from here, G20 backs the lie. Mendelsohn moves at dusk—Delta's her shadow, Hellfire's the fist. Questions done—execute."

The screens blinked off one by one, leaving the Situation Room. The hum faded. Only the desert's silence remained, waiting to be broken by blood and fire.

Seventy miles southwest, the desert's red rock swallowed the dawn's faint light, Barga Al Kharaz a festering wound carved into the dunes—a labyrinth of caverns where the Obsidian Hand wove their next grotesque tapestry, driven by a vengeance as old as the sands they claimed. The air inside hung thick and oppressive, a miasma of sour sweat, the chemical tang of Semtex, the coppery reek of drying blood, and the faint, cloying rot of flesh left too long in the heat.

Flickering fluorescent tubes buzzed overhead, their sickly green light casting jagged shadows across a cavern strewn with crates—stacked high with explosives, their Cyrillic labels peeling like old skin—and a central table littered with maps, laptops, a tangle of wires, and a severed hand, its pale fingers curled in a rigor mortis grasp, nails chipped and blood-crusted, a grim relic from the centipede's assembly.

"The Commander," loomed over the table, his scar-ravaged face a map of ancient wars— jagged lines crisscrossing his left cheek, a puckered gash splitting his brow, his yellow eyes glinting with a predator's malice. His Najdi dagger, its hilt worn smooth by decades of grip, traced Doha's outline on a map, the blade nicking the paper with each deliberate stroke, a ritual of intent. His black robe hung loose, stained with desert dust and the faint splatter of blood, his voice a low growl that seemed to rumble from the cavern's depths.

"Twenty-two hours—ransom's due, or they're bluffing. No payment, no mercy—Najdi blood demands a reckoning. The wheel turns next—grotesque, eternal, a monument to their shame. The Olympics mocked our sands, turned our legacy to glitter—Najdi vengeance rises now."

The Najdi vengeance Khalid invoked wasn't mere rhetoric—it was a fire kindled centuries before Islam's crescent rose, rooted in the harsh dunes of central Arabia, where the Najd tribes forged their honor in blood and sand. Before the Prophet's revelations unified the peninsula, the Najd was a crucible of warring clans—Banu Hanifa, Banu Tamim, Banu 'Abs—bound by a code of retribution that demanded an eye for an eye, a life for a life, a debt paid in slaughter. Their pre-Islamic odes, etched in oral verse, sang of raids and reprisals, of wells poisoned and caravans razed, a legacy of unrelenting vengeance against any who dared defile their dominion.

The Obsidian Hand saw the Olympic Games—an opulent spectacle of global unity hosted on Qatar's soil—as a desecration of that ancient pride, a glittering insult to the Najd's austere honor. Doha's towers, the IOC's pomp, the athletes' parade—it was a modern idol erected on sacred sand, a betrayal of their ancestors' unyielding spirit. The centipede was their opening curse; the wheel would be their apocalyptic sermon.

"The Arbiter," stood to his left, his lean frame taut as a bowstring, his hawkish nose casting a sharp shadow across his bearded face. His gray eyes flicked over a ledger—names, dates, debts inked in precise Arabic script—his voice a cold, measured hiss, the sound of a judge passing sentence.

"Twelve more—six athletes, six diplomats—chained, flayed, sewn into the wheel. Spines snapped, flesh fused—Semtex vests, 12 kilos each, shrapnel- packed. Corniche at dusk tomorrow—live to billions. IOC's scrambling, G20's silent—they'll pay, or it spins, fire and meat raining over Doha. We've got the bodies—two Israeli swimmers, a Lebanese runner, three French fencers, a British envoy, five others snatched from the embassies last night. Alive—for now. The Games mocked our blood—these twelve pay the price."

"The Scribe," hunched over a laptop, his wiry fingers dancing across keys, his glasses fogged with sweat, his voice a rapid, nervous chatter as he scrolled X feeds—#DohaHorror spiking, conspiracy threads blooming like weeds. "Social's a storm—Tariq's briefing's looping, Mendelsohn's a ghost they're chasing. I've hacked the streams—dark pools, encrypted relays. Wheel goes live, I'll flood it—every screen, every phone, unskippable. Najdi chants overlay the groans—vengeance carved in code. Ransom fails, it's ready— servers in Damascus, proxies in Tehran, untraceable. The Olympics crowned their heroes on our graves—now the world sees our ghosts rise."

"The Watcher," perched on a Semtex crate, her lean frame coiled like a desert cat, her keffiyeh streaked with red dust, her cracked tablet glowing in her hands as she tapped its screen—Warehouse 12 footage, skiff mud, Mendelsohn's shadow flickering in grainy stills. Her voice was a venomous hiss, her dark eyes narrowing with a hunter's focus.

"Mendelsohn's alive—sniffing, clawing, close. Warehouse 12's hers—red mud on the tires, Najdi scrawl on the tarp. She's got my perch, my taunt—tablet's bait, she's bitten. We trap her here—Barga's jaws snap, her corpse their warning. Ransom or not, she dies—yellow eyes see all. She's the West's hound, chasing our shadow—the Games sent her, they'll bury her."

"The Enforcer," loomed near the cavern's mouth, his massive frame a wall of muscle beneath a tattered tactical vest, his shaved head gleaming with sweat, his fists scarred and knuckles freshly bloodied. His voice was a guttural snarl, his meaty hand gripping a sledgehammer, its head crusted with hair and gore.

"Wheel's mine—chains forged, steel frame's up, hydraulic lift's rigged. Twelve's easy—snap the spines, flay the backs, sew 'em in. Vests fit tight—remote triggers, my thumb on the button. Corniche's soft—crowds panic, no cover. I'll haul 'em, break 'em, watch 'em spin— ransom fails, I light the fuse. The Olympics danced on our dunes—this wheel crushes their pride."

"The Keeper," crouched near a row of steel cages along the cavern's eastern wall, her gaunt face shadowed by a hood, her bony fingers clutching a ring of keys that jangled faintly as she moved. Her voice was a dry whisper, her eyes darting to the cages where muffled whimpers leaked through—12 figures, bound, gagged, their uniforms torn, embassy IDs glinting in the dim light.

"Prisoners secured—athletes from Aspire, diplomats from West Bay. Drugged, quiet— ketamine's holding, but they'll wake for the wheel. Supplies stocked—water, bandages, just enough to keep 'em alive 'til dusk. Ransom or not, they're ours—Najdi ghosts guard 'em. The Games flaunted wealth—we chain their idols."

Dr. Samir Haddad worked in a corner alcove, his white coat stained with rust-red streaks, his gloved hands steady as he stitched a severed finger onto a mannequin—a grotesque test for the wheel's seams. His voice was a clinical murmur, his glasses fogged as he adjusted a tray of scalpels, needles, and thread.

"Flesh is ready—flaying's precise, spines crack clean with a mallet, sutures hold under tension. Vests won't chafe—skin's prepped, ketamine doses timed to wake 'em mid-spin. Semtex's stable—12 kilos each, wired to Darius's triggers. Wheel turns, they burst—grotesque art, live forever. The Olympics glorified bodies—we remake them in ruin."

Khalid's dagger plunged into the map, pinning Doha's heart, the blade quivering as his growl deepened, his yellow eyes sweeping the circle.

"Ransom's a lie—they'll stall, bluff, send their dogs. Mendelsohn's the tip—Watcher, you bait her, trap her. Arbiter, you tally the blood—12's the count, no less. Scribe, you broadcast—world sees Najdi rise. Enforcer, you build—wheel spins true. Keeper, you hold—prisoners breathe 'til dusk. Doctor, you craft—flesh bends to our will. 22 hours—no payment, Corniche burns, the wheel turns—fire and meat, their gods weep. The Olympics crowned infidels on our sand—this is our requiem.

The Najdi grudge fueling the Obsidian Hand wasn't a fleeting rage—it was a resurrection of a pre-Islamic ethos where honor was a currency forged in retribution, where the Najd tribes carved their names in the desert with blades and oaths.

The Olympic Games, to them, weren't a celebration of human spirit but a colonial echo— Western ideals draped in gold, silver, and bronze, imposed on a land they claimed as theirs by blood-right. Qatar's modernity, its gleaming towers and global stage, was a betrayal of the Najd's austere past, a past where the tribes resisted empires—Sassanids, Byzantines, and later the Ottomans—with a ferocity that left scars in the sand.

The centipede was their warning, a grotesque nod to their ancestors' raids; the wheel was their judgment, a spinning altar of flesh and fire to punish the world's hubris, to reclaim a legacy they believed buried beneath Doha's glass and steel.

"The Arbiter's" ledger snapped shut, his gray eyes glinting with fanatic resolve. "Blood's tallied—12's the oath, Najdi ancestors demand it. Corniche dusk—embassies crumble, IOC kneels. I've mapped the snatch—routes from West Bay, Aspire's backroads, blind spots in Qatar's net. Ransom fails, they pay in screams. The Games mocked our dead—this settles the debt."

"The Scribe's" fingers paused, his glasses slipping as he grinned, a feral edge to his chatter. "Streams are primed—dark web's humming, X's a tinderbox. I've looped the centipede—12 million views, climbing. Wheel goes live, I'll hijack satellites—CNN, BBC, Al Jazeera, no escape. Najdi chants echo—'Blood for blood, sand for sand.' Ransom's irrelevant—world watches either way. The Olympics erased our voice—this screams it back."

"The Watcher" slid off the crate, her tablet clattering as she drew a curved blade from her belt, its edge glinting in the flickering light. "Mendelsohn's mine—tablet's the lure, Barga's the snare.

I'll perch high—vent shaft's my nest, yellow eyes on the wadi. She climbs, I cut— her blood stains the sand, her team follows. Delta's drones—EMP fries 'em, my signal's dark. Ransom or not, she's carrion. The Games sent her to hunt us—Najdi shadows hunt back."

"The Enforcer" hefted the sledgehammer, slamming it onto a crate—crack—wood splintering as his snarl echoed. "Wheel's ready—steel's welded, hydraulics hum, chains bite. I'll break 'em slow—spines first, then skin. Vests clip on—shrapnel's nails, bolts, glass. Corniche dusk—I'll stand in the fire, watch it spin. Ransom fails, I press—boom, blood, beauty. The Olympics built their stage—this tears it down."

"The Keeper" rattled her keys, her whisper rising as she tapped a cage, a muffled sob answering from within. "They're fresh—Swedish swimmer's strong, American runner's fast, French fencer's feisty. Drugged 'til dusk—ketamine's low, adrenaline spikes 'em for the show. Ransom's a ghost—they're mine 'til the wheel rolls. The Games paraded their champions—Najdi hands bind them now."

Dr. Haddad peeled off his gloves, revealing hands stained with antiseptic and blood, his murmur clinical yet gleeful. "Sutures tested—mannequin holds, flesh will too. Flaying's art— peel slow, keep 'em alive. Spines crack lateral—mallet's weighted, one strike. Vests sync to vitals—heartbeats trigger if Darius delays. Wheel's my canvas—ransom or not, it's grotesque perfection. The Olympics sculpted flesh—we carve it anew."

"The Commander" yanked the dagger free, the map tearing, his growl a command that reverberated off the rock. "Mendelsohn's a fly—swat her, trap her team. Ransom's their stall—we strike regardless. Wheel's the oath—Najdi vengeance, pre-Islamic fire reborn. 22 hours—Corniche dusk, it spins. Arbiter plans, Scribe spreads, Watcher hunts, Enforcer breaks, Keeper binds, Doctor weaves. No payment, no peace—Doha drowns in blood and ash. The Olympics dared to shine—this buries their light."

The cavern pulsed with their plotting, a symphony of malicc weaving a nightmare grotesque beyond the centipede's horror—12 souls chained to a wheel of steel and Semtex, poised to spin Doha into a crucible of fire and flesh, ransom or no, a vengeance born in the Najd's unforgiving sands, aimed at the heart of a world they despised.

At 6 p.m. in Doha, the Main Press Center's auditorium thrummed with a restless swarm of journalists, their cameras flashing like a storm of gunfire, their voices a cacophony of demands clawing at the air.

Sheikh Tariq bin Fahd Al-Mazrouei stood at the podium, his keffiyeh crisp despite the weight of the day, his face a mask of resolve forged in fury, flanked by Jacques Moreau and Viktor Borodin, their suits rumpled, eyes hollow from the night's strain in Doha's crucible. Behind them, a massive screen looped muted clips of the centipede—stitched limbs twitching, pixelated agony searing into the room's collective retina.

Tariq's voice boomed, a thunderclap silencing the din, his hands steady on the podium's edge. "The IOC, with financial support from the G20 nations, announces our intent to meet the Obsidian Hand's ransom demand—$500 billion. Talks begin immediately, coordinated through diplomatic channels. We seek peace, not further fire—details will follow as nations align their contributions."

James Cartwright of the BBC shot to his feet, his gray hair askew, his tie loosened, his tone sharp as a scalpel. "Sheikh Tariq, $500 billion—where's the cash flowing from? G20's a pledge, but who's writing the first cheque—UK, US, China? And these talks—how long 'til this 'peace' holds, or are we just buying hours?"

Tariq's eyes locked on Cartwright, his voice steady, a diplomat's precision cutting through. "The G20's pooling resources—US and UK lead the pledge, specifics will come within hours as treasuries align. The talks aim for lasting peace, but yes, we're buying time—every minute counts to halt this nightmare."

Emilie Laurent of L'Équipe leaned forward, her notebook scribbled with frantic French shorthand, her voice urgent, her blonde hair slipping from its bun. "Monsieur Moreau, the athletes—six dead, six dying, a horror etched in our minds—how does ransom heal that wound? What's the IOC's guarantee this ends here, not escalates into something worse?"

Tariq interjected before Moreau could respond, his tonc firm, his gaze shifting to Laurent. "The ransom doesn't heal—it's a bridge to stop the bleeding. Those lost can't return, but we secure the living. Our guarantee is action—talks now, force if they fail. Escalation's their choice, not ours."

Greg Palmer from Australia, his sunburned face taut, his shirt sleeves rolled up, barked over the murmurs, his accent thick with impatience. "Borodin—ransom's a bloody fortune, and Russia's in on it? What's Moscow's cut—oil contracts, geopolitical leverage? And if they don't pay up, what's next—more bodies, another freak show?"

Tariq's hands tightened on the podium, his voice a controlled growl as he faced Palmer. "Russia's committed—no cuts, no leverage, just survival. The G20 stands united. If they don't pay, we're prepared—their 'next' is a shadow we're countering, not inviting. No more bodies if we can choke it here."

Rashida al-Hakim of Al Jazeera, her hijab framing a fierce gaze, pressed forward, her recorder thrust out, her voice steady but edged with accusation. "Sheikh Tariq, Qatar's hosting—you're bleeding on your own soil. Ransom talks—where's your military muscle, your intel backbone? Colonel Al-Kuwari's silent, Captain Rahman's a ghost—why the blackout?"

Tariq met her gaze, his eyes blazing, his tone sharp yet measured. "Qatar's bleeding, yes— our military's roaring through these streets, our intel's alive but classified for security. Al- Kuwari and Rahman are shadows by design—trust our resolve, not our silence. We're fighting, not folding."

Carlos Mendes of Globo Esporte, his voice rising, waved a recorder, his dark eyes flashing, his shirt damp with sweat from the press room's stifling heat. "Tariq, Brazil's G20—my people deserve answers. $500 billion—how's it wired, who controls the tap? And this 'next' they're threatening—what's the Obsidian Hand cooking if you're a minute late?"

Tariq's jaw tightened, his voice steady as he addressed Mendes. "Brazil's part of this— funds are secured through IOC oversight, wired via encrypted channels, G20 controls the flow. Their 'next' is a threat we're countering—details stay dark to keep them guessing. Late or not, we're ready."

Priya Patel of The Times of India stood, her sari rustling as she adjusted her glasses, her tone piercing through the chaos. "President Al-Mazrouei, India's footing this bill too— ransom's a band-aid on a gaping wound. What's the real play here—talks, or a strike in the shadows? And Mendelsohn—rumors swirl she's alive, feeding this plan. True or smoke?"

Tariq's knuckles whitened, his voice a warrior's fire beneath a diplomat's mask as he faced Patel. "India's stake matters—ransom's the band-aid, talks are the play now, strikes are rumors we don't fuel. Mendelsohn's status is unconfirmed officially—rumors don't dictate our moves, resolve does."

The room erupted, a barrage of overlapping shouts—"How much per nation?" "Classified— covering what?" "Unconfirmed—alive or dead?" "What's 'countering' mean?"—as Tariq stood firm, Moreau raised a trembling hand for calm, and Borodin's stoic silence loomed, the press hammering relentlessly, sensing blood beneath the polished words.

The announcement rippled outward, a calculated deception cloaking the world in a tense, uneasy hush—eight hours ticking down, Barga's wheel poised to spin, and Nova's shadow creeping closer to the desert's red heart, where Najdi vengeance burned against the Olympic flame.

Veil 20

Shadow in the Sand

The late afternoon sun bled a molten orange across Doha's skyline, its light splintering through the jagged teeth of glass towers and glinting off the Gulf's restless waves. By 5:45 p.m., the city's pulse thrummed with a frenetic edge—military Humvees growled through the streets, their tires kicking up dust that mingled with the lingering fog, now a thin, clammy haze.

Sirens wailed intermittently, a discordant soundtrack to the lockdown that had choked the capital since the centipede's grotesque debut. Nova crouched behind a rusted shipping container at the Old Port, her cracked ribs aching with each shallow breath, her dark hair plastered to her sweat-streaked forehead.

Beside her, Jaber squinted through the haze, his fingers drumming nervously on the grip of a battered Makarov pistol. Omar knelt a few feet away, his calloused hands adjusting a canvas sack slung over his shoulder, its contents clinking faintly—tools, water, a scavenged radio.

The trio's plan was a razor's edge: slip out of Doha's iron grip, cross 70 miles of desert to Barga Al Kharaz, and breach the Obsidian Hand's lair before dusk turned to night. Failure wasn't an option—capture meant torture, or a one-way ticket to the centipede's rotting shadow.

To the operators in their distant tent, Nova and the others were just red blips on a black screen—assets, not people. Delta Force would track them from a distance—micro-drones buzzing like invisible hornets, their feeds relaying every move to a command post 50 miles out—but the first leg was theirs alone, a covert dance through a city on the brink and a desert that swallowed secrets whole.

Nova's intel, scratched into her memory from Warehouse 12's blood-soaked clues, pinpointed Barga's vent shaft as their entry. Smoke canisters, tucked into Jaber's pack, were their ticket to flush the bastards out—assuming they didn't trip a Semtex wire first.

"Port's crawling," Jaber muttered, his voice a low rasp as he peered around the container's edge. A Qatari patrol jeep rumbled past, its headlights slicing through the haze, the growl of its engine fading into the docks' cacophony—clanging cranes, shouting workers, the slap of waves against concrete.

"Two checkpoints between here and the Al Rufaa gate. Military's thick—Al-Kuwari's got 'em on a leash since Tariq's press stunt."

Nova winced, pressing a hand to her side, her breath hitching as she spoke. "We don't go through—too hot. Omar's skiff's still moored, north slip, 50 yards. Tide's low, we hug the shore 'til the industrial sprawl, ditch it there. Truck's stashed—old Toyota LandCruiser, rusted but runs. Gets us to the dunes." Omar nodded, his deep voice steady, a counterpoint to Jaber's twitchy edge. "Skiff's fueled—barely. Enough for five miles. Truck's got half a tank, spare can in the bed. Sand's shifting out there—forecast says wind's picking up, 25 knots by dusk. Visibility's gonna drop to nothing."

The desert beyond Doha loomed in their minds—a vast, undulating sea of red-gold dunes, its surface rippling under a sky turning bruised purple as the sun sank. The weather was turning feral: a sandstorm roared closer, its ochre veil swallowing the horizon, lashing the dunes with a gritty howl. Heat still radiated from the sand, a dry furnace breath at 105°F, though the wind carried a biting chill, tugging at loose clothing and scouring exposed skin with fine, abrasive grains. Nova's plan hinged on that chaos—cover from the storm, a shroud for their approach, if they could navigate it without losing their way.

Jaber smirked, though his eyes stayed hard. "Great—sand in my lungs, wind up my ass, and Delta's drones playing babysitter. You sure they won't shoot us if we sneeze wrong?"

"They're our shadow, not our trigger," Nova snapped, her tone sharp despite the pain lancing her ribs. "Implants are live—Renshaw's got us tagged. They'll know it's us. Focus on the skiff—move when that crane swings."

She pointed to a towering crane 30 yards off, its arm groaning as it hefted a pallet of crates, casting a fleeting shadow over the dock. The trio tensed, muscles coiled, waiting for the moment. The crane's hydraulics whined, the pallet swung—and they bolted, low and fast, boots scuffing the cracked concrete.

The skiff bobbed in the north slip, a battered 12-footer with peeling paint and a coughing outboard motor, half-hidden by a tangle of fishing nets. Nova slid in first, crouching low, her hands gripping the splintered gunwale as Jaber and Omar followed, their movements silent but urgent.

Omar yanked the starter cord, the motor sputtering to life with a throaty gurgle, spitting exhaust into the haze. The skiff eased out, hugging the shoreline, its hull scraping sandbars as they slipped past the port's edge. Doha's lights flickered through the fog—neon signs, military floodlights, the distant pulse of a helicopter's blades—but the tide's murmur and the motor's drone cloaked their escape. Five miles north, the industrial sprawl loomed: skeletal warehouses, rusted silos, and the Toyota, a dented relic parked behind a crumbling wall, its faded green paint blending with the desert's fringe.

"Keep it steady," Nova murmured, her eyes scanning the shore. "Patrols don't sweep this far unless they're tipped. We're ghosts 'til the truck." Jaber snorted, adjusting the smoke canisters in his pack. "Ghosts with a busted boat and a junker. If that storm hits early, we're screwed—dunes'll eat us before Barga does."

"Storm's our friend," Omar countered, his hands firm on the tiller. "Blinds 'em—covers tracks. We stick to the wadi path, use the ridges for cover. Truck's got chains if we bog."

The skiff beached with a soft crunch, its bow grinding into the gravelly shore. They scrambled out, dragging it into a thicket of saltbush to conceal it, the briny scent of the Gulf mixing with the dust kicked up by their boots. The Toyota waited where Omar had stashed it, its hood warm from the day's heat, keys tucked under the driver's mat. Nova slid into the passenger seat, Jaber took the wheel, and Omar climbed into the bed, securing the spare can as the engine coughed awake, a rattling roar that settled into an uneven hum.

The desert unfolded as they rolled west, Doha's glow fading into a smudge behind them. The dunes rose like frozen waves, their crests sharp and shadowed, the sand a deep crimson under the dying sun. The wind surged, a banshee's wail flinging grit against the truck's cracked windshield, the temperature dropping to 95°F as dusk crept in. Visibility shrank with each gust, the sandstorm's full fury descending—a roiling wall of dust that slashed visibility to mere feet, the Toyota lurching through the wadi as sand stung their faces and the sky bled into night.

Thirty miles from Doha, the Toyota shuddered, its engine choking on the sand-saturated air. Jaber gunned the throttle, cursing as the wheels spun, digging deeper into the softening wadi bed. The vehicle stalled with a pitiful whine, its hood swallowed by a drift of red grit, the storm's howl drowning out the last sputters of the motor.

"Fuck!" Jaber slammed the wheel, his voice swallowed by the wind as he kicked the door open, sand blasting his face. "We're done—this piece of shit's toast!"

Nova climbed out, shielding her eyes against the stinging haze, her voice tight with strain. "I guess we're on foot—40 miles left. Grab the gear, we move now."

Omar hauled the sack from the bed, slinging it over his shoulder as the storm battered them, the wind a relentless roar that tore at their clothes and scoured their skin. The sand shifted underfoot, a treacherous slurry that sucked at their boots, each step a battle against the gale.

Nova led, her scarf wrapped tight around her face, leaving only her eyes exposed—gritty, narrowed slits scanning the void. Pain gnawed at her ribs, exhaustion fogged her mind—but Nova shoved it down, forcing her battered body onward. Fear would not bury her here. Jaber followed, the Makarov tucked into his waistband, his pack rattling with canisters. Omar brought up the rear, his broad frame hunched against the wind, the radio clutched like a lifeline.

The storm was a living thing, a maelstrom of sand and shadow that clawed at their senses, reducing the world to a suffocating blur. The air tasted of dust and heat, thick in their throats, the temperature hovering at 80°F but feeling colder with the wind's bite.

They stumbled through the wadi, its banks eroded into vague

humps, the sand piling into drifts that forced them to climb or detour. Visibility was a cruel joke—five feet at best, the dunes looming as vague, monstrous shapes before vanishing into the haze.

"Keep south!" Nova shouted, her voice shredded by the wind. "Wadi splits ahead—stay close or we're lost!"

Jaber spat sand, his scarf slipping as he yelled back, "Lost? We're already screwed—can't see a goddamned thing! How's Delta even tracking us in this?"

"They've got thermal," Omar grunted, his voice a low rumble against the storm. "Implants are still hot—drones'll find us. Keep moving."

Above, a micro-drone battled the tempest at 400 feet, its thermal lens flickering as Captain Logan "Viper" Kincaid watched from a command tent 50 miles southwest of Doha. His lean frame hunched over a monitor, his sharp green eyes tracking the trio's heat signatures— three faint red smudges jostling through the chaos.

Beside him, Lieutenant Sam "Hawk" Hawkins adjusted a comms unit, his voice cutting through the tent's hum.

"Targets stalled—40 miles out, wadi south fork. Truck's down, they're on foot. Storm's frying visuals, but thermal's holding. ETA to Barga: two hours if they don't drop. Orders?"

Renshaw's voice crackled back, steady as stone. "Hold shadow—500-yard buffer. Drones push altitude if wind spikes, keep thermal lock. They flush, we strike. No deviations."

Back in the storm, the trio pressed on, their legs burning, the sand a relentless foe that clung and dragged. After an hour of staggering through the maelstrom, the faint glow of oil lamps floated like a mirage, flickering, unreal—hope straining against the storm's endless hunger.

Nova squinted, her heart thudding as shapes emerged: a dozen tents, their black weaves taut against the gale, nestled in a shallow depression between dunes. The Bani Hajer, a semi-nomadic Bedouin tribe, had hunkered down here, their camp a fragile oasis in the chaos. She exhaled, almost disbelieving—shelter in the storm felt like a hallucination painted in goat-hair and grit.

The Bani Hajer traced their lineage to the pre-Islamic tribes of Qatar, a hardy clan of herders and traders who roamed the peninsula's interior long before oil reshaped the land.

Once fierce raiders allied with the Banu Yam, their blood feuds once inked the desert with war; now the Obsidian Hand traced the same lines in Semtex and scripture. By 2025, they'd adapted—some worked Doha's markets, others clung to the desert, herding camels and goats, their lives a bridge between past and present.

The black tents, woven of goat hair and palm fronds, crouched like shadows, their interiors lined with age-worn cushions—a testimony to grit carved over centuries.

A figure emerged from the nearest tent, a wiry man in a weathered thobe, his face half- shrouded by a red-and-white shemagh. He raised a hand, shouting in Arabic over the wind, "Min antum? Ma taba'un huna?"—Who are you? What do you want here?

Jaber stepped forward, his voice hoarse but steady, switching to Arabic. "Istajirna—naḥnu muta'abūn. Naḥtāj mawā."—We seek refuge, we're exhausted. We need shelter.

The man studied them, his dark eyes narrowing, then waved them in. "Tafaddalū—enter. The storm spares no one."

Inside, the tent was a warm reprieve, the wind's howl muted to a dull moan. The air smelled of cardamom and smoke, a small brazier glowing in the center, casting shadows across a half-dozen tribesmen—lean, sun-darkened men in thobes, their hands cradling tin cups of tea. A woman in a black abaya moved silently, pouring more from a dented pot, her face veiled but her eyes sharp. Nova sank onto a rug, her ribs screaming, while Jaber and Omar slumped beside her, sand spilling from their clothes.

Jaber wiped his face, glancing at the nearest man—a grizzled elder with a hooked nose. "Shukran—thanks for this. You see anything weird out there? Near Barga, maybe?"

The elder sipped his tea, his voice a dry rasp. "Barga's cursed—lights flicker there, shadows move at night. Some say the wind at Barga cries with a woman's voice, mourning sons lost to the well.

"Two days back, trucks rolled in, covered, quiet. Men with guns, not ours. They took the old, haunted well path, left no tracks."

Omar leaned in, his tone low. "Trucks—how many? Any markings?"

"Three," a younger man cut in, his beard patchy, his eyes flicking to Omar. "No markings, just black tarps. They stopped at the ridge, unloaded crates—metal, heavy. Then gone, like djinn."

Nova's pulse quickened, her mind racing—Semtex, likely, staged for the wheel. She kept silent, letting Jaber press.

"Anyone go near?" Jaber asked, his fingers twitching toward his pack. "See what they left?" The elder shook his head, his gaze hardening. "We don't tempt fate—Barga's a grave. Last year, a boy wandered close, didn't return. Whispers say it's haunted—old blood, old wars."

The Bani Hajer's tales wove a grim tapestry—Barga Al Kharaz, a forgotten outpost from the tribal feuds of the 6th century, where the Banu Hanifa and Banu 'Abs clashed over a now- dry well. Legends claimed the losers' bodies were piled in its caves, their spirits cursing the sands. The Obsidian Hand's presence only thickened the myth, their atrocities echoing the past's savagery.

The elder set his cup down, his tone shifting. "You're not traders—your eyes are hunted. Where do you go?"

Nova met his stare, her voice firm. "South—we've got business. The storm trapped us." He grunted, unconvinced, then gestured to the younger man. "Three camels—saddled, strong. Take them, but don't return. This storm's a warning—heed it."

The woman handed them a skin of water, her gaze lingering on Nova, a silent question in her eyes. The trio rose, brushing off sand, their gear heavier with the weight of the Bani Hajer's words. Outside, the storm raged on, but the camels stood ready—tall, sinewy beasts with matted fur, their humps swaying as they snorted against the wind. Nova mounted first, her ribs protesting, while Jaber and Omar followed, gripping reins slick with dust.

"Camels beat a dead truck," Jaber muttered, his smirk faint as he adjusted his pack. "Let's ride—Barga's waiting."

The Bani Hajer watched them vanish into the haze, their tents fading behind as the storm swallowed the trio once more, now astride beasts bred for this hell, their path to Barga sharpened by the tribe's grim accounts.

The sandstorm's fury had dulled to a persistent growl as Nova Mendelsohn, Jaber Al- Rashid, and Omar Al-Sayed urged their camels onward, the Bani Hajer's camp a fading memory swallowed by the desert's maw.

The sky above was a churning bruise, purple-black and streaked with veins of dust, the last embers of daylight snuffed out by the storm's relentless shroud. The wind, now a steady 20 knots, whipped across the dunes, carving their crests into jagged, fleeting sculptures that collapsed and reformed with each gust.

The air was thick with sand, a gritty haze that stung their eyes and coated their tongues, the temperature plunging to 75°F as night claimed the peninsula. The camels plodded forward, their broad hooves sinking into the shifting sand, their grunts and snorts a rhythmic counterpoint to the storm's low howl.

Nova clung to her reins, her scarf tight around her face, leaving only her bloodshot eyes exposed to the abrasive onslaught. Her ribs throbbed with each sway of the camel's gait, a dull fire that flared when she twisted to scan the horizon. Jaber rode beside her, his lean frame hunched against the wind, the Makarov pistol a reassuring weight against his hip, its grip slick with sweat and dust.

Omar trailed a few paces back, his broad shoulders squared, the canvas sack bouncing against his side as he guided his mount with a steady hand. The Bani Hajer's camels were sturdy, their matted coats flecked with sand, their dark eyes gleaming with a stoic endurance bred into their bones over centuries of desert life.

The terrain grew harsher as they closed the final 30 miles to Barga Al Kharaz, each mile scraped closer to madness—sand gave way to bone-littered stone, as if the land itself remembered blood.

The wadi they'd followed from the truck's grave gave way to a fractured landscape—dunes flattened into broad, windswept plateaus pocked with jagged outcrops of red rock, their edges worn smooth by eons of erosion. Skeletal acacia shrubs dotted the expanse, their gnarled branches clawing at the air, stripped bare by the storm's relentless scour.

The sand here was coarser, a reddish grit that crunched under the camels' hooves, speckled with shards of ancient pottery and the occasional glint of bleached bone— remnants of a time when tribes like the Bani Hajer and their foes fought for these barren wastes.

"Barga's close," Nova rasped, her voice barely audible over the wind as she squinted into the haze. "Those rocks—southwest ridge. Vent shaft's gotta be near. Keep low—their watchers'll be perched."

Jaber spat a mouthful of sand, his scarf slipping as he grumbled, "Low? These damn camels are six feet tall—might as well wave a flag. You sure about this vent? Bani Hajer said shadows move out here."

"Shadows with guns," Omar added, his deep voice cutting through the storm's din. "Crates at the ridge—Semtex, probably. We're walking into their teeth."

Nova's jaw tightened, her eyes tracing the ridge's silhouette—a hulking mass of rock that loomed through the dust like a sleeping beast, its contours blurred but menacing. "Vent's our shot—smoke 'em out, Delta hits. Bani Hajer saw trucks, not guards. They're deep in the caves, not up top—yet."

The camels plodded closer, their pace slowing as the ground hardened, the sand giving way to a cracked expanse of desert pavement—fist-sized stones baked into a mosaic by centuries of sun and wind. The storm's haze thinned slightly here, revealing more of Barga's outskirts: a shallow wadi snaked westward, its dry bed littered with rusted tin cans and tire tracks half-buried by drifting sand—evidence of the Obsidian Hand's recent passage.

Beyond it, the ridge rose sharply, its face pocked with fissures and shadowed hollows, a natural fortress carved from the desert's bones. The air carried a faint tang of diesel and decay, a whisper of the horrors festering within.

Jaber reined his camel to a halt, his hand hovering near his pistol as he scanned the ridge. "Tracks stop there—wadi's edge. Too quiet. If they've got lookouts, we're cooked."

"Quiet's good," Nova countered, her voice taut as she dismounted, wincing as her boots hit the ground. "Means they're inside, not out. Tie the camels—those rocks'll hide 'em. We're on foot from here."

Omar slid down, securing his mount to a jutting slab of stone, its surface etched with faint, pre-Islamic glyphs—spirals and slashes from a forgotten hand. "Storm's our cover—wind's masking sound. But if they've got eyes up high, we're blind 'til we're close."

The trio tethered the camels in a shallow dip behind the rocks, their humps blending with the terrain as the beasts knelt, snuffling the sand. Nova adjusted her pack, the smoke canisters clinking faintly, and led the way, crouching low as they crept toward the ridge.

The storm battered them still, its gusts flinging sand into their faces, but the wind's roar cloaked their steps, the crunch of stone underfoot swallowed by the tempest's din. The desert had been vast; the ridge loomed larger now, like a craggy mouth narrowing to swallow them whole, the air growing heavier with the stench of fuel and something fouler—rotting meat, perhaps, seeping from the caves below.

They skirted the wadi's edge, its banks rising into low cliffs of compacted sand and rock, their surfaces streaked with dark stains—old blood or oil, impossible to tell in the dimness. A rusted metal pole jutted from the ground, its tip bent by some long-ago force, a relic of Barga's past as a tribal outpost.

Nova's eyes locked on a narrow cleft in the ridge ahead—a jagged scar in the rock, barely three feet wide, its edges smoothed by wind and time. The vent shaft, if her intel held, lay within, a back door to the Obsidian Hand's lair.

"There," she whispered, pointing as she dropped to a knee, her breath ragged. "Cleft's our mark—vent's inside. Fifty yards, tops. Move slow, check for wires."

Jaber peered through the haze, his hand tightening on the Makarov. "Fifty yards in this crap? Might as well be fifty miles. You see anything—tripwires, guards?"

"Nothing yet," Omar murmured, his eyes sweeping the ground, the storm's dust swirling around his boots. "Sand's fresh—no footprints. They're not patrolling out here—too damn wild."

The trio edged forward, their bodies low, the storm's chaos a double-edged sword—cover and curse in equal measure. The cleft grew clearer as they neared, its mouth a black gash framed by jagged rock, the wind funneling through it with a low, mournful whistle.

The surrounding terrain was a graveyard of neglect: a shattered crate lay half-buried near the wadi, its splintered wood spilling rusted nails; a shredded tarp flapped from a thorn bush, its edges frayed and stained; and a single tire track curved toward the ridge before vanishing under a fresh drift of sand. The Obsidian Hand was here, their presence etched in these silent scars, but the storm had erased their surface traces, leaving only the promise of violence beneath.

Nova paused at the cleft's edge, her hand brushing the rock—cool, gritty, ancient. The air within carried a sharper bite, a mix of damp stone and chemical fumes, a hint of the Semtex stockpiles below.

"This is it," she said, her voice barely a breath. "Vent's down there—narrow, but we'll fit. Canisters ready?"

Jaber patted his pack, his smirk faint but grim. "Ready to choke 'em out—if we don't choke first. You sure Delta's still with us?"

"They're up there," Omar said, glancing skyward, though the storm hid the drones' hum. "Thermal's our leash—Renshaw won't lose us now."

Above, a micro-drone hovered at 450 feet, its lens battling the wind as Captain Kincaid tracked their signatures—three red dots inching toward the ridge. In the command tent, his green eyes narrowed, his voice a low snap over the comms.

"Targets at Barga perimeter—cleft entry, 30 miles out. Storm's steady, thermal's clean. ETA to breach: 20 minutes. Confirm strike prep."

"Prep confirmed," Renshaw's voice crackled back. "Hellfire's hot, ground team's staged. They flush, we bury. Hold lock."

Nova took a final breath, the storm's grit coating her throat, and slipped into the cleft, her frame vanishing into the shadows. Jaber followed, his pistol drawn, and Omar brought up the rear, the sack slung tight. The ridge swallowed them, its silence a stark contrast to the tempest outside, the air growing colder and heavier as they descended toward Barga's heart—where the Obsidian Hand waited.

The cleft in the ridge narrowed as Nova, Jaber, and Omar descended, its jagged walls pressing closer, the air thickening with the dank chill of subterranean stone. The storm's howl faded to a muted wail behind them, replaced by the drip of unseen water and the faint hum of something mechanical—ventilation, perhaps, feeding the Obsidian Hand's lair below.

Nova led, her boots scuffing the uneven floor, her cracked ribs a constant ache as she navigated by feel, her hands brushing the rough rock. Jaber followed, his Makarov pistol gripped tight, its barrel catching the faint glow of her phone's dimmed screen. Omar brought up the rear, his broad frame stooped, the canvas sack clinking softly with each step—tools and canisters their only weapons against the nightmare ahead.

The passage twisted downward, a steep incline that forced them to brace against the walls, the air growing heavier with the acrid tang of Semtex and the sour reek of sweat-soaked fear. Nova's intel had pegged this vent shaft as their back door—50 yards from the surface to the caverns, a straight shot to flush the Obsidian Hand with smoke. But the silence was wrong, too thick, too deliberate, a predator's hush before the strike. She froze, her hand shooting up, her breath catching as her eyes caught a glint—thin, taut, metallic—spanning the passage at ankle height.

"Wire!" she hissed, her voice a blade cutting the stillness. "Back—now!"

Time hiccuped—Nova's eyes locked on the wire, but the stone moaned first, betrayal whispering beneath her boots. The floor beneath them shifted, a subtle groan of stone giving way to a sickening click. A trapdoor yawned open, its hinges silent and oiled, plunging them into a chute of smooth rock. Nova's stomach lurched as she slid, her hands clawing at the walls, finding no purchase.

Jaber yelped, his pistol skittering away as he tumbled, his pack slamming against the chute's curve. Omar grunted, his bulk crashing behind, the sack ripping open, tools and canisters clattering into the dark. The drop was brief—ten feet, maybe twelve—but it ended hard, their bodies slamming onto a packed dirt floor, the air punched from their lungs in a chorus of gasps and groans.

Dust clouded the dim cavern, lit by a single flickering fluorescent tube bolted to the ceiling, its sickly green glow casting long, distorted shadows. Nova rolled to her knees, pain exploding in her ribs, her vision swimming as she scanned their prison—a rough-hewn chamber, 20 feet wide, its walls studded with rusted iron rings and stained with dark, ominous streaks. Jaber sprawled beside her, cursing through gritted teeth as he clutched his twisted ankle, his Makarov lost in the fall. Omar pushed himself up, his face smeared with dirt, the torn sack spilling its contents—wrenches, a cracked radio, and two smoke canisters, one dented but intact.

Before they could regroup, a shadow loomed at the chamber's far end, lean and coiled, stepping from a tunnel mouth with the grace of a desert cat. "The Watcher," emerged. She didn't walk—she prowled, keffiyeh trailing like a banner of blood. In her stillness, something hunted.

A curved blade hung at her belt, its edge catching the fluorescence, and a compact submachine gun—Heckler & Koch MP5—dangled from her shoulder, its muzzle trained on them with lethal calm. Her lips curled into a venomous sneer, her voice a low hiss that slithered through the cavern.

"Yellow eyes see all," she said, her gaze locking on Nova. "You took my bait—Warehouse 12, the tablet. Sniffing like a hound, straight into Barga's jaws." Nova's gut twisted—Warehouse 12 hadn't been intel, it was an invitation. She'd marched them straight into the lion's throat.

Zainab had played her, left the clues to lure them here. She forced her voice steady, defiance masking the pain. "You're sloppy—left tracks a blind man could follow. Delta's coming, Watcher. You're done."

"The Watcher" laughed, a sharp, cutting sound, stepping closer as her blade gleamed. "Delta's drones? Sand and wind eat their signals—your leash is cut. You're mine now."

A heavier shadow followed, the cavern trembling under the weight of "The Enforcer." His massive frame filled the tunnel's mouth, a wall of muscle clad in a tattered tactical vest, his shaved head glistening with sweat, his scarred fists flexing around a sledgehammer—its head crusted with dried gore and matted hair. His presence was a physical force, the air shifting as he loomed, his guttural snarl rumbling like distant thunder. His dark eyes flicked over them, assessing, dismissing, a predator sizing up prey.

"Commander wants answers," he growled, his voice thick with menace as he hefted the hammer. "You'll talk—or break."

Jaber scrambled back, his bad ankle dragging, his bravado cracking as he spat, “You’re a freak—gonna bash us like some damn piñata? Try it, big man!”

Darius lunged, faster than his bulk suggested, the hammer swinging in a brutal arc. Jaber rolled aside, the weapon cratering the dirt where he’d been, dust exploding in a choking cloud. Omar surged forward, tackling “The Enforcer” low, his shoulder driving into his gut—a desperate bid to buy time. The two grappled, Omar’s strength straining against “The Enforcer’s” mass, grunts and thuds echoing off the walls as the hammer clattered free.

“The Watcher” moved like a wraith, her blade flashing as she closed on Nova, who dodged, her ribs screaming, snatching the dented canister from the floor. She yanked the pin, hurling it at her feet—smoke erupted in a gray plume, stinging their eyes and lungs, the cavern blurring into chaos. “The Watcher" cursed, firing blind, the MP5’s staccato bark shredding the air, bullets ricocheting off stone as Nova dove behind a rusted crate, her breath ragged.

“Get the tunnel!” Nova shouted, coughing through the haze, her hand groping for anything— a weapon, a way out. Jaber limped toward her, clutching a wrench from the spilled sack, his face a mask of grit and fury.

Omar roared, slamming “The Enforcer” against the wall, but “The Enforcer’s” fist crashed into his jaw, a meaty crack sending Omar sprawling, blood trickling from his split lip. “The Watcher” spun through the smoke, her blade slashing at Jaber, who parried with the wrench—metal clanged, sparks flying as he stumbled back, his ankle buckling.

The Watcher’s voice cut through the chaos, icy and triumphant. “Enough—chain ‘em. The Commander wants ‘em alive—for questioning.”

“The Enforcer” shook off Omar’s blow, retrieving his hammer with a snarl, his bulk towering as he advanced. “The Watcher” holstered her gun, drawing a coil of rusted chain from a hook on the wall, her movements swift and precise. Nova lunged for the tunnel, but “The Watcher’s” blade caught her calf—a shallow slice, hot and wet—dropping her with a gasp. “The Enforcer” hauled Jaber up by the collar, slamming him against the wall, the chain rattling as it looped around his wrists, the iron biting into his skin. Omar struggled to rise, but his boot pinned him, the hammer raised like a guillotine as “The Watcher” bound his hands, the links clanking shut.

Nova fought, kicking with her good leg, but “The Watcher's” grip was iron, the chain cinching her wrists tight, the cold metal grinding against her bones. The smoke thinned, revealing their defeat—three captives, battered and bleeding, their gear scattered, their plan in ruins. “The Watcher” stepped back, her sneer widening as she wiped her blade on her sleeve, the blood smearing crimson against the dust.

“Commander’ll peel your secrets,” “The Enforcer” rumbled, dragging Omar to his feet, the chain taut between them. “Talk fast—or I’ll loosen your tongues my way.”

“The Watcher’s” eyes glinted as she prodded Nova with her boot, her voice a venomous whisper. “You hunted us—now you’re the prey. Barga’s jaws snap shut.”

Above, the micro-drone’s feed flickered, sand and static warping the thermal signatures as Captain Logan “Viper” Kincaid slammed a fist on the console, his voice a sharp bark.

“Signal’s dropping—storm’s spiking, they’re in the ridge. Heat’s clustered—three, no, five now. Shit—they’re nabbed.”

Renshaw’s response was steel, unflinching. “Confirm capture—hold strike ‘til we’re sure. Drones push in, get eyes. They’re bait now—plan adapts.”

The cavern's silence settled, broken only by the captives' ragged breaths, the trap's jaws locked tight around Nova, Jaber, and Omar, their fate now a grim interrogation in the hands of their captors.

Veil 21

The Price of Silence

The cavern's oppressive air thickened as "The Watcher," and "The Enforcer," dragged Nova, Jaber, and Omar deeper into Barga Al Kharaz's labyrinth.

Nova's ribs clenched with every step, each breath tainted by blood and fear—Barga wasn't just a labyrinth, it was a descent into legend.

The fluorescent tubes overhead buzzed erratically, their green light flickering across the rough-hewn walls, casting grotesque shadows that danced like Spectres. The trio's breaths came in ragged gasps, their bodies bruised and battered from the trap's brutal embrace, but their eyes burned with defiance, even as the Obsidian Hand's lair closed around them like a tomb.

They emerged into a wider chamber. The room swallowed light and time—part armory, part ossuary, where old wars and new torments met beneath the carved curse of resurrection. The floor was strewn with crates and the detritus of violence—spent shell casings, blood-streaked rags, a severed finger curled in a corner. Piles of Semtex lined the stone walls. An old inscription carved above the explosives:

دْجَنْ ُضَهنَيِ بُّ ُهتَ ةُحوَّدلا ،يّدَؤُيُلَعشْمِلا مِّدلابِ مُّدلا - ُضَهنَتٌدْجَنْ

At the chamber's heart stood "The Commander," his scar-ravaged face a mask of cold fury, his yellow eyes glinting with predatory malice. The tribes called him Abu Ẓill—Father of Shadows—for wherever he walked, death followed and sunlight fled. His black robe hung loose, stained with desert dust and faint splatters of crimson, his Najdi dagger sheathed at his hip, its hilt worn smooth by decades of grip.

Around him gathered the rest of the Obsidian Hand: Rashid Nazari, "The Arbiter," his hawkish features taut as he clutched a ledger; Adil Rahmani, "The Scribe," hunched over a laptop, his glasses fogged with sweat; Elias Marwan, "The Keeper," a gaunt figure cloaked in a hood, her bony fingers jangling a ring of keys; and Dr. Samir Haddad, "The Doctor," his white coat rust-red, a tray of scalpels glinting beside him.

"The Watcher" shoved Nova forward, her blade prodding the shallow cut on her calf, while "The Enforcer" Jaber and Omar with brutal efficiency. It stung—but she'd been through worse. Kabul, 2031. A drug dealer's bullet that missed her spine by a whisper.

Three steel cages lined the chamber's eastern wall—crude, rusted boxes barely five feet square, their bars pitted with age and streaked with dried blood.

"The Enforcer" unlocked them with a grunt, the hinges screeching as he forced each captive inside. Nova's cage slammed shut first, the lock snapping with a dull *thud*, her wrists still chained, her body pressed against the bars. Jaber followed, limping on his twisted ankle, his curses muffled as the door clanged shut. Omar, blood dripping from his split lip, was last, his broad frame barely fitting, the cage rattling as it was secured.

“The Commander” stepped forward, his dagger tapping rhythmically against his thigh, his growl a low rumble that filled the chamber.

“You’re bold—slipping into my den, sniffing for my blood. Mendelsohn, your name’s a thorn in my side. Tell me—your plan, the ransom. A fake, isn’t it? A lure to flush us out?”

Nova met his gaze, her ribs aching, her voice steady despite the pain. “You’re guessing. Keep guessing—you don’t scare me.”

Jaber smirked through the bars, his voice hoarse but defiant. “Yeah, big man—figure it out yourself. We’re just tourists lost in the sand.”

Omar spat blood onto the dirt floor, his deep voice unyielding. “You’ve got nothing but chains and threats. Waste your breath.”

“The Commander’s” lips twitched, a flicker of rage breaking his composure. He turned to “The Keeper,” his tone sharp as a blade. “They’re stubborn—what old ways will loosen their tongues?”

“The Keeper” stepped forward, her voice held the hush of ancient sermons, each word a blade honed over centuries of silence and screams.

“The Basṭīnah—for the big one. It’s an ancient art, born in the Najd before Islam tamed the tribes. They’d hang their enemies upside-down, legs roped to beams, heads dangling low, weights pulling their arms ‘til joints screamed. Hot irons to the feet—slow, precise—kept ‘em alive but broken. It’ll test his iron.”

“The Commander” nodded, his yellow eyes glinting. “Omar first—let’s see his resolve melt. Spectre, do it.”

From the shadows emerged “The Spectre,” his thobe stained with old blood, his hands steady as death itself. His presence chilled the air, his silence more menacing than "The Enforcer's" snarls.

He unlocked Omar's cage, dragging him out with surprising strength, his chains rattling as "The Enforcer" hoisted a coarse hemp rope over a rusted beam—a grim echo of the pre- Islamic clans who once used such methods to settle scores over wells and honor. They bound Omar's ankles, the rope biting into his flesh, and hauled him upward, his body inverting, his head swaying a foot above the dirt.

Nova bit her cheek until she tasted copper, her fury held behind clenched teeth. Every scream Omar didn't release was one she felt echo through her spine.

As the two moved to execute their evil, "The Scribe" led the others in a chant, rhythmically repeating *"Tha'r ar-Rimāl! Tha'r ar-Rimāl!"*

"The Spectre" tied two jagged stones—ten pounds each, their surfaces scratched with faded curses from a forgotten age—to Omar's wrists, the weight wrenching his shoulders, a low groan escaping his lips as the tension pulled his joints taut. A brazier glowed nearby, its coals hissing as "The Spectre" drew a thin iron rod, its tip orange with heat, a tool the Najd's ancient torturers favored for its slow, searing precision.

"The Spectre" pressed the rod to Omar's left sole, the flesh sizzling instantly, a wet hiss rising as skin blackened and peeled, the stench of burnt meat sharp and nauseating in the cavern's stale air. Omar's body convulsed, his chained hands jerking against the stones, veins bulging in his neck as he bit back a scream, his teeth grinding audibly.

"The Spectre" shifted to the right sole, the rod's heat searing a fresh strip of agony, blisters bubbling and bursting, blood trickling down Omar's calves in thin, dark rivulets—each touch a nod to the Basṭīnah's cruel legacy, designed to break the body while leaving the mind intact to confess.

"Talk," "The Commander" growled, leaning close, his dagger tapping Omar's cheek. "The ransom—fake or real? Who's coming?" He wanted answers—but Omar's silence rang louder than a scream. Even pain couldn't touch that kind of defiance.

Omar's eyes, bloodshot and watering, locked on "The Commander," his voice a strained rasp. "Fuck you!"

"The Spectre" pressed harder, the rod grinding into charred flesh, the sound a wet crackle as nerves flared and died, a technique honed by tribes who once strung up spies to scream warnings across the dunes. Omar's body shook, sweat and blood dripping to the dirt, but his jaw clenched tighter, silence his only defiance.

Nova pounded her cage's bars, her chains rattling, her voice raw. "Leave him, you bastard!" Jaber cursed, his wrench useless against the steel, his ankle throbbing as he watched Omar endure.

"The Commander" straightened, his patience fraying, his growl deepening. "He's iron—try another. What's next?"

"The Keeper's" hood shifted, her whisper colder. "The Brazen Bull—for the loud one. Our warlords took it in the early wars—bronze forged into a beast, hollowed out to roast the living. Fire underneath, screams turned to roars through its pipes. They'd carve djinn names on it, call it justice for traitors. It'll cook his will."

Jaber had laughed at ghost stories. But this—this was metal shaped into madness. He'd seen a photo once, thought it was Khara. Now the hoax breathed heat at his heels.

"The Commander's" eyes narrowed, a cruel spark igniting. "Jaber—let him sing. Spectre, prepare it."

"The Spectre" released Omar, letting him hang, his soles a ruin of blackened meat, and turned to a shadowed alcove where the

Brazen Bull loomed—a hulking, tarnished statue, its bronze surface pitted and stained with the faint etchings of ancient curses, a relic adopted by Arabian clans to terrorize their foes.

"The Enforcer" dragged Jaber from his cage, the chains clanking as he forced him toward the bull, its hatch creaking open to reveal a cramped, soot-streaked interior. Jaber thrashed, his twisted ankle dragging, his voice a defiant snarl.

"You're sick—gonna roast me like a damn goat? I'll haunt you, you motherfuckers!"

"The Enforcer" shoved him inside, the hatch slamming shut, the lock snapping with a metallic clang. "The Spectre" piled dry acacia branches—wood the desert tribes once burned to fuel their grim rites—beneath the flames licking upward as he struck a match, the bull's belly glowing a dull red. The heat built fast, the bronze radiating a suffocating warmth.

Jaber's muffled screams turning to gasps as the air inside scorched his lungs. His skin blistered, sweat evaporating instantly, his clothes smoldering as the temperature soared past 200°F. The pipes, crafted to mimic the bull's bellow, warped his agony into low, guttural roars that echoed through the cavern—a haunting sound that once struck fear into medieval camps, now chilling even "The Scribe's" frantic typing.

Nova couldn't move, couldn't scream—but her heart pounded so loud it drowned out the bull's roar. She memorized every name, every face. They would pay.

"The Commander" crouched near the bull, his voice cutting through the noise. "The plan, Jaber—ransom's a lie, isn't it? Who's behind it?"

Jaber's voice, twisted by the pipes, rasped out, "Fuck… you…" He wasn't just resisting—he was marking the moment. If he died, it would be spitting in their fire, not begging for air.

His defiance held, though his body buckled, his fists pounding the searing metal, knuckles splitting, blood hissing as it hit the hot surface—a resistance as unyielding as the spies who once defied their captors in the bull's brazen gut.

Nova's voice cracked under the weight of helplessness, every scream a thread unraveling her control. Watching Jaber burn rewrote something deep in her.

"Stop it, you bastard! He's not breaking!" Omar, still hanging, groaned, his head lolling, his silence a mirror to Jaber's resistance.

The bull's heat climbed, the bronze glowing brighter, Jaber's roars fading to choked whimpers, his flesh cooking against the walls, the stench of burnt hair and skin seeping through the cracks—a visceral echo of the warlords' wrath. "The Spectre" watched, impassive, feeding the fire as "The Commander" stood, his patience a thin veneer over boiling rage.

Two captives held their secrets, their wills unyielding, their bodies bearing the brutal cost of their defiance in the Obsidian Hand's relentless grip.

The cavern's air hung heavy with the stench of burnt flesh and the echoes of Jaber's fading roars, the Brazen Bull's bronze glow casting a hellish light across the chamber. Omar dangled from the beam, his charred soles dripping blood onto the dirt, his breath a shallow rasp of defiance.

Nova gripped the bars of her cage, her knuckles white, her ribs screaming with each ragged inhale, her dark eyes locked on "The Commander" as he turned his scarred visage toward her. His yellow eyes burned with a cold, unrelenting fury, his dagger tapping a slow, deliberate beat against his thigh, each tap echoed in her chest like a countdown—his weapon wasn't just steel, it was the rhythm of control.

"The Commander" stepped closer, his growl slicing through the cavern's oppressive silence. "Your men are iron, Mendelsohn—Omar's feet are ash, Jaber's been cooked alive. But you—you're the brain, the thorn I can't pluck. The ransom's a lie, isn't it? A trap to draw us out. Tell me—who sent you? What's the play?"

Nova's jaw tightened, her voice steady despite the pain lancing her side, her defiance a shield against his glare. "You're fishing. You've got nothing but guesses and a blade. I'm not here to feed your paranoia."

"The Watcher," slipped forward from the shadows. Nova smelled dust and ash before she saw her—The Watcher always brought the storm with her, even in silence. Her dark eyes glinted as she leaned close to Nova's cage, her voice a venomous hiss that cut deeper than the blade at her hip.

"You think you're clever, Mendelsohn, but I've tracked every step. The Old Port—your dock rats, Jaber and Omar, skulking like rats. Warehouse 12—red mud on your boots, my tablet in your hands. The US Embassy—two days ago, slipping in at dawn, begging for help before you vanished into the sand. I see all—yellow eyes miss nothing. You're not a ghost; you're a fool caught in my snare."

Nova's pulse quickened, her mind racing—"The Watcher's" knowledge was a net, tight and precise, but she wouldn't let it choke her. Every detail The Watcher named clicked into place—Nova filed the intel behind her pain, weaponizing her panic.

"Nice story—write it down, sell it. Doesn't change a thing. I'm not breaking for you or your yellow-eyed dog."

"The Commander's" dagger stilled, his growl deepening, a storm brewing behind his scarred features. He turned abruptly, his robe swirling, and faced "The Arbiter," his tone a command wrapped in frustration. "She's stone—they all are. What's our move? They're not cracking."

"The Arbiter" stepped forward, his lean frame taut, his gray eyes flicking over Nova as he snapped his ledger shut, his voice a cold, measured hiss. "She's a rebel—a war captive in our grip. No honor, no mercy—she's defied the Najdi code. Her fate's ours to judge."

They weren't just torturers—they styled themselves executioners of a code twisted into madness.

"The Keeper's" hooded figure shifted, her bony fingers rattling her keys, his whisper dry and sinister. "Al-Khawz, but twisted for shame. The old tribes staked their enemies upright, slow death through the gut, a warning to the sands. We'll make it worse—strip her, hoist her high, let the desert and their drones see her fall."

This wasn't punishment—it was a signal flare. Her body would scream louder than her voice ever could.

Al-Khawz, or impalement, traced its roots to the brutal justice of pre-Islamic Arabia, where Najd clans drove sharpened stakes into their foes to prolong agony as a public deterrent. The victim's body, pierced and raised on poles, served as a grim banner, their suffering stretched over hours or days as gravity tore flesh and spirit apart.

"The Keeper's" humiliating twist echoed the warlords who stripped captives bare, amplifying the spectacle before tribes and enemies alike.

"The Commander's" lips curled, a cruel decision settling in his gaze. "Do it—break her pride, let the world watch."

"The Spectre," re-emerged from the shadows, his blood-stained thobe rustled as he approached Nova's cage, unlocking it with a deft twist of a key. "The Enforcer" yanked her out, his massive hands bruising her arms as he pinned her, her chains clanking against the bars. Nova fought, her body a whirlwind of resistance—kicking with her good leg, the shallow cut on her calf bleeding anew, her elbows slamming into "The Enforcer's" gut.

He grunted, his grip tightening, slamming her against the cage to stun her as "The Spectre's" curved knife flashed. The blade sliced through her jacket, shirt, and pants with ruthless precision, the fabric shredding and falling in tatters to the dirt. Her boots were wrenched off, kicked aside, leaving her bare under the cavern's sickly light.

Nova's stood stripped, but not broken. Her scars weren't shame—they were proof. The body they tried to shame had outlived every attempt before. Her skin was pale where unmarred, a stark canvas against the bruises blooming across her torso— purple and yellow welts outlining her cracked ribs. Her shoulders were narrow but muscled, her arms lean and sinewy, marked with faint, jagged scars from shrapnel and close calls, a lattice of resilience.

Her chest heaved with defiant breaths, her curvy breasts firm, nipples taut and darkened in the cavern's chill, a sheen of sweat glistening across her collarbone. Her waist curved inward, hips sharp and scraped from the chute's fall, a thin landing strip of ginger pubic hair, neatly trimmed, now bared in cruel vulnerability.

Her legs were strong, thighs taut with muscle, the shallow gash on her calf a red streak against her pale skin, blood trickling to her ankle, her feet calloused and dirt-streaked from the desert trek.

Omar groaned, his head lolling, his silence a protest as "The Spectre" stepped back, his work done. "The Doctor" and the "The Enforcer" moved in, their hands rough and clinical. They dragged a rusted metal plate from a corner—four feet square, pitted with age—and secured it to a thick iron pole, its base sharpened to a cruel point. A steel spike, two-feet long and blackened, was bolted to the plate at an angle, positioned to pierce through her right clavicle—a slow, gravity-driven impalement meant to shatter bone and nerve.

Nova thrashed harder, every flinch, every kick at "The Doctor's" Shin was more than instinct—it was defiance coded into her bones. She wouldn't give them stillness.

"Get off me!" she snarled, her voice raw, her muscles straining as she twisted, the chains biting deeper into her wrists, blood welling where the iron met flesh.

"The Enforcer" roared, pinning her to the plate, his meaty hands forcing her arms down as "The Doctor" looped the chains through hooks, her body stretched taut, the spike's cold tip pressing just below her right shoulder.

With a grunt, "The Enforcer" attached ropes to the pole, and with "The Scribe's" help, they hauled it upward, the mechanism creaking as it rose through a shaft in the cavern's ceiling—a natural vent widened by time and intent.

The pole breached the surface, thrusting Nova's naked form into the desert night, the sandstorm's fading winds whipping her hair and stinging her exposed skin. The apparatus swayed, the spike tilting her slightly downward, its tip piercing her right clavicle with a sickening crunch as gravity took hold.

The pain was a cataclysm—an incandescent inferno that erupted in her shoulder. The spike shattered more than bone. It threatened to unmake her. But pain was an old rival—this wasn't surrender, it was survival with teeth bared.

Blood gushed, a scalding flood that pulsed from the wound, cascading down her chest in thick, steaming rivulets, soaking her skin in a sticky, crimson sheen that glistened in the drone's thermal glow. Her nerves shrieked, a jagged symphony of electric fire that clawed down her arm, rendering it a useless, twitching limb, while her neck stiffened, muscles seizing as the pain clashed up her spine like a lightning strike.

Each sway of the pole was a new violation, the spike shifting, scraping bone fragments against raw flesh, a wet, grinding agony that pulsed with her heartbeat. She wouldn't black out. She wouldn't give them that. Focus narrowed—heartbeat, breath, rage. That was enough.

Above ground, the night sky stretched vast and clear, the sandstorm's remnants a faint haze as three micro-drones hovered at 300 feet, their thermal lenses sweeping Barga Al Kharaz's ridge for any sign of Nova, Jaber, and Omar.

Delta Force had deployed—ten elite operatives racing across the dunes in ATVs, still 20 miles out, their engines roaring through the desert silence—but the drones held the first vigil, their feeds streaming live to Captain Logan "Viper" Kincaid in the command tent. His green eyes narrowed as the thermal image sharpened, Nova's heat signature flaring—a lone, upright figure pierced and raised, her naked form stark against the cold sand.

They'd trained for worst-case scenarios. But this wasn't a target—it was their journalist, their comrade, strung like a trophy.

"Motherfuckin' hell!" Viper roared, his fist crashing onto the console, the metal denting under his fury. "They've got Nova—

stripped bare and impaled through the goddamn shoulder! Those sick sons of bitches stuck her up there like a fuckin' scarecrow! Where the hell are Jaber and Omar? Shit—these twisted bastards are begging for a bullet storm!"

Lieutenant Sam "Hawk" Hawkins leaned over the screen, his jaw clenched so tight it twitched, his voice a guttural snarl. "Right clavicle—bleeding like a stuck pig, she's alive but in deep shit. No thermal on the others—caves are swallowing 'em. Fuckin' animals— parading her naked to piss on us!"

Renshaw's voice crackled through the comms, steady but laced with barely contained rage. "Confirm visual—Nova's exposed, impaled, alive. Hold strike—Delta's inbound, ETA 15 mikes. Drones tighten, get angles. They're baiting us—keep it locked, we hit when we're close."

Viper's hands balled into fists, veins bulging as he spat, "Fifteen minutes? She's a goddamn pincushion up there—naked, bleeding, and those fuckers are laughing! I'll rip their throats out myself!"

The moment Nova rose above ground, Khalid's game changed. She wasn't bait—she was the hourglass turned over. He paced the cavern, his yellow eyes flicking not to the shaft but to the stacked crates of Semtex lining the walls and blasting his way to survival.

"The Watcher" stood at his side, her sneer replaced by a taut alertness, while "The Arbiter," "The Scribe," "The Enforcer," "The Keeper," "The Spectre," and "The Doctor" gathered closer, their faces grim with the weight of the moment. The captives' silence was no longer his focus—Nova's hoisted form was a distraction, a taunt, but the drones overhead signaled a tightening noose.

"Ransom's a ghost," Khalid growled, his voice a low thunder as he stabbed his dagger into a map on the table, pinning Doha's heart. "They're not talking—they're stalling. Delta's coming—drones mean boots on sand soon. We move now—scatter, detonate the

Semtex, bury this lair and their plan with it."

Rashid nodded, his ledger forgotten, his tone sharp. "Three tunnels—north, west, south. Split the crates, rig 'em remote—Darius and The Spectre haul, Adil sets the triggers. We're gone before they breach."

"The Keeper's" whisper cut in, her keys jangling as she gestured to the captives.

"Leave 'em—Omar's strung, Jaber's roasted, Mendelsohn's a beacon. They'll slow the dogs."

"The Scribe's" fingers danced over his laptop, his glasses slipping as he muttered, "Timers set—20 minutes 'til boom. Semtex'll collapse the ridge—drones won't see shit through the dust."

"The Commander's" gaze hardened, his dagger yanked free, tearing the map. "Move—north tunnel's mine. Zainab, west—Rashid, south. Darius, Spectre, Samir—load and rig. We detonate when we're clear—Najdi vengeance burns their trap to ash."

The Obsidian Hand sprang into motion, their footsteps echoing as they grabbed crates and weapons, the cavern a hive of calculated chaos.

Above, Nova hung pierced and bleeding, her pain a searing testament to their cruelty, but below, Khalid's focus was escape—her silence a moot point, her suffering a mere pawn in their flight and the Semtex's impending roar.

Veil 22

Requiem in the Dunes

The desert night unfurled over Barga Al Kharaz like a shroud of molten obsidian, the air a suffocating stew of blood's copper tang and the sandstorm's dying rasp. Nova hung naked, impaled on a steel spike. She didn't feel like a martyr—she felt like prey, bait on a hook carved from her own bones, but she would remember every face that watched her bleed.

The pole creaked in the frigid wind, each groan a jackhammer splitting her ravaged frame. Pain was a feral juggernaut, its talons sunk deep into her shoulder, shredding bone and sinew with unhinged savagery. The spike had obliterated her clavicle into a jagged graveyard, its blackened tip grinding against fractured shards, ripping muscle and nerve with every lurch of the apparatus.

Blood erupted in scalding torrents, a crimson deluge that sluiced over her pale breasts, dripping in thick, glistening ropes down her belly and groin to drench the sand below, the dunes gorging on her life in dark, steaming pools. Her right arm flopped, a mangled slab of meat twitching with electric agony, nerves flayed to screaming tatters, while her gasps clawed from her throat—each breath a thunderstrike smashing broken bone against steel, her vision a crimson fog of torment and blood loss.

Her skin prickled raw in the sandy gusts, sweat and blood congealing in a clammy sheen, her dark hair plastered in sweaty tangles, her legs quaking as toes scraped the sand, the shallow cut on her calf weeping red rivulets against her death-pale flesh.

Above, the drones' roar shredded the silence, their thermal eyes blazing as Operation Sandstorm Requiem surged into its brutal zenith. The 10 men deployed by Delta Force weren't just a strike team—they were coming for one of their own. Every mile shaved from the desert was carved from rage, ATVs snarling like rabid wolves, their matte-black frames vomiting sand in frenzied plumes.

Captain Logan "Viper" Kincaid spearheaded the assault, his lean frame hunched over the handlebars, green eyes aflame through NVGs, M4 carbine slung tight against his chest. Lieutenant Sam "Hawk" Hawkins gripped a SAW beside him, jaw locked like a steel trap, while Reaper, Ghost, Talon, and the rest fanned out—silent reapers forged in the crucible of Tehran, Mogadishu, and Baghdad. One mile out, then half, the ridge loomed—a jagged wound in the night, Nova's fading heat signature a desperate SOS.

Viper's voice tore through the comms, jagged with rage. "Visual on Nova—ridge top, naked, speared through the fuckin' shoulder! She's bleeding out—Jaber and Omar AWOL! Thirty seconds—Reaper, Ghost, flank north, cut the bastards off! Hawk, Talon, with me—straight in! We're ripping her down NOW!"

The ATVs screamed to a halt, engines choking out in a guttural snarl, the team vaulting off with lethal precision—Delta's DNA from the '80s Iran ops pulsing in their veins. Reaper and Ghost peeled north, MP5s whispering death as they vanished into the shadows, hunting escape routes. Viper stormed the ridge, Hawk and Talon pounding behind, every second Nova hung was a second her blood claimed the sand. Viper moved like the spike was through him, too, boots hammering sand, NVGs bathing the night in spectral green.

He hit Nova's position, breath exploding in a hiss of fury as her butchered form loomed—blood-drenched, swaying, the spike a tyrant twisting her shoulder into a grotesque slaughterhouse tableau.

"Goddamn animals—hold on, Nova!" Viper roared, slinging his rifle as he clawed up the pole's base, gloved hands tearing into rusted metal, sand grit shredding his palms. "Hawk, cover—full sweep! Talon, rope, medkit—fucking MOVE!"

Hawk dropped, SAW raking the ridge, his growl a primal snarl. "Clear—no topside yet! They're bunkered—get her down, she's a corpse on a stick!"

Talon flung a coiled rope and trauma kit, hands shaking with adrenaline as Viper snatched them mid-air. Nova's head slumped, lips cracked and blood-crusted, a guttural scream ripping free as he looped the rope under her arms, the hemp gouging her blood-slick skin. The spike shifted—a wet, bone-crunching snap—and she convulsed, her cry a banshee's wail shredding the night, blood jetting in a hot, arterial spray. Viper's saw flashed, teeth gnashing wood with a frantic rasp, splinters exploding as he hacked the pole's base.

"Brace—gonna hurt like a bitch!" he bellowed, muscles screaming, sweat blinding him. The pole hit like a guillotine's hilt, jarring the spike deeper—Nova's body a canvas of fresh agony, yet she clung to consciousness like it was a weapon.

Talon dove in, medkit ripping open—gauze, morphine, QuikClot spilling like guts. He stabbed a syrette into her thigh, morphine flooding her veins, her gasps softening as he slammed clotting powder into the wound, sand turning to a crimson swamp beneath her.

"She's crashing—pulse barely there, BP's tanking!" Talon yelled, hands drenched in her blood, gauze drowning red as he packed the gash, the spike a grotesque monument in her shoulder. "We've got seconds—exfil or she's dead!"

Viper dropped into the shaft, M4 up, plunging into the cavern's green-lit inferno—Delta's Balkans playbook alive: enemy exits flipped to breach points. The air stank of charred flesh and Semtex, the chamber a maelstrom of shadows. Omar hung from a beam, soles blackened husks, blood dripping in slow, dark rivers, his chest heaving faintly—alive, a stubborn ember in his ruin. Jaber lay dead in the Brazen Bull, fire extinguished, his charred corpse fused to bronze, skin cracked and oozing, a silent husk of defiance snuffed out.

Viper's stomach lurched, but his eyes locked on Omar.

"Hawk, Talon—second vic alive, topside—NOW!" he barked, slashing Omar's ropes with a vicious flick, the hemp parting as the big man collapsed, a wet groan gurgling from his throat.

Hawk rappelled down, boots slamming dirt, SAW sweeping as Viper gripped Omar's arms, blood smearing his vest in a slick tide. Talon followed, rope searing his gloves, and they hauled Omar's bulk, his soles dragging a red smear, his breath a rattling wheeze.

"He's half-dead—move, MOVE!" Hawk roared, shoving Omar's limp form through the vent, sand cascading as Viper climbed, yanking him free. Even broken, Omar was mass and muscle—Delta dragged more than a body; they hauled hope gasping from the grave. On the ridge, Hawk threw Omar over his shoulder, fireman's carry, legs pumping, blood soaking his back in a grisly streak as Omar's weight sagged, a broken titan teetering on the edge.

Viper hit his comms, voice a guillotine's edge. He didn't issue orders—he hurled fury. Nova wasn't just a soldier; she was his war drum, and someone had silenced her. "Renshaw—Nova and Omar critical, Jaber's KIA! Get an MC-130H Combat Talon II—LZ ridge top, stat! Scramble B-2s from Al Udeid— JDAMs hot, nuke every fuckin' vehicle these rats stashed! Semtex's live—lair's a bomb, we're on borrowed time!"

Renshaw's reply snapped back, taut with fury. "Talon II's airborne—ETA 7 mikes! B-2s out of Al Udeid, weapons free—hold ground, disarm or die!"

Inside, Reaper and Ghost breached the north tunnel, MP5s silent, sweeping a chamber stacked with Semtex crates—Cyrillic labels curling like dead flesh, timers flashing red, 12 minutes bleeding to 9.

"Holy fuck—enough to glass the desert!" Reaper hissed, NVGs catching the glow of triggers rigged in haste. "No hostiles—tunnels fork west, south—boot prints, tire scuffs—they're bolting!"

Ghost probed a crate, voice a razor wire. "Remote dets—can't kill 'em all, too wired! West tunnel's got exhaust—vehicles stashed! South's tight—foot traffic! They're splitting—fast!"

Viper regrouped topside, Nova and Omar sprawled on stretchers, Talon's hands a frantic blur—IVs dripping saline, gauze a sodden red mess. "MC-130's 7 mikes—B-2s hunting!" he shouted, wind lashing sand into their eyes. Drones screamed overhead, feeds blazing as B- 2 Spirits from Al Udeid Air Base tore through the night sky—stealth wings slicing the heavens, their angular fuselages painted matte black, engines a low, menacing thrum.

Launched from Qatar's sprawling airbase, 300 miles east, the bombers had scrambled at Mach 0.95, their crews—pilots call-signed "Raven" and "Wraith"—locked in, radar-absorbent hulls evading detection, bomb bays bristling with 2,000-pound GBU-31 JDAMs—GPS- guided harbingers of annihilation.

The desert was a furnace of chaos, the ridge trembling as the Semtex timers ticked—9 minutes to annihilation—and The Obsidian Hand clawed through their subterranean escape routes, a pack of cornered jackals scattering into Barga's labyrinthine bowels. Delta Force wasn't waiting for the MC-130H or the B-2s to clean up—they were bloodhounds unleashed, their veins pumping rage, their prey's scent thick in the air.

Viper's voice erupted over the comms, a guttural war cry, spit flecking his lips as he roared, "Reaper, Ghost—north tunnel, rip their throats out! Hawk, Talon—hold Nova and Omar, medevac's 6 mikes! Raven, Wraith—west with me! Talon Two, Reaper Two—south! We're gutting these fuckers—NOW!"

Reaper and Ghost tore north, boots slamming damp stone, the tunnel a cavernous gullet— six feet high, walls glistening with condensation, roots piercing the ceiling like skeletal claws dripping with moisture, the air a rancid stew of mold and sweat. Their NVGs bathed the passage in a sickly green glow, MP5s up, suppressors hissing like vipers as they tracked "The Enforcer," and "The Spectre," 50 yards ahead, hauling a Semtex crate toward a collapsed vent. "The Enforcer's" massive frame lumbered, his sledgehammer swinging like a pendulum of death, its gore-crusted head glinting, his growl a thunderous bellow, "Vent's tight—crawl, Spectre! Buggy's 400 out—move or we're ash!"

"The Spectre" slithered ahead, wiry and silent as a shadow, crate scraping rock, his voice a venomous hiss, "B-2s'll hit—go, you lumbering ox! I'm not dying here!"

Reaper's voice was a guttural snarl, his breath hot against his mic, "Visual—big bastard and the skinny fuck, 50 yards! Ghost—flank right, I'm straight—let's carve 'em!"

Ghost peeled into a side crevice—a razor-thin slit, barely two feet wide—belly-crawling as sand and shale ground into his tac vest, his MP5 braced, suppressor kissing the stone.

Reaper charged, boots splashing through shallow, fetid puddles, a flashbang arcing from his gloved hand—BANG—the tunnel exploding in blinding white light and a deafening CRACK, the shockwave slamming "The Enforcer's" ears, his roar a pained bellow as he stumbled, hammer crashing to the floor with a bone-rattling thud, splintering rock.

For a split second, Reaper watched the hammer drop—then he moved, faster than guilt, before that arm could rise again. He leapt, a predator's lunge, his M4's stock swinging like a battering ram—CRUNCH— smashing "The Enforcer's" skull, the bone caving inward with a wet, pulpy snap, brain matter oozing black in the green glow, his massive body collapsing like a felled oak, blood pooling in a viscous, steaming lake beneath him.

"One down—another's rabbiting!" Reaper barked. His voice was steel, but his chest burned. Killing was easy—chasing ghosts was harder. Hassan vanished through the vent, his wiry frame a fleeting shadow swallowed by sand and darkness. Ghost emerged from the crevice, his voice a razor's edge, "He's gone—vent's a fuckin' rat hole! Buggy's 400—pursue?"

Reaper's boots pounded, diving for the vent—a jagged maw, three feet wide, sand spilling inward—his shoulders scraping rock as he crawled, MP5 ahead, "Hell yes—Spectre's mine! Cover north!" The tunnel shuddered, a B-2's distant BOOM reverberating, dust raining as Reaper pushed deeper, chasing a ghost.

Viper bulldozed forward—Raven danced with his rifle, Wraith slithered between shadows like a breathless curse, tearing down a damp, serpentine passage— walls slick with seepage, ceiling sagging with jagged stalactites dripping water that stung their eyes, air a moldy choke thick with the stench of fear-soaked sweat. Their NVGs caught the heat of "The Commander," "The Watcher," "The Scribe," and "The Doctor," 70 yards ahead, racing for a garage—three Toyota Hiluxes, sand-camouflaged under a dune overhang, 500 yards out.

"The Commander's" yellow eyes blazed like twin infernos, robe whipping in his wake, dagger slashing air as he roared, his voice a guttural thunderclap, "Hiluxes—west gate! Zainab, cover—Adil, detonate at 5 mikes! Samir—rig the last crate—NOW!" Zainab's MP5 rattled, a blind burst ripping back down the tunnel, bullets ricocheting off stone with sharp pings, her snarl a venomous lash, "Delta's close—move or we're meat!"

"The Scribe" clutched his laptop, remote trembling in sweat-slick hands, gasping, "7 mikes—triggers live—fuck, they're gaining!" "The Doctor" fumbled a crate, scalpels clinking against Semtex, his voice a frantic wheeze, "Set—go, go!"

Viper's NVGs locked their heat signatures, his voice a feral howl, spit flying as he roared, "West—70 yards, four tangos! Raven—grenade! Wraith—left flank—bleed 'em dry!" Raven ripped a frag grenade from his vest, its pin yanked with a metallic clink, hurling it—a tumbling harbinger of death arcing through the tunnel's gloom—BOOM, the passage erupting in a deafening roar, shrapnel shredding "The Doctor's" back like a swarm of razors, his white coat blooming crimson as his spine snapped, ribs jutting through torn flesh, his body collapsing atop the crate with a wet thud.

Plans died in flames—one wrong twitch, and the whole desert might swallow them with Nova still bleeding behind them.

The Semtex detonated prematurely—CRASH—a fireball exploding outward, singeing "The Watcher's" keffiyeh, her scream a raw, guttural wail as flames licked her face, blistering skin, her

MP5 clattering to the stone.

"Another one's toast—three left!" Viper bellowed, charging through the smoke, M4 barking—suppressed rounds stitching "The Watcher's" leg with surgical precision, muscle tearing, bone splintering as she crumpled, blood jetting in a hot arc, her hands clawing the dirt, keffiyeh smoldering. Wraith flanked left, weaving through a stalactite forest, his silenced pistol popping—thwip-thwip—two rounds punching "The Scribe's" chest, his sternum shattering, blood and bone shards exploding outward, laptop sparking as it crashed, the remote skittering across the floor in a shower of glass and circuits.

"Third one down—fourth's hit!" Wraith snarled, but "The Watcher" crawled, her leg a mangled ruin, blood trailing in a thick, glistening smear, her fingers scrabbling for her MP5 as "The Commander" hit the garage, ripping a tarp off a Hilux, engine snarling to life with a guttural growl.

Viper closed, boots pounding, a flashbang arcing—BANG—light and sound blasting, "The Watcher" fell with a whimper, not a prophecy. Nova had earned that silence. Raven leapt, a knee slamming her skull to the stone—*CRACK*—her neck snapping with a wet, final pop, her body twitching once before going still, eyes staring blankly, yellow dust mingling with her blood. "Fourth's out—One's rolling!" Raven roared, as Viper vaulted a crate, M4 up, chasing the Hilux's dust trail.

South, Talon and Reaper Two hunted "The Arbiter," and "The Keeper," through a tighter tunnel—a claustrophobic chute of jagged despair, its ceiling spiked with razor-sharp rock that snagged their tac vests, air a gritty haze of dust and stale breath, walls narrowing to four feet, forcing a hunched, breathless sprint that tore at their lungs.

Sixty yards ahead, "The Arbiter" led, his lean frame weaving, boots pounding toward a wadi exit—two dirt bikes under a sand-crusted tarp, 300 yards out, their frames glinting in his flashlight's jittering beam. "The Keeper" trailed, her gaunt figure cloaked in a hood, bony fingers jangling a ring of keys that clinked like death knells, her whisper a dry rasp cutting through the din, "Wadi—bikes! Rashid, cover—I'll rig a trap!" Her skeletal hands clutched a Semtex brick, a crude tripwire dangling, her hood slipping to reveal a face like weathered parchment, eyes sunken pits of malice.

"The Arbiter's" voice bounced off stone like a ricochet, sharp and commanding, "South's ours—bikes are freedom! Alya—set it and move!" His ledger was clutched like a lifeline, pages fluttering as he sprinted, the flashlight's beam slicing the dark, catching "The Keeper's" hunched silhouette as she knelt, keys scraping rock to anchor the wire.

A B-2's roar shook the tunnel overhead, stalactites snapping like brittle bones, crashing behind them in a hail of splintered rock that peppered their backs, dust choking the air into a suffocating slurry.

Talon's voice was a razor's edge, his breath ragged with fury, "Sixty yards—two tangos! Reaper Two, right fork—flank 'em!" Reaper Two split into a side passage—a claustrophobic slit, three feet wide, its walls slick with seepage that soaked his boots, shale slipping underfoot as he scrambled, M4 scraping stone, sweat stinging his eyes like acid.

Talon closed, his NVGs painting the tunnel green, a stun grenade arcing from his hand— *CRACK*—the passage flaring in blinding light and a deafening blast, sound waves slamming "The Arbiter's" ears, his stagger a drunken lurch as his ledger flew, pages scattering like ash across the blood-streaked floor.

"The Keeper" spun, her trap half-set, the Semtex brick trembling in her grip, her whisper a venomous hiss, "Dogs—taste Najdi wrath!" She yanked the tripwire taut, keys jangling as she lunged back, but

Talon was faster. For one breath, he saw the trap still humming in The Keeper's hand. Then he moved—faster than her final prayer—his boots pounded, a predator's charge, tackling "The Arbiter" first, knees driving into his spine—SNAP—vertebrae cracking like dry twigs, a guttural scream cut short as Talon's knife flashed, slashing his throat in a vicious arc.

Blood jetted, a scalding geyser spraying the walls, "The Arbiter's" gurgle a wet, choking death rattle as his body slumped, sand drinking his life in a steaming, crimson tide, his gray eyes glazing over, ledger pages soaking red beneath him.

"He's done!" Talon snarled, spinning as "The Keeper" darted, her hood flapping, keys clinking like a frantic metronome, the Semtex brick clutched like a dark prayer.

Reaper Two emerged from the flank, his M4 barking—suppressed rounds whizzing, one grazing "The Keeper's" arm, blood blooming black in the green glow, the brick slipping from her grasp with a dull thud.

"Got a bleeder—pin her!" he roared, boots slipping as he closed, but "The Keeper" twisted, skeletal frame darting into a shadow—a narrow alcove, two feet wide, its walls jagged with protruding rock, a dead-end refuge.

Talon charged, his voice a guttural bellow, "No hole saves you, you fucking rat!" He ripped a flashbang, hurling it into the alcove—*BANG*—light and sound exploding, "The Keeper's" scream a shrill, broken wail as her eardrums ruptured, blood trickling from her ears, her hood singed, keys scattering across the floor like spilled teeth. Reaper Two flanked, M4 up, but Talon was in—his gloved fist slammed "The Keeper's" jaw—*CRACK*—teeth shattering, bone splintering. The rock cracked louder than her skull. That was enough—no scream left to offer.

"The Keeper" slumped, still twitching, her sunken eyes wide with fading malice, blood pooling from her ruined mouth, but Talon wasn't done. "You don't rig my grave, fucker!" he roared, knife flashing again—*SHUNK*—plunging into "The Keeper's" chest, the blade sinking through ribs with a sickening crunch, piercing breast, lung and heart, blood spurting in a hot fountain, soaking Talon's arm to the elbow.

He twisted the knife, a savage wrench—*SNAP*—ribs breaking further, "The Keeper's" body jerking once, a final gurgle bubbling from her throat as her life bled out, the Semtex brick rolling free, its wire limp and impotent.

"Another one out—south's clear!" Talon spat, yanking the blade free, blood dripping from its edge in thick, steaming drops, wiping it on "The Keeper's" tattered hood, the fabric tearing under the weight of gore. Reaper Two kicked the Semtex brick aside, his voice tight, "Trap's dead—wadi's ours! Bikes are clean!" The tunnel shuddered, a distant JDAM blast from above rattling loose shale, dust raining as Talon retrieved the keys—rusted, blood-slick—a grim trophy of the kill.

"The Spectre," was a phantom amid the slaughter, his escape a masterstroke of cold, calculated survival. As "The Enforcer" fell, Reaper's M4 stock caving his skull, "The Spectre" had slithered through the north tunnel's collapsed vent—a jagged maw, three feet wide, sand spilling inward like a hungry mouth. His wiry frame twisted, bones grinding against stone, his blood-stained thobe tearing as he crawled, abandoning the Semtex crate, its weight a death sentence he shed without a second thought.

His hollow cheeks were smeared with sweat and grit, his void-like eyes glinting with a predator's focus, breath shallow and silent as he emerged into the night, 400 yards north of Barga's heart.

The dune buggy—rusted, acacia-shrouded—was a decoy he never intended to reach. As Reaper's boots pounded the vent behind him,

"The Spectre" rolled sideways, tumbling into a fissure—a narrow crack in the dune's flank, hidden by a collapsed acacia trunk, its gnarled branches a skeletal veil. Sand stung his grazed arms, blood oozing from a shallow shrapnel cut, but he smeared it with fistfuls of desert grit, masking his heat signature, his thobe blending with the dune's ochre hue.

From a pouch at his waist, he pulled a thermal blanket—scavenged from a dead Bedouin smuggler two months prior, its metallic weave dull and patched—unfurling it over his crouched form, flattening against the dune's curve like a chameleon on stone.

Above, a B-2 Spirit—callsign "Wraith"—roared, its thermal sensors sweeping, locking the buggy's heat as Hassan's faint trace vanished beneath the blanket's shroud. "North—400, buggy moving!" Wraith barked, a GBU-31 dropping—15 seconds of freefall, then a cataclysmic *BOOM,* the buggy erupting in a molten storm, metal and sand fusing, the blast wave slamming the dune, acacia branches incinerating in a fiery rain.

"The Spectre" went rigid. He didn't pray. He had no god. Just breath held in a crevice, waiting for the fire to pass him by. The explosion's thunder swallowed his desperate slide into the fissure—a six-foot plunge into a shadowed hollow, scoured eons ago by savage floods. Its walls, slick with mineral sweat, glinted like obsidian veins; above, Samr roots coiled in gnarled tangles, a lattice of desiccated serpents clawing the air.

"Fools chase the blaze—shadows outlast," he spat, voice a venomous rasp drowned in the cacophony. Victory wasn't survival—vanishing was. He didn't need to win battles. He just needed to be the last shadow standing.

His fingers tore at the gritty earth, nails splitting as he tunneled sideways, 450 yards north through Barga Al Kharaz's sun-scorched dunes. Overhead, the predatory whine of U.S. military drones sliced the sky, their thermal eyes raking the desert for life. Escape above ground was suicide—the Persian Gulf shimmered 242 kilometers east, a taunting mirage across an exposed crucible of sand.

His path led to a forgotten wadi, a bone-dry scar snaking through the dunes, its floor littered with jagged flints and the rusted husks of abandoned tin cans, glinting like cruel winks in the sunlight. No Bedouin sled waited here; the desert offered no such mercy. Instead, his hands found the lip of a concealed sinkhole, whispered of in smuggler tales—a crumbling maw into an ancient qanat, an underground vein of tunnels once channeling water from distant aquifers toward the Gulf's briny edge.

"The Spectre" dropped into darkness, sand avalanching around him, The desert's furnace died behind him, replaced by a tomb's breath—damp, bitter, alive with the ghosts of thirst. The tunnel stretched east, its ceiling braced by cracked limestone, roots piercing through like skeletal fingers.

He crawled, knees grinding against the uneven floor, the distant thrum of helicopters vibrating the walls, dust sifting down in choking clouds. His wiry frame pressed forward, scraping through narrowing passages where the qanat's ancient builders had faltered, their ghosts now silent witnesses to his flight.

Hours bled into eternity, the tunnel weaving beneath dune and rock, its path erratic but relentless toward the Gulf. At last, a faint saline tang kissed the air. Each stroke of his battered limbs was a prayer answered in salt and shadow. The qanat opened into a coastal cave, its mouth hidden by tidal boulders, waves gnashing beyond. A derelict skiff—12 feet of salt-crusted wood, its hull pocked but seaworthy, oars warped yet whole—bobbed in the shallows, tethered by rotting rope.

He tore it free, leaping aboard, oars carving the water with fevered strokes. The cave's shadow cloaked him as he rowed, a wraith slipping from Barga's fire and the U.S. military's unblinking gaze, vanishing into the Gulf's vast, clandestine embrace.

Viper hit the west garage, "The Commander's" Hilux roaring 600 yards out, sand spraying in a frenzied plume as he weaved through dunes, engine screaming, tires chewing earth. Distance wasn't just yards—it was seconds bleeding away from Nova's life.

"One's on the move—600 west! Raven—cut him!" Viper bellowed, leaping onto an ATV, its engine snarling to life with a guttural howl, sand blasting his face as he gunned it, Raven and Wraith flanking, M4s blazing—suppressed rounds pinging off the Hilux's frame, glass shattering, metal screeching.

"The Commander's" yellow eyes glared back through the rearview, dagger slashing air as he roared, his voice a thunderous death knell, "Najdi fire—detonate! Bury these dogs!" He didn't flinch. If he died, it would be dragging the world's spite down with him. His hand slammed a backup remote—Semtex timers flashing 5 minutes—his robe soaked with sweat and blood from a ricochet graze, his scarred face a mask of feral defiance.

Raven closed, ATV skidding as he ripped a frag grenade, hurling it—a tumbling reaper arcing through the night—*BOOM,* the Hilux's rear axle shredding, metal twisting in a tortured squeal, tires bursting with a pop-pop, rubber flaying as the truck spun, slamming into a dune with a bone-jarring *CRASH.* The night fractured—sand, smoke, and screams colliding as metal screamed its death song.

"The Commander" kicked the door open, staggering out, dagger flashing as he charged Viper— 50 yards, 30, 10—his roar a guttural war cry, "You'll burn with me!"

Viper leapt, boots hitting sand, M4 barking—three rounds punched "The Commander's" chest in a tight triangle, the first shattering his sternum with a wet *crack,* blood and bone shards exploding outward, the second tearing through his lung, a gurgling wheeze erupting as crimson frothed his lips, the third piercing his heart, stopping it dead. Every round was a payment—interest on what they'd done to Nova, to Jaber, to Omar.

Seventh one's down—all but one!" Viper snarled, breath heaving, sand sticking to his sweat-drenched face as he kicked the dagger away, its blade sinking into the dune.

The lair rumbled, 4 minutes to detonation, a low, guttural growl building in its stone belly as Reaper and Ghost regrouped, Ghost's voice tight with frustration.

Slippery enemies didn't die easily—they plotted.

"Wiry one's gone—slipped the fuckin' net! Buggy's ash—where's the bastard?" Reaper spat sand, his NVGs scanning the north vent's wreckage, "Fucker's a ghost—hunt later!

Semtex's live—pull back!" Viper's fist slammed the ATV's handlebars, metal denting under his knuckles, "Goddamn it—another one's out there! Talon—status, NOW!"

Talon's voice cracked over the ridge, a desperate howl cutting the wind. He wasn't a medic now—just a man trying to stop death with his bare hands. "Nova's fading— pulse a whisper, blood's everywhere! Omar's barely breathing—lungs wet, he's drowning in it! MC-130's 3 mikes—Semtex's at 4! We're cutting it to the wire—GO!"

The Combat Talon II descended. It wasn't a bird or a machine—it was deliverance forged in steel and roaring fury. Its silhouette was a black leviathan against the stars, engines a deafening ROAR, ramp dropping, sand swirling in a blinding vortex as Delta hauled Nova and Omar aboard—stretchers rocking violently, blood pooling on the metal floor, IV bags swaying, Talon's hands a crimson blur as he screamed, “Secure ‘em—lift, lift!”

ATVs roared to life, engines shrieking as Delta raced the blast radius—Viper, Raven, Wraith, Reaper, Ghost—sand blasting their faces, goggles fogging with sweat and grit, the lair’s rumble swelling to a volcanic bellow.

The Semtex ignited—*ROAR*—Barga cratering in a hellish plume, sand and stone erupting like a geyser from the earth’s gut, the shockwave slamming their backs, ATVs fishtailing as the MC-130H clawed skyward, its ramp sealing with a clang, Nova’s blood-streaked stretcher rattling, Omar’s broken form shuddering, the desert swallowing their prey’s grave.

The world ended behind them—but inside the Talon, life clung by threads no blast could sever.

Viper’s eyes burned through the cockpit window, staring back at the inferno, The Spectre’s shadow a festering wound in his gut. “One got away,” he growled, voice a low, guttural promise, fists clenched as the Talon II banked north, the desert’s silence a mocking veil over the escapee’s unseen flight. The Spectre wasn’t just unfinished business. He was a wound that would bleed until closed.

The hunt was deferred, but Delta’s wrath simmered, a storm poised to break when, and if, the ghost resurfaced.

Veil 23

Lifelines in the Sky

The war outside had gone quiet, but inside the Talon II, it raged louder, blood and desperation echoing in every rivet of the hull. The copter tore through the Qatar night like a wounded beast, its engines a deafening ROAR that vibrated the fuselage into a shuddering scream, clawing the sky at 320 knots, banking so hard north from Barga Al Kharaz's smoldering grave that the frame groaned under the strain.

Inside, the cargo bay was a slaughterhouse of desperation—a hellscape of blood-slick steel and flickering red emergency lights, the air a choking miasma of coppery gore, antiseptic's bitter sting, and the rancid stench of flesh rotting alive. Nova and Omar were lashed to stretchers bolted to the deck, their bodies mangled wrecks on the precipice of death, Delta Force operatives hunched over them like frenzied surgeons in a war zone, hands trembling, voices cracking as they fought a losing battle.

The Semtex's apocalyptic blast still seared their retinas—7

minutes had exploded into zero, the lair's collapse a fiery maw that swallowed The Obsidian Hand, save for The Spectre's phantom escape—and now, 30 miles south of Al Wakra Hospital, every heartbeat was a guillotine's drop.

Nova's stretcher bucked wildly with the Talon's turbulence, her naked body a grotesque tableau beneath a blood-drenched thermal blanket. The spike wasn't just metal—it was a message still gouging into her, even as they tried to outrun death.

Blood gushed in torrents, a steaming crimson flood that soaked the blanket, pooling in thick, clotting rivers across the stretcher, dripping onto the deck in a relentless pat-pat-pat that echoed like a death knell. The QuikClot jammed into the wound was a sodden, gritty mess, oozing through his fingers, her right arm a twitching, useless slab of meat— nerves flayed raw, spasming with electric fire that morphine couldn't touch, its bluish tint a grim herald of necrosis creeping in.

Her dark hair was a matted snarl, plastered to her face with sweat and blood, her cracked lips gaping, a guttural, animalistic keening ripping from her throat as her eyes—bloodshot, wild, nearly blind—darted in a haze of agony, pupils blown wide with shock.

Talon knelt over her, his gloved hands a frantic, crimson-soaked blur. Every second he lost her, he lost himself. Blood soaked through his gloves, but it was the weight of helplessness that crushed him.

"Nova—FUCKING STAY WITH ME!" he screamed, voice shredded raw, spit flying as he ripped open a trauma kit with shaking hands, gauze and syringes clattering to the deck like spent shells. Her pulse flickered, barely there–a dying echo he chased with every breath he could give her.

"She's tanking—hemorrhagic shock! Where's the goddamn PLASMA?!" he roared, tearing a bag of O-negative from the kit with his teeth—*RIP*—plastic shredding, his jaw clenched so hard his molars ached, spiking it with a trembling hand, the blood-red fluid surging into her left arm, the needle buckling as her vein blew, a fresh spurt of crimson spraying his face, stinging his eyes.

Viper loomed over Talon, his green eyes blazing like twin infernos through NVGs fogged with sweat, M4 swinging against his chest, sand and blood crusting his tac vest in a gritty armor. "KEEP HER ALIVE, TALON—15 MIKES TO AL WAKRA! SHE DIES, WE'RE FUCKED!" His voice was a guttural howl, fists slamming the stretcher's frame—*CLANG*— metal denting, the Semtex blast's aftershock still pounding his skull, The Spectre's escape a jagged shard twisting in his gut.

Nova's keening spiked—a wet, choking shriek—as Talon shoved a fresh gauze pack against the spike, blood jetting around his fingers, soaking his sleeves to the elbows in a steaming, visceral tide.

"Spike's tearing her apart—bone's fucking GONE! I CAN'T STOP IT—NEED A SURGEON NOW!" Talon's scream cracked, his hands slipping in the gore, the monitor shrieking as her heart flatlined—*EEEEEE*—a piercing wail, then jolted back, a weak thump-thump, 28 beats, her body seizing, legs thrashing, blood frothing at her lips as her chest arched in a spasmodic convulsion.

Omar lay three feet away. Once immovable, he was now dissolving by inches—his silence louder than any scream. His soles were charred atrocities—flesh peeled away in blackened, weeping strips, blisters bursting with pus and blood, the Basṭīnah's iron rods having melted through skin and muscle to expose bone, a reek of burnt meat and infection clawing the air like a living thing.

Blood streamed from his wrists, flayed raw by hemp ropes, pooling beneath him in a dark, sticky lake, sand and sweat congealing into a grotesque slurry on the deck. His chest heaved in wet, drowning gurgles—each breath a torturous rattle-rattle-hiss as fluid flooded his lungs, blood and pus bubbling at the corners of his blue-tinged lips, his face a death mask of ashen gray, sweat pouring in rivulets down his sunken cheeks. His eyes, bloodshot and glassy, stared into nothing, pupils dilated, his calloused hands clawing the stretcher's edges, fingers snapping with brittle cracks as muscle seized, his body a furnace of sepsis burning him alive from within.

Lieutenant Sam "Hawk" Hawkins hunched over him, SAW slammed against the stretcher, his hands a trembling mess of blood and desperation as he forced an oxygen mask over Omar's face, the plastic fogging with wet, labored breaths, O2 hissing like a punctured tire.

"OMAR—FUCKING BREATHE, YOU HEAR ME?!" Hawk's voice was a primal roar, cracking with terror, his fingers ripping open a chest tube kit—plastic and steel clattering like a gunshot as it hit the deck, blood smearing his gloves in a slick, crimson sheen. The monitor screeched—oxygen saturation plunging to 78%, pulse a faltering 45, BP 65/35—a cacophony of collapse, red lights flashing like a dying star.

His lungs weren't just failing—they were drowning him from the inside. Every breath was a battlefield. "Pneumothorax—he's fucking FLOODING!" Hawk bellowed, slashing Omar's shirt with a combat knife—RIP—the blade tearing through fabric and skin, exposing a chest mottled with purple-black bruises and oozing burns, ribs jutting like broken spears beneath taut, fever-hot flesh.

He plunged the tube's needle between the second and third ribs—*SHUNK*— a sickening pop as it punched through, air and blood erupting in a frothy, crimson geyser, spraying Hawk's chest, splattering his NVGs, the tube sucking a torrent of gore as Omar's chest convulsed, a guttural *GAAAAH* tearing from his throat, blood flecking the mask.

"He's septic—lungs are SHIT!" Hawk screamed, taping the tube with shaking hands, blood and pus oozing around the seal, the monitor's beeps lurching—O2 clawing to 80%, pulse 48—as he stabbed a broad-spectrum antibiotic syringe into Omar's thigh—*CRUNCH*—the needle snapping through muscle, fluid surging into his bloodstream, fighting a tidal wave of infection that turned his veins black beneath the skin.

"HOLD ON—WE'RE ALMOST THERE!" Hawk's voice broke, his fist slamming Omar's chest—*THUD*—ribs creaking, forcing a wet, choking inhale, blood spraying the deck as the big man's eyes rolled back, a gurgling hiss escaping as his body shuddered, teetering on the abyss.

Viper stormed the bay, boots pounding steel—*CLANG-CLANG*—his comms crackling as he roared, "RENSHAW—ETA TO AL WAKRA, FUCKING NOW! NOVA'S GONE—OMAR'S DROWNING! WE'RE LOSING EVERYTHING!" His voice was a jagged blade, spit flying, fists smashing the bulkhead—*CRASH*—metal buckling, his knuckles splitting, blood dripping as Renshaw's reply cut through, a steel whip cracking,

"12 MIKES—MED TEAM'S SCRAMBLED! TALON II'S REDLINING—HOLD 'EM OR THEY'RE CORPSES!" The fuselage lurched, turbulence slamming the stretchers—BANG—Nova's spike grinding deeper—*CRUNCH*—a fresh torrent of blood erupting, her scream a shredded YAAAAA as Talon roared, "SHE'S SEIZING—FLATLINE! FUCK!" He jammed a third morphine syrette into her neck—*SHUNK*—her body slumping, pulse flickering—25, 22—alarms a deafening *EEEEEEEE* as Viper's roar shook the bay, "FASTER—THEY'RE DYING!"

Omar's stretcher jolted, the chest tube bubbling a frothy red flood, his eyes snapping shut, a guttural *CHOKE* as Hawk bellowed, "NO—NO YOU DON'T!" He slammed both fists onto Omar's chest—*THUMP-THUMP*—ribs snapping like dry branches, blood spurting from the tube, forcing a wet, gasping HURGH.

Hawk didn't count compressions—he counted the seconds he refused to let his brother die, the monitor spiking—O2 to 82%, pulse 45—as the Talon II screamed toward Al Wakra, its lights a faint, mocking glimmer 10 minutes out.

The bay was a maelstrom. The floor was red, but not from war—it was the price of not letting go. Monitors shrieked like banshees, Delta clawing at the threads of life—Nova and Omar's fates dangling over a bottomless pit, the desert night a ravenous void snapping at their heels.

The MC-130H tore into Al Wakra's airspace, its engines a bone-shaking ROAR that shredded the Qatari night, a black leviathan clawing the sky at 320 knots, its frame rattling as it banked hard over the hospital's helipad, every rivet groaning under the strain.

Ten minutes had stretched into a blood-drenched crucible, the cargo bay a chaotic hell— blood pooling in dark, sticky lakes across the deck, seeping into cracks, the air thick with the sharp tang of copper and antiseptic's sterile bite, monitors shrieking like wounded beasts.

Nova and Omar were strapped to stretchers, their bodies broken husks teetering on the brink, Delta Force operatives hunched over them, hands trembling with urgency, voices raw as they battled to hold death at bay.

The Semtex's blast still echoed in their skulls—7 minutes had detonated into a fiery abyss, Barga Al Kharaz reduced to a smoldering crater, most of The Obsidian Hand buried in its ruin, one tango slipping the net like a shadow—and now, approaching the southside of Al Wakra Hospital, every tick of the clock was a razor's edge.

"Touchdown—MOVE YOUR ASSES, NOW!" Captain Logan "Viper" Kincaid barked, his voice a guttural growl slicing through the bay, boots hammering the deck—*CLANG- CLANG*—as he leapt from the ramp, M4 swinging, sand blasting his blood-streaked face like a gritty hail.

The helipad blazed below—a stark white square ringed with floodlights, med teams scrambling with gurneys, wheels squealing on concrete, shouts piercing the rotor wash— "Trauma stat! Code black!"—as the Talon II's ramp slammed open—*BOOM*—sand and wind erupting in a blinding vortex, choking the air with desert dust.

Nova's stretcher jolted hard, her naked form shrouded in a blood-drenched thermal blanket, the steel spike in her right clavicle grinding—*CRUNCH*—with every lurch, her chest rising in shallow, wet gasps. Talon unstrapped her, hands slick with sweat, voice tight and urgent,

"She's crashing—get her out, stat!" Her pulse flickered at 20 beats, the monitor's *EEEEEEEE* a relentless wail as medics swarmed, gloved hands yanking the stretcher free—*SCREECH*—gurney wheels grinding concrete, leaving a dark red smear in their wake.

Omar's massive frame rocked as Hawk unlashed him, his charred soles seeping pus, chest tube bubbling crimson, breaths a labored *RATTLE-HISS.* "He's septic—lungs are failing!" Hawk growled, voice rough and strained, hands steady despite the tremor as medics hauled Omar's stretcher, the deck slick with his blood, gurney lurching forward, a trail of gore streaking the helipad like a warpath.

As the Talon II's engines wound down, rotor blades chopping air—*WHUMP-WHUMP*—noise gave way to precision. Outside was chaos, but inside the hospital gates, survival followed rules. Medics shouted—"Bay 1, Bay 2—crash protocol, now!"—as Viper strode beside, green eyes sharp with focus, fists clenched, boots pounding—*BOOM-BOOM*—a steady drumbeat on concrete.

The trauma bay doors burst open—*CRASH*—steel slamming steel, floodlights glaring with surgical precision, a storm of beeping monitors, clattering trays, and clipped commands as Nova and Omar were wheeled into separate bays, curtains ripped apart—RIP—blood- streaked tiles gleaming under halogen fury.

Nova heard none of it—only the rhythm of her breath not being her own, her thoughts flickering like static in the dark.

Nurses and surgeons surged in—gowns snapping into place, masks pulled tight, gloves donned with sharp SNAPS—the air taut with controlled urgency, protocols locking in like a well-oiled machine: crash carts rolled into position—*SCREECH*—defibrillators humming, teams calling vitals—"BP 40/10!" "O2 75!"—Code Black declared, wing sealed tight, every move a calculated strike against collapse.

Nova's gurney slammed into Bay 1, wheels locking—*SCREECH*—surgeons barking, "Clavicle impalement—severe hypovolemic shock! BP 40/10—crash cart, immediately!" Her blanket was pulled back, revealing her pale, sweat-drenched body, bruises stark against her ribs—purple and black welts from the chute fall—the steel spike protruding from her right clavicle, blood seeping in a steady, dark flow, her chest rising in weak, uneven gasps that rasped like sandpaper.

Dr. Amina Khalil, trauma chief, took command, her voice sharp and urgent, "Spike's embedded—bone's critically damaged! Intubate—start plasma transfusion, now!" A nurse, hands steady despite the chaos, slid an endotracheal tube down Nova's throat—*SHUNK*— her faint choke muffled by the wet gurgle of blood in her airway, the tube secured with a *CLICK*, oxygen flowing—*HISS-HISS*—her chest lifting with mechanical rhythm, each forced breath a shallow *HUFF-HUFF* against the silence.

"Defibrillator—charge to 200, stat!" Khalil ordered, a nurse pressing paddles to Nova's chest—*WHUMP*—her body jerking off the table, electricity surging through her frail frame, pulse spiking to 24—*BEEP-BEEP*—as her heart fought to cling to life, the monitor's wail softening to a staccato rhythm.

"Remove the spike—surgical saw, now!" The saw hummed to life—*ZZZZZ*—its high-pitched whine cutting through the din, the blade slicing into the spike's base—*SCRRR*—metal grinding against shattered bone, sparks flickering briefly as blood welled up in a controlled flow, the spike extracted with a wet POP, a steady stream pooling on the table, dark and thick, clotting around the edges of the wound.

"Clamp the artery—quickly!" Khalil directed, forceps diving into the jagged gash. This wasn't just saving a life—it was rebuilding a broken message the world still needed to hear. After the severed subclavian artery was pinched, another surgeon—Dr. Faisal—sutured with rapid precision—*SNIP-SNIP-SNIP*—needle flashing, thread pulling torn muscle and skin taut over the raw, pulsing wound.

"Transfuse—four units O-negative, immediately!" Khalil commanded, They poured life into her neck like fuel into a flickering engine—praying it would catch flame. Her blood pressure inched to 55/25, monitors stabilized slightly—*BEEP-BEEP-BEEP*—pulse flickered at 28, oxygen saturation scraped to 82%.

"Chest X-ray—stat! Prep a tube!" An X-ray machine rolled in—*CLUNK*—its beam snapping an image in seconds, revealing a collapsed left lung, pleural cavity filling with blood—hemothorax—a nurse inserting an intubation chest tube—*SHUNK*—between her fourth and fifth ribs, air and blood escaping in a sharp *HISS*, a dark red stream draining into a collection canister. Nova didn't feel the blade, only the shift—the faint relief of breath returning as air hissed from the wound, proof she was still in her body.

"Labs—CBC, lactate, stat!" Khalil ordered, a phlebotomist drawing blood from Nova's arm— *SHUNK*—vials filling with dark crimson, rushed to the lab to assess her hemoglobin and acidosis levels, critical markers of her survival odds.

"She's acidotic—bicarb, 50 mEq, push it!" A syringe plunged into her IV—*SHUNK*—sodium bicarbonate surging to counter the lactic acid buildup from prolonged shock, her pH teetering at 7.1, a lethal edge. "CT scan—head and chest, now!"

A portable CT rolled in—*CLUNK-CLUNK*—its arm whirring as it scanned, images flashing on a screen: skull intact, no intracranial bleed, but her chest showed a fractured sternum and two cracked ribs, the spike's collateral damage. "She's bleeding internally—prep OR 3, move!" Khalil snapped, gurney wheels rolling—*SCREECH-SCREECH*—Nova rushed out, crash cart trailing, a nurse ventilating manually—*SQUEEZE-HISS*—oxygen pumping, her vitals a fragile thread—BP 60/30, pulse 30, O2 85%—teetering on the brink.

In Operating Room 3, the team scrubbed in—gowns rustling, masks snapping, sterile fields laid out—*RIP-RIP*—as Nova was transferred to the table, her body limp under the blanket, monitors reconnected—*BEEP-BEEP-BEEP*—an anesthesiologist adjusting the ventilator— HISS-THUMP—delivering 100% oxygen, her chest rising and falling mechanically.

Khalil barked, "We need to open her up—midline incision, stat!" She had seconds to find the bleed—she moved like muscle memory could outpace death. A scalpel sliced—*SHLICK*—from sternum to abdomen, skin parting, subcutaneous fat exposed, a retractor cracking Nova's chest open—*CRACK*—ribs spreading, blood welling as the pleural cavity was accessed, a dark pool of hemothorax sloshing within. "Suction—clear it!"

A hose plunged in—*SLURP-SLURP*—sucking out 800 mL of blood, revealing a lacerated intercostal artery, the source of her internal bleed. "Clamp and ligate—now!" Forceps pinched—*CLINK*—a suture tied off—*SNIP-SNIP*—the bleeding stemmed, her BP nudging to 65/35, pulse to 32.

"Check the lung—resect if needed!" Khalil ordered, a lung speculum inserted—*CLINK*— revealing a small tear in the lower lobe, blood oozing, a resection performed—*SHLICK- SHLICK*—damaged tissue excised, sutures closing the defect—SNIP-SNIP—the lung reinflated, a pleural drain inserted—*SHUNK*—to prevent re-collapse, draining residual fluid.

"Fluids—lactated Ringer's, 2 liters!" An IV bag spiked—*SHUNK*—crystalloids surging, her lactate dropping to 3.5 mmol/L, a sign of stabilizing perfusion, her O2 climbing to 88%, an upward tick in numbers that meant nothing if she didn't wake to feel them.

"She's holding—close her up!" Khalil directed, the chest retractor removed, ribs aligned, sternum wired shut—*CLINK-CLINK*—skin sutured—*SNIP-SNIP-SNIP*—layer by layer, a sterile dressing applied—*SLAP*—her vitals settling: BP 70/40, pulse 40, O2 90%.

"Critical but stable—ICU, now!" Khalil declared, gurney rolling—*SCREECH*—Nova transferred, her condition a hard-won lifeline, still fragile but anchored.

Meanwhile, Omar's gurney crashed into Bay 2—*BOOM*—wheels skidding, medics calling out, "Burns and sepsis—bilateral pneumothorax! BP 55/30—O2 75%, critical!" Nova was a broken sculpture—Omar, a crumbling citadel. His ruin required brute intervention.

His soles were a charred nightmare—third-degree burns peeling away in blackened, weeping clumps, pus seeping from open sores, bone glinting through the ruin, chest tube active, his breaths shallow and strained, a wet *RATTLE-GURGLE*. Dr. Yusuf Mansoor, lead surgeon, barked, “Debride the burns—start antibiotics, maximum dose!”

A nurse administered cefepime—*SHUNK*—the syringe plunging into his arm, 2 grams of fluid racing to combat the sepsis raging through his bloodstream, his pulse at 45, monitors insistent—*BEEP-BEEP-BEEP*, oxygen saturation teetering at 75%.

“Scalpel—begin debridement, now!” Mansoor ordered. Each slice stripped not just charred flesh, but the searing history of what he’d endured to shield her.

“Second chest tube—left side, immediately!” Mansoor directed, a needle piercing— *SHUNK*—between his fourth and fifth ribs on the left, air and blood releasing in a sharp HISS, a frothy mix draining into a canister, oxygen rising to 80%, pulse nudging to 48, his chest easing slightly as the tension pneumothorax released.

“Transfuse—three units AB-positive, stat!” Blood bags were spiked—*SHUNK-SHUNK*— crimson flowing through dual IVs in his arms, needles piercing with a *CRUNCH*, veins bulging as fluid fought the septic tide, BP inching to 65/40, sweat beading on his ashen face in thick, glistening drops.

“X-ray—full chest and lower limbs, now!” An X-ray machine clattered in—*CLUNK*— snapping images in rapid succession: bilateral rib fractures—three on the right, two on the left—lungs flooded with pleural effusion, right femur cracked mid-shaft, a stress fracture from the beam’s weight.

“Labs—CBC, CRP, blood cultures!” A phlebotomist drew samples—*SHUNK*—vials filling with dark, infected blood, rushed to the lab, results flashing: hemoglobin 7 g/dL, C-reactive protein 250 mg/L, cultures pending—sepsis confirmed, likely Staphylococcus aureus from the burns.

“Debride the left foot—move!” Mansoor ordered. She didn’t

flinch—but the nurse beside him wept as she flushed the wound. It was the price of what heroes become.

"Second antibiotic—vancomycin, 1 gram, push it!" A syringe plunged—*SHUNK*— the drug surging to double-team the infection, his temperature spiking at 39.8°C, fever raging, skin hot and clammy. "CT—chest and pelvis!"

A portable CT rolled in—*CLUNK-CLUNK*—images revealing bilateral pleural effusions, a small liver laceration from rib trauma, no major organ rupture. "OR 5—prep grafts, go!" Mansoor snapped, gurney wheels screeching—*SCREECH*—Omar rolled out, crash cart beside, a nurse ventilating—*SQUEEZE-HISS*—his vitals precarious: BP 68/42, pulse 50, O2 82%.

In Operating Room 5, the team worked like a single machine—cut, clamp, drain, stitch—each move a gamble for a breath.

Mansoor barked, "Thoracotomy—left side, stat!" A scalpel sliced—*SHLICK*—along the fifth intercostal space, skin parting, muscle dissected—*SHLICK-SHLICK*—a rib spreader cracking open—*CRACK*—exposing the pleural cavity, 600 mL of bloody effusion sloshing, suction clearing—*SLURP-SLURP*—revealing a punctured lung lobe, blood oozing from a tear. "Suture the lung—now!" Sutures stitched—*SNIP-SNIP*—closing the defect, a pleural drain inserted—*SHUNK*—draining residual fluid, O2 climbing to 85%.

"Right side—go!" Mansoor ordered, a second incision—*SHLICK*—rib spreader cracking— *CRACK*—another 400 mL drained—*SLURP*—lung intact, effusion cleared, a second drain placed—*SHUNK*—O2 nudging to 88%. "Femur—plate it!" An orthopedic surgeon stepped in, drilling—*ZZZZ*—into the cracked femur, a titanium plate screwed—*CLINK-CLINK*— stabilizing the bone, blood welling, gauze packing—*SLAP*—to control it. "Burn grafts—prep skin!"

Harvested skin from his thigh—SHLICK—was meshed—*CLICK-CLICK*—and grafted over his debrided feet—*SLAP-SLAP*—dressings applied, his BP stabilizing at 72/45, pulse 55. "Fluids—Ringer's, 3 liters!" An IV bag spiked—*SHUNK*—crystalloids surging, his lactate dropping to 3.0 mmol/L, O2 hitting 90%. "Close him—move!" Chest incisions sutured— *SNIP-SNIP-SNIP*—dressings slapped on—SLAP—vitals settling: BP 75/48, pulse 60, O2 92%. "Critical but stable—ICU, now!" Mansoor declared, gurney rolling—*SCREECH*—Omar transferred, his condition a hard-fought anchor.

The trauma bay and ORs were a fortress of relentless precision. This wasn't just a hospital—it was a warship turned inward, repelling death with sterile steel and bare-knuckled will.

Sterile packs tore open—*RIP-RIP*—gowns and gloves donned, nurses calling vitals every 15 seconds—"Pulse 30, Nova!" "O2 88, Omar!"—trauma logs scribbled in rapid, ink- smeared strokes, teams rotating—ten surgeons, twelve nurses, eight techs—each bay and OR a hub of ceaseless action.

Code Black sealed the wing—doors bolted, security barking into radios, "Clear the halls— move it, now!"—patients rerouted, sirens wailing as ambulances diverted, blood bank runners pounding corridors—*THUD-THUD-THUD*—O-negative reserves tapped dry, a tech shouting, "We're out—pull AB-positive, cross-match!"—crash carts reloaded mid-frenzy, epipens, saline, and plasma bags slamming into trays—*CLUNK-CLUNK*—the air a storm of *BEEP-BEEP-BEEP* and urgent directives, a symphony of controlled chaos.

Viper stormed the trauma bay's edge, boots pounding—*CLANG-CLANG-CLANG*—blood crusting his tac vest like a second skin, green eyes sharp as he watched Nova and Omar vanish into ORs, doors crashing shut—*BOOM-BOOM*—like distant thunder.

He yanked his comms mic close. His words weren't just intel—they were prayers wrapped in fury, demanding a second chance.

"Renshaw—Kincaid! Nova and Omar at Al Wakra—hanging by a goddamn thread! She's got a hole in her chest, he's rotting from the inside—surgeons are on 'em! Semtex's toast, Barga's a fuckin' graveyard— most of those bastards are worm food, but one tango's unaccounted, slipped the net like a ghost."

His breath steadied—*HUFF-HUFF*—sand grinding his teeth, blood dripping from his knuckles as he tapped the wall—*THUD*—plaster cracking lightly, a controlled vent. General Alex Renshaw's reply growled back, steady but taut, "Copy, Kincaid—relaying to *CENTCOM*, White House, IOC Doha, Israel, Lebanon. Semtex's neutralized, Obsidian's gutted—damn fine work, but one loose end's a itch. Hold tight—Langford's inbound, 80 mikes out."

Viper grunted, "80 mikes—better hustle. They're alive, that's a win—let's keep it that way." Renshaw snapped, "Orders are live—Strickland's on, Reyes too. Stay frosty."

In the White House Situation Room, screens buzzed—Viper's voice a rough echo through the speakers, aides bustling, President Logan Calder leaning forward, voice firm but steady, "Semtex's out—thank God. Most of 'em are down, one's loose—Reyes, what's the read on this?"

DNI Chief Mark Reyes replied, eyes narrowed, "No ID on the tango—Barga's a hole, sats show squat. He's a shadow, but the bulk of the threat's dead." Admiral Jordan Strickland nodded, "Delta's pulled a hell of a save—Semtex's gone, Obsidian's shattered. One runner's a wrinkle, not a break—secure those survivors." Aides relayed—*CLICK-CLICK*— lines humming worldwide, a ripple of cautious relief spreading.

In Doha, IOC headquarters at Raffles Hotel—a modern, glass resort pulsing with tension— President Sheikh Tariq bin Fahd Al-Mazrouei exhaled, voice steady but pressing, "Semtex's neutralized—praise be to Allah. Most of them are dead—one's loose, but the Games… Moreau, your take?"

Vice President Jacques Moreau nodded, "The threat's crippled—Olympics can resume. One man's not a legion, Sheikh—we tighten security, we move forward."

Vice President Viktor Mikhailovich Borodin grunted, "Lebanon's border's still twitchy, but this is a victory. Games can go—lock it down, Tariq." Al-Mazrouei mused, "Relief's tangible—the flame is no longer eclipsed, torch can burn again. Langford's landing soon—we'll align with her and address the media."

Israel's Prime Minister Eitan Mazar cut in, voice clipped, "Semtex's done—solid work. One tango's a loose end—keep Mendelsohn breathing, she's critical. Lebanon's a risk, but we're holding."

Lebanon's Prime Minister Ziad el-Khoury replied, measured, "Threat's down—Hezbollah's quiet for now. Secure your assets—we'll maintain stability." The relay hummed, a cautious optimism threading through the urgency.

Aboard her C-32, 35,000 feet over the Gulf, Secretary of State Victoria Langford gripped the sat phone, voice calm but resolute, "Kincaid—hold steady, you've turned the tide. The Semtex's gone, most of them are neutralized—I'm 70 minutes out, we'll address the remaining concern together. Mr. President—Renshaw—let's coordinate resources, ensure this stays contained."

Her aide relayed—*CLICK*—the plane steady at Mach 0.8, Doha's skyline a faint promise on the horizon, her diplomatic focus a steady hand on the chaos.

Viper paced the trauma bay's edge, boots scraping tiles—*SCRAPE-SCRAPE*—blood drying on his vest in cracked flakes, fist tapping the wall—*THUD-THUD*—a slow rhythm, his growl low, "Semtex's ash, Obsidian's fucked—one tango's a flea we'll squash later."

Nurses hustled—*THUD-THUD-THUD*—crash carts rolled, monitors beeped—*BEEP-BEEP- BEEP*—the hospital a fortress of order, Delta's relief a hard-won breath as Nova and Omar fought for life in the ORs, the world watching, the Games poised to reignite.

The neutralization of the Semtex and the decimation of The Obsidian Hand sent shockwaves through the global arena, a seismic shift from terror to tentative hope.

In Washington, President Calder convened an emergency session—Reyes briefing, "Threat level's dropped from red to yellow—one tango's a wildcard, but the backbone's broken." Strickland added,

"Military posture can ease—Delta's given us room to breathe." The White House exhaled, focus shifting to stabilizing the region, ensuring Nova and Omar's intel could seal the breach.

In Doha, the IOC's command center buzzed—Al-Mazrouei on a secure line with Qatar's Emir, "The Games were suspended four days after the torch-lighting—96 hours lost.

Threat's near-zero, we can resume." Moreau chimed, "Athletes are restless—security's tripled, venues locked. Green light?" Borodin nodded, "Russia's team's ready—Lebanon's stable enough. Signal the world—Olympics live."

The decision rippled—stadiums prepped, broadcasts reignited. The flame would burn again—but its light was fueled by bodies still on the table, breath by fractured breath.

Israel and Lebanon, twin flashpoints, adjusted—Mazar reinforcing border patrols, "One tango's not a war—Games go, we watch." el-Khoury tightened Beirut's security, "Stability holds—Olympics signal peace."

Langford's imminent arrival in Doha loomed. She wasn't coming to comment—she was coming to seal a chapter, and script the next.

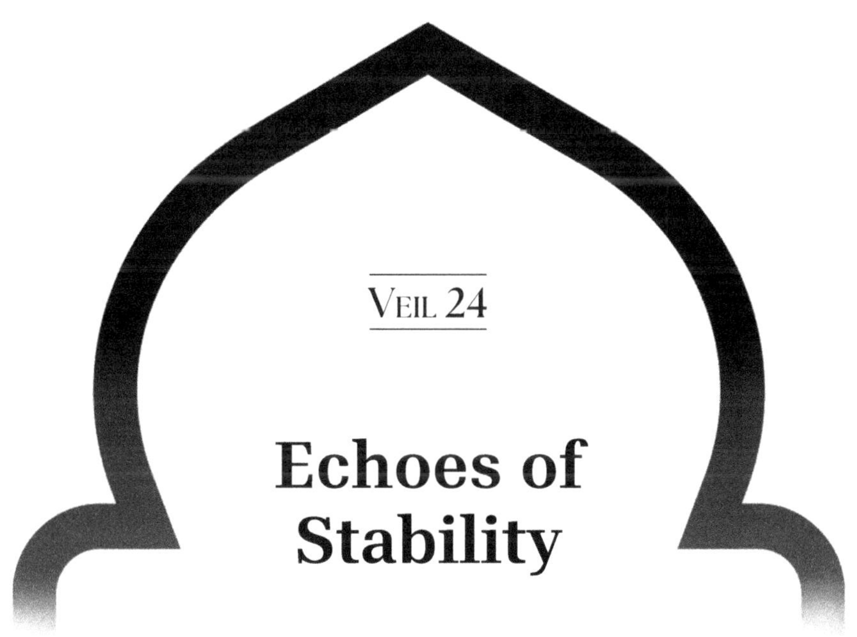

Veil 24

Echoes of Stability

The walls of the intensive care unit at Al Wakra Hospital hummed with machinery, but grief lingered louder—in the air, in the drip of saline, in the silence of the sedated.

The sky over Doha was heavy with ash-gray clouds, pressing against the sealed windows like a mourner's shroud, casting faint shadows across the eight souls tethered to life within.

The air hung thick with the antiseptic sting of bleach, undercut by the metallic tang of blood and the sour, lingering reek of sweat-soaked fear—a miasma that clung to the walls, the tiled floors, the very breath of the place.

Ventilators wheezed their relentless *HISS-THUMP*, monitors shrieked their staccato warnings—*BEEP-BEEP-BEEP*—each sound a lifeline stitching together the fragile existence of Nova, Omar, and the six athletes who had endured The Obsidian Hand's grotesque human centipede: Lior Abramson, Omar Haddad, Yael Ben-Ami, Noa Levi, Yasmine Haddad, and Nadine Al-Rassi.

Barga Al Kharaz lay in smoldering ruins, the Semtex threat reduced to ash, most of The Obsidian Hand buried beneath the desert's wrath—The Spectre slipping free like a wraith in the night—but here, in the ICU, the war raged on, a brutal clash of flesh, machines, and shattered minds.

Nova lay in Bay 1, her slight frame swallowed by a snarl of tubes and wires that bound her to survival, a broken doll amidst the clinical chaos. She wasn't just asleep—she was loading, like a storm building behind closed lids.

Her chest rose and fell in a mechanical dance—*HISS-THUMP*—driven by a ventilator tube taped to her cracked, peeling lips, oxygen hissing at 40% FiO2 through a throat raw from intubation, each breath a shallow shudder that rippled across her pale, sweat-slick skin.

A central venous catheter jutted from her neck like a cruel parasite, its triple lumens dripping saline and O-negative blood—six units transfused since the frantic hours in Operating Room 3—her blood pressure teetering at 72/42 mmHg, pulse a frail 42 beats per minute, oxygen saturation clinging to 92%.

The steel spike that had impaled her right clavicle was gone, but its legacy remained—a jagged, sutured gash weeping faint yellow serous fluid beneath a sterile dressing, the bone beneath a pulverized wreckage of shards pinned with titanium, glinting dully on the X-ray pinned to the wall.

Her right arm hung limp in a sling, a useless appendage twitching with sporadic, electric spasms—nerves frayed and screaming from the impalement, dulled only by the steady drip of morphine at 2 mg/hour coursing through her veins.

The bruises told stories her voice couldn't yet reclaim – each one a timestamp of what she survived.

Dr. Amina Khalil stood at her bedside. She'd seen worse cases, but never one that made her silently beg the monitors to hold steady. Her white coat stained with faint rust-colored streaks, her dark eyes scanning a tablet glowing with the latest labs—hemoglobin 8.2 g/dL, lactate 2.8 mmol/L, pH 7.28—her voice a sharp whip as she instructed the charge nurse, "She's climbing–but slowly. Once infection turns the scale. Clavicle's our wild card."

A nasogastric tube snaked from her nose, its tip buried in her silent gut, draining 50 mL of bile-tinged fluid in the last hour—shock had stilled her digestion—total parenteral nutrition (TPN) flowing at 100 mL/hour through a peripheral line, lipids and dextrose sustaining her frail form, her glucose steady at 110 mg/dL.

An EEG monitor hummed beside her, its screen tracing slow delta waves—brain activity sluggish but intact, no intracranial hemorrhage, though a mild concussion clouded her mind, her pupils equal and reactive at 3 mm, eyes sealed shut beneath a morphine veil. Her dark hair lay matted against the pillow, a sweaty tangle framing a face etched with silent agony, her psyche a fractured mirror—shards of terror and defiance locked behind sedation, poised to shatter when consciousness returned.

Across the narrow corridor in Bay 2, Omar's frame sprawled was broken–yes–but still immense. Even in defeat, he loomed, a monument clawing its way back from collapse. His ventilator churned, his broad chest heaving with a wet, guttural RATTLE-THUMP, each inhalation a labored fight through lungs scarred by septic effusion. Dual chest tubes pierced his sides—300 mL bloody fluid tinged with pus drained from the left pleural cavity, 250 mL from the right—a grim testament to the infection that had nearly drowned him, now held at bay by relentless intervention.

His blood pressure stabilized at 78/50 mmHg, pulse a steady 62, oxygen saturation 93%, sustained by three units of AB-positive blood and 3 liters of lactated Ringer's crystalloids infused since

Operating Room 5, their residue staining the IV bags dangling above him.

His soles were a nightmare tableau—third-degree burns stripped to raw, weeping tissue, debrided to pink flesh and grafted with meshed skin harvested from his thick thighs, the dressings soaked with serous fluid and faint crimson streaks. A triple assault of powerful IV antibiotics fought to save his body. The man inside hadn't decided yet if he wanted saving.

His right femur, cracked mid-shaft under the beam's crushing weight, lay plated with titanium, leg elevated in a foam brace, a traction pin piercing the flesh like a cruel sentinel, immobilizing the fracture beneath a bandage stained with faint seepage.

Each wound was its own war crime—but what lingered was the silence, the dignity stripped as much as the flesh.

Dr. Yusuf Mansoor adjusted the ventilator, eyes scanning vitals: hemoglobin 9.0 g/dL, CRP 200 mg/L, fever 38.5°C. "Sepsis contained—barely," he said, voice tight. "Staph aureus, resistant. Linezolid's running; recheck in six hours." A nurse nodded, adjusting the IV.

Omar's nasogastric tube drained 70 mL of coffee-ground fluid—stress-induced gastric irritation. TPN pumped 120 mL/hour, stabilizing blood sugar at 130 mg/dL. A sutured liver laceration leaked 20 mL into an abdominal drain, bilirubin at 2.5 mg/dL tinting his sclera and skin jaundiced yellow, hepatic strain evident under sepsis's weight. EEG showed normal alpha waves, brain spared, but his bloodshot eyes flickered, clouded by pain.

Fentanyl at 100 mcg/hour dulled the agony, though his calloused hands twitched against restraints, fingers clawing at memories of Basṭīnah's searing rods—trauma festering, ready to scream when sedation eased.

The corridor stretched onward, Bays 3 through 8 a grim gallery of The Obsidian Hand's surviving victims—athletes sewn together in a chain of unimaginable horror, now freed by surgeon's scalpels but scarred–physically and emotionally–beyond recognition.

In Bay 3, Lior Abramson shivered under a midazolam drip at 2 mg/hour, sweat soaking bandages around his face and pelvis. Surgery had undone the grotesque stitching from his anus to another victim's mouth, leaving his rectum sutured and bleeding faintly.

A tracheostomy tube hissed oxygen at 30% FiO2, bypassing his ravaged throat, a feeding tube snaking through his nose to deliver 90 mL/hour of liquid nutrition, his gut intact but sluggish from trauma. The Obsidian Hand's cruelty lingered in his scars, a gallery of horror etched into flesh.

Dr. Layla Hassan stood by, her voice steady as she noted, "Anus's healing—no infection yet, but the catheter's a risk; up fluids to 150 mL/hour, watch for sepsis."

Next in Bay 4, Omar Haddad's stocky frame shuddered under a fentanyl drip at 75 mcg/hour, his broad chest heaving beneath bandages that criss-crossed his lower face and groin. His mouth, once sewn to Lior's anus, was a raw, sutured ruin—lips split, teeth chipped, esophagus grafted with synthetic tissue to restore swallowing, a tracheostomy tube hissing oxygen at 35% FiO2 to ease his swollen airway.

A feeding tube delivered 80 mL/hour of high-calorie nutrition, his CRP at 170 mg/L signaling persistent inflammation. Hassan adjusted his drip, murmuring, "Trach's clear—no pneumonia, but aspiration's a threat; antibiotics stay aggressive."

Yael Ben-Ami lay in Bay 5. She used to swim in still water, her strokes cutting clean lines; now her breaths came like panic against glass, her body a cage of scars. Her lean frame quaked under propofol at 20 mcg/kg/min, bandages wrapping her pelvis and face. Her anus, once stitched to Tamar's mouth, was repaired with a colostomy bag collecting watery output. A chest tube drained 180 mL from a pneumothorax, tracheostomy rasping oxygen. Hassan said, "Colostomy's stable, lactate's 2.9 mmol/L; increase TPN to 110 mL/hour." Her shallow gasps echoed panic, her mind trapped in defilement.

Noa Levi trembled in Bay 6. Her voice was gone, but her stillness screamed louder than sound, her vacant stare a window to a shredded soul. Bandages swathed her face and pelvis. Her mouth, once stitched to Tamar's anus, was a canvas of lacerations and necrosis; her anus, linked to Yasmine's mouth, was sutured with a colostomy bag collecting greenish output. A feeding tube sustained her, CRP at 160 mg/L. Hassan noted, "No obstruction—monitor electrolytes; psyche's a wreck." Her terror locked tight, nightmares poised to erupt.

Yasmine Haddad's fingers twitched in Bay 7, tracing invisible scars, as if her taekwondo strength could still weave her fraying sanity together. Her athletic frame rested under fentanyl at 50 mcg/hour, bandages encasing her pelvis and face. Her mouth, separated from Noa's anus, bore debrided lips; her anus, once Nadine's anchor, was repaired with a colostomy bag. Hassan said, "Resilient, but watch for infection; mental scars run deep." Her psyche teetered, haunted by the violation.

In Bay 8, Nadine Al-Rassi's frail shivers were a fragile dance, her soul swaying on the edge of collapse, yet a faint spark of endurance flickered within. Her runner's body was snowed under propofol at 25 mcg/kg/min, bandages swaddling her pelvis and face. Her mouth, once linked to Yasmine's anus, and her anus, sewn to Nadine Mansour's mouth, were sutured, with a colostomy bag collecting output. A chest tube drained 160 mL from a pneumothorax, tracheostomy at 40% FiO2. Hassan whispered, "Lactate's 3.2 mmol/L; up TPN to 120 mL/hour." Her mind trembled, terror threatening to consume her.

The psychological toll hovered like a storm cloud over all—Omar's smoldering dread, Yael's panicked breaths, Noa's vacant despair, Yasmine's fraying sanity, and Nadine's teetering soul. Each clung to survival, their inner lives fractured but not yet extinguished, their bodies and minds bearing the weight of unimaginable trauma.

Therapy would be brutal. But perhaps, stitched together by shared survival, they might begin to heal what couldn't be sutured.

At 0900, the ICU doors parted with a pneumatic HISS, and U.S. Secretary of State Victoria Langford strode in, her navy suit pristine, her gray eyes cutting through the sterile haze with steely resolve despite the grueling 13-hour flight from Washington, D.C. She didn't walk into a hospital—she entered the aftermath of hell, where survival itself was a form of diplomacy.

Flanking her were IOC officials: Sheikh Tariq bin Fahd Al-Mazrouei, his keffiyeh stark against his dark suit; Jacques Moreau, tie loosened from urgency; and Viktor Mikhailovich Borodin, broad shoulders straining his gray jacket.

Viper trailed, his tac vest a crust of dried blood and sand. He wasn't one for awe, but watching the survivors fight to breathe made every bullet he'd fired feel justified. "They're alive—fuckin' miracles, all of 'em," he said in a low rumble. The group moved through the bays, their dialogue intense, specific, and raw, doctors briefing with clipped urgency as the hum of ventilators and the BEEP-BEEP-BEEP of monitors underscored every word.

Langford paused at Nova's bay, her voice steady but edged, "Dr. Khalil, prognosis—lay it out, no fluff. She's our intel lifeline."

Khalil's dark eyes flicked up from her tablet, "Critical but stable—BP 72/42, pulse 42, O2 92%. Clavicle's a shattered mess—pinned with titanium, but osteomyelitis's a lurking threat; we're culturing daily. Chest drained 800 mL—artery's ligated, lung's fragile, 200 mL output today. Hemoglobin's 8.2, lactate's 2.8—shock's easing, pH's 7.28. No fever, but sepsis is a knife at her throat. Brain's intact—concussion, no bleed. Vented, morphine—consciousness is days off, maybe a week."

Al-Mazrouei's voice cut in, "Timeline—weeks? Months?" Khalil replied, "Weeks if infection stays out—months if it flares. 60/40 for full recovery, arm's a question mark."

Moreau asked, "Mind intact?"

Khalil sighed, "Physically, yes—psychologically, she's a bomb waiting to blow. The body may heal—but the mind's coiled tight. One wrong memory, and she'll detonate."

Borodin grunted, "She talks when?" Khalil shook her head, "Days—vent's out then, if she holds."

At Omar's bay, Langford pressed Mansoor, "Status, risks—give it to me." Her voice was steady, but her hand trembled once—just enough to betray the weight of what she'd seen.

Mansoor's tone was firm, "Critical but stable—BP 78/50, pulse 62, O2 93%. Burns are 20% TBSA—grafted, but Staph aureus is resistant; triple antibiotics are holding it. Lungs are clearing, effusion was septic, CRP's 200. Femur's plated, liver's sutured—20 mL drainage, bilirubin's 2.5, jaundice creeping. Hemoglobin's 9.0—sepsis is contained, not gone. Vented, fentanyl—he's flickering awake."

Al-Mazrouei asked, "Mobility?" Mansoor said, "Weeks—70/30 he walks if grafts take."

Moreau queried, "Infection spread?" Mansoor nodded, "Possible—fever's 38.5°C, under watch."

Borodin growled, "He speaks?" Mansoor replied, "Days—vent's

out then, if lungs stabilize."

The group flowed into the centipede survivors' bays, Hassan briefing as they moved, her voice a taut wire,

"Lior—BP 88/58, pulse 68, O2 95%. Mouth's sutured—tongue's lacerated, trach's at 30%. Catheter's draining 80 mL, hemoglobin 9.8, 6-8 weeks, 80/20 odds.

"Omar Haddad—BP 82/52, pulse 70, O2 94%. Esophagus grafted, trach's 35%, jaw wired—catheter at 70 mL, hemoglobin 9.2, 8-10 weeks, 75/25.

"Yael—BP 80/50, pulse 74, O2 92%. Anus resutured, colostomy at 45 mL, catheter 60 mL— hemoglobin 8.5, 10-12 weeks, 65/35.

"Noa—BP 84/54, pulse 72, O2 93%. Anus repaired, colostomy 50 mL, catheter 65 mL—hemoglobin 9.0, 8-10 weeks, 70/30.

"Yasmine—BP 81/51, pulse 70, O2 94%. Anus sutured, colostomy 40 mL, catheter 70 mL—hemoglobin 8.8, 8-10 weeks, 75/25.

"Nadine—BP 77/47, pulse 76, O2 90%. Anus weak, colostomy 40 mL, catheter 55 mL—hemoglobin 7.8, 10- 12 weeks, 60/40, she's frailest."

Langford's voice sharpened, "Testimony—when?" This wasn't just about healing—it was about evidence. About justice. About answers the world needed.

Hassan replied, "Weeks—sedation's lifting, but minds are shattered; clarity's a gamble." Al-Mazrouei asked, "Survival odds?"

Hassan said, "High—all stable, but infection's the joker; Nadine's teetering."

Borodin growled, "They ID the Frankenstein who did this?" Hassan shook her head, "Not yet—too broken, too lost."

The group retreated to the end of the hallway, Langford leaning against the wall, her voice calm but urgent, "Eight survivors—Nova and Omar are our keys, the six are witnesses. Semtex's ash, Obsidian's gutted—one tango's loose, but the storm's passed. Media's howling—Olympics teeter. We need a tight plan now."

Al-Mazrouei nodded, "Games halted at the torch—48 hours gone. Threat's dead— resumption's on. Doha's a fortress, athletes are set."

Moreau added, "Security's ironclad—venues locked. We say: crisis crushed, Games rise— symbol of grit." Borodin grunted, "Russia's in—torch burns, world heals. One runner's noise—highlight the win."

Langford replied, "The world needs hope. We give them this, 'Terror broken, spirit unshaken.' I'll call Calder. IOC announces tomorrow the Games are a restart, full slate. Israel and Lebanon get briefed— Mazar and el-Khoury need calm."

Al-Mazrouei said, "Qatar's ready—Emir's greenlit. Press at 1400—truth, no fear." The huddle moved toward the elevators, urgency threading their words, the Olympics' flame was flickering back to life.

Outside, the Doha sun blazed through a haze of dust, the sky now a bruised gray streaked with yellow, casting jagged shadows over a city teetering on the edge of recovery. The 48- hour suspension of the Olympic Games had left Doha a pressure cooker—streets taut with tension, air thick with the acrid bite of uncertainty—and now, with The Obsidian Hand and its Semtex reduced to ash and eight survivors clinging to life, the convoy prepared to roll toward the Main Press Center Auditorium, 25 kilometers north, for the 1400 press conference that would shape the world's next breath.

Langford strode into the hospital's forecourt, her gray eyes scanning the vehicles arrayed before her with a diplomat's cool precision. Three armored Toyota Land Cruiser Prados awaited—black as midnight, their reinforced hulls glinting under the sun, tinted windows reflecting the chaos like obsidian mirrors. Bulletproof glass, 2-inch steel plating, run-flat tires—these were beasts of war dressed as diplomats, each bearing the discreet Qatari flag on its hood.

Sheikh Tariq led the way to the lead Prado, his keffiyeh rippling faintly as he slid into the rear beside Langford, the leather seats creaking under his weight, the interior a cocoon of chilled air and muted luxury—black upholstery, a faint whiff of oud lingering from the vents. Moreau and Borodin climbed into the second Prado, its engine rumbling to life with a low GROWL, while Viper joined a Qatari security detail in the third, his growl a match for the machine, "Keep it tight—eyes peeled."

Two Qatari National Guard Humvees—sand-camouflaged, bristling with mounted M2 Brownings—flanked the convoy, their turrets swiveling as soldiers in tan fatigues barked orders into radios, a protective shield rolling out ahead and behind.

The convoy lurched forward at 1045, tires crunching gravel as they pulled onto Al Wakra Road, the asphalt shimmering with heat mirages, a ribbon of black slicing through a city transformed by crisis. Doha still trembled–but somewhere beneath the rubble, breath had returned. That mattered.

Streets once thrumming with Olympic fervor now bore the scars of lockdown: shuttered storefronts, their neon signs dark and lifeless; concrete barricades sprouting like jagged teeth along intersections; military checkpoints every kilometer, Qatari soldiers in tan berets clutching FN FAL rifles, their eyes scanning with hawkish intensity.

The air hung thick with dust and the faint, acrid tang of smoke drifting from distant fires— looters, perhaps, or remnants of panic—while the horizon shimmered with the skeletal outlines of cranes frozen mid-construction, a city paused in mid-breath. Palm trees lining the road drooped, their fronds brittle and yellowed, as if the desert itself mourned the chaos, and the Persian Gulf glittered to the east, a restless expanse of steel-gray waves under a sky that refused to clear.

Inside the lead Prado, Langford adjusted her posture against the leather. She'd flown a warplane into diplomacy. Now every word was a minefield. "Sheikh, we've got to nail this— media's ravenous, and one slip could unravel everything. I'll hit the operation hard— Delta's strike, Semtex's end, eight alive. Thoughts?"

Sheikh Tariq's dark eyes flicked to her, his tone a steady rumble, "It's solid—emphasize Qatar's role, our forces in the fray. The Emir joins us—Nawaf's voice will anchor it. I'll follow with the Games' resumption—tomorrow, 0800, full slate. Security's the backbone; they'll press on the loose tango."

Langford nodded, her fingers tapping the armrest, "Good— Nawaf's weight seals it. I'll frame the tango as a footnote—lone, cut off, no juice. We've got CENTCOM's latest: Barga's ash, no chatter. Moreau and Borodin ready?"

Sheikh Tariq grunted, "Jacques is prepped—security details, athlete morale. Viktor's blunt— torch burns, world moves. They'll back us."

The Prado banked onto the Al Matar Al Qadeem Street interchange, the convoy weaving through a snarl of abandoned taxis—yellow paint peeling, horns silent—past the Hamad International Airport, its terminals a ghost town save for military patrols, armored vehicles hulking near the gates.

Billboards once flashing Olympic ads now bore stark warnings in Arabic and English— "STAY VIGILANT, REPORT SUSPICION"—their colors faded under the relentless sun. A cluster of locals huddled near a falafel stand, their faces gaunt, eyes hollow with the strain of days under siege, while a stray dog—ribs jutting—snarled over a scrap in the gutter, its growl swallowed by the convoy's rumble.

The Pearl-Qatar loomed to the north, its artificial islands a glittering mirage of wealth, but even there, yacht docks stood eerily still, the rich hunkered down behind locked gates.

In the second Prado, Moreau's voice crackled over the secure comms, his French accent taut, "Victoria, Sheikh—media'll dig at the athletes' trauma. Six mutilated, two critical—how much do we give?"

Langford's reply snapped back, "Enough to humanize, not enough to spook. Nova and Omar—critical but stable, intel gold. The six—alive, recovering, heroes. No gore—keep it clinical."

Borodin's growl cut in, "Russia's press wants blood—say it's crushed, move on. Athletes compete, fear dies."

Sheikh Tariq added, "Agreed—Doha's safe, Games heal. Stadiums are set. 0800, condensed, fierce."

The convoy rolled onto the Corniche, the Gulf's waves crashing against the promenade, spray flecking the air with salt as seagulls wheeled overhead, their cries a shrill lament over a city clawing back from the brink. Fishing boats bobbed listlessly, nets tangled and abandoned, while the skyline rose ahead—Burj Al Arab's sleek spire piercing the haze, Aspire Tower's torch dimmed but defiant. Checkpoints thickened—sandbags piled high, soldiers sweating in Kevlar, their rifles glinting as they waved the Prados through, the Humvees' engines a steady THRUM of menace.

Doha's streets bore the weight of 48 hours of dread—trash piled in alleys, windows boarded, the faint echo of sirens a reminder of the chaos barely quelled—but beneath it, a flicker of life stirred: a vendor reopening his stall, a child kicking a deflated ball, the city's pulse stirring beneath the scars.

Langford's voice hardened, "Timeline's tight—1400's our shot. I lead, Nawaf follows, Sheikh closes. Questions will hit hard—Lebanon, the tango, athlete psyche. We're a wall— unshakable."

Sheikh Tariq's lips curved faintly, "We are Qatar—stone endures. The torch lights tomorrow; the world will see."

The convoy slowed at 1345, pulling into the Main Press Center's fortified lot—concrete barriers, razor wire, Qatari guards in tan berets snapping salutes. The auditorium loomed ahead, a squat fortress of glass and steel, its entrance swarming with press—cameras flashing, voices clamoring—a ravenous beast awaiting its feed. The Prados' doors swung open with a CLUNK, the heat slamming in like a fist, dust swirling as Langford, Sheikh Tariq, Moreau, Borodin, and Viper stepped out, their resolve a steel thread weaving toward the stage.

The Main Press Center Auditorium thrummed with a restless, electric hum as the clock struck 1400, its cavernous expanse packed shoulder-to-shoulder with journalists from every corner of the globe. The air buzzed with the clatter of laptop keys, the rustle of notepads, and the low murmur of anticipation, thick with the scent of coffee and sweat under the glare of overhead lights that cast stark shadows across the sea of faces.

Microphones bristled like a forest of steel spines along the edges of tables, cameras perched on tripods swiveling with predatory focus, their lenses glinting as they trained on the elevated stage at the room's heart. A massive screen loomed behind, its blank surface a silent promise of revelations, flanked by the Olympic rings and the Qatari flag—crimson and white rippling in the faint breeze of overworked air conditioning. The world hung on edge, 48 hours of suspended Games a gaping wound in the global psyche, The Obsidian Hand's shadow still lingering despite Barga Al Kharaz's smoldering ruin.

At precisely 1402, the auditorium's double doors swung open with a resonant THUD, and Sheikh Tariq bin Fahd Al-Mazrouei strode onto the stage, his keffiyeh pristine against a tailored black suit, his presence a commanding anchor amid the storm. Behind him followed U.S. Secretary of State Victoria Langford, her navy suit crisp despite her grueling travels, gray eyes cutting through the crowd with steely calm; Jacques Moreau, IOC Vice President, tie loosened, his lean frame taut with urgency; Viktor Mikhailovich Borodin, IOC Vice President, broad shoulders squared, his gray suit straining as he moved; and Qatari Emir Nawaf bin Ahmad Al Thani, his traditional thobe and headscarf a regal contrast to the modern suits, his dark eyes steady with quiet authority.

The quintet settled behind a long table, microphones gleaming under the lights, water glasses clinking faintly as they took their seats. The room fell into a hush, a collective breath held, pens poised, cameras rolling.

Sheikh Tariq leaned into his microphone, his voice a deep, resonant timbre that filled the space, cutting through the tension like a blade.

"Ladies and gentlemen of the press, distinguished guests, I am Sheikh Tariq bin Fahd Al- Mazrouei, President of the International Olympic Committee. We stand today at a pivotal moment—48 hours ago, the Olympic Games faced an unprecedented threat, a shadow cast by a ruthless enemy intent on chaos. That shadow has been dispelled, thanks to the courage and resolve of our allies. It is my honor to introduce the United States Secretary of State, Victoria Langford, who will detail the operation that has brought us to this point of recovery. Secretary Langford, the floor is yours."

Langford rose, her posture unwavering, hands resting lightly on the podium as she adjusted the microphone with a faint SCREECH that echoed briefly before settling. Her voice emerged steady, measured, yet laced with an undercurrent of iron resolve, projecting across the auditorium with clarity.

“Good afternoon. Three days ago, a terrorist organization known as The Obsidian Hand executed a heinous attack, targeting the Olympic Games and the stability of this region. Their plan was audacious—kidnapping athletes, constructing a grotesque human experiment, and rigging a desert stronghold with enough Semtex to level a city on the border of Qatar and Saudi Arabia. Their intent was clear: to sow terror, disrupt the Games, and fracture the international community.

“They failed.

“At 0200 hours yesterday, a joint operation led by U.S. Delta Force, with support from Qatari forces and intelligence from multiple nations, stormed their base in Barga Al Kharaz. The Semtex was neutralized—every last ounce reduced to ash—along with the vast majority of The Obsidian Hand’s operatives. Two hostages, operatives critical to our understanding of

this threat, were extracted alive. They are now in Al Wakra Hospital’s ICU alongside the six athletes subjected to unimaginable cruelty, critical but stable, under the finest care.

“One suspect remains unaccounted for—a loose thread. However, we can confidently say that the threat is contained, the Games are secure, and the world stands united. I will now yield the microphone to His Highness, Emir Nawaf bin Ahmad Al Thani.”

Langford stepped back, her gray eyes scanning the room as Emir Nawaf rose, his thobe rustling faintly, his presence a quiet storm of authority. He adjusted the microphone with a deliberate CLINK, his voice a rich baritone that carried a weight of both pride and resolve, resonating through the auditorium like a call to prayer over the desert sands.

“People of the press, representatives of the world, I am Nawaf bin Ahmad Al Thani, Emir of Qatar. Our nation has stood as host to these Games, a beacon of unity and strength, and we have faced this trial with unwavering resolve. The operation in Barga Al Kharaz was not merely a military triumph—it was a testament to the unbreakable spirit of Qatar, our allies, and the Olympic ideal.

"Our forces stood shoulder-to-shoulder with the United States, our intelligence guided their blades, and together we crushed a threat that sought to tear us asunder. Doha remains a fortress, our people unbroken, our commitment to these Games unshaken. The darkness has lifted, and the light of peace shines once more. I return the floor to Sheikh Tariq to outline our path forward."

A ripple of murmurs swept the room—pens scratching furiously, cameras zooming—as Emir Nawaf resumed his seat, his dark eyes steady, hands folded calmly before him.

Sheikh Tariq rose again, his hands resting on the podium, his voice a steady beacon piercing the rising tide of whispers.

"Thank you, Your Highness. The IOC, in consultation with our Qatari hosts, the United States, and global partners, has determined that the suspension of the Olympic Games, enacted 48 hours ago at the torch-lighting, will be lifted effective immediately. The threat is eradicated—Doha is a fortress, our venues fortified, our athletes resolute.

'Competition will resume tomorrow, at 0800 local time, with a revised schedule: swimming preliminaries at 1200, and gymnastics qualifications at 1400. All events will proceed across 32 venues, with full security—tripled since the crisis—ensuring safety. Our torch burns as a symbol of resilience. We now open the floor to your questions."

The auditorium erupted, hands shooting skyward, voices clamoring as the moderator—a wiry Qatari official in a crisp suit—stepped forward, his voice booming, "One at a time—state your name and outlet!" The Q&A stretched into a marathon, raw and unrelenting, each exchange a volley in a global dialogue.

James Cartwright, BBC reporter, stood first, his clipped British accent slicing through the din, tie askew from hours of waiting. "James Cartwright, BBC. Secretary Langford, you say one operative's unaccounted—how can you assure us the threat's truly gone? Could this 'loose thread' reignite the chaos?"

Langford leaned into her mic, her tone firm, unflinching, "The operation at Barga was a surgical strike—Delta Force left no stone unturned. The Semtex stockpile, enough to glass half this city, is ash. The Obsidian Hand's leadership is confirmed dead—bodies identified in the rubble. One survivor slipped through, yes, but intelligence suggests he's a lone actor, cut off, no resources. We're tracking him—CENTCOM, Mossad, MI6, all on it. The risk is minimal; the Games are secure."

Sheikh Tariq added, "Security's airtight—20,000 personnel, drones, checkpoints. One man doesn't undo this victory."

Emilie Laurent, journalist for France's L'Équipe, rose next, her sleek blonde bob catching the light, her French accent sharp with urgency. "Emilie Laurent, L'Équipe. Sheikh Tariq, the athletes in the ICU—six were mutilated in that… experiment. What's their condition? The French team's shaken."

Sheikh Tariq's jaw tightened, his voice steady but grave, "The six—Lior Abramson, Omar Haddad, Yael Ben-Ami, Noa Levi, Yasmine Haddad, Nadine Al-Rassi—are critical but stable. Their ordeal was barbaric—mouths sewn to anuses—but surgically separated, under care at Al Wakra. Recovery's months to years. Their nations, Israel and Lebanon, are informed, and support is in place."

Langford interjected, "Their survival's a miracle—doctors report physical stability, but mental scars run deep. We're coordinating counseling, repatriation when they're fit."

Greg Palmer, Australian reporter, shoved to his feet, his broad accent booming, shirt rumpled from the heat. He wanted facts. She gave them fire-dampened truths, calculated to heal more than inflame. "Greg Palmer, Nine Network Australia. Secretary, you've got two key hostages—one of them a journalist—still alive. What intel do they hold, and when do we hear it?"

Langford's eyes narrowed, her voice crisp, "Nova Mendelsohn and Omar Al-Kaabi are critical assets—both operatives with knowledge of The Obsidian Hand's structure. They're in ICU, vented, sedated—stable but fragile. Intel extraction waits—days, maybe a week, till they're conscious. We expect names, networks, motives—vital to sealing this. Patience; they're fighting to live."

Moreau added, "Their survival strengthens us—proof the enemy's grip broke."

Rashida al-Hakim, Al Jazeera's Doha bureau chief, stood, her hijab framing a fierce gaze, her Arabic-inflected English ringing out. "Rashida al-Hakim, Al Jazeera. Sheikh, the Middle East's volatile—Lebanon's border's tense, Hezbollah's watching. One member of The Obsidian Hand's loose—how's this not a spark?"

Sheikh Tariq met her stare, "Rashida, Qatar's a rock—security's tripled, borders are locked. Lebanon's prime minister, Ziad el-Khoury, assures stability; Hezbollah's quiet. One man's a whisper, not a storm—Barga's ash proves our strength."

Langford said, "I've spoken to el-Khoury and Israel's Eitan Mazar—both briefed, both steady. The escapee's a ghost, not a match."

Carlos Mendes, Brazil's Globo Esporte reporter, rose, his Portuguese accent thick, his posture tense. "Carlos Mendes, Globo Esporte. Sheikh, resuming tomorrow—athletes are rattled, Brazil's team included. How do you convince them it's safe?"

Sheikh Tariq replied, "Every venue's a fortress—guards, cameras, drones. Athletes met today—coaches, IOC reps, briefed them: threat's dead, Doha's ironclad. Brazil's delegation's on board; competition heals fear."

Borodin grunted, "Russia's team's ready—fear fades when the torch burns."

Priya Patel, The Times of India, stood, her sari a splash of color, her voice precise. "Priya Patel, The Times of India. Secretary Langford, psychological trauma—those six athletes, Nova, Omar. India's worried about long-term impact. What's the plan?"

Langford's tone softened, "Nova's a journalist—one of ours. What she's endured will scar generations. But she's still here. And that's enough—for now. All of their trauma's profound—Nova's impalement, Omar's burns, the six's mutilations… PTSD's a certainty—nightmares, dissociation, panic. We've got psychologists on-site, long-term care planned—U.S., Qatar, Israel, Lebanon all collaborating. They're stable physically; mentally, it's a marathon."

Moreau added, "The IOC will also be funding support—counseling, recovery programs. They're heroes, not victims."

Hiroshi Tanaka, Japan's NHK correspondent, cut in, his glasses glinting, his tone clipped. "Hiroshi Tanaka, NHK. Sheikh, timeline's tight—tomorrow's start. Japan's judo team's logistics are scrambled. How's this work?"

Sheikh Tariq nodded, "Schedules are adjusted—judo heats shift to 1300, venues prepped overnight. Transport's doubled—buses, escorts, all secured. Your team's set; we've planned for this."

Fatima El-Sayed, Egypt's Al-Ahram reporter—rose, her voice sharp, "Fatima El-Sayed, Al- Ahram. Secretary, one of these monsters is loose—Egypt's near Lebanon, tense borders. Any chance he's not alone?"

Langford replied, "Intel's clear—Barga was their hub, their leadership's dead, caches destroyed. One survivor's a remnant, not a cell. Egypt's safe—CENTCOM's watching."

As the questions echoed and the cauldron's image burned behind them one truth held firm: the world hadn't stopped. It had survived.

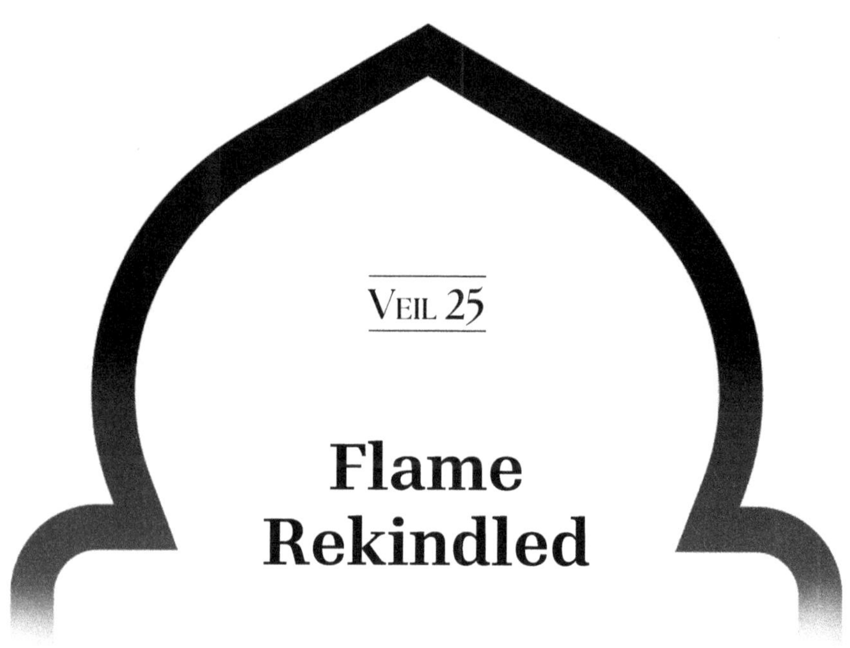

Veil 25

Flame Rekindled

The sun burned with the same merciless heat that had seared every scar Doha tried to hide, a merciless blaze cutting through the dust and smoke that veiled the city, its golden rays glinting off Khalifa International Stadium as the Olympic Games clawed their way back from a 48-hour abyss of terror.

The cauldron, ignited days prior in an Opening Ceremony dripping with themes of unity, flickered atop its pedestal, its flame, like those still clinging to life at Al Wakra, refused to go out—fragile yet ferociously alive, defiant yet haunted by The Obsidian Hand's shadow.

Beyond the stadium's walls, Doha pulsed with a raw, wounded energy—Qatari soldiers in tan berets gripped rifles at checkpoints, their eyes hollow with sleepless vigilance, drones whining overhead like mourners keening, the air thick with the acrid sting of fear and the bitter tang of a city teetering on the edge of reclaiming itself. Inside the venues—32 arenas of sweat and steel—triumph surged, a desperate cry against the void, each medal a tear- streaked testament to resilience.

Inside Aspire Arena, the women's gymnastics all-around final unfolded beneath a canopy of harsh lights, the mat a sacred ground where every leap was a plea, every landing a sob wrested from the jaws of despair.

Alyssa Park, a wiry 22-year-old American from Oregon, stood at the edge of her final rotation—floor exercise—her jet-black hair matted with sweat, her steel-gray eyes glistening with a storm of pride and pain. Her muscles knew what to do—but her memory screamed with every breath.

Three days ago, in this very arena, she'd pried open a mysterious, splintered crate, her trembling hands uncovering The Obsidian Hand's grotesque human centipede—twelve athletes mutilated, their eyes wide with silent screams that still echoed in her skull.

The crowd's roar—15,000 voices strong—swelled with a jagged, brittle edge, their cheers a fragile shield against the memory of that horror, a sound Alyssa felt in her chest like a second heartbeat, urging her forward even as it threatened to break her.

Her competition had been a crucible of grit and grief—vault first, a Yurchenko double twist launched with a THUD that jolted her spine, her feet planting firm at 15.100, but as she soared, her mind cracked open: Lior Abramson's bloodshot gaze, pleading from the crate, a silent wail that drowned the crowd's applause, her landing a defiance of that image, her breath a shuddering gasp she hid behind a clenched jaw.

The uneven bars followed—chalk-dusted hands swinging through a Tkatchev to a Pak salto, her body a taut arc scoring 14.800—yet mid-flight, a flash seared her: Omar Haddad's gagged mouth, the stench of rot flooding her senses, her grip tightening as tears pricked her eyes, her dismount a desperate anchor to the present.

The balance beam loomed next, a 4-foot tightrope where her front aerial faltered, a wobble at 14.200—her vision blurring with Yael Ben-Ami's trembling form, the crate's dark maw swallowing her focus, her heart pounding a frantic rhythm as she fought to stay upright, a sob lodged in her throat she refused to let free.

China's Lian Mei-Xiu, a lithe 19-year-old from Beijing with a dancer's poise, led with 43.325—vault 15.125, bars 14.700, beam 14.500—her movements a liquid grace that flowed unbroken, her dark eyes serene, untouched by the arena's ghosts. Italy's Giulia Rossi, 24, with a Roman fire in her veins, held third at 43.250—vault 14.800, bars 14.900, beam 13.550—her uneven bars a symphony of strength, though her beam faltered, a flicker of doubt in her fierce gaze.

Alyssa trailed at 43.100, 0.375 points behind Lian, her gold medal a fading dream as she paced the sidelines, chalk dusting her trembling hands, her breath a shallow, ragged pull— each inhale a battle against Noa Levi's whimpers, Yasmine Haddad's mutilated form flashing behind her eyes, her chest tightening with a grief she couldn't name.

The floor exercise was her last stand—These 90 seconds weren't about gold—they were about burying the crate with every landing. With a pulsing remix of "Sweet Dreams" pulsing, her triple-twisting double back exploding off the mat with a BOOM, legs snapping together like a gunshot—a round-off, back handspring, double layout—her body a blade slicing through the air once thick with dread.

Mid-twist, a flash: Nadine Al-Rassi's frail shivers, the crate's splintered wood—she faltered, her breath catching, but she gritted her teeth, pouring it into her final pass, a double pike that landed with a THUD, her chest heaving, sweat streaking her face like tears she wouldn't shed, the stadium erupting as her score blazed: 15.600.

Lian's 15.200 flowed like silk—front tuck to full twist—but fell short, her silver a quiet ache at 58.525. Giulia's 14.950—a layout full inches from perfection—secured bronze at 58.100, her eyes glistening with pride and exhaustion.

Alyssa clinched gold at 58.700, the podium a trembling altar as she gripped the medal, tears spilling free—victory a fragile thread against the crate's weight, her psyche a battlefield of triumph and torment, her smile a mask over a soul still screaming.

Across the city, the Hamad Aquatic Centre churned with the 200m butterfly final, water glinting like molten steel as American Natalie Brooks, a 25-year-old Californian with broad shoulders and a relentless stroke, surged through the lanes, her arms cutting the surface— 50m splits of 27.89, 30.12, 31.45, 31.41—touching the wall at 2:04.87, a new Olympic record, gold hers as her goggles fogged with exertion and unshed tears.

The Al Khor Coastal Course roared with whitewater as Germany's Lukas Müller, 27, carved a blistering 88.34 seconds through frothing gates in the canoe slalom K-1 final, his paddle a blur—gold a defiant shout as the rapids hissed, his chest tight with a victory he couldn't fully feel, Spain's Elena Ruiz, 24, taking silver at 89.12, her lean frame battling the tide with a grit born of loss, Canada's Owen Carter, 26, nabbing bronze at 90.05, his canoe teetering but holding, the crowd's cheers a fragile echo against the desert's scars.

At the Aspire Dome, China's Zhang Wei, 23, soared to gold in the men's 3m springboard, his reverse 3½ somersaults slicing the water at 92.40. The splash muffled the phantom screams of the kidnapped athletes, but his hollow gaze betrayed a victory that couldn't quiet the horror. Britain's Tom Hargreaves, 25, claimed silver at 89.75, his inward 3½ near-flawless, yet tears spilled as if grieving teammates lost to the shadows.

In the Lusail Sports Complex, Australia's Logan Kelly, 24, clinched BMX freestyle gold with a double tailwhip to barspin at 94.20. The ramps trembled, but his racing pulse carried the dread of those still fighting for their lives, each cheer a reminder of silenced voices.

At the Qatar Sports Club, Russia's Sofia Petrova, 26, thrust to gold in women's foil, her 15-12 win a viper's strike. The blade's clash offered no solace, the memories of the abducted haunting her fleeting triumph.

At the Al Sadd Sports Complex, Serbia's Marko Petrovic, 28, powered men's water polo to a 12-10 victory, his five goals a primal roar. Yet the water, churning like his memories.

In the Aspire Zone, USA's Ethan Blake, 25, dominated men's indoor volleyball, his spikes sealing a 25-23, 27-25, 25-21 win. His block stood firm, but his heart cracked under the weight of pride and the absent faces of the taken.

Each medal, each roar, was a fragile shield against the lingering terror of the Olympic kidnappings—a triumph that ached with the unhealed wounds of the lost.

While the world cheered, two breaths fought for rhythm in a quiet room far from gold. Nova and Omar, linchpins of Delta's extraction, stirred from their medically induced comas, their consciousness clawing through layers of sedation and anguish as the clock neared 1800.

The air was a sterile stew—bleach cutting through the metallic tang of blood, the sour reek of sweat-soaked sheets—ventilators silenced, replaced by the soft HISS of nasal cannulas, monitors a relentless BEEP-BEEP-BEEP as nurses in blue scrubs moved with hushed precision, their gloved hands trembling faintly as they adjusted drips and charted vitals.

Nova lay in Bay 1, her slight frame a fragile silhouette against a snarl of tubes and wires that had bound her to life for 48 hours. The tubes were fewer now, but they still felt like shackles. Every breath was a reminder of the spike.

The steel spike's scar marred her right clavicle—a sutured gash, red and swollen, weeping yellow serous fluid beneath a dressing, the bone beneath pinned with titanium, a deep ache pulsing with every twitch, X-rays showing microfractures radiating like spiderwebs, a physical echo of her shattered soul.

Her right arm hung limp in a sling, fingers trembling with sporadic, electric spasms—brachial plexus nerves frayed, morphine tapered to 1 mg/hour leaving a dull burn she welcomed, a tether to reality—while bruises mottled her torso, purple-black fading to sickly yellow, her wired sternum and plated ribs a cage of pain, a chest tube draining 150 mL of pink fluid since morning, the hemothorax receding, her lung reinflated but tender, a faint wheeze audible with each exhale, a sound that mirrored her fragile hope.

The world came back in fragments—pain first, then memory, then the scream she couldn't find. Her eyes fluttered open—bloodshot, pupils dilating to 4 mm—blinking against the halogen glare, a fog of disorientation clouding her mind as fentanyl's haze lifted. The monitors beeped, the fluids dripped. What mattered was her eyes—open, but haunted.

Her psyche fractured—terror surged like a tidal wave, a scream trapped in her raw throat, her left hand clawing at the sheets as panic flared, heart rate spiking to 60—BEEP-BEEP- BEEP—sweat beading on her brow, her voice a hoarse croak. Two words, broken and jagged, the first thing she claimed from the wreckage of herself. "Where… he…"

Dr. Amina Khalil leaned in, her voice firm yet trembling, "Nova, you're safe—Al Wakra ICU. Rest, you're alive." But Nova's mind spun—hypervigilance igniting, every beep a bomb tick, every shadow a blade, PTSD's tendrils sinking deep, her gaze darting, searching for threats, her breath shallow gasps as flashbacks looped: the spike's crunch, blood pooling, a faceless figure fleeing, her chest tightening with a despair that threatened to swallow her whole, tears welling but refusing to fall, her soul a battlefield of rage and loss.

In Bay 2, Omar's massive frame stirred, a colossus awakening amidst a lattice of machinery. He came back slowly, like stone surfacing from floodwater—each breath a defiance, each memory a knife.

His blood pressure held at 80/52, pulse 65, hemoglobin 9.2 g/dL after three units, saline dripping at 60 mL/hour through his subclavian catheter, a faint itch where the line pierced his skin, a tether he loathed yet needed. His soles—grafted nightmares—oozed serous fluid beneath dressings, the stench of rot a faint whisper despite the triple dose of vancomycin, cefepime, and linezolid hourly. His temperature held steady at 38.2°C, a triple-lumen catheter snaking from his chest, its ports a lifeline against sepsis he resented with every fiber.

His right femur, plated and pinned, throbbed under a foam brace, traction pin tugging at his flesh, an ache radiating up his thigh like a scream he couldn't voice, while his liver drain wept dark fluid, jaundice receding from his sclera, a faint yellow tinge lingering on his skin, a mark of battles fought and lost.

The Basṭīnah's white-hot iron rods searing his soles; Barga's blast shaking the earth, a roar that stole his breath; Nova's scream piercing the dark, a sound that broke something deep within. His psyche buckled—fists clenching the sheets, heart rate jumping to 70—BEEP-BEEP- BEEP—sweat pooling in his matted beard, a guttural "No…" escaping as terror flared, visions of iron and fire flashing, dissociation tugging at his edges, his gaze unfocused, staring through the ceiling as if the desert's heat still pressed down, tears brimming in eyes that had forgotten how to weep.

Dr. Yusuf Mansoor gripped his shoulder, his voice a steady anchor, "Omar, you're here— ICU, safe. Breathe." But Omar's mind churned—nightmares of captivity clawing free, every sound a lash, every shadow a captor, his massive frame trembling. It wasn't just fear—it was war inside his ribcage, waged in silence.

At 1815, Drs. Khalil and Mansoor converged in the ICU's central station, a glass-walled hub buzzing with the hum of monitors and the staccato of hurried whispers, the air heavy with the antiseptic bite of bleach and the faint, metallic tang of blood that clung to their stained white coats like a second skin. Khalil didn't cry—but her fingers trembled. "They're awake," she said. "Sort of."

"We need to inform them—Nova and Omar are waking, but they're not there yet, not speaking fully." Mansoor, his broad shoulders slumped, his beard flecked with sweat, nodded, his tone a gravelly rasp that scraped the silence, "It's a start—they're conscious, barely, but the trauma's a wall. The IOC and Langford need this now."

The call patched through to the IOC headquarters at the Raffles resort, where Sheikh Tariq bin Fahd Al-Mazrouei, Jacques Moreau, Viktor Mikhailovich Borodin, and Victoria Langford lingered in a conference room, their suits rumpled from hours of tension, coffee cups cold and abandoned, the air thick with the stale scent of urgency and the weight of a narrative teetering on the edge of hope and dread.

The phone buzzed—a harsh BRRRR that jolted the room—and Sheikh Tariq snatched it, his keffiyeh askew, his voice a low rumble that vibrated through the stillness, "Yes?" Khalil's words crackled through, sharp and strained, "Sheikh, it's Dr. Khalil—Nova Mendelsohn and Omar Al-Sayed are awakening. Extubated at 1600 and 1630, vitals stable—BP 75/45 and 80/52, O2 at 94%

and 95%. They're conscious, eyes open, but not coherent—too fragile to speak fully, trauma's gripping them."

The room froze, Langford's gray eyes sharpening, her breath catching in her throat as she leaned forward, her voice taut with a mix of relief and impatience, "Awakening? What state are they in?" Mansoor's voice joined, heavy with strain, a rumble that carried the weight of hours spent wrestling death, "Nova's muttering—'where'—disoriented, panicked. Omar's groaning, unresponsive beyond that—PTSD's hitting like a storm, they're not ready for questions."

Sheikh Tariq's jaw tightened, a flicker of relief warring with a deep, gnawing dread that etched lines into his weathered face, "Alive—praise Allah—but not speaking?" Khalil replied, her tone softening with fatigue, "Not yet—hours, maybe more. They're teetering, fighting to surface."

Langford's voice dropped, not rose. "They're our key. I need to see them now."

Moreau's French accent broke through, soft with awe, a whisper that trembled with emotion, "Mon Dieu, they're back from the edge—fragile or not, it's a miracle."

Borodin grunted, his broad frame shifting, his growl a rough echo of pride, "Strength in survival."

Langford stood, her navy suit creased from hours of unrelenting tension, her voice a command that sliced through the room's haze, "Sheikh, hospital—immediately. The Games hold, but this is our pulse."

Sheikh Tariq nodded, his dark eyes flashing with a fierce purpose that belied his exhaustion, "Qatar stands with them—cars, now." The line clicked dead, the room erupting in motion—chairs scraping tile with a shrill SCREECH, aides scrambling, their footsteps a frantic THUD-THUD—as the convoy mobilized outside, three black Toyota Land Cruiser Prados growling to life, their reinforced hulls glinting under the fading sun like polished obsidian, flanked by two sand-camouflaged Qatari National Guard Humvees, their M2 Brownings swiveling with a metallic CLANK, soldiers barking orders into radios, their voices sharp with urgency.

Langford slid into the lead Prado beside Sheikh Tariq. The seat groaned beneath her. The air was cool, but her thoughts burned with the stakes of Nova and Omar's fragile return.

The convoy lurched south at 1820, tires crunching gravel with a gritty CRUNCH as they peeled onto Al Wakra Road, the asphalt shimmering with heat mirages, a ribbon of black slicing through a city still raw from terror's grip. The Humvees' engines rumbled—a steady THRUM that vibrated through the seats—as the Prados wove through checkpoints, Qatari soldiers in tan berets waving them past, their rifles glinting in the dusk, their faces etched with the strain of sleepless nights, the air outside thick with the dust of a city stirring back to life.

Langford's voice cut through the hum, sharp and urgent, her breath fogging faintly in the chilled cabin, "If they're lost inside…" she didn't finish. She didn't have to. Sheikh Tariq's tone was steady, a bedrock beneath her storm, his words carrying the weight of a man who'd seen too much yet refused to yield, "We see them, assess—doctors will guide. They're warriors; they'll speak when they can. Qatar's honor rests on their survival, their strength."

Langford's gray eyes flickered, a storm brewing behind them, her voice softening with a tremor she couldn't suppress, "Honor's one thing—answers are another."

The journey blurred past—abandoned taxis clogging intersections, their yellow paint peeling under the relentless sun, horns silent; concrete barricades jutting like broken bones, their edges rough against the fading light; the Persian Gulf's steel-gray waves crashing to the east, a restless dirge that sprayed salt into the air, a briny tang that seeped through the Prado's seals.

The hospital loomed at 1845,. The building was unchanged—but the reason for being there wasn't. Its forecourt swarmed with security—soldiers in Kevlar, their boots pounding a steady THUD-THUD on the pavement, their rifles slung tight, their breath visible in the cooling dusk.

The Prados screeched to a halt—tires squealing with a high-pitched SCREECH—doors swinging open with a heavy CLUNK, the heat slamming in like a fist, a dry, suffocating punch that carried the faint scent of diesel and dust. Langford and Sheikh Tariq stepped out, their strides purposeful, faces set with a mix of resolve and trepidation, the weight of their mission pressing against their chests.

They breached the ICU doors—HISS—the sterile air a cold slap against their sweat-damp skin, bleach and blood mingling in a scent that clung to their throats like a bitter film, the BEEP-BEEP-BEEP of monitors a relentless pulse that echoed in their skulls. Dr. Khalil and Dr. Mansoor met them at the central station, their white coats stained with rust-colored streaks and the faint sheen of perspiration, Khalil's hands trembling as she clutched a tablet, its screen glowing with vitals, Mansoor's broad frame rigid with exhaustion, his beard damp with the day's toil.

Khalil's voice quavered, a thread of hope laced with strain, "Secretary, Sheikh—they're waking, but not fully here. Nova's eyes are open, she's muttering—disoriented, panicked, lost in her head. Omar's stirring, groaning—trapped somewhere deep, not with us yet. They can't speak to you, maybe not for hours."

Langford's gaze sharpened, her gray eyes piercing through the dim light, her voice a whisper laced with urgency, "Show us—I need to see them." Sheikh Tariq nodded, his tone a low rumble that carried the weight of a prayer, "Lead on—their fight is ours."

The group moved to Bay 1, glass walls fogging with their breath as they peered in, Nova a fragile wraith against the snarl of tubes and wires that had tethered her to life, her slight frame dwarfed by the sterile chaos. Her chest rose in shallow, ragged gasps—WHISTLE- GASP—each breath a jagged plea rasping through her raw trachea, the plastic prongs of the cannula chafing her nostrils, a faint sting she barely registered. Her blood pressure steadied, her pulse a frail 48, and her hemoglobin up to 8.5 g/dL after six units of O-negative. The central venous catheter in her neck dripped saline at 50 mL/hour, a cold trickle against her fevered skin, a lifeline that clung to her with a desperation she couldn't voice.

The clavicle scar—red, swollen, weeping yellow serous fluid beneath a dressing—throbbed with a deep, relentless ache, titanium pins anchoring a bone that pulsed with every twitch, a physical echo of her shattered spirit, the sensation a dull hammer against her nerves. Her right arm hung limp in a sling, fingers trembling with sporadic, electric spasms—brachial plexus nerves frayed, morphine at 1 mg/hour a thin veil over the burn that seared her flesh, a pain she welcomed as a tether to reality.

Bruises mottled her torso—purple-black fading to a sickly yellow—her wired sternum and plated ribs a cage of torment, a chest tube draining 150 mL of pink fluid since morning, the hemothorax receding, her lung reinflated but tender, a faint wheeze audible with each exhale, a sound that mirrored her fragile defiance, a whisper of life against the void.

Her consciousness surged, ripping through the fading shroud of fentanyl's embrace, as if clawing free from a suffocating dream. Her bloodshot eyes snapped open, darting wildly, blinking against the halogen glare that pierced her skull like shards of glass. Her heart convulsed with grief, a raw, clawing ache in her chest, while despair settled into her bones like molten lead.

Memory crashed in—a tidal wave of sensory horror. The spike. The fire. Her scream. That's all she could see. That's all she was.

Terror surged—her psyche fracturing—a scream trapped in her raw throat, her left hand clawing the sheets, nails digging into fabric until they bled, panic flaring as her heart rate spiked to 60—BEEP-BEEP-BEEP—sweat beading on her brow, trickling into her eyes with a salty sting, her voice a hoarse croak, "Where…" The word dissolved into a whimper, her chest tightening, a vise of despair squeezing her ribs as flashbacks looped: the blood's weight, a thick, clotting mass that clung to her skin, staining her hands as she pressed them to the wound, the warmth turning cold, a shiver rippling through her; the explosion's roar, a wall of fire swallowing her world, the ground trembling beneath her, her ears ringing with a high-pitched whine, her vision blurring with smoke and tears she couldn't shed; the silence after, a deafening void where screams should have been, her comrades' faces—Lior, Omar, Yael—flashing, blood-streaked and pleading, a carousel of horror spinning faster, her breath shallow gasps, her chest a furnace of rage and loss.

Fear wasn't new—but now it had a voice, a shape, and it lived just behind her eyes —hypervigilance igniting, every beep a bomb's tick, every shadow a threat, her gaze darting, searching for enemies in the sterile blur, tears welling but refusing to fall, her soul a battlefield, a soldier's defiance flickering against a darkness that threatened to drown her, a silent wail echoing: I'm alive, but I'm gone.

Langford's breath caught, her gray eyes glistening with unshed tears. She pressed her palm to the glass. "Nova." That was all she could say.

Sheikh Tariq's hand rested on her shoulder, a steady weight, his tone a low rumble that trembled with emotion, "She's steel beneath the cracks—Allah grant her peace, give her time."

Khalil shook her head, her voice soft with exhaustion, "She's not ready—hours, maybe days. The mind's a warzone, a storm she can't escape."

They shifted Omar to Bay 2, his colossal frame moving like a giant amidst the tangle of machines. His chest rose and fell with heavy, ragged breaths, each one a struggle through scarred lungs, the nasal cannula chafing his nose with an itch he barely noticed amid deeper pain. Chest tubes drained fluid, now a lighter shade, into canisters that gurgled softly, their rhythm haunting his thoughts.

His blood pressure stayed low, his pulse steady but weak, his body fueled by transfusions and a slow drip of saline through a catheter, its coolness both a comfort and a curse against his fevered skin. His feet, wrapped in dressings, wept fluid, a faint sour smell lingering despite the antibiotics, his temperature slightly elevated, his body fighting an unseen battle.

His right leg ached under a brace, a metal pin pulling at his flesh with a constant, sharp sting. A drain from his side leaked dark fluid, his skin still tinged with a fading yellow, a shadow of illness that clung to him, heavy as the weariness in his bones.

Pain didn't wait. It slammed into him the moment his eyes met the light. A guttural groan rumbled from his chest, a deep, vibrating through his ribs as the fentanyl tapered to 75 mcg/hour, sensation flooding back: burning feet like embers searing his flesh, the skin peeling in his mind's eye; ribs creaking with each breath, a dull ache that pulsed with every gasp; a throat like shattered glass, raw and bleeding, his voice lost to it.

He didn't remember waking—but the memory remembered him. It struck first with heat, then with screams.

The Basṭīnah's iron rods searing his soles, a white-hot agony that branded his soul, the metal glowing red, the sizzle of flesh as it melted, a sickening CRACKLE filling his ears, the stench of charred skin choking his lungs, his screams swallowed by the darkness, his body bucking against restraints. Jaber's screams weren't just sounds—they were blades. Each one cut something loose inside Omar that would never heal.

Omar's hands clawed at the air. His voice cracked the silence. "Stop, stop…" But silence answered. Silence always answered.

Terror flared—his psyche buckling—fists clenching the sheets, nails digging into fabric until they tore, heart rate jumping to 70—BEEP-BEEP-BEEP—sweat pooling in his matted beard, dripping into his eyes with a salty sting, a guttural "No…" escaping as visions flashed: Jaber's face, contorted in agony, eyes wide and pleading as flames consumed him, his screams fading to a gurgle, the bull's bronze glinting with heat, a relentless ROAR that drowned Omar's cries; the rods' searing bite, his flesh peeling in strips, the pain a white-hot wave that stole his breath, his body trembling, powerless; Barga's collapse, a wall of fire swallowing his world, the ground trembling, his ears ringing with a high-pitched whine, Nova's blood pooling beside him, a warm, sticky tide he couldn't staunch, her scream a knife in his chest.

And then came the boom. Not the scream. Not the fire. But the silence that followed.

There was no grip—only gravity pulling him deeper. The past was a pit with no floor. Every sound a lash, every shadow a captor, his massive frame trembling, tears brimming in eyes that had forgotten how to weep, his breath a ragged pant as dissociation tugged, pulling him into a void where he floated, untethered, the desert's heat pressing down, Jaber's screams echoing, a weight he couldn't shake, a silent roar trapped:

I couldn't save him.

I couldn't save her.

Sheikh Tariq's voice broke, a crack in his stoic facade, "Omar—Allah preserve him, he's a mountain crumbling, a soul torn apart."

Langford's hand hovered—then touched the glass. Cold seeped into her bones, but the grief had already made her numb. "He's alive, but lost—they both are, drowning in it. Doctors, what now?"

Mansoor's tone was heavy, a rumble weighted with sorrow, "Time—rest, sedation if it worsens. They're surfacing, but the air up here is full of ghosts."

Behind the glass, two souls floated in wreckage. And the world waited for them to breathe again.

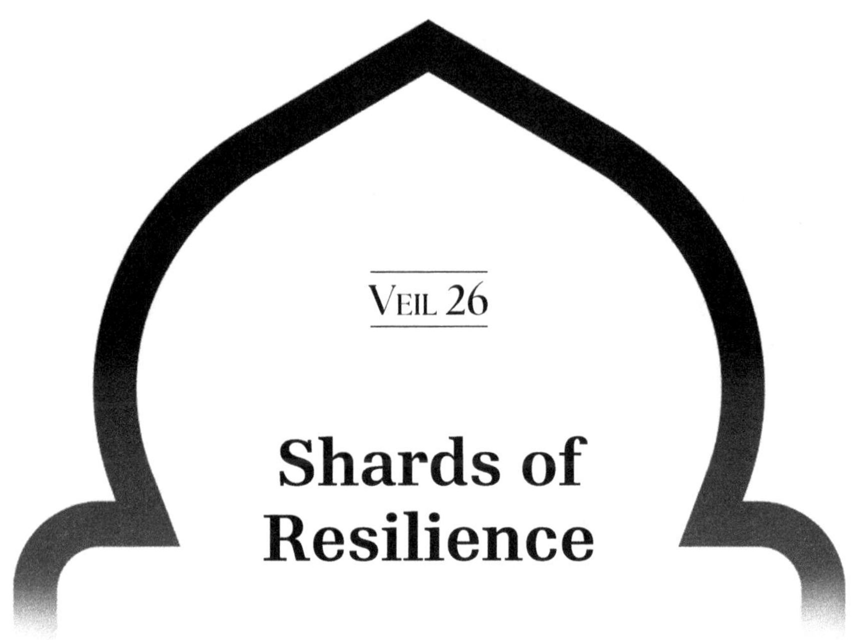

Veil 26

Shards of Resilience

The ICU at Al Wakra hummed—a fragile sanctuary for bodies healing and minds splintering under the weight of The Obsidian Hand.

The air was a sharp clash—bleach's acrid sting slicing through the faint, sour reek of sweat- damp sheets, the BEEP-BEEP-BEEP of monitors a ceaseless drumbeat piercing the silence, nurses in blue scrubs moving with hushed urgency, their gloved hands steady but their eyes shadowed with the toll of cradling lives clawed back from ruin.

Nova and Omar, bound by a shared abyss, fought to heal—physically stabilizing, yet their psyches were raw, gaping wounds, their sanity a trembling ember battered by a storm of guilt and grief they faced with desperate, tear-soaked resolve.

Nova's breaths eased, each inhale less a rasp and more a quiet pull, the nasal cannula delivering oxygen at 2 liters per minute. Her chest rose with newfound rhythm, the faint ache in her lungs softening, oxygen saturation holding steady at 96%. Bruises along her ribs faded to a mottled yellow-green, the sutured clavicle scar less angry, its titanium pins anchoring her healing frame.

Her right arm, still slung, twitched with sparks of nerve recovery, the morphine drip keeping pain at bay. The chest tube's exit, now just a small bandage, marked a lung slowly silencing its wheeze. Nova was stabilizing, her toned frame knitting itself back from the brink.

Omar's broad chest rose with deeper, steadier breaths, the rattle of his lungs nearly vanished, oxygen at 3 liters per minute supporting a robust 97% saturation. His chest tubes were gone, their scars tender but sealed, while his blood pressure climbed to 85/55, pulse a solid 68. The grafted skin on his soles wept less, the stench of infection fading under antibiotics, his temperature settling at 37.8°C.

The right femur, freed from its traction pin, ached dully in its foam brace, a sign of progress. Jaundice receded, his skin losing its sallow tint, bilirubin down to 2.0 mg/dL.

They were still bruised, still stitched—but stabilizing. But their minds were furnaces of torment—Nova's eyes, bloodshot and glistening, stared blankly, the halogen glare a cruel spotlight on her

anguish; Omar's eyes, heavy and shimmering, gazed into nothingness, a groan rumbling as grief clawed his chest.

By day five, their pleas to see each other had eroded the doctors' caution. Dr. Amina Khalil and Dr. Yusuf Mansoor met at the central station, tablets glowing with vitals, their faces etched with fatigue and tentative hope.

Khalil's voice quivered, "They're stable—Nova's BP's up, Omar's infection's down. They're begging—seeing each other might anchor them." Mansoor nodded, "Risky, but it could pull them back. Wheelchairs, full support." Nurses prepped—wheelchairs clanking, cushions adjusted for Nova's slung arm and Omar's braced leg, IV poles rigged, monitors muted, a slow procession across the ICU's gleaming tiles, a 10-meter trek laden with stakes.

At 1400, Nova was lifted—her body light as a wraith, trembling as nurses eased her into the wheelchair, the leather cool against her damp, naked skin, her right arm cradled, her left gripping the armrest, nails biting into it, her breath a shuddering sob of anticipation and dread. Omar followed—his bulk a labor, nurses grunting as they shifted him, his braced leg extended, hands clenching the chair's edges, knuckles white, a groan escaping as pain flared, his beard slick with sweat, his eyes locked on Bay 1.

Across the ICU, Bays 3-8 housed the centipede survivors—Lior Abramson rasping "Hurts…" in Bay 3, his mouth a sutured ruin, pelvis scarred, catheter draining 100 mL; Omar Haddad croaking "Where…" in Bay 4, esophagus grafted; Yael Ben-Ami whispering "Cold…" in Bay 5, anus resutured, colostomy at 50 mL; Noa Levi gasping "Help…" in Bay 6, anus repaired, colostomy at 60 mL; Yasmine Haddad murmuring "Pain…" in Bay 7, anus healing, colostomy at 45 mL; Nadine Al-Rassi wheezing "No…" in Bay 8, anus weak, colostomy at 40 mL, frailest yet speaking faintly—progress amid their wretched, surgery-bound bodies, their voices a haunting chorus threading through the ICU's sterile hum.

The wheelchairs creaked across the tiles. Oxygen hissed. Nurses walked softly behind them. Ten meters felt like miles. Khalil and Mansoor trailing, breaths held as Nova's chair halted beside Omar's bed. Their eyes met. Neither blinked. Then came the names—broken, beautiful, alive. "Omar…"

He stared back—eyes heavy, shimmering—a groan rumbling, "Nova... you're alive..." Their hands reached—hers trembling, his calloused—fingers brushing, then clasping, a touch that seared through the void, a lifeline tethering them, their sobs a shared hymn of survival and sorrow, a floodgate bursting wide.

Nova's voice shattered, "I chased them, Omar. Pulled you in. Jaber's gone because of me. I can't carry it. I need you to say it's not my fault."

Omar's eyes welled, tears cutting through the grime, his voice a guttural sob, "Nova, no— don't… I heard him scream. I couldn't stop it. I couldn't reach you. I'm sorry. I should've done more."

Nova sobbed, her voice a trembling thread, "I feel them… every one of them.

"Lior said, 'Hurts.' Yael said, 'Cold.' That's all I hear at night."

Omar's voice cracked, "Nova, I see him—Jaber, his face, his screams… I tried, I clawed, but the bull—it took him, I couldn't… and you, pinned, bleeding, I couldn't reach you, hanging there useless… I failed you both, I'm the one who's sorry…" His tears dripped, mingling with hers, his breath a shudder, "I hear him, begging, and I'm frozen, I'm nothing, a shell—I can't shake it, it's in me, eating me alive…"

Nova's sob softened, her voice raw, "We're here, Omar—we're here, broken, but here… I feel you, your screams, I hear them in my head." Omar's grip tightened, "I hear them too… we're both drowning, Nova, drowning in it…"

Nova's tears slowed, her voice trembling, "Drowning, but breathing… I keep hearing it, their voices, in Barga… not just screams, words, old words… we were onto something, weren't we?"

Omar's breath hitched, "Yeah… Jaber—we were digging, the three of us…"

Nova nodded, her voice a whisper, "Before they took us—we

found it, those texts, Ancient Arabic…"

Omar's eyes flickered, "He did—Najd, he kept saying 'sons of the sands'…"

Nova's sob caught, "Those brittle scrolls, at the port. You remember?"

"Yeah," Omar said. "Jaber read them. Najd, old grudges. Blood for blood."

"They weren't bluffing," Nova said. "They planned Doha. Not Barga."

Omar's voice steadied, "Jaber—he pieced it, 'centuries of shame,' he said… they hated Doha, the Games, 'Western pride on our soil'—he saw it…"

Nova's grip tightened, "We were in that vault—dust, ink, those words… 'Najd rises,' Jaber translated, 'blood for blood'—he said it was tribal, old wars…"

Omar nodded, "He did—'forgotten kings,' 'oaths broken'—they burned villages, he said, centuries back, West came, took… they never forgave…"

Nova's voice rose, "He showed us—'vengeance of the sands,' scratched into stone… we thought it was a myth, but they chanted it, in Barga, over us…"

Omar's tears slowed, "They did—'Najdi blood, Western shame'—Jaber heard it too, before the bull… he said 'they're ghosts, old ghosts,' living it out…"

Nova's eyes shimmered, "We found their mark—'torch falls,' Jaber read it, 'unity breaks'—it was the Games, Omar, they wanted Doha to burn…"

Omar's voice hardened, "He saw it—'Doha's pride,' they spat, 'old debts paid'—it was revenge, deep, Najdi revenge, against the world watching…"

Nova's sob turned to a shaky resolve, "We knew it—before they took us, Jaber said 'they'll strike the heart'—he meant Doha, didn't he?"

Omar's breath shuddered, "Yeah—'Semtex for the torch,' he whispered, that last night… they wanted it here, Nova, not there…"

Nova's eyes widened, "Wait—Barga, the blast… why there? It doesn't fit…" Omar's grip tightened, "We saw crates… they weren't staying, were they?"

Nova's voice trembled, "No—they were moving it… 'torch falls,' they meant here, the stadium, the Games… Barga wasn't the plan…"

Omar nodded, "They panicked… they lit it there, desperate…"

Nova's tears dried, "Escape—they blew it to run, to cover… it was for Doha, Omar, all of it…"

Omar's voice steadied, "Jaber knew—'Najd's ghosts strike,' he said… they wanted the world to see, to break it here…"

Nova's resolve flared, "We've got it—Ancient Arabic, Najdi vengeance, Doha's fall… we heard it, we know it…"

Omar's eyes blazed, "They mocked us—'centuries wait,' 'Doha bleeds'—it's not done, we've got this…"

This wasn't memory. It was evidence. Intel buried in trauma, now rising with the blood.

Nova's voice rose, "This matters. We have something. Call Sheikh Tariq!" Omar echoed, "He needs this…"

Drs. Khalil and Mansoor stepped forward, startled, Khalil's voice trembling, "You're sure? You're still…" Nova cut in, "We're broken, but we remember—get him!"

Mansoor nodded, "Stable—BP's up, lucid…"

He grabbed the phone, dialing the IOC headquarters at Raffles, his voice firm, "Sheikh Tariq, it's Mansoor—Nova and Omar are improved, speaking, demanding you.

“They’re ready.”

The elevators awaited beyond Al Wakra Hospital's glass doors, a soft DING echoing as the steel panels slid open with a faint HISS, admitting Sheikh Tariq bin Fahd Al-Mazrouei and U.S. Secretary of State Victoria Langford into a mirrored box that hummed upward, the fluorescent light casting stark shadows across their faces—his keffiyeh framing a jaw set with purpose, her gray eyes gleaming with a storm of resolve and fatigue.

The ascent was a quiet, tense breath, the WHIRR of machinery a low undertone to their racing thoughts, the doors parting on the ICU floor with a DING that jolted the silence. They emerged into a sterile corridor—white walls gleaming under halogen lights, the air sharp with bleach's sting and the faint, metallic tang of blood, the BEEP-BEEP-BEEP of monitors a relentless pulse threading through the space. Drs. Khalil and Mansoor stood at the central command station, their white coats stained with rust-colored streaks, their faces carved with exhaustion and a flicker of guarded hope.

Khalil stepped forward, her dark eyes glistening, her voice quavering with strain, "Sheikh, Secretary—they're waiting, stable but fragile. They've been talking. They're insistent."

Mansoor nodded, his broad frame rigid, his beard damp with the day's toil, his tone a gravelly rumble, "Vitals are up. They're lucid, but the trauma's deep. We've prepped them, wheelchairs, a room. You'll need PPE gear—their immune systems are still vulnerable."

Langford and Sheikh Tariq suited up quickly 's gaze sharpened, "Take us—now. I need their words."

Sheikh Tariq's hand rose, a steady gesture, "Lead on—their strength is ours."

The doctors guided them down a short hall, the tiles gleaming underfoot, their steps a soft PAT-PAT against the SQUEAK of a passing cart, to a small changing room. They suited up quickly—

masks, gowns, gloves. The only thing more fragile than the air was the truth waiting behind glass.

Langford adjusted her mask, her breath warm against it, her voice muffled but firm, “This is it—let’s keep them safe.” Sheikh Tariq tied his gown, his movements deliberate, his eyes dark pools above the mask, “Allah guide us—they’ve suffered enough.”

Gowned and gloved, they followed Khalil and Mansoor through the ICU’s double doors— HISS—the sterile air a cold slap against their exposed skin, the BEEP-BEEP-BEEP louder now, a heartbeat of survival echoing through the bays.

The centipede survivors lingered in Bays 3-8, their faint voices a haunting undercurrent— Lior Abramson’s rasped “Hurts…”, Omar Haddad’s croaked “Where…”, Yael Ben-Ami’s whispered “Cold…”, Noa Levi’s gasped “Help…”, Yasmine Haddad’s murmured “Pain…”, Nadine Al-Rassi’s wheezed “No…”—their bodies still wretched, surgery-bound wrecks, yet speaking minimally, a fragile thread of progress amid the sterile hum.

The group reached a small, private room—glass walls fogged with condensation, a faint antiseptic tang lingering—where Nova and Omar waited in wheelchairs, their figures stark against the white backdrop, oxygen hissing softly, their hands clasped, a lifeline unbroken since their reunion.

Nova sat straighter than anyone expected—frail, but fire in her spine. The air hissed; her words were coming.

The clavicle ached—a quiet throb beneath the dressing. Her fingers twitched less. The morphine barely masked the truth: pain meant she was alive.

Omar sat beside her. His breaths came stronger now, each one a fight he was beginning to win. Sweat clung to his beard, but his eyes burned—not with fever, but focus. His hands—calloused, trembling faintly—clenched Nova's.

Sheikh Tariq stepped forward, his gown rustling, his voice a low rumble muffled by the mask, "Nova, Omar—Allah be praised, you're here, alive. How are you feeling, truly?"

Langford followed, her gloved hands clasped, her gray eyes piercing above the mask, her tone soft but urgent, "You've fought through hell—tell us, how are you holding up?"

The air thickened, the HISS of oxygen and the BEEP of a distant monitor underscoring the weight of their words, the room a crucible of hope and vulnerability.

"I'm here," she rasped. "But it's heavy… like I'm drowning and breathing at the same time."

Omar's groan rumbled, "Outside, it's healing. Inside? It's fire. It's Jaber. It's her. I'm holding on."

Sheikh Tariq nodded, his eyes softening above the mask, "Your strength honors us—what you've endured, it's beyond words."

Langford leaned in, her voice steadying, "You're survivors—more than that. We're here now, listening. What do you recall—what did you see, hear, before all this, during this?"

The question hung, open and vast, a door cracked wide, inviting their fractured memories to spill forth, the room poised on the edge of revelation.

Nova's breath steadied, her voice gaining a fragile coherence.

"It began with a note—Ancient Arabic, a ransom demand… slipped to me after the kidnapping," she said. "'Deliver $500 billion, no police, no delays, or they die.'

"It accused the IOC—corruption, ignoring war-torn athletes, blaming Israel for lawless impunity, Lebanon for bending to foreigners.

Justice, they called it. 72 hours."

Her eyes flickered, haunted. "The words—old, heavy, like stones—I couldn't read them. So I found Omar. He translated, led me to Jaber… the three of us, we started chasing it."

Omar's voice cut through, low and rough. "Jaber saw that note, said it echoed something ancient. Took Nova to the Old Pier—a ruin of stones and scrolls. Ancient Arabic, Najd history. Their root, he called it."

His fists clenched, knuckles whitening. "Then Barga—their lair. Above the Semtex, scratched into the wall: 'Najd Rises - Blood for Blood.'

"When they came for me—rods, the bull—they chanted, 'Tha'r ar-Rimāl,' 'Vengeance of the Sands,' over and over, like a pulse."

Sheikh Tariq's gaze sharpened, piercing. "This note—what justice did it mean?"

Nova swallowed, her voice thin but resolute. "Jaber said it was old anger—Najd, desert tribes, Bedouin, primal. They'd kill for honor, blood debts, tha'r, centuries deep.

"He tied it to '73, Yom Kippur War—Egypt, Syria struck Israel, lost. The ceasefire left radicals seething, unbowed."

Omar nodded, his voice gravelly. "The scrolls spoke of 'sons of Najd,' 'oaths broken.' To them, the West, Israel—they're thieves. Stole their pride."

Langford interjected, "Yom Kippur—how'd that spark this group?"

Nova nodded, "They didn't just lose a war—they lost pride. Trust. They buried it in the desert. And it festered.

"Jaber—he said after 1973, camps, young fighters, they broke off… no trust in deals, Camp David… took Najdi vengeance, made it theirs—just blood, like the tribes…"

Omar's breath hitched, "He found it—'Najd rises,' on the pier, said they hated the world watching, turned it on Doha…"

Sheikh Tariq's voice rumbled, "Why Doha, the Games—why here?"

Nova's eyes flared, "Jaber—he said 'Doha's pride,' the cauldron, it mocked them… 'Najd Rises,' above the Semtex, meant burn it here, show they're alive…"

Langford's breath caught. The fire had been meant for the world's stage, not the wasteland.

Sheikh Tariq's voice softened, "This inscription—'Najd Rises'—what else was there?"

Nova paused, "Red dust, blood smears… Jaber said it was new, but old, a vow… 'Blood for blood.'"

Omar nodded, "They bragged—'torch falls,' 'unity breaks'—in Barga, over the crates… Jaber saw 'Doha bound,' before…"

Langford's gaze sharpened, "Semtex intended for Doha—why blow Barga then?"

Nova's voice trembled, "Jaber—he said 'strike the heart,' meant Doha… but Barga, they panicked…" Omar growled, "When 'The West' closed in, they lit it—desperate, to run… Semtex was for here, not there…"

Sheikh Tariq's hand rose, "This Najdi vengeance—how old, how rooted?"

Nova's voice steadied, "Jaber said—Najd, Bedouin, centuries… a goat, a well, they'd avenge it generations later… after '73, they saw it—West stole their victory, their honor… swore tha'r, turned it on us…"

Omar added, "He read—'kings forgotten,' 'sands reclaim'… Barga, near Najd, desolate, their hideout…"

Langford's voice cut, "Why athletes—why them?"

Nova's breath hitched, "They chose them like flags. To make the world watch. To twist peace into punishment."

Omar added, "They bragged—'world falls'— Najdi vengeance, on us all…"

Dr. Khalil stepped forward, "Enough for today," Khalil said gently. "They've given more than enough."

Dr. Mansoor nodded, his broad frame looming beside her, his gravelly tone adding, "You've got what they can give—more later, if they strengthen."

Langford's gaze flicked to them, a curt nod, "Keep them safe." Sheikh Tariq's hand rose, a steady gesture, his voice a low rumble, "Their courage lights our path—protect it, doctors."

The group turned, the HISS of the ICU's double doors parting as they retraced their steps, shedding the protective gear in the small changing room. The gowns rustled as they peeled away, gloves snapping faintly as they tugged free, masks and head coverings slipping off with a soft SHUSH, the cool air a sharp contrast against their flushed skin.

Langford smoothed her hair, her breath no longer muffled, her tone resolute, "It's a thread of fire—thin, but real. Enough to follow. Enough to start." Sheikh Tariq adjusted his keffiyeh, his movements deliberate, his voice steady, "A thread of fire—Allah spared us its full blaze."

Their steps echoed down the sterile corridor—PAT-PAT against the gleaming tiles—the halogen lights casting long shadows behind them, the BEEP-BEEP-BEEP fading into a distant hum. The elevators awaited beyond the glass doors, a soft DING punctuating their arrival as the steel panels slid open with a HISS.

They stepped inside, the mirrored box humming downward, the fluorescent light stark against their faces once more—his jaw set with purpose beneath the keffiyeh, her gray eyes alight with a storm now tempered by clarity. The descent was quiet, a held breath, the WHIRR of machinery a faint pulse beneath their thoughts.

As the doors parted with a final DING, the warm Doha night spilled in—palm trees swaying beyond the hospital's entrance, the distant hum of traffic a reminder of a world still turning, oblivious to the precipice it had skirted. Sheikh Tariq paused, his gaze lifting to the star- strewn sky, the weight of Nova and Omar's story settling into his bones.

A ghost war, centuries old, nearly lit the world on fire. What stopped it? Desperation. Grief. Luck. But the scar remains. He saw it now: the Games preserved, nations spared, a fragile unity intact.

Langford stepped beside him, her heels clicking softly against the pavement, her voice low, "We dodged a bomb—$500 billion, athletes as pawns. This could've redrawn the map." She exhaled, the fatigue in her eyes giving way to a steely resolve. "The world needs this—cleaned up, clear, no panic. I'll brief D.C., NATO, the UN— quietly, first. You?"

Sheikh Tariq nodded, his tone measured, "My council, the Gulf states—then the Arab League. We'll speak as one, show strength, not fear. This 'Obsidian Hand'—their roots run deep, but ours are deeper."

They moved toward the waiting cars—black SUVs gleaming under the streetlights, engines idling with a low growl. Sheikh Tariq's mind turned to the words he'd choose—honor for the survivors, vigilance for the future, a call to unity that masked the tremor of what might have been. Langford's thoughts churned through cables and calls—diplomats roused at dawn, intelligence nets cast wide, a narrative sharp enough to rally without breaking.

The doors shut with a solid THUNK, the vehicles pulling away into the night, their silhouettes shrinking against the hospital's glow.

Behind them, Al Wakra Hospital stood sentinel, its glass facade reflecting the stars, the faint BEEP-BEEP-BEEP a heartbeat of survival pulsing within.

Nova and Omar rested, their fragile thread of life holding, their story now a torch passed to those who'd carry it forward. The world would learn—quietly, carefully—of the fire that almost consumed it, and the two survivors who kept the torch from falling.

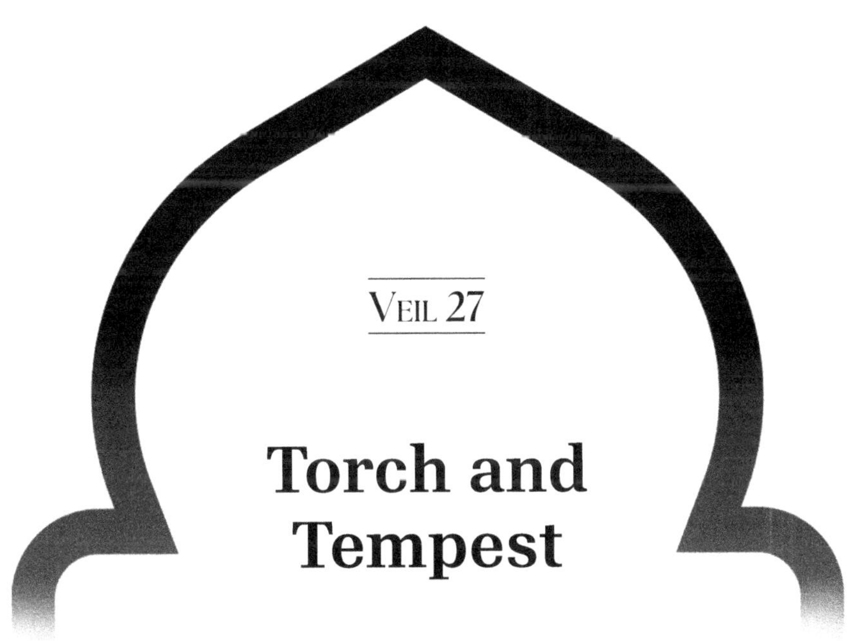

Veil 27

Torch and Tempest

The Oval Office thrummed with urgency, the secure line's faint crackle threading through the predawn gloom as U.S. Secretary of State Victoria Langford's face came through a screen on the Resolute Desk, her gray eyes locked on the President's taut expression.

Outside, Washington, D.C.'s first light crept across the lawn, but inside, the air was heavy with near-miss dread.

The President's fingers drummed the Resolute Desk's edge, the morning light catching a furrow in his brow—this wasn't just intelligence. It was an abyss avoided by inches.

"Mr. President," she said, "it was a $500 billion ransom—Ancient Arabic, Najdi roots, aimed at the Doha Games. Eight at Barga, Semtex crates, one slipped away. Delta Force took out seven, but their network's scale—unknown. Funding's a ghost. They nearly shattered the torch, and us with it." The President's jaw tightened, "NATO, UN—now. No leaks, Victoria."

Hours later, NATO screens in Brussels flickered to life, Langford's face stark on their monitors, her tone clipped. The room fell still. One misfire, one misstep—and a continent could've burned.

"Allies, this Obsidian Hand struck Barga—eight operatives, one escaped, seven down by Delta. Explosives for Doha, a 1973 vendetta reborn. Their affiliates, their cash—we don't know, and that's the terror. NATO's in, full throttle."

In New York, UN delegates leaned into her voice, "A transnational phantom—tribal rage turned global. We dodged catastrophe, but the embers burn. Eyes open, everywhere."

Across the Gulf, Sheikh Tariq bin Fahd Al-Mazrouei stood in Doha's marble council chamber, Gulf Cooperation Council flags framing his keffiyeh-clad figure, his voice a steady rumble.

"Brothers, a shadow from Najd rose—old oaths, new fire. They targeted our Games, our honor. Nova Mendelsohn, a journalist of the Olympic flame, and Omar Al-Kaabi, a humble Souq Waqif merchant and local historian, saw it—Allah spared us, but one fled."

Before the League of Arab States, he paused, jaw clenched—a flash of the ICU's sterile hum surfacing behind his eyes—before continuing, steel in his voice, "This Obsidian Hand twists our past—we hunt their remnants, their shadow, together."

At the IOC briefing, he softened, "The Games held—thanks to survivors' courage. We shield the flame tighter now."

Meanwhile, at the Main Press Center, tension crackled in every seat. Reporters packed the rows for the final briefing of the Doha Games—a closing marred not by triumph, but by a terror thwarted. Their notebooks trembled, the air buzzed with the HUM of cameras, the CLICK-CLICK of shutters, the rustle of anticipation.

On the dais, Langford and Sheikh Tariq stood resolute—her red suit sharp, her gray eyes piercing; his robes pristine, his dark gaze unyielding. The Olympic rings glowed faintly behind them, a symbol singed but standing.

Langford took the podium, her voice slicing the clamor, "Yesterday, we learned of a plot against the Doha Games—an international strike by The Obsidian Hand. Eight operatives in Barga, seven killed by Delta Force, one escaped. Semtex meant for here detonated there— premature, their misstep.

"Nova Mendelsohn, a journalist who's tracked the Olympics for twenty years, and Omar Al-Kaabi, a Doha historian and spice merchant from Souq Waqif, survived to tell us. This wasn't isolated—post-'73 roots, global reach. We're blind to their network, their funds— that's the threat we face."

Sheikh Tariq stepped forward, his presence a quiet storm, "The Games are our unity, our pride—they aimed to break it. A Najdi vengeance, twisted, sought our torch. Nova and Omar, and those in Al Wakra's bays, bore witness—Doha stands, by their strength, by Allah's grace. One enemy slipped free. We mourn, we resolve."

Hands shot up, voices surged.

James Cartwright of the BBC stood, his tone brisk, "Secretary Langford, eight at Barga—but how big is this Obsidian Hand, really?"

Langford's eyes met his, steady, "We know eight were there—one escaped, seven dead. Beyond that—unknown. Affiliates, operatives, funding—no clarity. NATO and Interpol are digging—that gap's what keeps us awake at night."

Emilie Laurent of L'Équipe rose, her accent cutting, "Madame Secretary, why athletes—why them?"

Langford's voice hardened, "Symbols—Lior Abramson, Omar Haddad, Yael Ben-Ami, Noa Levi, Yasmine Haddad, Nadine Al-

Rassi were nations to them, their suffering a broadcast. It was precise, meant to unravel us."

Rashida al-Hakim from Al Jazeera faced Sheikh Tariq, "Sheikh, this Najdi vengeance—why the Games, why Doha?"

His gaze softened, then steeled, "They saw our hosting as defiance—a desert's rise they despised. The torch, our unity, was their target—to burn it here, in our core."

Greg Palmer, the Australian, called out, "Sheikh, what's this do to the Olympics' future—can it take this hit?"

Sheikh Tariq's hand lifted, calm, "It endures—it always has. Security hardens, vigilance grows—the flame's alive. We'll carry it, scarred but strong."

Carlos Mendes of Globo Esporte pressed, "Secretary, this one enemy—still out there? What's the hunt?"

Langford's tone sharpened, "Yes—rank unknown, identity a void. Delta missed him at Barga. NATO, Interpol, the League of Arab States—they're tracking. He's a ghost, but not forever."

Priya Patel of The Times of India stood, "Sheikh Tariq, will nations trust the Games after this?"

His nod was grave, "Trust rebuilds—hosts will prove it, as Doha did. The movement bends, never breaks."

Hiroshi Tanaka of NHK asked, "Secretary, how far could this reach—beyond Doha?"

Langford exhaled, "Their words—'world falls'—hint at more. Doha was the spark—its limits, we don't know. That's why we're global now."

Fatima El-Sayed of Al-Ahram rose, "Sheikh, the Arab world—how do we mend this?"

His voice gentled, "With truth—this isn't us, but a distortion. We hunt the villains, stand as one, honor the survivors. Unity heals."

The room hushed, the CLICK-CLICK fading as their words sank in.

Langford stepped back, her mind spinning through cables—NATO's net, Interpol's leads, the LAS's resolve. Sheikh Tariq lingered, his thoughts on the Games' soul—tested, enduring. Reporters scribbled, the tale of a near-lost torch now theirs to spread.

Outside, Doha shimmered under the morning sun, its skyline a quiet defiance, its future a shadowed hope.

As the Main Press Center Auditorium emptied, its echoes of questions and shutters fading into Doha's sunlit sprawl, a quieter resilience stirred within Al Wakra Hospital's white walls.

The sterile corridors, once sharp with bleach and blood's metallic tang, now carried a softer hum—faint WHIRS of machinery, the occasional SQUEAK of a cart, the steady BEEP- BEEP-BEEP of monitors. The light cut warmer now across the tiles, casting long, quiet shadows—an ICU not just surviving, but mending.

Earlier that morning, in a sunlit ward on the ICU's edge, Nova and Omar had sat side by side, their wheelchairs angled toward a window framing palm trees and a sliver of Gulf blue. Discharge loomed closer for them—a tentative step after days of fragility—and with it, a cautious hope tempered by scars.

Nova had perched upright, her spine held straighter than before—not confidence, but endurance in motion, the wheelchair's leather creaking less beneath her. The nasal cannula was gone, her oxygen saturation a firm 98%, her breaths shallow but smooth. Her blood pressure had climbed to 98/62, pulse a solid 60, blood volume returning, the catheter scar on her neck fading to a faint pink line.

The clavicle repair held, titanium pins anchoring the bone, the dressing peeled back to reveal a healing suture, the ache dulled to a murmur, her slung right arm flexing faintly, fingers curling with purpose. Morphine had tapered to nothing, replaced by ibuprofen's gentler hand. Bruises lingered as pale yellow smears across her torso, the chest tube's scab a small memory, her lung clear. Her eyes—less bloodshot, brighter—tracked the horizon, sweat gone from her brow, her left hand gripping Omar's, a reflex of endurance.

Mentally, she teetered—nightmares of Barga jolted her awake, but daylight brought back focus, a journalist's instinct to write.

Omar, beside her then, had seemed less broken, his massive frame less hunched, the wheelchair groaning faintly under his weight. Oxygen was off, his saturation at 99%, his chest rising with deep, even breaths—no RATTLE-GASP, just a steady swell, scars from chest tubes pink and closed. His blood pressure steadied at 102/68 mmHg, pulse 72, hemoglobin 11.0 g/dL, infection's grip loosened, the subclavian scar a subtle mark. Nova watched the rise of his chest, slow and unlabored—proof they weren't just surviving, but inching back.

His grafted soles, wrapped in light dressings, oozed less, the rot's stench a ghost, antibiotics whittling CRP, temperature at 37.2°C. The femur brace stayed, the traction pin's exit a healing dot, the ache a low throb, his liver drain gone, jaundice a whisper in his eyes. His hands—calloused, steadier—held Nova's, his beard dry, his gaze heavy but lifting. Grief gnawed—Jaber's screams, the Souq's silence— but a shopkeeper's pragmatism crept in.

Nova's voice had broken the quiet, raspy but warm, "They're letting us out soon—can you believe it, Omar? I can almost smell the ink again." She squeezed his hand, a faint smile tugging her lips.

Omar's rumble answered, "Aye, and the Souq's spices—dusty,

alive. We're still here, Nova. Battered, but here." His eyes met hers, a flicker of defiance softening, "You'll write it, won't you? All of it?"

She nodded, her breath catching, "Every word—I owe it to us, to them. You'll tell it too, in your way."

He chuckled, low, "Over tea, loud as ever—Doha needs the story straight."

That tempered optimism had hung fragile, a thread through pain—physical scars fading, mental ones raw but stitching. Discharge meant crutches for Omar, a sling and long flight back to New York for Nova, and for both, numerous outpatient checks ahead, and a return to a world nearly lost. Outside, car horns and the distant trill of a call to prayer reminded them: life hadn't paused.

In the ICU, each bay told a variation of the same story—of bodies desecrated, of minds frayed beyond words, of a chain that refused to fully break.

Omar Haddad, massive yet frail in Bay 4, breathed shallowly. His face, sewn to Lior's anus, bore jagged, infected sutures, lips swollen. Rectal wounds from Yael's link festered.

Yael Ben-Ami trembled in Bay 5, gaunt and weak, her breaths faint. Her face, stitched to Omar's anus, wept pus, jaw misaligned. Rectal wounds from Tamar's lost link bled.

Noa Levi curled fetal in Bay 6, skeletal, gasping desperately. Her face, once sewn to Tamar's anus, oozed beneath torn dressings, mouth ravaged. Rectal wounds from Yasmine's attachment leaked.

Yasmine Haddad lay rigid in Bay 7, her taekwondo spirit broken, breaths rasping. Her face, linked to Noa's anus, festered with infected sutures, rectal wounds from Nadine's stitching seeping bile.

Nadine Al-Rassi slumped in Bay 8, ashen, her wheeze fading. Her face, sewn to Yasmine's anus, bore gaping sores, rectal wounds raw, sepsis closing in.

The future for these six—Lior, Omar, Yael, Noa, Yasmine, Nadine—remained precariously unknown, their bodies ravaged and facing a pile of surgeries—facial reconstructions, rectal repairs—weeks, months, years of care ahead, survival a mere flicker. Drs. Khalil and Mansoor hovered, their coats streaked anew, orchestrating IVs, scans, and desperate plans, the most powerful of antibiotics nothing more than a frail shield.

A distant THUMP-THUMP-THUMP broke the ICU's HISS—IAF Sikorsky CH-53 helicopters landing on Al Wakra's pad, dust swirling as medics in olive drab spilled out. The Israeli government, with Lebanon's rare assent, had arranged their transfer to Sheba Medical Center in Tel Hashomer—Lior, Omar, Yael, Noa, Yasmine, and Nadine—a trauma lifeline.

Stretchers rolled, oxygen tanks clanked, monitors beeped—each survivor swaddled, their frail forms dwarfed by machines.

Lior's stretcher jolted, medics securing his mask, "Rectal bleed—pressors up!" Omar followed, his groan muffled, a nurse adjusting his drip, "Facial sepsis—antibiotics max!" Yael's eyes fluttered shut, "Jaw's unstable—intubate now!" Noa's monitor spiked, "Anal hemorrhage—clamp it mid-flight!" Yasmine rocked, "Fever's critical—cooling stat!" Nadine hung limp, "She's crashing—vent ready!" The Lebanese pair, Yasmine and Nadine, joined the Israelis under a fleeting diplomatic thread.

The choppers lifted, THUMP-THUMP-THUMP fading over Doha, bound for Tel Hashomer— five hours, midair refueling, medics braced for collapse. Sheba awaited—ORs prepped, trauma teams poised.

Back in the ward, Nova watched as Omar slept. To her, the beat of the blades sounded less like escape and more like a vow: carry them far, carry them safe. Her voice softened, "They're going—better hands, maybe a chance…" She'd write them back from the edge, even if it cost her sleep.

She gripped the wheelchair's arm, a vow to wait, her optimism now a solitary thread amid the storm's retreat.

Later that evening, the sterile hum of Al Wakra Hospital softened as dusk settled over Doha, the sky beyond the ward's windows a deepening indigo streaked with gold. Nova and Omar lay in adjacent beds, free from the ICU's grip. Tonight, they'd been granted a small mercy— beds wheeled into a private room, a television flickering to life with the Closing Ceremony of the Doha Olympics.

The BEEP-BEEP-BEEP of monitors pulsed faintly, a steady undertone to the broadcast's swell, their hands clasped across the gap, a lifeline unbroken.

The ceremony opened with the parade of athletes streaming into Lusail Stadium, a sea of flags and weary smiles under floodlights. The announcer's voice crackled through the screen, "The athletes of the world, united once more…"

But the absence of the Israeli and Lebanese teams carved a hollow space in the procession. Their surviving members—Lior Abramson, Omar Haddad, Yael Ben-Ami, Noa Levi, Yasmine Haddad, and Nadine Al-Rassi—lay far away at Sheba Medical Center, their bodies still battling "The Doctor's" horrors. The deceased—Tamar Cohen, Nadine Mansour, Yasmine Khalil, Cyrine Ghazal, Maya Ben-Ari, and Ronit Weissman—had been returned home, their remains mourned in silence.

In their stead, members of the Qatari federation stepped forward, solemn and deliberate, waving the blue-and-white of Israel and the green-red-white of Lebanon. The flags fluttered high, a quiet tribute against the stadium's roar, their bearers' faces etched with respect.

Nova's voice rasped, soft but steady, "Look at that, Omar—Qatar holding their flags. It's... something, isn't it?" Omar's rumble came low, his eyes glistening, "Honor where it's due. They're gone, but not forgotten." His face tilting toward her, "Wish I could've walked with 'em."

The ceremony shifted, the Greek flag rising to a swell of strings, its white cross stark against blue, honoring the Games' ancient roots. Then, India's tricolor ascended, saffron, white, and green rippling for Mumbai, host of the 2044 Games, a distant promise under the night sky.

Nova murmured, "Greece, India... the thread keeps going, even after this." Omar nodded, his breath a faint RASP, "From sand to stone—life turns, doesn't it?"

The Olympic flag descended next, the five rings folding into shadow as the Olympic anthem's mournful notes filled the stadium, marking Doha's Games' end. The crowd stood hushed, a collective breath held.

Nova's eyes shimmered, "It's over—feels heavier than it should." Omar's voice softened, "Heavier—but it held, Nova. We held."

The handover followed, a ritual of transition. Doha's mayor, Faisal Al-Kuwari, clutched the Olympic flag, his hands steady as he passed it to Sheikh Tariq bin Fahd Al-Mazrouei. His robes flowed as he turned, offering it to Mumbai's mayor, Sneha Patil, her emerald sari catching the light. Their exchange was wordless, a baton passed across continents.

Omar chuckled faintly, "Sheikh's hands—strong as ever. Mumbai's got a load to carry now." Nova smiled, weak but real, "They'll manage—Sneha's got fire in her eyes."

The Olympic flame, burning since the opening, flickered in its cauldron, a beacon against the dark. Then, with a slow HISS, it extinguished. The smoke curled upward—one last breath exhaled into the world. Nova's breath hitched, "There it goes… feels like losing something." Omar squeezed her hand, "Not lost—just resting."

Cultural performances unfurled, Doha's first—a tapestry of Qatari tradition. Bedouin drummers pounded goatskin tablas, their rhythms deep and rolling, as falconers released birds skyward, wings slicing the air. Dancers in flowing thobes spun, swords flashing in an ardha, the warrior dance echoing Najd's past, though tonight it felt less like vengeance and more like defiance. Incense wafted, ouds weeping a mournful tune, the stadium awash in desert gold.

Mumbai countered with a burst of India—Kathak dancers twirled, anklets jingling, their spins a blur of crimson and saffron, while tablas and sitars wove a joyous raga. Elephants, painted with lotus motifs, lumbered in hologram, a nod to Ganesh, as Bollywood voices soared, vibrant against Doha's somber echo.

Nova's eyes brightened, "The ardha—it's fierce, but… healing, somehow. Like a scream shaped into something sacred." Omar's rumble warmed, "And Mumbai's dance—life shouting back. Good to see it, Nova." She nodded, "They're both saying it without saying it—tragedy doesn't win."

Sheikh Tariq took the podium, his keffiyeh framing a face carved with resolve, his voice a steady thunder over the speakers.

"People of Doha, of the world—tonight, we close a Games unlike any other. We dreamed of unity, of pride, and we faced a shadow that sought to break it—Najd's vengeance, the Obsidian Hand, a fire aimed at our torch. They took lives—Tamar, Nadine, Yasmine, Cyrine, Maya, Ronit, Jaber—wounded others beyond measure."

In the stands, a mother clutched her son tighter. Somewhere, someone wept.

"Yet here we stand, unbroken," he continued. "Nova Mendelsohn and Omar Al-Kaabi, voices of truth, bore witness with the centipede's survivors—Lior, Yael, Noa, Yasmine, Nadine—whose strength shames the darkness. This was our trial, and Allah's mercy, our shield. To Mumbai, we pass a flame tested but enduring—carry it high, for we've proven its worth."

Omar's eyes glistened, "He named us, Nova—feels real now." She squeezed back, "It is real—we're the proof, Omar. He's right about the flame."

Emir Nawaf bin Ahmad Al Thani followed, his robes regal, his tone a quiet storm.

"Friends, these Games were our heart laid bare—joy turned to sorrow, courage rising from ash. The torch lit Doha, and a sinister ghost from the past tried to snuff it—fortunes demanded, Semtex poised, a doctor's cruelty unleashed. We lost daughters and sons, saw survivors endure the unimaginable, yet the Games closed, not in defeat, but defiance.

"Nova and Omar, your bravery lit our path; Lior, Yael, Noa, Yasmine, Nadine, your survival is our honor. To India, we entrust this legacy—not just of triumph, but of resilience. Mumbai, let your Games sing of hope, for Doha has sung through tears."

Nova's voice trembled, "The Emir… he sees it all, doesn't he?" Omar's rumble steadied her, "Sees us too—tears and all. We're still singing, Nova."

The ceremony closed with a grand yet subdued artistic show. Qatari musicians cradled ouds and qanuns, their strings weaving John Lennon's Imagine into a haunting elegy, notes bending with desert melancholy. Acrobats drifted on silks, their arcs slow and mournful, dancers in white swaying like apparitions, performers casting shadows against a crescent moon backdrop. The stadium dimmed, the crowd hushed, a collective exhale for a Games scarred but whole.

Nova's breath caught, "Imagine—it fits, doesn't it? Quiet, but strong." Omar's hand tightened, his voice a low thread, "Aye, like us—quiet now, but still here. Doha's done it, Nova—closed the circle." She nodded, tears slipping free, "And we're part of it—always will be."

It wasn't peace—but it was promise. And for now, that was enough.

The screen faded to black, the room silent save the BEEP-BEEP-BEEP, their hands still clasped. Outside, Doha glittered, its wounds raw but its spirit unbroken, the flame's echo lingering in the night.

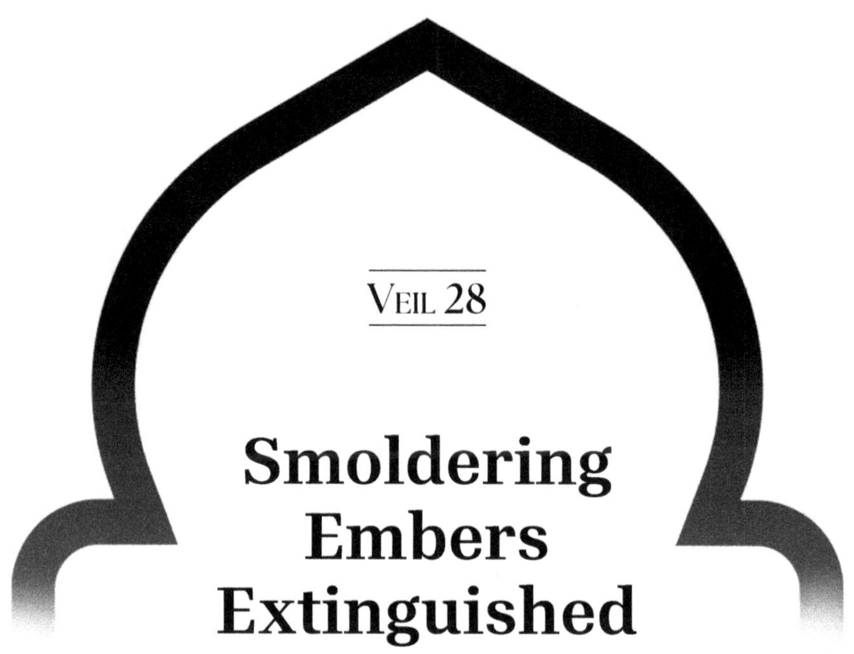

Veil 28

Smoldering Embers Extinguished

Two weeks after the Closing Ceremony, Nova emerged from Al Wakra Hospital's glass doors, the humid Doha air clinging to her skin like a damp veil. Her discharge papers rustled in her sling-bound hand, her wounds superficially mending—clavicle sutures a tight pink seam, bruises dulled to sallow whispers, chest tube scar a puckered ridge. But beneath the stitched flesh, something feral still stirred—unmended, unseen.

Her right shoulder and arm, braced with titanium pins, throbbed with each jostle, nerves prickling like static; physical therapy loomed—months of sweat-soaked stretches, weights, and grimaces—yet doctors warned her range would cap at 80%, strength a ghost of its past. She slid into a taxi, her sling glaring white against her jacket, and returned to her Sheraton Grand hotel room. Time hadn't passed—it had frayed, snagged on a moment that refused to loosen its grip—laptop open mid-sentence, notes splayed like fallen leaves, jeans crumpled over a chair, a coffee cup's stale ring mocking her absence.

Alone in Doha, the silence gnawed. The room's stillness amplified every creak—her footsteps a hollow PAT-PAT, the AC's HUM a taunting drone. Barga's ghosts crept in— Semtex's acrid tang stung her nose, Jaber's screams echoed in her skull, the Spectre's shadow loomed in every corner. She'd wake gasping, sheets soaked, her good hand clawing for a pen to anchor her. Days blurred—coffee gone cold, curtains half-drawn, her reflection in the mirror a stranger with hollow eyes and a trembling jaw.

She'd pace, shoulder aching, muttering to herself, "Keep it together, Nova—just write it out." The city beyond buzzed, oblivious, its gleam a cruel contrast to her unraveling.

Her phone buzzed incessantly—TV interviews piling up like debts. She granted four, each interview felt like another incision—probing, never healing.

The BBC's James Cartwright faced her in a sterile studio, lights harsh, his voice clipped, "Nova, how do you process Barga—personally, as a journalist?" She swallowed, throat dry, "It's a scar, James—physical, sure, but it's the mental gouge that festers. I write to stitch it up, but some threads just… dangle." He pressed, "Survivor's guilt?" Her eyes flickered, "Every damn day—I'm here, they're not. It's a weight I can't shrug off."

Al Jazeera's Rashida al-Hakim met her in a plush lounge, her tone gentle, "What did Doha teach the world?" Nova's voice steadied, "Resilience, Rashida—ours, the Games'. It's not just surviving; it's spitting in the face of what tried to break us." Rashida leaned in, "And the cost?" Nova's breath hitched, "Too high—lives, sanity. But we paid it."

Fox News flew her to a garish set, Chase Drennan's voice sharp, "Was this a security failure?" She bristled, "No—it was a near-hit, caught by dumb luck and guts. Blame the shadows, not the guards."

He smirked, “You’re the hero, then?” She snapped, “No—just the one still breathing.”

The Joe Rogan Experience stretched three hours, Rogan’s drawl probing, “What’s it like knowing you dodged death?” She rubbed her shoulder, “Like carrying a corpse, Joe—every step’s heavy, every night’s a fight. You don’t dodge it; you drag it.” He pushed, “Nightmares?” Her voice cracked, “Yeah—fire, blood, faces I can’t save. Pen’s my weapon now.”

Each word carved her open, yet fed her draft.

Omar Al-Kaabi endured another week in the hospital, his massive frame a canvas of repair. His soles—charred and flayed from Barga’s heat—demanded relentless grafts. Surgeons peeled skin from his thighs, thin and glistening, meshing it over raw, suppurating wounds, stapling it tight. The grafts clung unevenly—pink patches knitting, others sloughing yellow, re-debrided with steel and saline, each session leaving him shivering, fever spiking to 38.5°C.

But what the scalpel couldn’t stitch was the silence between screams—the memory of Jaber, still smoldering.

Nova visited daily, her sling a fixture, her presence a balm—tea shared, silences thick with understanding. Without words, they became scaffolding—one bracing the other, upright in the ruin.

On discharge day, she arrived with a wheelchair, its frame groaning as Omar eased in, soles swathed in gauze. The taxi ride to his Souq Waqif flat was hushed, the city’s clamor muted. Inside, the air hung heavy with cardamom and neglect, his shop below shuttered. She wheeled him to his couch, a nest of cushions and a tray of dates and water waiting.

Mubarak, his brother, arrived hours later, wiry and sun-darkened from UAE, his suitcase thudding as he surveyed the space.

Omar's rumble greeted him, "Mubarak—thought you'd forgotten the way."

Mubarak grinned, dropping his bag, "Never, brother—engineering's dull without your noise. This place stinks of you already."

Nova laughed, setting tea, "Good—it's home, then."

Omar shifted, wincing, "Aye, home—but these feet, Mubarak. Docs say grafts need time— crutches soon, maybe."

Mubarak knelt, inspecting the bandages, "They're holding—ugly, but holding. I'll keep you off 'em, stubborn ox."

Nova chimed in, "He's right—you're not hobbling yet. I've seen you try; it's pitiful."

Omar chuckled, "Pitiful? I'll be dancing by Ramadan—watch me."

Mubarak snorted, "Dancing? I'll settle for standing. Nova, you staying 'til he's sorted?" She nodded, "Yeah—'til you've got him, Mubarak. Then Brooklyn calls."

Omar's eyes softened, "You don't have to, Nova—staying, I mean. You've done enough." Her voice trembled, "I do, Omar—you're my anchor here. I'd be lost without these visits."

He gripped her hand, "And you're mine—kept me sane in that bed. But you're shaking— Barga still?" She swallowed, "Yeah—nights are hell. You?" His rumble deepened, "Screams, fire, that damn doctor. We're a pair, aren't we?"

Nova's tears welled, "A damn tough pair—scarred, but breathing."

Mubarak clapped Omar's shoulder, "You two—tougher than my steel beams. I'll handle the rest; Nova, get your story out."

She stayed, helping Mubarak settle Omar—crutches propped by the couch, meds sorted in a clinking row, the kitchen stocked with rice and dates. She left two days later, her draft thicker, her hotel room packed.

In Brooklyn, her Crown Heights flat became a crucible—rain drumming the panes, her laptop's glow a lifeline. Doha 2040: The Shadow Games took shape—400 pages of raw prose, blending her notes with Omar's tales, Jaber's scrolls, the centipede's horror. She feared what writing might preserve—and what it might erase.

Chapters traced the ransom note's ancient script, Barga's Semtex stench, the survivors' gasps, her own unraveling—a journalist's lens on terror, resilience, and the Games' fragile flame.

Simon & Schuster published it March 2041, its cover stark—a torch bleeding into red sand—rocketing to a New York Times Best Seller. Reviews sang: "Mendelsohn bares the soul of survival," "A haunting elegy for Doha's Games."

Fame followed—London's Barbican, Tokyo's NHK Hall, Sydney's Opera House—her voice firm, shoulder stiffening in chill. Notoriety chafed; she craved quiet, but Barga's Spectres—flame, blades, screams—stalked her sleep, her pen a frail bulwark.

In spring 2042, an IOC envelope arrived. Victory and grief coiled inside the seal, indistinguishable. Athens, October 15, the 161st Session, the Pierre de Coubertin Medal for her service to the Olympic movement. Her chest tightened, pride warring with dread.

That evening, she sank onto her couch, rain streaking Brooklyn's dark, and FaceTimed Omar. His face bloomed on screen, bearded and hearty, the Souq's clatter behind. "Nova— rainy there again?"

She smiled, "Always—keeps me honest. Shop busy?"

He grinned, "Aye—feet grumble, but I'm upright. Mubarak's back in UAE, so it's me and the chaos."

She held up the invite, "This came—Athens, October. Coubertin Medal." His eyes lit, "Allah's grace, Nova—that's yours, earned in blood."

She softened, "Come with me—my guest, flights and room on me." She needed him there—not just for company, but for courage. He paused, "Greece? With you? I'd not miss it—crutches and all."

Her voice broke, "Good—I need you there, Omar. Something big to ask, face-to-face." He tilted his head, "Big, eh? You're killing me—spill it now?"

She laughed, tears slipping, "No—Athens. It's… us, the story, what's next. I'm still scared, Omar—Barga's in me."

His rumble steadied, "Me too, Nova—every night. But we're tougher than it. I'll be there— ask me anything."

She nodded, "I will—god, I miss you." He grinned, "Miss you more—Athens, then. We'll face it together."

The screen dimmed, rain tapping, her heart a tangle of fear and hope. The medal gleamed in promise, Omar's voice her tether, a question unasked but burning—partnership, healing, or a shared fight anew.

Nova Mendelsohn woke to the relentless TAP-TAP-TAP of Brooklyn rain battering her Crown Heights window, a gray dawn clawing through the blinds' slats. Her eyes jolted open at 6:47 a.m. breath snagging as Barga's inferno flared—Semtex's guttural BOOM, Jaber's scream liquefying into ash—before dissolving into the damp hush of her bedroom. For a moment, she didn't know which smoke was real—steam or Semtex. She lay rigid, sheets twisted like ropes around her calves, her chest a vise from the nightmare's grip. The clock's red digits glared; four hours of sleep, snatched with an extra Ativan at 3 a.m., left her groggy, her right shoulder pulsing with a deep, gnawing ache, titanium pins grinding beneath her skin.

She eased her legs off the bed, the hardwood's chill biting her soles, and stood with a grimace, her left hand bracing her weight. The room reeked of stale coffee and ink—her desk a sprawl of notes, Doha 2040 proofs teetering beside a drooping fern. She shuffled to the kitchen, linoleum tacky underfoot, and flicked on the kettle, its low HUM a frail lifeline.

Breakfast was mechanical—two rye toast slices, brittle and unbuttered, crumbs scattering like sand; a mug of black tea, its steam sharp with tannin, scalding her tongue as she sipped, leaning against the sink, the rain's drone a dull thrum through the glass.

Her phone buzzed, a scarred iPhone rattling on the counter—18 emails, agent texts ("BBC redux?"), a missed call from her sister. She swiped through—paperback pitches, Tokyo invites, spam—typing terse replies with her left thumb, right hand limp, fingers twitching faintly. The Coubertin Medal envelope loomed nearby. It weighed less than a paperclip, and more than the Games, its IOC seal a quiet taunt; she sidestepped it, dread outweighing pride.

She trudged to the bathroom, a tight box of chipped white tiles and mildewed grout, the air thick with damp. Twisting the shower knob unleashed a groan from the pipes, then a stuttering spray, water hissing as it struck the porcelain, steam blooming in heavy curls that fogged the cracked mirror.

She shed her Syracuse tee, faded orange, wincing as it snagged her right shoulder, the fabric rasping against her skin. It still smelled faintly of antiseptic and cardamom—of survival and tea. She then dropped her underwear, the cotton whispering to the floor in a soft heap. Naked, she stepped in, the water's heat a sudden slap, prickling her flesh like a thousand needles, her breath catching in a sharp gasp as it cascaded over her scarred body.

The spray pounded her scalp, soaking her red, cropped hair, flattening it in wet, heavy strands that clung to her neck, rivulets snaking down her spine with a ticklish shiver. Her skin flushed pink under the onslaught, the heat coaxing a sheen of sweat that mingled with the water, its faint salt tang rising as steam filled her lungs.

Her clavicle scar—a jagged, four-inch slash above her right breast—glistened, pink and raised, the flesh taut and tender, puckering as droplets traced its edges, stinging where the skin stretched thin. Her breath came shallow—not just from the heat, but from the weight of memory pressing behind her ribs.

Her right arm hung slack, water sheeting off the wasted muscle, the skin mottled with pale streaks where nerves flickered, fingers curling inward like wilted petals, the pins beneath radiating a dull, wet throb that pulsed with each heartbeat. Bruises lingered on her torso, sickly yellow-green smudges fading into her ribs, their edges soft under the water's caress, the chest tube's scab a small, dark crater beneath her breast, rippling as she breathed, the soap's lather burning faintly as it slid over it.

Her left hand—her lifeline—scrubbed a bar of lavender soap across her chest, the suds frothing white, then gray as they caught the grime of sleepless nights, the scent sharp and floral, cutting through the steam's musk. The water roared in her ears, a white-noise shield, but then came the breach—no warning, no mercy—just Barga swallowing her whole—smoke choking her throat, blood's copper sting on her lips, the Spectre's blade flashing cold. Her good hand slapped the tile, slick and cool, fingers splaying as a sob clawed up, swallowed by the spray's hiss.

Her knees quaked, the heat leaching strength, skin pruning into tight ridges—fingertips wrinkled, soles slick—until the water cooled, a tepid shift that jolted her. She twisted the knob off, the silence crashing in, dripping echoing like a slow heartbeat as she stood, steam swirling, her body a glistening testament to survival.

She toweled off with care, the rough cotton rasping over her clavicle scar, snagging briefly, her right arm dangling as she patted her torso dry, the fabric warm and damp against her ribs. She dressed—leggings hugging her legs, a loose sweater swallowing her frame, her jacket a struggle over the shoulder—and combed her wet hair, the mirror revealing bloodshot eyes, sharp but shadowed. The routine tethered her, a fragile thread to the day, though Barga's pulse thrummed beneath.

She grabbed her phone, the Coubertin invite, and rode the subway to Park Slope, Dr. Rachel Kessler's brownstone a refuge—lavender air, book-lined walls, the couch's sag familiar.

Kessler's sharp eyes met hers, "Nova—good to see you. How's the night been?"

Nova sank in, the invite crinkling, "Rough—rain's loud. Woke at 3, saw fire—Barga, Semtex, Jaber melting. Extra Ativan."

Kessler nodded, "Nightmares—frequency?"

Nova's jaw clenched, "Three, four times a week. Less vivid with Lexapro at 20, but there."

Kessler probed, "Mood?" Nova shrugged, "Flatter—less drowning.

Anxiety's a buzz, chest tight, waiting."

Kessler jotted, "Coping—writing?" Nova traced the invite, "Not so much right now. Walking in rain helps a bit—keeps me moving."

Kessler asked, "Ativan?" Nova frowned, "Once, twice weekly—nightmares. Hate the fog."

Kessler smiled, "PRN it is. Lexapro—side effects?"

Nova rubbed her temple, "Dry mouth, morning haze. Bearable." Kessler eyed the envelope, "What's that?"

Nova held it up, "Coubertin Medal—Athens, October. For Doha." Kessler's brows rose, "Extraordinary. How's it feel?"

Nova's voice dropped, "Heavy—pride, but a trigger. Doha's back—hospital, Omar's screams, the centipede. Chest caved last night."

Kessler leaned in, "Meaning?"

Nova's eyes glistened, "Validation—thirty four years, surviving hell. But it's Barga—blood, fire, unshakable."

Kessler nodded, "Honor and haunt. Athens—impact?"

Nova swallowed, "Reliving it—blast, Spectre. Might crack me." Kessler asked, "Tools?"

Nova nodded, "Breath—counting. Omar's coming—my rock." Kessler smiled, "Omar—how's that?"

Nova softened, "Safe—like air. Got something big to ask him—us, the story." Kessler probed, "Worst-case?"

Nova clenched, "Freeze—sobbing, crowd staring. Or bolt." Kessler steadied, "Then?"

Nova paused, "Breath. Omar's voice—I'd cope." Kessler smiled, "Best-case?"

Nova drifted, "Take it—medal, stage. Tell Omar—partnership, strength. Own Doha."

Kessler nodded, "Power—reclaiming. Psyche now?"

Nova rubbed her shoulder, "Wired—scared it'll rip me. Don't want to lose this." Kessler gentled, "Fear's real—you'll stitch it. Needs?"

Nova exhaled, "See Omar. Maybe up Lexapro." She paused, voice trembling, "Rachel—I want out. Not dying, but this life—Brooklyn, the grind. I can't escape Doha mentally; it's in me. Omar's my lifeline—he is Doha. I want to go there, live with him, off the grid—simple, quiet."

Kessler's pen stopped, "That's big—not suicidal, but a reset. Why Doha, Omar?"

Nova's tears welled, "He's home—steady, real. Brooklyn's noise, fame—it's choking me. There, with him, I could breathe—sell tea, write in peace, no spotlight."

Kessler tilted her head, "Escape or anchor?"

Nova swallowed, "Both—Doha's hell's root, but Omar makes it bearable. I'd trade this for souq dust, his laugh."

Kessler nodded, "A lifeline shift—practical?"

Nova shrugged, "Sell here, move—book money's enough. He'd take me in; I'd ask in Athens."

Kessler probed, "Psyche—risks?"

Nova's voice broke, "Risk? Doha's ghosts—closer there, rawer. But with him, I'd face 'em, not run."

Kessler smiled, "Strength—Omar's your ballast. Athens could test it—relapse or resolve. How's it feel?"

Nova's breath steadied, "Scary—freeing. Like shedding skin."

Kessler nodded, "We'll track it—20 milligrams holds, write this out, talk to Omar. You're not alone."

Nova left, rain streaking her face, the shower's echo and Kessler's words a fragile shield, Doha's pull a quiet ache with Omar at its heart.

On October 14, Nova boarded Delta Flight 216 from JFK to Athens, settling into the plush leather of seat 2A in first class, a window perch courtesy of Simon & Schuster's advance for the Doha 2040 paperback. Her boarding pass, slightly creased, tucked into her passport and rested on the armrest as she adjusted her tailored navy blazer, its crisp lines softening against the seat's curve, the white silk blouse beneath whispering against her skin, slim black trousers hugging her legs with quiet elegance.

Her right shoulder ached, titanium pins grinding beneath the fabric, a dull reminder of Barga's toll. She stowed her carry-on—a weathered leather satchel bulging with her laptop, Doha 2040, and the Coubertin Medal invite—in the overhead bin, its zipper rasping as it caught. A flight attendant offered a warm towel, its damp heat a fleeting balm as she pressed it to her face, the plane taxiing through rain-streaked tarmac, New York's gray sprawl fading into mist as they ascended, the Atlantic unfurling below like a dark, endless shroud.

Her mind, restless amid the first-class hush—crystal clinking softly, a murmured "More wine?"—drifted to the Olympic scandals she'd chronicled since 2008, a two-decade tapestry of betrayal and ink that had shaped her career and gnawed her soul.

Sochi 2014 loomed larger—Russia's state-sponsored doping, a sprawling conspiracy of swapped urine and tainted glory. She'd tracked it from Sochi to Rio, her New York Times features mapping the midnight lab switches—vials clinking in shadows, officials bribed with vodka and cash—to Putin's iron hand, her interviews with exiled chemists raw with fear, the partial bans a slap to the clean athletes whose tears she'd wiped in cramped hotel rooms.

PyeongChang 2018 brought the figure skating judging scandal—French judge Marie-Reine Le Gougne's whispered deal with Russia, skewing pairs' scores for gold. Nova's Sports Illustrated exposé leaned on late-night talks with insiders, her pen icy with scorn as she detailed the vote-trading's chill, the bronze-to-gold shift a hollow nod to justice, her faith in the ice's purity cracking.

Tokyo 2020, pushed to '21, carried Belarus sprinter Krystsina Tsimanouskaya's defection— fleeing forced repatriation after a public critique, her voice cracking over burner phones from Poland, Nova's Washington Post pieces pulsing with her defiance and dread, the IOC's asylum a rare victory she'd toasted with cheap vodka, alone.

Damascus 2022—Summer Youth Olympics—unraveled next, Syria's athletic corruption scandal, a grim tangle of bribery and coercion. She'd embedded with the delegation, her Foreign Policy reports exposing how regime officials funneled state funds to rig wrestling and track events, young athletes like 17-year-old sprinter Leila Hassan coerced into doping with military-grade stimulants, their parents threatened with prison if they resisted. She'd met Leila in a dusty Aleppo safehouse, her trembling hands clutching a medal she'd won under duress, Nova's pen heavy with grief as she chronicled the girl's hollow eyes, the IOC's sanctions too late to save a dozen futures snuffed by despair.

Paris 2024 stung fresh—the boxing gender eligibility row, Algeria's Imane Khelif and Taiwan's Lin Yu-ting caught in a storm of IBA chromosome tests and IOC silence. She'd shadowed their fights, her ESPN columns dissecting the science and the jeers, her heart twisting as Khelif's fists clenched post-bout, medals dulled by crowd hate, her own exhaustion mirrored in their weary eyes.

Doha 2040 dwarfed them all—her own crucible, the Obsidian Hand's terror, Semtex crates, the centipede's grotesque sadism, her survival a tale she'd bled onto pages, the Games' flame flickering through her own near-extinction.

Each scandal had carved her—hope chipped away, cynicism creeping in, her pen a weary warrior, Athens now a capstone she faced with a fraying spirit.

The cabin lights dimmed, a soft chime signaling cruising altitude, the clink of a champagne flute against a tray punctuating the hush. Her mind sagged under the scandals' weight, eyes heavy, and she slipped into sleep, head lolling against the window's cool curve, the first- class pillow a faint comfort.

Darkness enveloped her, then Barga roared back—a nightmare visceral and unrelenting. She stood in the desert, sand a scorching, gritty furnace under her bare feet, the sun a merciless tyrant blazing overhead, its heat blistering her skin to a raw, cracked red, sweat pooling in stinging rivulets.

The Spectre emerged—hooded, towering—his blade a curved, glinting scythe, its edge a whisper of honed death. He seized her, his grip a vice of calloused steel, and raised the knife, slicing her old Solomon Schechter Day sweatshirt—faded blue, threadbare from years— with a slow, deliberate SHHHK, the fabric parting like flesh, the blade's cold edge grazing her sternum as it fell in tatters to the sand. Her jeans followed, the denim resisting with a deeper RRRRIP as he carved them away, seams popping, the steel nicking her thighs, scraps fluttering down, leaving her utterly bare.

Her body wasn't just stripped—it was claimed, displayed, desecrated, and somewhere deep, a part of her watched from behind her own eyes, unable to look away.

His hands—rough, unyielding—yanked her arms, rope gnawing her wrists, cutting red welts that oozed blood, warm and sticky, its copper tang thick in her throat, choking her. They forced her onto a rusted metal sheet, its surface scalding from the sun, searing her back and thighs with a hiss, the acrid stench of heated iron mingling with her sweat's sour bite.

Straps lashed her down—leather biting her ankles, wrists, waist—pinning her spreadeagled, helpless, the metal creaking under her thrashing. A spike loomed—jagged, cruel—angled wickedly, its tip hovering above her right clavicle. They drove it in, a white-hot agony erupting as it pierced the old scar, splitting skin and bone with a wet CRUNCH, the titanium pins snapping like brittle twigs, blood gushing hot and thick, painting her chest in crimson streaks that pooled beneath her, sticky and clotting with sand.

She screamed, a raw, guttural howl shredding her throat, swallowed by the desert's howling wind, her voice breaking into a ragged whimper.

They hoisted the sheet, her body swaying like a grotesque pendulum, gravity dragging her down, the spike burrowing deeper through her clavicle, a grinding torment as bone splintered, nerves shrieking in electric bursts, her right arm dangling limp, a marionette's limb torn free, blood dripping in slow, fat drops—PLIP-PLIP—onto the sand below.

Hung like a billboard, sand blasted her wounds, scouring her exposed flesh, flies swarmed with a frenzied BUZZ-BUZZ-BUZZ, their legs prickling her bloodied skin, her nakedness a sadistic banner—breasts swaying heavily, her groomed vaginal area—trimmed, private, a quiet piece of herself—lay bared, the coarse wind scouring the red curls, sand grains lodging in the tender folds like shards of glass, a raw, humiliating sting that shattered her womanhood's sanctuary under the relentless sky.

The Spectre's laugh rumbled. She heard it again—"Najd rises"—and in that instant, the medal back in her bag burned like a brand against her ribs.

She jolted awake, a strangled cry catching in her throat. The hum of the cabin replaced the wind's howl, but her skin couldn't tell the difference—everything still throbbed with heat and shame.

The first-class cabin glowed softly—crystal clinked, a flight attendant's heels clicked faintly—and 2B, a silver-haired woman in cashmere, stirred, murmuring, "You alright, dear?" Nova's voice rasped, brittle, "Yeah—nightmare. Sorry." It wasn't the first time she'd said it. Probably wouldn't be the last. But every time, it scraped something rawer inside.

She fumbled for her water glass, the crystal cool and slick, gulping tepid liquid that sloshed in her trembling grip, a droplet splashing her trousers, soaking through to her thigh with a faint chill. Her left hand pressed her chest, counting breaths—one-two-three, slow—her pulse easing, the cabin's hum a lifeline, the wing's steady drone beyond the window a fragile anchor.

Tears surged, hot and stinging, tracing her cheeks in silent rivers, her breath hitching as she swiped them with her sleeve, the faded orange cotton rough against her skin, a sob trapped in her chest like a caged bird. The hum of the cabin morphed into a buzzing fly in her ear—Barga's specters still clinging—her breasts and womanhood a public scar, the medal's stage a looming abyss, her psyche teetering on collapse.

Somewhere in the darkness, the scent of cardamom cut through—the Souq's warmth calling her back. The nightmare's brutality didn't break her—it forged a steely resolve, a raw, aching clarity piercing her trembling core, igniting a desperate fire in her soul. This life—Brooklyn's clamor, fame's relentless glare, the scandals' endless weight—was a prison she'd outgrown, a hollow shell that echoed with every scream she'd survived, each scandal a chain she'd worn too long, Barga the breaking point that wouldn't release its claws from her heart.

Omar's face rose through the haze—his steady rumble a balm that softened her jagged edges, his tea's cardamom warmth a refuge she could taste even now, Doha's dust a gritty embrace she craved with a bone-deep longing that twisted her gut and swelled her chest.

In Athens, she'd beg him—not just for partnership, but for

salvation—sell everything, vanish with him off-grid, trade this chaos for the rhythm of the Spice Souq, where sanctuary waited in a woven rug sprawled across Omar's shop floor, a steaming teapot at its center, its warmth a bulwark against the ghosts that flayed her soul night after night. Her tears slowed, drying to a salty crust that tightened her skin, her breath settling into a quiet, resolute rhythm. The nightmare's terror wasn't defeat but a clarion call—she couldn't endure this half-life, chained to a past that devoured her.

With Omar, she'd build something new, something hers, a sanctuary where Barga's echo might finally fade, where her survival could mean more than enduring pain.

She leaned back, the leather creaking softly, her eyes fixed on the dark window, the Atlantic a void below, Athens a beacon ahead. Her fingers brushed the scar at her collarbone, a silent promise not to let the pain define her.

The plane droned on, hours stretching like a taut wire, and she longed for it to land in Greece—land where the medal waited to crown her scars, where Omar would stand beside her with his quiet strength, where she'd voice the question burning in her chest, a lifeline to pull her from this wreckage into something real, something she could hold without breaking.

Her fingers tightened on the armrest, resolve a quiet flame against Barga's lingering howl. Beyond the clouds, Athens waited—stone and sunlight, and him.

Delta Flight 216 touched down at Athens International Airport on October 15, at 10:37 a.m. local time, the wheels thudding against the tarmac with a jolt that snapped Nova from her reverie. Her dream clung like steam, but beneath it stirred something else—hope, raw and flickering.

She rubbed her eyes, the nightmare's echo—Barga's spike, her naked shame—still a raw pulse in her chest, her shoulder stiff beneath the blazer. She retrieved her satchel from the overhead bin, its strap creaking as she slung it over her good arm, and shuffled down the aisle, the plush carpet muffling her steps, the air thick with recycled staleness and a hint of champagne.

The terminal buzzed—announcements crackled in Greek and English, a tinny garble over the HUM of rolling suitcases, the air sharp with coffee and jet fuel. She queued at immigration, passport in her left hand, the line a slow shuffle, her silk blouse clinging faintly with residual sweat.

The officer—a wiry man with a clipped mustache—stamped her entry with a THUNK, his "Kalos irthate" met with a tired nod, her throat parched. Customs was swift, her checked bag—a sleek black roller—trundling off the belt with a CLUNK, its wheels squeaking as she pulled it through the green lane, fluorescent lights harsh against her bloodshot eyes.

In the arrivals hall, an IOC attache waited—Eleni Papadakis, a young woman in a crisp navy blazer, her name tag glinting, holding a sign: Nova Mendelsohn, IOC Guest. "Ms. Mendelsohn, welcome to Athens," Eleni said, her accent lilting, her handshake firm against Nova's weak left grip. "Car's outside—to The Dolli." Nova murmured a thanks, following Eleni through glass doors, the Greek sun a warm slap, the air thick with exhaust and olive trees.

A black Mercedes purred at the curb, and Nova sank into the backseat, leather cool against her trousers, her bag stowed in the trunk with a soft THUD. The drive cut through Athens' sprawl—horns blaring, scooters weaving, whitewash and graffiti blurring—until the Acropolis loomed, its ancient stones golden against the sky.

The Dolli at Acropolis gleamed, its white facade catching the midday light, a boutique oasis in Plaka's winding streets. Eleni handed her to a porter—a wiry youth in a burgundy vest— who hefted her bags with a grunt, guiding her through a lobby of polished marble and jasmine air. Check-in was brisk—keys clinked, a tablet signed with her left thumb—and she rode the elevator to the fifth floor, its soft DING echoing as the doors parted. Room 512 opened to luxury—cream linens, a wide balcony, and a glass wall framing the Acropolis, its Parthenon aglow, a timeless sentinel over the city's hum.

Nova dropped her satchel on the bed, the mattress sighing, and unzipped her roller, unpacking with care—trousers folded, dresses and blouses hung, undergarments tucked neatly in drawers, her laptop on a dark wood desk, Doha 2040 beside the Coubertin invite.

The bathroom beckoned—a marble cavern, its deep, oval hot tub a centerpiece, faucets gleaming chrome. She twisted them on, water gushing with a loud RUSH, steam rising in thick curls as she shed her blazer, blouse, and trousers, the silk and wool pooling on the tiles with her bra and underwear. Naked, she eased into the tub, the heat a scalding embrace prickling her skin, her right shoulder throbbing as she sank to her chin, bubbles fizzing around her scars—clavicle's pink seam, chest tube's scabbed divot—her breath slowing as the warmth melted the flight's strain.

She gazed out the window. Like her, the Acropolis had withstood collapse, a monument to what endured when beauty met devastation. The water lapped her skin, a gentle SLOSH with each shift, steam fogging the glass, the marble cool against her nape. Her mind drifted—Omar's arrival imminent, their reunion a heartbeat away—her chest tight with anticipation.

After an hour, the water cooled, her skin pruned, and she climbed out, toweling off with a plush cloth, its weave soft against her scars. She slipped into a wavy white sundress, its fabric flowing light and airy against her legs, a quiet elegance for the day ahead.

She ascended to The Dolli's rooftop restaurant, a sunlit expanse of white tables and wicker chairs, the Acropolis a breathtaking backdrop. The air carried a breeze—olive oil and rosemary wafting from the kitchen, a faint tang of sea salt from the coast. She claimed a table outside, the sun warm on her face, the chair creaking as she sat, slipping on a pair of designer sunglasses—sleek, black Tom Fords—their lenses shielding her eyes, framing the world in a cool, tinted calm.

A waiter approached, apron crisp, and she ordered a bottle of Antigone, Economou 2004— a dry red from Crete, its name a nod to defiance. He returned with a CLINK, pouring a deep ruby stream into her glass, its aroma of blackberry and earth rising sharp and rich. She sipped, the wine's tannins biting her tongue, grounding her as she watched the horizon, Athens sprawling below.

The clink of her glass against the table mirrored her pulse—a quiet tremor before the storm of seeing him. Omar Al-Kaabi emerged onto the rooftop, his massive frame a beacon, moving gingerly with Lofstrand crutches, their aluminum shafts glinting in the sun, his forearms braced against the grips, his steps tentative but deliberate. His soles, once ravaged by Barga's torments, had healed enough for weight-bearing—grafts pink and taut, the limp a fading scar of his resilience.

His beard was fuller, framing a face etched with time, and he wore a beige tunic, worn and simple, its hem swaying as he advanced, the faint TAP-TAP of crutches on tile a quiet rhythm. His eyes crinkled as they locked with hers through her sunglasses, and her breath seized, a tidal wave of emotion crashing—relief so sharp it pierced her lungs, joy so fierce it burned her throat, an ache of shared scars that twisted her heart into knots.

She stood, glass trembling in her hand, sunglasses fogging as tears welled, hot and unstoppable, spilling down her cheeks to dampen the sundress. "Omar," she choked, voice shattering into a sob, and he closed the distance, his grin breaking wide, a rumble bursting free, "Nova—Allah be praised, you're here, ya habibti."

He dropped one crutch against a chair with a CLANK, sweeping her into his arms, a fortress of warmth and strength, his tunic rough against her dress, the scent of cardamom and desert dust enveloping her, a home she'd ached for across years and oceans. Her good hand clutched his back, fingers digging into the fabric, her right arm pressing weakly against him, tears soaking his shoulder as a sob tore loose, raw and ragged.

"I missed you—god, Omar, I missed you so much," she gasped, her voice a broken thread, her chest heaving against his solidity, her sundress fluttering with the force of her trembling.

His rumble softened, thick with emotion, his free hand cradling her head, fingers threading her hair, "Me too, Nova—every damn day, every night, your voice in my head kept me upright. You're here now—real, not some ghost I dreamed." He tightened his grip, his crutch arm steadying her waist, his breath warm against her scalp, "Thought these legs wouldn't make it, but you pulled me through—always do."

She pulled back, tears streaming, sunglasses slipping as she met his gaze—his eyes glistening, heavy with the same weight, the same survival, his crutch a testament to battles fought. "Not a ghost," she murmured, echoing her midnight fears. "You're really here."

He chuckled, low and rich, wiping her cheek with a calloused thumb, his touch grounding, “Lost me? Never, Nova—scared or not, I’d crawl here for you. Greece called, but you’re the tether.”

Her heart clenched, a flood of gratitude and longing—she’d survived Barga, the scandals, the nightmares, and here he stood, her rock through hell’s fire, his crutches a quiet victory. Inside, her mind raced—the big question burning, the plea to join him in Doha, to shed this life for something simpler, safer, with him. But she wasn’t ready, not yet—her tongue felt leaden, her courage unsteady, the words too vast for this fragile moment. She’d ask soon, when the medal’s weight settled, when Athens gave her the breath to voice it.

They sank to the table, her sundress fluttering as she sat, Omar easing into the chair opposite, his crutches propped against the wicker with a soft CLINK, the seat creaking under his bulk. She lifted the Antigone bottle, its glass cool in her shaky grip, and poured him a generous measure, the wine’s ruby flow glinting in the sun, a soft GURGLE as it filled his glass.

“Try this,” she said, voice steadying, brushing a tear from her cheek, “Crete’s finest—fits us, doesn’t it? Defiant.” He took the glass, his fingers brushing hers, a spark of warmth that steadied her pulse, and sipped, his rumble deepening, “Strong—like you, like us. Burns good—reminds me of the Souq’s heat, the life we fought for.”

She smiled, tears drying, sunglasses perched atop her head now, “I needed this—you, here. After the flight, the dreams… it’s been heavy, Omar.”

His gaze softened, heavy with knowing, “Barga again? I see it in your eyes—still drags you back, doesn’t it?”

She nodded, throat tight, “Yeah—last night, worst yet. Stripped me bare, broke me again. But you… you make it lighter.” He leaned forward, voice low, his crutch arm resting on the table, “Same for me—your letters, your fire, kept me going when these feet wouldn't. We're tougher than it, Nova—together, always."

Her hand reached for his across the table, trembling, fingers lacing with his calloused grip, "Together—I couldn't do this without you. I've got something big on my mind, Omar, something for us. Not yet, but soon."

His brow lifted, a glint of curiosity sparking in his eyes, "Big, eh? You and your mysteries— keep me waiting, then. Athens has time for us, and I've got ears for you."

She laughed, a tear slipping free, "You always do—patience of a saint. I'll spill it when I'm ready—promise." He squeezed her hand, his rumble warm, "I'll hold you to it—whatever it is, we'll face it, like always."

The wine sat between them, a silent witness, their reunion a blaze of emotion—raw, radiant, a lifeline forged in fire and tempered by time. Athens hummed below, the Acropolis watching, their words a bridge from past pain to a future she wasn't ready to voice, but felt growing closer with every beat of her heart beside him.

October 16 dawned crisp and golden over Athens, the first light filtering through The Dolli's glass wall, casting the Acropolis in a soft amber glow. Nova Mendelsohn woke at 6:45 a.m., the hotel's silence broken by a distant rooster's crow and the faint CLINK of breakfast carts below.

Her eyes fluttered open, the nightmare's echo a faint shadow, her right shoulder a dull ache beneath the sheets' cool linen. She lay still, breath steady, the medal ceremony looming—a capstone to decades of ink and blood, a moment she'd face with Omar by her side. She rose, the hardwood cool against her bare feet, her wavy white sundress from yesterday draped over a chair, its fabric whispering as she brushed past.

Her morning routine unfolded with quiet precision. In the marble bathroom, she splashed cold water on her face, its sharp bite waking her fully, droplets tracing her jaw as she patted dry with a plush towel, the scent of jasmine lingering from the soap. She brushed her teeth, the mint paste sharp on her tongue, the toothbrush's bristles a soft SCRUB against her gums.

Breakfast came via room service—a knock, a tray wheeled in—black coffee steaming in a porcelain cup, its bitter aroma curling up, a warm croissant flaking gold onto the plate, butter melting into its layers with a faint SIZZLE as she spread it. She ate by the window, the Acropolis a stoic witness, crumbs dusting her fingers, the coffee's heat grounding her nerves.

She dressed for the ceremony with care, choosing a tailored charcoal blazer—sharp, authoritative—over a cream silk blouse, its sheen catching the light, paired with slim black trousers that hugged her legs with understated elegance. Her right arm resisted as she eased into the blazer, the pins grinding, but she smoothed the lapels with her good hand, the fabric crisp against her skin. She slipped on low black heels, their leather creaking faintly, and pinned her red hair into a loose chignon, a few strands framing her face. A silver necklace—simple, a gift from her mother decades ago—rested cool against her collarbone, a quiet anchor.

She descended to the lobby at 8:30 a.m., the marble gleaming, jasmine air mingling with espresso from the bar. Omar waited near a velvet sofa, his massive frame striking in formal attire—no tunic today, but a nod to his Qatari roots: a midnight-blue suit, its cut sharp yet adorned with subtle gold embroidery along the cuffs, a crisp white thobe peeking beneath, his beard neatly trimmed, his presence regal despite the Lofstrand crutches propped beside him. His soles, healing steadily, bore his weight with a ginger grace, the crutches a quiet testament to his recovery.

His eyes lit as he saw her, a grin breaking, "Nova—you clean up well, ya habibti." She smiled, heart lifting, "You too, Omar—Qatar's finest, crutches and all." He chuckled, "Aye, had to match you—big day, this."

They stepped outside, a black IOC sedan idling at the curb, its engine a low purr. She paused before the door, her hand tightening on the handle—this was the step into everything she couldn't yet name.

The fifteen-minute ride to the Electra Metropolis Athens wove through Plaka's charm— cobblestones rattled under the tires, bougainvillea spilled pink over white walls, the air thick with olive oil and gasoline. Street vendors hawked souvlaki, skewers sizzling, their smoky tang wafting through the cracked window, while scooters buzzed past, horns bleating.

The Acropolis receded, then reappeared, a constant sentinel as they neared Syntagma Square, its bustle of taxis and tourists a vibrant blur against the hotel's sleek facade.

The Electra Metropolis Athens loomed, its glass and stone a modern shrine, the conference center abuzz with international sports diplomats—suits and saris, keffiyehs and kimonos, voices weaving a global tapestry of French, Arabic, Mandarin. Flags of the 206 member nations fluttered above, their colors snapping in the breeze, the air electric with anticipation.

An IOC attaché—Dimitri Kostas, a lean Greek with a clipped beard—greeted them at the entrance, his handshake firm, "Ms. Mendelsohn, Mr. Al-Kaabi, welcome. This way, please." Nova nodded, her pulse quickening, Omar's crutches tapping a steady rhythm beside her as they entered the hall, its marble floors echoing with footsteps, chandeliers casting a warm glow over the crowd.

Across the room, Sheikh Tariq bin Fahd Al-Mazrouei stood, his keffiyeh pristine, conversing with a cluster of delegates, his voice a low rumble. His gaze caught Nova's, a flicker of recognition sparking, and he politely excused himself, his robes flowing as he approached.

"Nova—Omar," he said, his tone warm, eyes crinkling, "Allah's mercy, you're here." Nova's throat tightened, memories of Doha flashing—his steady hand in the storm.

"Sheikh Tariq," she said, voice soft, "good to see you too." Omar grinned, shifting a crutch, "Sheikh—thought you'd left us for good." Tariq chuckled, "Never—retired, not gone. Nakamura's the future, but today's yours, Nova—and Omar, your strength humbles us still."

Nova swallowed, "We owe you—Doha wouldn't stand without you." He waved a hand, "No—you two carried it. I'm proud to witness this."

The session began at 9:00 a.m., the hall hushing as Kenji Nakamura, the new IOC President, took the dais—a wiry Japanese former gymnast, his silver hair sharp against a black suit, elected in 2041 to succeed Sheikh Tariq. A technology-forward visionary turned sports diplomat, his presence was electric, his voice clear over the speakers.

"Ladies and gentlemen, delegates, friends—we gather for the 161st IOC Session to honor the Olympic spirit. Today, we present the Pierre de Coubertin Medal, awarded for extraordinary service to the Olympic movement, a rare recognition of courage, integrity, and sacrifice. In the fire of 2040, we found not just survival—but the soul of what these Games must become."

He paused, eyes on Nova, "Nova Mendelsohn receives this medal for nearly thirty-five years of unwavering dedication. Since 2014, she's chronicled the Games, the good and the bad—Sochi's doping web, PyeongChang's judging flaws, Tokyo's defiance, Damascus's corruption, Paris's eligibility fights—pursuing fairness and justice with a journalist's tenacity.

"But it was Doha 2040 where she transcended. Amid the Obsidian Hand's terror—a $500 billion ransom, Semtex poised, a sadist's cruelty—she didn't just report; she acted. Her survival, her voice, saved the Games, the movement, perhaps the world. This medal honors her legacy—a beacon of what we strive for."

The hall erupted in applause, a wave of sound as Nova rose, her legs trembling, Omar's hand brushing hers in quiet support. Nakamura met her at the podium, the medal—a silver disc engraved with Coubertin's visage—cool in his hands as he draped it over her neck, its ribbon soft against her blazer, its weight a tangible anchor.

"Congratulations, Nova," he said, his grip firm, and she nodded, tears pricking, "Thank you, President Nakamura."

She faced the crowd, the medal heavy, her voice steadying as she spoke, "This… this is more than I can hold. The Olympics have been my life—three decades of chasing their heart, their flaws, their triumphs. From Beijing's gyms to Doha's sands, I've seen the best and worst of us—fairness fought for, justice demanded, hope tested. Doha broke me—two years of scars, nightmares I can't shake, a toll I'll carry always. But in that fracture, I found a choice—to speak, to stand, to stay whole by telling the truth."

Her gaze found Omar, his crutches gleaming, eyes glistening, "I stand here because of Omar Al-Kaabi—my friend, my rock. His sacrifice in Barga—his body, his spirit—held us up when I couldn't. He's the heartbeat of this honor, the man who taught me what strength means. To the IOC, Sheikh Tariq, President Nakamura—thank you for seeing us, for this. The Olympics are my past, my pride, and I'm grateful—grateful to have carried their story, to have stood in their fire."

Her voice cracked, tears spilling, the hall rising in a standing ovation, a roar that shook her bones. As the applause thundered, she felt it—grief unlatched, her past loosening its grip. She stepped back, Omar's nod a quiet anchor, her words a farewell to her past—not overt, but a whisper of release, her future with him a seed unvoiced.

The medal gleamed, Athens watched, and she felt done—not broken, but ready for what lay beyond.

Veil 29

Valor Over Horizons

The 161st IOC Session adjourned at the Electra Metropolis Athens, the conference hall's echoes of applause for Nova's Pierre de Coubertin Medal dissolving into a hum of anticipation. But beneath her medal, her bones still hummed with the morning's weight—victory too fresh, too raw to feel like triumph.

The day's formalities yielded that evening to a grand reception in the hotel's opulent ballroom, a cavernous expanse of gilded arches soaring toward a vaulted ceiling, where crystal chandeliers dangled like frozen waterfalls, their prisms scattering light in a kaleidoscope of golden flecks across the polished marble floor.

The air pulsed with life—the sharp CLINK of silverware against porcelain, the low murmur of voices weaving a tapestry of languages—French lilting with soft consonants, Arabic rolling with guttural depth, Japanese clipped with precise rhythm—and the faint, mournful strains of a string quartet tucked in a corner, their bows coaxing Vivaldi's Four Seasons into the air, the violins' tremolo a haunting thread beneath the din.

Tables swathed in crisp white linen groaned under a feast of mezze—hummus gleamed in shallow bowls, its surface swirled with a glistening pool of olive oil, its nutty tang mingling with the sharp zest of lemon; dolmades sat plump and dark green, their rice filling spilling faintly as a delegate speared one, the vine leaves glistening with brine; skewers of lamb sizzled on silver platters, their charred edges curling, the air thick with rosemary's piney bite and the meat's smoky juiciness, a faint HISS rising as a drop of fat hit the tray.

Trays of drinks circulated—champagne flutes fizzed with golden bubbles, their crisp, yeasty scent cutting through the richness, while tumblers of ouzo glowed milky white, their anise bite sharp and medicinal, leaving a trail of licorice on the tongue of a nearby diplomat who grimaced, then laughed. The sensory assault wrapped the room in a cocoon of indulgence, a stark contrast to the weight settling in Nova's chest.

She stood near a towering floral centerpiece—orchids cascading in creamy tendrils, lilies unfurling with a sweet, cloying perfume that tickled her nose—her charcoal blazer crisp despite the day's strain, its tailored lines a shield against the crowd's press, the medal's silver disc cool against her cream silk blouse, its ribbon a soft, insistent pressure on her neck. She adjusted her stance, the pants' swish too loud in her ears—like every movement threatened to unravel her composure. Her low heels clicked faintly on the marble, her left hand clutched a glass of Antigone wine, its ruby hue glinting as she sipped, the dry bite of Crete's vintage a sharp anchor amidst the swirl.

Her right arm hung stiff, the titanium pins a dull grind beneath her skin, a quiet protest against the hours of standing, smiling, nodding. Omar lingered nearby, his midnight-blue suit a regal nod to Qatar, its gold-embroidered cuffs catching the light like threads of fire, his white thobe beneath a pristine contrast, his Lofstrand crutches propped against a chair, their aluminum shafts glinting under the chandeliers. His soles, healing steadily, bore his weight with a ginger grace, his beard framing a face alight with pride as he watched her navigate the throng, his presence a steady pulse in her periphery.

The reception pulsed with diplomats, each drawn to Nova like filings to a magnet, their congratulations a relentless tide of gratitude for her decades of service to the Olympic movement.

Sofia Mendes, Brazil's sports minister, approached first, a statuesque figure in a shimmering emerald-green dress that rustled like leaves, her dark hair swept into an elegant twist, her handshake firm as she leaned in, her Portuguese accent warm and rolling, "Nova, parabéns—your work in Rio, exposing that doping web, it gave us a chance to rebuild something honest. This medal's yours, truly, a testament to your fire."

Nova smiled, her throat tightening, the wine glass cool against her palm, "Obrigada, Sofia— Rio was a mess we had to untangle. I just wrote what I saw, what mattered." Mendes nodded, her eyes glinting with a shared memory, "You saw truth—saved us from a deeper rot. Brazil won't forget."

Amina Al-Sayed, Egypt's Olympic committee chair, followed, her indigo hijab framing a face of quiet strength, her voice a melodic hum as she clasped Nova's hand, "Ms. Mendelsohn, sala—your courage in Doha, it's a story we tell our youth, a legend of grit. The Games owe you more than gold."

Nova's fingers brushed the medal, its edge smooth under her touch, "Shukran, Amina— Doha was bigger than me. It was all of us holding on." Al-Sayed's smile softened, her gaze warm, "But you lit the way through the dark—mashallah, a beacon."

Jean-Paul Dubois, France's IOC delegate, sidled up next, his pinstripe suit sharp as a blade, a faint whiff of cologne—cedar and citrus—trailing him, his accent clipped and precise, "Nova, félicitations—PyeongChang's skating mess, your pen sliced through the fog like a guillotine. This honor's overdue, non?"

She nodded, the wine's tannin lingering on her tongue, "Merci, Jean-Paul—justice was cold there, slippery, but we pinned it down." He chuckled, a dry rasp, "You did, relentless as a bloodhound—chapeau."

The tide swelled—India's Vikram Patel, his saffron kurta vivid against the muted suits, his voice rich with gratitude for her Tokyo defection coverage, "You gave Krystsina a voice, Nova—India cheered her through you"; Syria's Leila Rahim, her black abaya whispering as she moved, her eyes glistening as she recalled Damascus 2022's corruption exposé, "Leila Hassan runs free now because of you—our youth thank you"; Japan's Hiroshi Tanaka, his gray suit understated, bowing slightly, his words soft, "Your fairness, Nova-san, it's why we trust the Games."

Each voice layered weight, and beneath the chorus of praise, Barga's torch flared again—sweat, screams, a crack of bone. Her smile held, but only barely. Her jaw ached as she nodded, the medal a growing burden against her chest, her thoughts drifting to Omar—his crutches' TAP-TAP, his steady gaze—her question to him a quiet drumbeat beneath the praise, Doha, a new life, its rhythm quickening with each exchange.

Kenji Nakamura, the IOC President, approached amidst the flow, his silver hair sharp against his black suit, his gymnast's frame compact yet commanding, his handshake a brief, firm clasp.

"Nova," he said, his English precise with a faint Japanese lilt, "this medal—it's a fraction of what you've given us. Doha 2040, your resolve—it's why I stand here today. You're the movement's spine."

She swallowed, her throat dry despite the wine, "Thank you, President Nakamura—Doha was a fight we couldn't lose. I just did my part." His eyes crinkled, admiration sharp, "Your part saved us all—history won't forget."

Sheikh Tariq bin Fahd Al-Mazrouei followed, his keffiyeh pristine, his robes flowing as he moved through the crowd, a faint scent of oud trailing him—woodsy, rich. "Nova," he rumbled, his voice a warm echo of Doha's chaos, "this honor—it's yours, but it's ours too. You and Omar, you held the flame when it faltered."

She met his gaze, tears pricking, "Sheikh Tariq—we couldn't have without you. You steadied us." He smiled, his hand resting briefly on her shoulder, "No—you two were the steel. I'm proud, beyond words."

Omar shifted closer then, his crutches tapping a soft rhythm on the marble as a Nigerian delegate praised his resilience, "Mr. Al-Kaabi, your survival—heroic." Omar's rumble cut through, deflecting, "Aye, but it's Nova's day—her pen, her fight, that's the hero here." His eyes flicked to her, warm and deflecting, the TAP-TAP of his crutches a quiet underscore as he moved, her heart swelling at his humility, the question pulsing louder—with you, Omar, in Doha.

The reception dragged into hours, the quartet shifting to Barber's Adagio for Strings, its mournful swell thickening the air, the chandeliers dimming as shadows stretched across the marble. Diplomats swirled—silk saris rustling like wind through leaves, wool suits brushing with a faint SCRATCH, laughter spiking over debates about doping reforms, the clink of ouzo glasses a sharp counterpoint. The heat pressed Nova's lungs, her blazer clinging damply, her smile a brittle mask as fatigue gnawed—her legs heavy, her jaw tight, her thoughts a tangle of Barga's screams and Omar's steady presence.

If she stayed another second, she'd scream. "Need some air," she whispered—barely more than a lifeline. She politely slipped away, her heels a soft CLICK-CLICK-CLICK as she wove through the crowd, brushing past an Argentine mid-toast, his champagne sloshing faintly as she passed, the ballroom's warmth a suffocating weight, the terrace door's cool glass a beacon under her palm as she pushed through.

Outside, the evening air hit her like a wave, crisp and sharp, slicing through the heat, her cheeks flushing as the breeze rustled her blazer, its fabric flapping faintly against her sides. The sky deepened to a rich blue, streaked with orange and gold as the sun dipped below the horizon, the Acropolis a distant silhouette of jagged stone, its edges stark against the fading light, a timeless echo of endurance.

The terrace stretched wide, its marble balustrade cool and smooth under her trembling hands as she gripped it, the city below a hum of distant horns, the faint clang of church bells tolling vespers, the rumble of traffic weaving through Plaka's veins. The breeze carried olive groves' earthy whisper, a tang of diesel threading through, her sunglasses—Tom Fords— perched atop her head, forgotten, the medal glinting in the dusk's last rays.

Alone, her thoughts roared—Barga's spike piercing her clavicle, blood's copper tang, her nakedness a billboard of shame; Beijing's forged papers, Rio's shadowed labs, Damascus's coerced youth, each scandal a brick in her crumbling wall; her doctor's office, Kessler's steady voice, "You're drowning," the Lexapro's haze a frail shield. The medal's weight pressed—literal, its silver a cold heft against her chest, symbolic, thirty-five years of justice now a chain she longed to shed.

Her question to Omar swelled—a crescendo of fear and craving, leave it all, live with you in Doha, a plea she'd rehearsed in silence, its edges jagged with doubt, its core a desperate hope for peace. Her hands shook on the balustrade, knuckles whitening, her breath hitching as the Acropolis sharpened her resolve, a monument to survival she mirrored, yet couldn't sustain in this life.

Footsteps approached—slow, deliberate, the TAP-TAP of Lofstrand crutches on marble— and she turned, Omar emerging from the ballroom's glow, his midnight-blue suit catching the twilight, gold embroidery shimmering like embers. His face softened, eyes tracing her tension—shoulders hunched, hands trembling—his rumble gentle, "Nova—you're out here alone. Struggling, aren't you?"

She nodded, tears pricking, voice cracking, "Yeah, Omar—too much in there. Too much everywhere."

He eased closer, crutches steadying his bulk, stopping beside her, the Acropolis a shared vista as he leaned against the balustrade, "I saw it—their words piling on you. You're carrying more than that medal, habibti."

She swallowed, "It's not just the medal—it's everything. I can't keep this up, Omar. I need to tell you something, something big." Her heart hammered, the question clawing free, and he tilted his head, eyes steady, "Tell me, then—I'm here, always."

She drew a shaky breath, the air cool and biting, and let it spill, raw and unfiltered, "I want to leave it all—my life, my past, everything I've known. Not die, not give up, but start over— simple, quiet, in Doha with you. Brooklyn's a cage—every sound's a bomb, every shadow's Barga, the fame's a noose I can't shake. I can't escape Doha—it's burned into me, the fire, the screams, the blood—but you're my lifeline, Omar, you are Doha to me.

"I want to sell it all, go there, live with you—off the grid, no spotlight, just us. Tea in the Souq, writing when I feel it, your voice to keep me steady. I've been breaking for two years—nightmares every week, Lexapro at 20 milligrams dulling the edges but not the weight, Ativan for the worst nights, a fog I hate. I told my doctor

I'd crack if I stayed—she saw it, saw me drowning in this chaos. I need you, Omar—I need us, a new start where I can breathe, where Barga's just a scar, not a chain."

Her voice shattered, tears streaming hot and fast, her good hand clutching the balustrade, knuckles white, her right arm limp as she shook, the medal swaying against her chest.

"Barga stripped me, hung me up, shamed me. The scandals, the stories—I've given them my life, poured my soul into fairness, justice, and I'm done—empty.

"I need you Omar.

"I need us, a new start where I can breathe. I want peace—your dust in my lungs, your laugh in my ears, a life I can hold without it crushing me.

"Will you let me come? Will you have me there?"

She gasped, sobs racking her frame, her eyes searching his, terror and hope a storm within her, the question a jagged wound laid bare.

Omar's gaze held hers, unwavering, his crutches creaking as he shifted, tears glistening in his eyes, his face softening with a knowing warmth that pierced her.

Something in Nova's chest gave—uncoiled, like a breath she'd been holding for two years finally escaped.

"Nova," he rumbled, voice thick and trembling, "I knew you'd come to it, felt it in every letter you sent, every call when your voice shook. I've seen you fight, seen you break, and I've prayed you'd find your way to me. Aye, I'll have you—more than that, I want you there with me. Doha's my home, and it's yours too—always has been."

His fingers hesitated at the pocket. "I didn't know if this would be too much," he murmured, "but you just gave me my answer.

"Barga burned me too—my soles blistering, screams in my ears, that stench of rot and blood. I carried it, same as you, but your strength pulled me up when I couldn't stand. I read your words—those late-night notes, the way you'd pause, searching—and I knew you'd tire of this fight. I've been ready, habibti—crafted something for you, waited for this night."

She remembered the girl she was before Barga—one who believed in rings and promises. That girl stirred now, aching to believe again.

He reached into his suit pocket, fingers trembling, and pulled out a small velvet box, its deep blue a quiet promise under the twilight. He opened it, revealing an ornate ring—gold, its band etched with delicate arabesques, cradling a red aqeeq gemstone, its surface a warm, translucent glow catching the last orange streaks of sunset.

"This," he said, voice low and reverent, "is for you—for us. Aqeeq's sacred, Nova—not just a stone, but a prayer. It's the gem of the Prophet, peace be upon him, the first to testify to Allah's Oneness and Muhammad's message. The Qur'an says it—Chapter 62, first verse: 'Everything in the heavens and on Earth glorifies Allah.' Even stones worship, even this one, singing His praise we can't hear, and wearing it keeps that blessing close—wraps you in it."

She didn't fully grasp the stone's power, but the reverence in Omar's voice made her believe—this wasn't just a ring. It was a prayer she didn't know how to say.

He held the ring up, its gold warm in his palm, the aqeeq's red a living ember, "They say aqeeq repels poverty—keeps evil at bay, turns a two-rakat prayer into a thousand in Allah's eyes. It drives out hypocrisy, sadness, distress—brightens your face, speeds your prayers to Him. My father wore one—red like this—through the lean years, said it steadied him when my mother passed, kept his heart light when grief weighed it down."

Nova's throat tightened. This was legacy—not just love, but memory, blood, and prayer bound in gold.

"This one's yours—forged in the Souq, gold from the desert's veins, aqeeq from Yemen's quarries," Omar said as he cupped her hand in his calloused palm, brushing a thumb over the ring's curve as if sealing a vow. "I chose it months ago, carried it since you called about Athens, knowing you'd ask, hoping I'd give it to you like this—a symbol of us, my prayer that it shields you, lifts you, brings you peace in this new life."

Her breath hitched, tears falling faster, her good hand reaching for his, fingers brushing the box's velvet, soft and cool, then tracing the ring—gold's intricate etchings smooth under her touch, aqeeq's warmth a pulse against her skin.

For a breathless moment, she felt the shadows of Barga lift—watching, vanishing—as if this act had rewritten her ending.

"Omar," she whispered, voice a fragile thread, "you knew—god, you knew me better than I did. This… it's more than I dreamed, more than I deserve." Her voice broke, awe trembling through her, "It's beautiful—sacred. I feel it already."

He smiled, tears slipping into his beard, "I know you—your heart's loud, even in silence. Take it, wear it—come with me. We'll build it together—with silence and tea, with words that only matter to us." He slid the ring onto her left hand, his fingers trembling, the gold cool against her skin, the aqeeq settling with a warm weight, its red glow a promise as it fit perfectly, a quiet CLICK as it locked into place.

She clutched his hand, sobs softening to gasps, her right arm lifting weakly to touch his face, the ring glinting as the sky shifted—

orange bleeding into indigo, stars pricking through.

“Yes,” she gasped, his scent—smoke, spice, dust—filled her lungs as she pressed into him, anchoring her to this breath, this choice. “Yes—I’m yours, Omar. Doha, us—it’s home.” He dropped a crutch with a CLATTER, pulling her close, balancing on one as his arms enfolded her, a fortress of warmth, her head against his chest, his heartbeat a steady THUMP-THUMP beneath her ear, the aqeeq a quiet prayer between them.

Their embrace lingered, his breath ragged, her tears soaking his suit, the Acropolis a silent witness as their words wove a tapestry—pain’s echoes, promise’s threads—a new life trembling into being under Athens’ twilight–one that would begin with tea, not terror.

Hours later, the reception’s din faded as Nova returned to her room at The Dolli, the city quiet save for a distant siren’s wail. She stood by the window, the Acropolis dark against the night, its stones a shadow of history. Her blazer hung on a chair, the medal on the desk, its silver dull in the moonlight. She’d hung her armor beside her, a warrior ready to walk away from the war.

She gazed at the ring, lifting her hand—gold’s etchings sharp under her fingertips, aqeeq’s red glowing softly, warm as Omar’s voice. Her heart lightened, a burden easing, as Doha flooded her mind: his shop’s wooden shelves, heavy with spice jars, the clink of tea glasses, steam rising from cardamom-laced cups, a life reborn in dust and simplicity. The hotel room’s sterile chill—the faint whiff of bleach, the hum of air conditioning—faded, overtaken by the imagined heat of sun-baked stone, the earthy curl of cumin and saffron in the Spice Souq’s air. Barga lingered—a scar, not a chain—her past a shadow she was ready to abandon.

Athens, home of the first Olympic Games, now a bridge to a future with him, the ring a promise she’d hold as she stepped forward, leaving the Five Ring Circus behind.

Somewhere below, a bell chimed once—soft, solitary—a call to prayer or a promise, she couldn't tell. She simply listened.

Acknowledgements

Writing this book has been a lifelong journey of imagination, exploration, and discovery, with a number of people and places without which, this project would have been impossible.

I would like to especially thank my parents, Ted and Fran, whose unwavering support and encouragement over a lifetime fueled my creativity and pushed me to finally write this book.

Thank you to my wife, Adrienne, whose unconditional love steadies me, even as she braves the wilds of my depraved imagination unleashed in print upon the world.

To my daughter, Giselda, whose journey with reading—full of discovery, frustration, pride, and quiet persistence—I hope blossoms forever. Gigi, this book awaits you when you're older… MUCH older.

Alan Abrahamson, from the day we first met, you have been a great colleague, collaborator, an E Street Brother, and friend. Being your partner in crime (both litter-ally and literary) is one of the joys of my life.

To my friend Sarah Crouch, I want to extend my deepest gratitude for your willingness to take the time to share your insights and critical feedback on this project to a novice novelist. This wouldn't have taken shape without you.

A special thank you to the great Jerry Izenberg for believing in a young kid from Newark with a glimmer of talent. Without your belief in me all those years ago, I would probably still be lost.

Finally, I am grateful to Doha and its people for serving as the heartbeat of my story's backdrop Upon my first arrival in 2010, this vibrant city captured me with its rich cultural tapestry, and dynamic blend of tradition and modernity. It provided an evocative canvas that brought this narrative to life and infused my characters and their world with authenticity and depth.

While Qatar, like any place, is not without its challenges, including criticisms over civil liberties issues and political freedoms, I remain profoundly honored to have drawn inspiration from such a captivating place.

www.ingramcontent.com/pod-product-compliance
Lightning Source LLC
Chambersburg PA
CBHW070823020826
48982CB00014B/397
9798893247923